MURDER CREEK PRESS

A Southern Mystery Publisher

OR ELSE...!

PETER D. TATTERSALL

MURDER CREEK PRESS

A Southern Mystery Publisher

New Orleans | Staunton

MURDER CREEK PRESS

New Orleans & Staunton
P. O. Box 1998
11 E. Beverley Street, Suite 8
Staunton, Virginia 24401
http://www.murdercreekpress.com
murdercreekpress@ntelos.net

Printed in the United States of America

1 2 3 4 5 6 7 8 9

Library of Congress Cataloging-in-Publication Data:
Tattersall, Peter D.
ISBN= 13: 978-0-615-14441-2

For Nell, my loving wife; sons Tom and Peter, Jr. and Nolan my daughter, and to Lloyd Allen Beattie.

They could have left, they probably should have left... Thank God they didn't.

ACKNOWLEDGEMENTS

Lyn and Bill Rainbow; for a quiet farm to write and their warm friendship. To Rannah Gray and Marc Chimes for their unwavering support and Dana Rae Pomeroy, Dev Singer and Jody Grogan, my editors; and Michael Vayvada of Ace Communication Arts whose help and advice was invaluable.

The late John Franks; as good a man to train for as ever lived and a wonderful friend and human. To my best pal who died during the writing of this book, Melville Church III, with whom I shared 50 years of fun; and Louis Wiley whose use of the cup I endured during our wonderful mornings by the rail in Middleburg. To Charlie Bishop who lifted me up.

And to my last two fellow skates still standing, John D. Adams IV and T. Mason Grasty, friends through so much.

There are thoroughbreds and all the rest are horses;
there are foxhounds and all the rest are dogs.

Eric W. Tattersall – 1948

CHAPTER ONE

On a freezing Boston morning in 2003 I was curled up in my ancient recliner covered by a fleece-lined horse blanket. It was my forty-first birthday, and I was trying to escape reality in my tack room of Suffolk Downs' Barn 15.

With morning training completed I contemplated the dark prospects of my future. Hidden from the harsh weather, it was becoming daily more apparent my once-promising career as a thoroughbred trainer was teetering on the edge of collapse. My string of charges had once numbered almost two dozen, but was now down to three cheap claimers, all my own. Tracks such as Saratoga, Aqueduct and Belmont Park had been my favorite places to run, but I'm now struggling to survive at Boston's decaying Suffolk Downs, located on a sliver of land between Logan Airport and the dying resort of Revere Beach. The Atlantic Ocean is so close the small infield lake becomes a mud hole at low tide and fills with water when the tide is high. This morning, both the lake and main track were frozen and snow-covered.

I had Count Basie playing high enough to drown out the barn noises, so I only faintly heard the knocking on my tack room door. Sure that it was a creditor, probably the feedman, blacksmith or hay dealer, I sank lower under the shield of my horse blanket like a child cowering from the belt. As the knocking got louder, I felt a gust of Arctic air sweep under my blanket.

"Mr. O'Hearn, could you come out from under that thing and talk with me?"

I didn't recognize the strange, business-like voice. Peering over the edge of the blanket I was face to face with someone right out of a Bogart movie. He wore a black hat, a double-breasted overcoat and had a pencil-thin mustache, the kind

Jimmy Buffett sang about. His beady, piercing eyes showed irritation and impatience.

This guy was not accustomed to being kept waiting. He moved from foot to foot, rubbing his hands together saying, "My name is Milos Santos, Mr. O'Hearn. Can we go somewhere warm to talk? I have a good deal for you… I think."

Now, I was in trouble. No one in his right mind offers a good deal to a man in my financial position, unless it's tainted. With my bank balance, even sorta honest looks pretty good. I pulled my six–three, two hundred and forty pound frame from my recliner, shook the man's hand and led the way out the door into the snow.

The barn sidewalk had been cleared, but the drifts on either side stand about four feet high with the accumulation of winter-hardened snow. We carefully picked our way across the street and up the salted steps leading to the track kitchen, the hub of all activity on this and every track's backside.

After training hours, the track is closed and prepared for the afternoon's racing. The kitchen is crowded, but rather subdued. Coffee-stained *Racing Forms* cover the tabletops and the bill of fare has been changed from fast breakfast food to a starch-laden lunch. The floor is littered with papers, food wrappers and coffee cups from the mid-morning break. The far corners serve as holding pens for the transient help, many homeless trying to stay out of the cold. Half-filled coffee cups look like small grave markers in front of the forlorn faces that tell the defining stories of racing's "lost souls". Destitute hot walkers, tired and exhausted, rest aching feet or sleep with their heads on the tables, some with tired arms hanging toward the floor, as they dream of ways to keep their "24-hour buzz" going.

Music and shouting echoed from an adjacent game and

bar room, where a pool table with torn, soiled green felt is surrounded by dozens of various money-gobbling machines which take abuse from exercise riders and grooms. Beer bottles slam against glass and fists pound the video games.

Oblivious to it all, I led this strange looking man into the darkened bar, where empty stools rise like stalagmites through the poorly lit watering hole.

"Too early for a beer?" I ask.

He declines. "I'd give my arm for something hot... a coffee light, maybe?"

Overhearing us, the bartender brings the dreadful looking milk and coffee combination and a Sam Adams. Santos looks at me over the steaming coffee, which he holds with both hands for his own warmth. " Mr. O'Hearn, I'll be blunt and to the point. I'm a CPA. My employer loves horse racing. From time to time, he runs horses up and down the East Coast. He's been out of the game for several years, but now wants to start a small outfit here at Suffolk Downs."

He takes a sip of coffee, careful not to soil his sharkskin suit and silk tie or muss his facial hair. "We've been looking for a trainer and have found out quite a bit about you. My employer, who will remain in the background as to all racing matters, thinks you're the man for the job. We know these are tough times for you, financially, and think we can form a profitable relationship."

Another careful sip.

"If you agree to do the paperwork our way, and be very careful not to involve my employer or disclose his interest in the stable, we'll offer you the chance to train five or six horses. We already have a license, in my name, as the owner of di Vinci Stable and know exactly what type of horses we want.

You can look at some we've picked out and will be free to buy others you want with our approval."

"Why me, Mr. Santos? You can find trainers around here with a hotter hand than mine, hungry for horses."

"Your cupboard may be bare now, Colin. We've been watching you for some time. You win races with the few horses you have, and you always run to win. We've been short-changed by too many trainers. They lie to cover up injuries and their training mistakes, for fear we might move our horses and they'd lose the day money.

"My employer is tired of being cheated. He's had cheap horses and good ones, usually without success. We also know you work wonders with sore horses and have one of the best percentages around. We want to buy a few good horses with problems. Some from Miami and others we've picked out in New York. Under your care in Boston where they can run on bute, they should clean up. My boss is betting you can patch up good horses and we can beat this kind around here. I'd rather start with young, clean horses, but it's his money and he likes to do things his way."

"Good horses, even problem horses, cost money, Mr. Santos. How much do you figure to spend for these five or six horses?"

"At least $250,000 to start. We'd also buy one very good horse, raising the budget to $500,000, if he could be a Mass Cap contender in the spring."

I struggled to hold onto my stool and raised my beer for another, searching for time to digest what was happening. "That's a lot of money for Suffolk Downs."

"That's a lot of money for anywhere."

I waved off my Sam Adams and switched to scotch, by

raising three fingers to show how much straight-up Dewar's I needed.

"We don't want to break any laws, just have a little fun. If we're lucky we'd like to win some races and maybe make a little money. The fewer questions you ask about the money and where it comes from, the better off you'll be.

A hot flash passed quickly through me. At this point, I should have gotten up and walked out.

He went on, " We realize you don't want to train bad horses that have no chance to get the job done. There are a few horses we feel strongly about and certain trainers we want to buy from. Do you know Paco Gomez at Calder or Carlos Reyes at Aqueduct?"

I shook my head. "I've seen their names in the *Form*, but I've never had any dealings with either of them. How about I check out the horses you have in mind first, and then talk with a few trainers I've known for years and trust?"

"That sounds reasonable. We'll give you cash or cashier's checks for less than $10,000. The boss has a problem with money trails and anything over that amount is reportable. If things go as we plan, you'll eventually meet the boss. Don't feel left out, he's touchy about making new friends.

"We've already put money in our account with the Horseman's Bookkeeper and signed this authorized agent form, so you can withdraw funds and pay bills as you see fit," he said.

"Milos, I have a few hard and fast rules myself. I don't cut corners and charge fifty a day, tops at this track. You might think we can get by for less and you're right. But, you can pay me now or you can pay me later. I'm going to get my fifty a day one way or another. I'm tired of losing money so owners won't bitch at me. Besides, it sounds like you guys can afford it.

"And, Milos, I've never pulled a horse. When I walk a horse over there, like you said, I go to win. I don't drug my horses, unless my vet says I can pass the spit box. Neither of us needs someone looking over our shoulder with a bad test. Most of the safe drugs the vet's give around here are just to run up the bill and don't give a legit trainer much of an edge. I choose my own medication and it's usually legal. I don't let the vets train my horses.

"I don't give a shit if you bet on your horses or another horse in our race, but I never bet on my horses. I'll do just fine with the day money and my ten percent. I run strictly for the pot and that's it. You and your man will never tell me when or where to run your horses. I'm the trainer and those decisions are mine. Also, you'll have no say over who I ride.

"I'm old-fashioned. Everything I do, I learned a long time ago. I'm a third generation horseman, and don't think much has changed since my grandfather was training in Ireland. Patience is the key. Every horse gets the same treatment whether it's a stake horse or a cheap claimer.

"I know this sounds like I'm being hardheaded and over bearing. I am. I won't tell your man how to handle his business, and he's not going to tell me how to train horses."

"Well, I guess we have a deal. These are my phone numbers and the best times to call me. I have your cell and home number in Winthrop. This will get you started," he said as he pushing a large envelope across the bar.

"How do you know I live in Winthrop?"

"We know almost everything about you, Colin. We've watched and studied you for some time before coming to you with this offer."

"Just for the hell of it all, tell me, was I your first choice?"

"You were our only choice. Oh, one other thing. Don't discuss our arrangement with anyone. It's no one's business how or what we do. It could be bad for you if we find that word of our arrangement gets around.

"Just buy the horses we agree on and run them where they belong. I like to get my picture taken, even if the boss doesn't," he said, getting up from his bar stool.

Shrugging into his overcoat he said, "I'll fax you with some horses to look over. You need to make plans to get to Calder in the next few days. We have a guy there to show you around. Don't pay any attention to him. Keep our business to yourself. His name is Mike Sullivan, and he's a lightweight."

Santos picked his way through the kitchen madness, pulling his hat down before braving the cold. I ordered three more fingers of Dewar's and opened the brown envelope. It was full of hundred dollar bills. I was afraid to count, with so many hard cases around the bar. There was a note with the money.

"We've put $10,000 in our account for various expenses. We've also put a $5,000 advance in your account. The money enclosed is for the purchase of the first few horses. There's always more money available. Just ask. Good luck."

I couldn't stand the tension, so I hurried to the head and locked myself in a stall to count the money. It came to $200,000 in cash! I went cold all over, not from the weather, but from fear and excitement. Thank God I had on a ski jacket with an inside zipper pocket. I stuffed the envelope in the pocket and zipped it. I left the head feeling panic take me over. I calculated how much Dewar's it would take to shake the feeling, but realized I'd never be able to walk across the road to Barn 15, if I tried to wash it away.

I felt like everyone on the backside was watching as I walked back to my tack room to seek solace under my blanket. At least my faithful groom Jock would be back from his dinner and we could talk over what had just happened. After all these years, I don't think I could function without Jock. To hell with what Santos told me. Not telling my best friend was out of the question.

This was turning out to be one hell of a birthday!

CHAPTER TWO

When I turned the dead bolt and stepped inside, I almost passed out. The heat from the hot air blower combined with the Dewar's and Milos Santos almost made me flash. I cracked a beer from my fridge and collapsed into my recliner, with sweat covering my forehead and pouring down my sides.

How could I go from being completely broke, borrowing money from Jock for feed and hay, to almost passing out with $200,000 in my pocket? I began thinking for a safe place to put the dough. I decided to use my old tack trunk that served as a table for my television and coffee pot. It was filled with old, decaying tack, including a few saddles at the bottom. After fighting through the mildew and dust, I managed to stuff all but about ten grand into an old steeplechase saddle. I had a new bolt-cutter resistant lock in my toolbox and used it to secure the trunk.

I was back in the chair with my beer when I heard Jock's key in the dead bolt.

"See you've got the new lock on the trunk. What you hiding in there? Must be drugs, 'cause they say all the money that slimy guy gave you is in the horseman's box."

There's no use trying to hide anything from Jock. He has always known my every move, usually before I make it.

"Shit, Jock, what good does it do for me to hide something and you know where it is, just walking through the door?"

"Us thieves notice new locks, Colin. Especially when half the backside already knows you're getting new horses and have money in the box."

"How'd that get out?"

"Well, the vet and blacksmith both stopped me and thanked me for the bookkeeper paying their bills. You know Alice; she's already spending your new money before you get your hands on it," the big black man said.

"Anyway, put the old lock on the trunk and whatever's left of the money that crook gave you will be safe. I'm the only one who knows you hide everything from your booze to your stash, in there. No need to call attention to what's left of it with a fancy new lock."

I dug into my pocket, counted out five, one-hundred-dollar bills and held them out to Jock.

"What's this for? The feed bill, the money you borrowed last week or my back salary?"

"Quit acting like such a smart ass, Jock. It's really something good for us. This guy is serious. He wants me to buy five or six nice horses. And quit calling him a crook. Next thing you know, I'll be doing it."

I told him the whole story. Unlike me, he was not impressed.

"Colin, doing business on the sly with them types ain't what we're all about. I'd rather starve than eat from the hand of a guy like him."

"Look, Jock, like I told you, I laid down the rules. It's going to be fine. You won't believe how much I have to spend on the new horses," I said anxiously.

"There you go again, Colin, talking money, when I'm talking right and wrong. If this guy is hiding from the Racing Commission and using you to spend his cash in a third guy's name, somethin' ain't right. Suit yourself, son. You be goin' to do what you want to anyway, no matter what anyone else thinks. Like always, I'll be here to pick you up," he said, slamming the door to the shed row.

Jock was right about always being there for me. From the day a sheriff's deputy picked him up as an abandoned child and left him in my father's Virginia courtroom, he'd been family. He lost his leg making hay when I fell under the tractor. He jumped in front of the bailer to keep me from getting killed. His leg had been chewed to pieces before another worker could turn the machine off.

At six-seven and over three hundred pounds, Jock's impressive to say the least. His steel gray hair and erect posture give him stature unlike any man on the backside. The size of his heart and his mild, caring manner with the horses are his best qualities.

When I was a student at Woodberry Forest prep school and the University of Virginia, Jock drove my father, who had ALS, to every track, boxing and wrestling meet, to watch me compete. After my dad died, I left law school and joined the Special Forces just before Desert Storm. Jock stayed at home and looked after the farm.

My father had been an Irish steeplechase rider who became an attorney after his days as a jockey were over. Jock's never told me, but I'm sure he made some kind of deathbed promise to the Judge to look out for me. Unlike me, he's saved every dime he could and still has the money he inherited from the Judge, and it's invested as my father instructed.

My mother was killed in an accident visiting my grand-mother in New Orleans when I was seven. When the Judge died, his will required all the horses and all but fifty acres of our family farm in Augusta County be sold at auction. Jock and I refer to the fifty acres as our anchor for the day we leave racing. I pay the taxes annually on the property, but neither of us has returned to look at the place since the funeral. The bank takes a fee to look after the property.

Jock's my rock when I'm in trouble and my banker when I'm broke. He's one of the strongest and toughest men I've ever

known. I'll wager no man on the backside of Suffolk Downs
has more friends or is better respected. He lives in a small
room between the feed room and my office and acts as night
watchman, my groom and mentor. In our salad days when
we had twenty horses at the major tracks, he was the assistant
trainer and foreman. Now, with so few horses, the two of us
work every task as one.

I left the office to check on the horses and found Jock
standing outside the stall of Lost Promise, an old gray gelding.

"Run him as soon as you can, Colin. He's on the bit now
and pretty sound. I think he'll win and somebody might take
him for $12,500."

"With the new horses coming in, I'm going to run him this
week for $7,500 and hope to lose him. I think I'll just sell or
cuff the other two to somebody."

"You know, Colin, Charlie Clark and Grady O'Brien are
down to their last horse. Why don't you cuff the two old mares
to them? The boys would be damn grateful."

"You bet, Jock. Ask them next time you see them. Three
grand buys both. They only have to pay me if one of the horses
wins. They can keep the place and show money to help 'em out."

Jock didn't answer, but I knew he was pleased. Charlie and
Grady are two older gay trainers, who've been together at the
New England tracks for years. They train a few cheap horses
out of the very last barn at the rear of the backside. Jock keeps
an eye out to make sure they're not abused or treated badly. I
count them as two of my better friends on the backside, and
they know it.

I looked to see what treat Jock had for his horses and found
diced carrots. He carried them in the deep pockets of his
denim jacket along with a mane comb, hoof pick and various

ends of bandage rolls and candy, usually peppermints. He always carries a small soft brush to use around the forehead and eyes instead of a harder, larger one the horses hate.

Jock's peppermints and lifesavers stick to the side of the feed tubs in the freezing weather. Diced carrots don't. Our hay nets are hung much lower than most trainers. The horses get all the mixture of alfalfa and timothy hay they want, especially in cold weather, since constant chewing helps a horse keep warm. When fed from a high net or a corner rack near the ceiling, bits and pieces fall into the horses' eyes. Nothing is worse than runny, irritated eyes that turn icy in the cold weather. I always smile to myself when I see Jock get a handful of oats from his other pocket and pour it over the hay bag.

Jock and I are "throwbacks". Everything in the barn, like screens, racks, buckets, hayforks and rakes are hung in perfect line. The sweat sheets and coolers are folded to show our logo of a jockey leaning on the stable name. Even during training hours the coolers are hung on hooks and nothing leather is allowed to touch the ground.

We use all leather in our barn. We clean it together every day after training hours. Most barn help considers it a chore but Jock and I like to talk and clean tack. We talk about the horses, and as the old timers used to say, "visit".

Nylon halters, bridles and shanks may be cheaper and wear longer, but, in addition to being unsightly, they're unsafe. They don't break when a horse gets a foot or leg caught. You don't want to see what's left of an exercise rider's leg, twisted in nylon reins after a spill. It's just the opposite when we use the walker for the older horses. We use nylon halters over the leather to keep an unruly horse from breaking the leather and running off. Either Jock or I watch the walker at all times. It's accident going somewhere to happen.

Before leaving for my favorite evening gin joint, I glanced down the half-empty shed row, trying to imagine what it would look like in a week.

CHAPTER THREE

The Shamrock is a horsemen's bar in the Beachmont section just off Bennington Street. My Irish pal, Evan Kennedy, owns the place. If I was casting for a South Boston movie and needed someone to play the owner of a used auto parts shop, Evan would get the part. He stands a shade under six feet and is overfed. His jet-black hair stays slicked to his head with a Jack Palance flip and an old yellow pencil run through the greasy mop. His red complexion tells of a lifetime of hard drinking. I have my suspicion high blood pressure and a pending heart attack add to his crimson look.

For a racetrack where Italians and Irishmen argue, fight and generally try to piss off each other whenever they're together, The Shamrock is a neutral watering hole. Evan established long ago that his bar is a place to relax and let off steam after a day on the backside. Getting out of line over heritage is not tolerated. The laughter is infectious, and the bar's "Fear Factor" is zero. Horsemen, many quick to anger, usually go along with the bar's relaxed atmosphere.

Jockeys and agents work the room for rides. Trainers work each other, looking for an edge or a tip on a possible claim or sale. Many of the card games have had the same players for years. No one misses the banging of pool sticks and pinball machines so prevalent in the track kitchen and rougher bars that cater to grooms and exercise riders.

The loudest voice in the bar is usually Cosey Costas, my least favorite fellow trainer, known for his arrogance and bullying personality. Costas came from West Virginia several years ago and brought his aggressive attitude with him. His main client is Connie Tass, a Russian "baker" from the South End who's known to be one of Boston's most ruthless mobsters.

For a city that historically loves its Irish and Italian

dominated crime structure, Boston has been rocked over the
last decade with the growing gangs of Russian, Oriental and
Latino criminals who resort to random violence to make an
impression on their peers. In areas such as Beachmont, Orient
Heights, Revere and Revere Beach, the calm streets where
children used to play after dark have become dangerous,
forcing older residents to become couch dwellers and constant
TV watchers. Local family bars and restaurants still thrive, but
there's a feeling of danger in many areas, the kind where youth
gangs sell their wares under street lights.

Costas is a huge, heavy set, crude-looking bull of a man,
an ex-coal miner. He's never had the nerve to confront me
straight up, but I know he trashes me as a snob and tells
anyone who'll listen that I think I'm too good for Suffolk's
backside.

When I walked into The Shamrock, I could hear him
running off at the mouth at his regular card table near the door
to the back parking lot. I gave him a long stare as Evan said,
"Booze or beer, Colin?"

"Dewar's tall, Evan."

I glanced around the room and noticed my vet, Emmy
Townsend, seated at a small corner table staring through her
beer, as far away from Costas as she could get.

"How long has Emmy been back there?"

"She was at the bar and had a burger when she first came
in, but she had some words with Costas and moved into the
corner. He's been trashing her from his table non-stop. Seems
she warned Costas not to run an old, sore mare today and
he told her to go to hell. The mare fell and she had to put her
down. You know Emmy; she takes things like that real personal. She gave Costas a piece of her mind and told him to shove

his horses, she'd never come back under his shed row."

I'll never know why Emmy stays at Suffolk Downs. She's a graduate of the New Bolton Center Vet School and could work at any racetrack in the country. Emmy's a striking woman with a mane of long blond hair. She's one of the most powerful women I've known, with the bone structure of a diva. She hides her best features with large horn-rimmed glasses and a refusal to wear make-up. Her hair usually pours out the back of a Red Sox cap. Loose fitting sweaters and khakis make it impossible to guess her figure. Deep green eyes only hint of the volume of emotions buried inside. On occasion, particularly when drunk and lonely, I fantasize about Emmy's womanly attributes and wonder if she's as shy as she appears.

I walked to Emmy's table and pulled out a chair. "Could a gentleman buy a beautiful woman a fresh beer?"

She looked at me in surprise. "You ass, Colin. It's been three years, and now you're going to hit on me?"

"What keeps you around here, Emmy? You could practice anywhere."

"If I asked you the same thing, you'd tell me you have to go where your horses take you." She hesitated a moment, ignoring my question. "I hear you may have some better horses soon. They gonna' take you out of Boston... and leave me behind?"

She glanced toward the back door as the noise factor grew. "I hate Costas. He's a real shit."

"You want me to go over there and kick his fat ass for you?"

"You'd do that?" she asked.

"You don't know what I'd do for a fancy Texas girl like you," I answered, grinning at our flirting.

She took a long drink from her beer and studied me. "Why haven't you ever looked at me? You know, like a guy looks at a woman's ass. Half the men on the track have visually undressed me, but never you. I get the impression my only attraction to you is my ability to take care of your horses."

I stared at her, as she continued.

"You know, Colin, I've tried to catch your eye, at times. Left my jacket off more than once, to give you a good shot at my boobs. You never even looked at me."

I blushed. "Emmy, cut it out. You're embarrassing me... us. You've never talked like this."

She shrugged. "I'm a divorced woman. Haven't had a date since I got to Boston. You're a single man. Sometimes, I think we could have a little action." She choked on a bitter laugh. "Oh, God... I'm making a fool of myself. Must be the beer."

I leaned across the table. "To tell you the truth, Emmy, I've looked at you plenty of times. A lot of guesswork, though. You hide yourself pretty good."

She sat back in her chair. "In a previous lifetime, I was an alternate on the Olympic downhill ski team and trained at the Olympic Village in Colorado. I met and married a big, bad professional from Denmark. He made me quit skiing and treated me badly enough to scar me for life. There were drugs. He dominated my life, belittling me, getting physical. Finally, when I called the cops, he went back to Denmark and left us. Thank God."

"Us?"

"I have a four-year-old daughter, Colin. That's why I drive in from Derry every day. I have a live-in to care for Aimee. It's better for her there — slower, a better life.

"Anyway, I guess you'd say I'm man shy. I hate most men. But you're different... a gentleman, a nice guy... the way you care for Jock, and the little guys you take up for on the backside. You give me faith there might be a decent man in my future."

Her statement ended on a questioning note. I took a deep breath and tried to explain.

"It's not you, Emmy. I have this unfinished thing with someone in Aiken, where I wintered my horses for years. I owe us at least a chance to see if we can work anything out. If not, I need to bring closure to it. I'm going down there to look at some horses this week. When I get back, maybe things will be different. I have to give it a try."

She smiled. "See, I said you were a nice guy."

During the short lull in our conversation, Costas' voice cut the air.

"Nah, he's not hitting on the dyke vet. He likes guys, like them queers back in the corner barn. They say he's going broke. Heard he's moving in with the gay guys to save money. I'm going to take over Barn 15."

As I rose from my seat, Evan called, "Take it outside if you have to Colin."

Costas stood up as I turned from my chair. In two strides, I hit him with my shoulder to his gut, crashing through the door and onto the ice in the parking lot. I landed on top of him and worked his face over. When he rolled, turning face down to avoid the blows, I grabbed his hair and banged his head into the icy surface, which turned a faint red from his bleeding. Ignoring his groans, I pulled him to his feet and forced him head first into the dumpster, slamming the plastic lid on his head a few times, for good measure.

"Never, ever talk about Emmy or me again, shithead, or you won't walk away when I'm through with you."

When I walked back into the bar, Emmy was standing by the front door, with my ski jacket and two glasses of scotch.

I followed her out the door to her van.

"You did that for me, didn't you?"

I tried to laugh, but my jaw hurt. Costas had gotten in a lucky shot.

She killed her drink in one gulp, and then kissed me, warmly and wetly, letting her palm rest on my thigh. "Call me when you get back from Aiken," she said, before getting into her van and waving goodbye.

Then she was gone, heading for the interstate to New Hampshire and her Aimee. "What a waste of time the past few years," I thought to myself.

CHAPTER FOUR

Even without a fire on a cold winter night, my small Winthrop cottage overlooking the ocean is one of the warmest places I have ever lived. Call it chronic nesting, but that's just me.

Small oil paintings inherited from my father hang in every nook and cranny of the cottage. A Civil War painting by Florida artist Gilbert Gaul of a war torn Confederate soldier leaning on a wooden rail fence, has hung over the fireplace where ever I've lived. The forlorn look on the soldier's face has mirrored my own since I returned from Desert Storm.

The Gaul oil and a wonderful, small etching by Mary Cassett are the only non-sporting art in my cottage. I was lighting the fatwood in the tiny fireplace when the phone rang. Nadine and Killer were going wild barking and scratching at the back door.

There's probably no worse combination of dogs than a Jack Russell terrier and a whippet. Killer is the sanest whippet I've ever encountered, but that's not saying much. When he runs the backyard, I'm astounded as he leaps and hangs in midair. Short-legged Nadine covers a lot of ground, but is no match for Killer. What she lacks in jumping ability, she makes up barking and growling, her two best attributes.

The dogs jumped all over me, almost causing me to drop the pasta I'd brought home from the Italian joint in downtown Winthrop. I held the box over my head, dripping gravy onto my jacket as the dogs pounded me. I couldn't care less. I had new horses in my future and a pocket full of cash. As I put the pasta on the counter, I thought of the money in the tack trunk at the barn. I knew with Jock on the lookout, it was safer than in the local bank.

"Hello," I growled into the phone.

"You Colin O'Hearn?" asked the caller.

It was a low, secretive voice, giving off the impression he wanted only me to hear him.

"What's left of him," I laughed.

There was a pause, like I had disarmed my caller.

"Mr. Santos told me to call you. I'm Sullivan, from Miami."

He continued before I could answer, "What kind of horses you looking for O'Hearn?"

"Fast ones ready to run," I answered, slightly annoyed that Santos had not told me Sullivan would be bothering me at home.

"From what Mr. Santos told me, I think I have what you want."

"Who are you with, Mr. Sullivan?"

"I sell a lot of horses privately around Calder and Gulfstream."

"I've done a lot of business with some very good trainers from Gulfstream and Calder, but I don't recall ever hearing your name."

"Mr. Santos will vouch for me, O'Hearn," his voice challenged.

"I'll tell you what, Mr. Sullivan. I'll give you my fax number and you can send me the pedigrees, prices and any *Racing Form* clips if they've run recently," I said flatly.

"I'll see what I can get together. If Mr. Santos says he wants my horses, you'll be down here to pick 'em up," he snapped.

"Mr. Sullivan, the terms of my agreement with Mr. Santos are between us, but I can assure you, the final decision on any horses I train will be left to me."

Before he could answer, I said, "Just send me the faxes, Sullivan, and thanks."

"I'll see you in Miami, O'Hearn," he said as he hung up.

I cracked a Sam Adams, pushed the dogs off the sofa and started dinner with Dan Rather. I finished the last meatball as a Cheers rerun began.

The fax machine made its noise and spit out a half dozen pages from Sullivan.

I switched back to a tall Dewar's and began to read the faxes when the phone rang again. It was Santos.

"Well, Colin, I understand you've talked with Sullivan and he sent you some faxes. What do you think?"

"I'm surprised. Some of the horses might be useful if sound."

"We've been shopping for horses in training for awhile, and our connections in Miami passed these along."

He went on, "Sullivan's just a tool we use to stay out of the direct line when doing business. We've bought several horses in Miami. An idiot like Sullivan can come in handy."

I said, "I know of a few older horses in Aiken that are ready to go back to New York and Kentucky after a winter of rehab. I'd like to take a look at them, if you don't mind."

After a pause he said, "On the way back from Miami, go to Aiken if you like. Just take a look at the ones we have lined up in Florida first."

After he hung up, I got on the computer and made flight reservations to Miami and a connection to Atlanta. I booked a car to Aiken and then a flight back to Boston directly from Atlanta. I had unfinished business with Annie Collins in Aiken.

Annie was the best thing that ever happened to me. She'd left the show ring after graduating from Hollins College and headed to Aiken, where she took to galloping thoroughbreds like a fish to water. She could ride anything with hair on it and was one of the few female riders the trainers would put on their tougher colts. Many of the seasoned horses brought all their bad manners to Aiken for the winter after a long season of racing the toughest of company. Annie had a way of calming them the first time up and keeping them within themselves throughout the winter. Rather than working for one trainer, she freelanced and was never short of work. Several trainers with the nation's best fillies would wait late in the morning for Annie, knowing their best were in the safest hands.

I'd fallen hard for her. She had strawberry blond hair, long and frizzy-curly in damp weather. She called it her Irish look. Her calf and thigh muscles were well developed, her arms thin and sinewy, but strong enough she could throw a two-hundred-pound man. She walked a horseman's walk, slightly bent from a dozen falls she ignored. She walked with a slight limp, which became a shuffle when the weather turned cold and rainy. Her strong hands bulged with coarse veins, yet she was soft and assuring at the same time.

We'd shipped from Aiken to New York and Saratoga for three years, sharing a lover's bond we were sure would last forever. We laughed and loved in a robust manner that made many envious. I lost myself in her strength of character and her passion in bed. We were avid readers, and books were always scattered throughout the house and stables.

Our friends never figured out why we'd broken up several years ago at Saratoga. Rumors held it was another woman and my excessive drinking. The rumors were right.

The "other woman" wanted me to train for her. She meant nothing to me. Our affair lasted a few nights. I confessed to Annie.

She cried and moped, sleeping on the sofa at night. After three days, she walked into the kitchen at five o'clock in the morning, tears running down her face, and landed a closed

fist punch to my mouth most men couldn't match. My chair
tumbled over backward and hot coffee poured across my
crotch. By the time I stopped screaming and got to my feet, the
finest woman I've ever known had walked out of the house,
gotten into her packed car and drove away.

I hadn't seen or spoken to her since. She went directly from
Saratoga to Aiken where she settled in year round. I had one
letter from her. Five lines. She told me Aiken was her place,
not mine, and begged me not to return the next winter and not
to contact her. Ever.

I wrote to her once, but the letter came back.

I doubted Annie would take me back, but I had to try. At
the least, I had to try and see her. There had been too many
cold and lonely nights in the last several years. Too many times
I'd reached for her in the dark. I'd slept with a few other women,
but it was like drinking flat coke, compared to loving Annie.

CHAPTER FIVE

Nadine, like most Jack Russells, will sleep forever if you let her. Killer, unlike most whippets, is a combination guard dog and alarm clock. Dawn is his waking hour and he never sleeps past it. Dawn for me is too late. Like other horsemen, 4:45 AM is time to be splashing water on my face and scraping my teeth. When Killer started licking my face, I knew I was in trouble. I'd slept so well even Nadine was whining by the back door when my feet hit the floor.

I blew off my shower and was out the door in record time. After a quick stop for my regular black coffee and donuts at Harry's Bakery under the train overpass outside the back gate, I parked my pickup outside Barn 15 and threaded my way across the ice into my shed row.

"About time, Colin. The old horse is ready and you be holdin' Steve back," Jock said.

Just then Steve Casey, who doubles as my morning exercise rider and afternoon jock, rounded the turn at the far end of the shed row with a loud bang. Lost Promise, the cranky claimer who'd seen better days, kicked the neighbor's wheelbarrow as he passed.

"Damn it, you worthless skate. Straighten up and save it for the track," Steve cursed. They knew each other from a hundred mornings together. The cranky, seven-year old gray was sending Steve a message.

The pair passed Jock and he warned me, "You better get that man to write this horse something or he's going to leave his race on the track in the next few mornings."

"He's in for Saturday, Jock. That gives me time to get to Calder and look at horses and be back in time to saddle him."

"That deal with the man in the shiny suit still on, Colin?"

"Until I hear different. He called me last night, all excited.

I'm going to the airport as soon as I watch this horse go. You'll have to handle everything until I get back, Jock."

"So what else is different? I've been doing stables every afternoon for twelve years, Colin. You better tell Steve what you want these horses to do in the morning, while you're gone. Even after all this time, he gets a little heady when he thinks I'm trying to be you... .fat chance I'd ever want to be you!," Jock laughed.

I left to brave the cold trackside. Twenty yards ahead, Steve sat chilly as possible as the gray horse pulled him from side to side up the icy horse path to the track. Other horses were scattering at his antics and I was full of reasons why I loved my business so much.

Since the first day the Judge had turned me loose to handle the training chores, I could count on one hand the number of times either Jock or I had not been with the horses to and from the track when they trained. We watched them with eyes peeled for a strange step or any other sign that things were just not right.

In this day of the declining horsemen, few trainers could get much out of following or, as we say, tracking horses. Most are lucky to catch a bad step. Jock and I watch that each footprint is spaced properly. Coming home, we look at how they move. We look for soundness and breathing and, most of all, the wear on the ace bandages as they hit the ground. If the dirt is excessive on one side or missing from one bandage while the other is run down and filthy, the horse is getting off one foot or leg and putting all his weight on the other.

The Judge called these markings on the bandages targets. I've saved many a horse from serious problems by following them home and getting right on the developing problems.

There's a big difference between someone with a trainer's license and a horseman who's been schooled under an old-timer. A good horseman worth his salt is on to trouble before it blossoms into a full-blown injury. Good trainers develop a sixth sense by training horses the old fashioned way. The Judge's favorite saying was, "If something doesn't look quite right, then something is wrong. Trouble always gives notice."

If I could get Lost Promise claimed Saturday and the boys took the other two horses on the cuff, I'd have a fresh, empty shedrow before my new horses arrived I planned to give Steve my word he'd continue to ride for me, no matter how good the new horses were. There are better riders than Steve in the jock's room, but I have loyalty to someone who's stuck with me through thick and thin.

There are bitter games played among trainers, owners, jockeys and their agents. When a jockey "gets off " a horse that has run well for him, it can cause hard feelings between agents and trainers. It's called "spinning" a trainer. He thinks he has a regular rider and finds out, after the entries close, that the jockey has taken off his horse to ride another, possibly a lesser horse. Then feelings can run high if a jockey rides regularly for one trainer and gets a winning "catch ride"; often the jock's agent will spin the winning horse and keep his commitment to the regular trainer who may have a dozen head. The trainer who is spun from his winning horse is often irate at the jock's agent. It's just track politics, but it can lead to hard feelings.

By the break, my three charges had trained, were cooled out, and Jock was doing them up. I was at my usual kitchen table with Arch Hale, Steve's agent. We're a trio, Evan Kennedy, Arch Hale and myself. Arch has spent his entire adult life and part of his childhood around racetracks, the last thirty at Suffolk.

Only five-ten, he carries over three hundred pounds like a dump truck without a driver. People see his carrot colored head come rumbling through the kitchen or grandstand and they just move aside. Like Evan, Arch has the face of a drinker and is probably closer to a heart attack than Evan. Standing side by side, their faces look like two carriage lamps outside a whorehouse.

Arch was bitching about the weather, bad horses and loud trainers. I was immersed in my *Racing Form,* making sure no horses were running that I might want to claim. I always talk about claiming another trainer's horses, just to keep them on edge and weary. I seldom do. I was ignoring Arch's mumbled bitching, thinking about my plane trip to Miami and what lay ahead, when he said something that made my head snap up.

"They say you got a new man... lots of money and lots of muscle."

"What the hell's that supposed to mean?"

"I was at The Shamrock late last night, after you had put on your show and left. Costas came back in from the parking lot, looking like a truck had hit him. He was mouthing off that my alcoholic friend had better look out for that guy Santos, you were seen huddling with at the track kitchen."

"He's been trying to get between you and me over Steve since the start of the meet," Arch added.

"I didn't know that. I know he's ridden Steve a few times, but never when I needed him."

"Why'd you go after him like that, Colin? He's always mouthing off and he hates those queer guys. It's just whiskey and bullshit talking. One of his owners came in after you popped him. That hard-nosed Russian, Connie Tass, was mad as hell you whipped up on Costas. He owns a bakery in the

South End, and some people say he's a loan-shark and all kinds of other shit. You know what that means, Colin? Collectors and rough guys.

"Anyway, they were talking about getting even with you. Both of 'em got drunk and Evan had to calm 'em down."

"Arch, I'm a big boy and I'm not afraid of a bunch of bar drunks, but thanks for the warning," I said, trying to sound confident.

I changed the subject. "I put Steve on Lost Promise in the $7,500 going a route for Saturday. I'm going out of town today, but I'll be back for the race."

"Yeah, I know. You're headed to Miami for that Santos guy."

"Who the hell told you that?"

"I heard Costas tell Tass. I told you he knows everything those Italians are up to. I think there's bad blood between Tass and the guy Santos works for from the North End."

With a worried look, my pal Arch heaved his frame up from the table and bellowed across the rowdy track kitchen, "Come on now, Steve, we gotta make a living. I'll meet you at Barn 7 to breeze one first after the break. Track ought to be harrowed by now!"

It took me a few minutes to drink the last of my coffee, fold my *Racing Form,* then ease toward the door. I shivered when I stepped out into the bright sunlight breaking through the clearing sky. I wasn't actually cold. Deep down inside, Costas and Tass bothered me. The last thing I needed was to get in a pissing contest between the Russian and my new owner. I don't think Santos is tough enough to handle Tass, but something told me my phantom owner might be a horse of another color.

My plane didn't leave until noon. After I left the dogs at the kennel, I stopped by The Shamrock for a beer and sandwich.

The first guy I saw was Steve Casey, and I could tell there was something on his mind. I made my way through the early lunch crowd and settled in a booth in the back of the room. Steve eased off his stool and came to sit across from me.

"I hear you're going to Miami this afternoon to look at horses. Why didn't you tell me this morning?"

"Where'd you hear that?"

"You know how jocks talk. They say you paid the vet and feed man already. I'm just hoping that we'll be getting some better horses, that's all. Tell me what's going on, Colin."

"I'm not sure just yet, Steve. But you can bet I'll be staying with you. You've been good to me, riding on the cuff in the mornings, even when I couldn't afford to pay you. There might be hotter jocks and they'll all be trying to steal your new mounts. But it's like I told Arch, your job with me is sound, pal."

"What kind of horses?"

"Like I said, son, I'm not too sure. Probably five or six and nothing but high claimers and allowance horses, if I can buy what the man wants," I assured him.

"No shit, Colin — real horses!"

Steve was past his prime, but he still had soft hands and used good common sense during a race. Better yet, he rides to orders and never gets too excited. He's one of the reasons I told Santos I had the final word, when it came to naming riders. He's never flashy, just steady.

When I paid Steve once a month, because money was short, he'd never complained. He knew when I had it, he'd get paid. I slipped five, one-hundred-dollar bills under the table. He didn't count it, just got up, put it in his jeans and thanked me.

"I could tell by the way you walked in here, Colin, that

things were going to be different. You had your head up and I knew you were holdin'. "

He tapped me on my arm. "I knew it... I knew it. We're going to be just fine... just fine."

I felt even better as I pulled my truck out of the parking lot and made the ten-minute run to Logan Airport.

CHAPTER SIX

The bulbous-eyed FBI agent Martin Watson slammed down the receiver of his desk phone and bellowed to his secretary through his half-opened door. "Mary Ann, get Fred Hardy of the Federal Strike Force in Miami on the phone!"

Watson, the longest serving agent in the Boston FBI office has been in charge of the search for Whitey Bulger, since his disappearance a decade ago. The Bay Area mobster, one of America's ten most wanted criminals, was said to be in Europe with his girlfriend, so Watson has plenty of time to dabble in other projects.

One of Watson's favorite such projects was his longtime pal Vito Corsetti, who has been in the sights of the Miami-based Hardy. One of Watson's least favorite fellow agents, Hardy had begun working with the FBI under Watson in Boston, but carefully politicked his way on to the Miami Organized Crime Task Force. He was after Corsetti for money laundering Florida drug proceeds. As the Boston agent picked up the phone, he cringed at Hardy's high-pitched voice, "What's on your mind, Watson?"

"You know that fellow Milos Santos you guys have been watching?"

"He's not a priority, but there's been some strange cash movements between Boston and Miami in a few of our drug cases, and Santos' name keeps popping up. We see him get it and then the money just disappears. We've never have been able to catch him laundering."

Hardy hesitated a moment, "He's a CPA for businesses in Boston owned by people on our watch list. When Miami money goes into those restaurants, it vanishes. We can't find out how it returns to Miami after being cleaned. Santos has turned up in some photos and videos of guys we'd love to tag.

You got something I can use?"

Watson, a heavy man with eyebrows like toothbrushes hidden behind thick, Tom Kite-like glasses, lit another of his never- ending line of cigarettes. He coughed and mumbled into the phone, "Santos's name turned up on one of my lists from a strange source today."

"What kind of list?"

"The Massachusetts State Racing Commission's licensing list. He's been granted an owner's license to race at Suffolk Downs. He's going to race under the stable name di Vinci Stable."

Hardy paused and said, "Any names on the permit, like a partnership?"

"No, just him. Probably nothing. The only other name on the application is his trainer, a local guy named Colin O'Hearn. Probably means nothing. Just wanted you to know his name crossed my desk," Watson said wanting the conversation to end.

"Fax me a copy of the license form and keep an eye on him. By the way, what has he got to do with your investigation?"

"As you know, Whitey Bulger is this office's prime target. His brother, who used to be president of the state senate, is now the head of the university system. He's supposed to be straight, but we watch him like a hawk. We cross his name with all the boards and commissions, including licensing permits. The computer kicked out Santos when he received a racing license. It's probably nothing, but Santos works for one of Whitey's old connections, Vito Corsetti, the owner of Little Venice Restaurant," he said between coughs.

"Thanks for the heads up, Watson. I'll keep you posted."

After breaking off the Boston call, Hardy popped the thick

rubber band on his left wrist. He used it when he got pressured or nervous. What he really wanted was a cigarette. He'd been off them for more than a year. Snapping the rubber band a couple more times, he turned to his computer.

After calling up his file on persons of interest, he added, "Colin O'Hearn, Suffolk Downs" to his watch list.

At the same time Hardy was adding Colin O'Hearn's name to his watch list, Martin Watson closed the door to his office and made a call on his private cell phone.

"Jimmy, tell the man to be careful with Santos and the racing action. I got a call from an agent in Miami. They picked up on Santos getting a license from the Racing Commission. Just watch what money you spend and where. By the way, we're due one of our lunches at the bank parking lot soon."

"Okay, Friday for lunch."

After hanging up, Watson thought about his long time arrangement with Vito Corsetti. The old man had been good to him for many years. In return, he'd kept Corsetti informed about any action in his or his friends' direction by the FBI. It had been several months since he'd had anything to report. Stirring the fire by getting Hardy moving in that direction was a way to make sure the old man at Little Venice Restaurant knew he was watching out for him.

It was a thin line, but he'd crossed it many years ago. His late wife had made frequent very expensive visits to a hospital for her drinking problem, and they were not covered by his insurance. Without the money Vito paid him on the sly, he'd also never have been able to send his two boys through college. They were no longer students, but he'd continued to rationalize lining his pockets with Vito's unreported cash.

The FBI and press always marveled that Bulger evaded

capture and was always two steps ahead of the law. Many knew Bulger had friends in high places, but had never figured out where to look.

CHAPTER SEVEN

I had three drinks and a sandwich before my half-empty flight dropped out of the clouds approaching the Miami airport. After getting off the plane I carried my briefcase and my only luggage, a shoulder bag, to the ground transportation exit.

I spotted a short man furiously chewing gum with a sign in his hand bearing my name. He was more bald than not and had a droopy mustache and a high forehead. Maybe 35, he looked 50 and very nervous.

This had to be Mike Sullivan.

As I approached him, Sullivan spoke loudly. "You must be O'Hearn. Mike Sullivan here. Glad you made it. I've got a bunch a horses to show you at Calder."

He pumped my hand with a sweaty grip. I was over-dressed for the warm Miami weather in my ski jacket. I handed him three of the past performances he'd sent me. "These three are the only horses I'm interested in, Sullivan. I've been over the others and they won't fit."

"But a few of the others are real bargains. I picked them out myself. Trainers are waiting. They'll be disappointed."

I looked him right in the eye and leveled with him. "Sullivan, I have to train these horses and I know what I'm looking for. If I didn't know better, the ones you're pushing are daily specials you must be getting a cut on. Don't embarrass both of us by wasting my time looking at horses I don't want to train."

"You're all wrong about that, O'Hearn," he snapped without much conviction.

He fell into a surly silence as we got into his car, a ten-year-old Caddy that needed more work than it was worth. I'd slipped into a light jacket that matched my khakis and a crewneck sweater. My battered yellow Aiken Training Track

cap completed the outfit. Any horseman at any sale, from
Kentucky to California, would see I had "hard-boot" written
all over me.

Sullivan tried to chat me up on the way from the airport,
but I wasn't much help. The less he knew, the better off I was.
I said a few nice things about the weather and the improve-
ments to Calder Racecourse since I was last there, but nothing
about horses.

He'd given up trying to impress me by the time we passed
through the stable gate and into the Calder barn area. I noticed
he received less than welcome glances from the two guards.
That told me a great deal about his status on the backside. No
one waved to him as we threaded our way through the hedges
and barns. Not a single wave or smile from a usually friendly
backside convinced me he was one of the dreaded black cats
found around racetracks. That was the last straw.

"Instead of taking me to Barn 17, just drop me off at the
track kitchen, where you can wait for me. I want to inspect
these horses on my own."

"You can't do that. Mr. Santos will be mad as hell if I'm not
with you."

"Mr. Santos is going to be mad as hell if I call him and tell
him you're being a pain in the ass and getting in my way. I've
been all over this track for years. I know all the trainers of the
horses I've selected. I'd rather be alone," I said firmly.

He sulked and gripped the steering wheel like it was my
neck and he was choking it to death.

I tried to soothe him, "Look Mike, you'll get your commission. Mr. Santos told me that himself. But he also said I could
go it alone and for you to call him if you've got a problem."

I slipped him fifty dollars and said, "Now, be a good guy

and go get a beer in the track kitchen."

Before he could say anything, I got out of the car and walked away quickly like a man who's made a loan and is trying to get away before the banker changes his mind.

CHAPTER EIGHT

Mary Ann didn't knock before entering Watson's office. She weaved through a thick cloud of cigar smoke, as she approached his desk.

"Mr. Watson, you're going to kill me with that darned cigar smoke. I think I'd rather die from your cigarettes. At least it wouldn't take as long as from those awful stogies."

"First you want me to slow down on the smoke, now it's the smell. I don't know how your old man puts up with your bitching, Mary Ann."

"He loves me and I know it, even if he does gamble both our paychecks away sometimes," she said sadly.

If she didn't work for the Feds, her husband would have been floating in Boston's cold harbor waters long ago. A compulsive gambler, his antics had almost ruined their marriage. Only her staunch Catholic background and a mother who controlled her with an iron fist kept her married to Thomas Murphy.

"Does Tom still bet the ponies?" Watson asked, as he ground out his half-smoked cigar. Mary Ann knew the early death of the cigar was a sign he was appeasing her.

"You scared him to death about his gambling at those places in the North End last year. It didn't cure him altogether. He thinks he's keeping his word by staying away from the bookies. He goes to the OTB and to the track. I think he just likes hanging out at Suffolk Downs. He's met some old retired guys that go everyday. They pour over the papers and read those darned charts," she rambled.

Watson took a fresh pack of Camels from his top drawer and turned it over in his fat hand while looking out the window.

"You wanted something when you came in here, I assume?"

"That new name we added to the watch list is on the

printout this morning. Colin O'Hearn. He's on a flight to Miami as we speak. Didn't you just talk to Mr. Hardy in Miami about him?"

"Hardy and his hard-on in Miami."

"Mr. Watson... "

"Call Hardy for me again, Mary Ann. Maybe he knows something more about our Mr. O'Hearn and that slime ball Santos."

After Mary Ann placed the call, Watson picked up and said, "Look, Fred, the printout on the flights out of Boston has that horse trainer we talked about heading to Miami. Thought you might be interested."

"You guys are faster than us, Watson. He wouldn't have come across our desk for a day or two, if then. Why do you think he's coming here?"

"Hard to tell, Fred. Maybe it's just horse business. Funny thing though, my background check showed him to be a broke-dick horse trainer with a lot of education and a drinking problem."

"Maybe he's come into a new source of funds. You don't fly to Miami to buy horses unless you have some real scratch. I'd love for it to be dirty cash," Hardy added.

Watson said nothing in return. He'd let Hardy offer what he was thinking without prodding. It was his way to give as little as possible and listen.

"I have a few drug folks watching at Calder. Maybe I can see if O'Hearn shows up with cash. It's the only local racetrack open this time of year," Hardy continued.

"How are you going to know if he's there or not?" Watson asked.

"Visitors have to sign in with security at the stable gate. I've got somebody in the security office. She'll know."

Watson rang off. Hardy got through to the security office
and found his contact.

"He checked in through the gate early this afternoon. He
put down inspecting horses as his reason and listed two barns.
I can take a ride in my golf cart in a minute and spot him.
Strangers on the backside stand out around here. No one's
moving around much until feeding time. We're dark today.
It's slow around here with no racing," she explained.

"Just watch him, honey. Tell me where he goes and who he
sees. If money changes hands, I want to know. Maybe a groom
or the horseman's bookkeeper will know who and how he
pays."

It took Hardy's security snitch less than ten minutes to spot
Colin with a visitor's pass clipped to his jacket walking into
Barn 17. She parked her golf cart under a shade tree right next
to a muck pit, took out a newspaper and watched the stranger.
He walked up to a man and began talking as if they were old
friends.

The trainer, an old-timer named Matt Lewis, only had a few
horses. One was a promising allowance colt named Cherokee
Moon. The gossip around the track was that Lewis was trying
to sell a colt that had broken his maiden by seven or eight
lengths the week before. The old man needed money and it
was the only hot horse he had in his barn. She was sure the
man she was told to watch was going after the young colt.

Lewis was no fool. If he could sell the colt after one start, he
might be able to buy three older useful horses and spread out
some of the cost risk in his barn. If he had another few months
like the last few, he'd be out of business. The security guard
knew who Lewis was, but not why he'd sell his best prospect,
save that he had bills outstanding around the backside.

Lewis knew the colt wasn't without his problems. He had a knot on his shin and probably should be fired and rested. He didn't have time for either. Lewis was ready to gamble, if a chance to make some ready money came up. He'd been thrilled when Colin called him from the plane telling him he was on his way to Calder to buy some horses in training. Colin was a good enough trainer that he'd see the knot, but he wouldn't let it totally discourage him. He'd be able to handle it and still get some run out of the colt.

Lewis had bought the flighty colt for $7,500 at the Ocala sale last fall. Since the colt had won his first start with such flair, Colin might jump at him. Lewis was hoping the Boston trainer had a client's money to spend. That way, he'd be more willing to pay a better price for Cherokee Moon. Either way, he was glad to see his old pal walking under his shed row on a slow afternoon when he was in the mood to sell his only good horse.

CHAPTER NINE

I hadn't seen Matt Lewis since we were both at Delaware Park about six years earlier. Our handshake was genuine and our conversation about Cherokee Moon was short and to the point.

The groom brought the flashy chestnut son of Cherokee Run from his stall looking bright and healthy. He had a very attractive head with a dish between his eyes which I found appealing. As much as I liked his head, I made a mental note of the horse's eyes. He had too much white around the iris and was constantly looking from one place to another. He never concentrated on anything. He was probably a scatterbrain.

I've have always disliked white-eyed chestnuts. Every really nasty colt I've had over the years was a chicken-gutted, white-eyed chestnut. They'll paw you with their front feet and tend to rear at the slightest movement. They sometimes flip over the minute you push them around. Often, despite all their faults, they're very fast. The key is to avoid trouble. I could look at this colt and could tell Jock could take the edge off him with his gentle touch. The Latino groom was jerking the shank and shaking the chain to keep the colt at a distance as they walked. The colt was light boned and small of stature but he had a lot going for him. He had a stout chest and was beautifully muscled. If Matt Lewis was nothing else, he was a fine conditioner.

"I watched his race the other day on TV," I said. "He's not much when it comes to rating. Just ran away from the other horses."

"No question about that, Colin. He's just speed. I'm afraid to guess if he'll go a route of ground. That's why I'm selling him," the trainer added.

I knew Lewis well and respected him. There was no real sales talk between us. I believed him when he said he needed money. I knew the worried look in his eye. I didn't think the colt was Florida stakes caliber, but he would do well in Boston. Despite his temperament and eye, he was a good mover and covered the ground freely.

He fit the bill. When Lewis said he wanted forty thousand, I never batted an eye. Matt was down on his luck, as I'd been many times, and I knew not to try to barter my pal down. We shook hands on the deal and I gave him the name of a veterinarian I had used in the past. Arrangements were made for x-rays of all four legs and for the horse to be scoped.

"Can you get it done this afternoon?" I asked.

"It's dark today, but I saw Dr. Mills around here about an hour ago. He's probably at his office by the receiving barn. I'll go there from here." Lewis said.

As I walked away from Lewis' barn, I recognized a vanning agent I knew walking between barns.

"Hey, Charlie Pierce!" I called.

The van agent hurried over.

"Damn, Colin, I was looking for you. I heard you were on the grounds to buy horses and I wanted to tell you that I have a van going to Philly and Boston in two days."

"How'd you know I was here, Charlie?"

"The guy from our Boston office called and said to look out for you. You know the old racetrack pipeline," Charlie chuckled. He was an ex-jock who'd once made his living on the New England circuit and now had a good thing going after retiring to Florida. I told Charlie he'd probably have two or three to ship from Calder to Boston. I also mentioned that I might have a horse or two to pick up in Aiken.

"Your old stomping grounds, Aiken. Loved it there myself in the '70s. Remember, I went there with Mack Miller after I hung up my tack in New England," Charlie said with a fond smile.

Running into Charlie wasn't surprising. Networking has always been part of the racetrack. I watched him head toward Lewis' barn and knew he'd handle all the details. What seemed strange to me was a woman security guard had her nose in a newspaper under a tree across from Lewis' barn. She was there when I went into the barn and still reading the same paper an hour later.

The newspaper and golf cart weren't unusual. What bothered me was the length of time the guard had been sitting in the same spot, next to a smelly manure pit. It's not the most pleasant place for a woman to catch up on an hour's reading on a hot afternoon.

If something doesn't look right, I thought, something's probably wrong. If it looks like a duck, walks like a duck, has webbed feet and a bill, it's probably a duck.

CHAPTER TEN

The difference between Lewis' proper shed row and the madhouse run by Paco Gomez was the difference between night and day.

Gomez's forty-stall barn had loud Latin music blaring from a half dozen different radio stations. Latin grooms in tank tops, if any shirt at all, roamed the barn in some sort of feeding ritual. Horses were slapped, chased with plastic pitchforks and subjected to all sorts of verbal abuse. Some horses had three or four different-colored bandages held up by masking tape. Broken or bent screens or webbings were hung with no rhyme or reason, some held up by baling twine rather than screw-eyes.

Overseeing this maze of activity was a huge trainer wearing several gold rings and various gold chains hanging outside his tank top. He wore cutoffs and sandals. His goatee was scruffy and unkempt. Like most of his staff, he was smoking under his shed row as I approached.

Gomez waved me to where he was standing in the center of the madhouse, saying, "You must be the guy from Boston."

"Right, I'm Colin O'Hearn. I hear you have a few horses to show me."

It took me a half-hour to closely go over the four horses Gomez brought out for me to inspect. Two that I had charts on were unsound and of no value to me. The charts showed they once were good quality racehorses, but they had no recent, decent form. Both badly needed rest and either blistering or firing. Time was not my ally in this venture. They would not do.

He showed me a four-year-old stake horse named Deeper River, a son of Riverman who had won over three hundred thousand, including a Grade III Florida stake. He walked soundly, but I was sure he was full of butazolidin, acepromazine or both. His eyes were red and he hung low between his legs, seemingly uninterested in the task at hand.

He'd been bowed, but it was old and high. I could handle it, with Jock's help. He showed signs of overwork and poor feeding habits. His dull coat matched his behavior, but he appealed to me. I was sure I could move him up.

"Mr. Santos really wants this horse."

Crystal Run, a five-year-old allowance mare who had been useful in New York, would be very tough in Boston. The mare, a dark bay with no color, was the type I loved to train. A very classy mare, she had some ankles which showed wear and probably had a bone chip or two judging from the jewelry on the outside of one ankle in the front and one in the back.

She moved soundly, but that meant nothing coming from this barn, where the needle obviously was a way of life. She carried her head and had a way of looking that made me melt. She'd make someone a fine broodmare one day when she was through racing. The fact that she was stakes-placed and had earned a shade over two hundred thousand with seven wins would look very good on a catalog page, even now.

"Milos said this mare and the other horse you liked were the ones he wanted the most. The colt is seventy-five thousand and the mare is fifty," he mumbled to me from very close so that his grooms wouldn't hear. Grooms usually got a small percentage of the sale price. I could tell none of Paco Gomez's grooms was in for a payday.

The dull condition of the Gomez stock didn't surprise me. Although trainers of his ilk won tons of races, most consider horses to be disposable as a Bic razor. Blood doping, milkshakes and many other drugs I'd never heard of were common at all racetracks. They were over the line for me and always would be. To latecomers in the game like Gomez, they were a way of life. Dr. Mills would probably tout me off any blood-doped horses. I'd known him almost twenty years and he was straight as a string.

"If you want me to vet these two horses, I'll give you seventy-thousand for the pair," I said.

"Eighty five," he countered.

"Done," I said as I stuck out my hand.

He walked away without a word or handshake, just gave me a backhand wave of approval.

Two hours later, Dr. Mills stood at a table cluttered with x-rays in the corner of his office. Both horses had manageable chips and Deeper River's bow was set. He told me the big horse also had stifle problems and had been tapped several times.

"Paco's too cheap to blood dope, but he'll shake in a minute. He doesn't win all those races by being a choirboy, but he's not the worst around here either, Colin. You and Jock can handle anything wrong with these two.

"I know Crystal Run well. She has a heart as big as a hand melon and the way you feed, she'll turn around in no time."

I paid Dr. Mills with cash and returned to Gomez' barn, where I gave him the eighty-five grand in cash. He took it without counting, as if he knew exactly what was coming.

It went so smoothly, I was sure it was prearranged.

After I paid Matt Lewis, we bid our fond farewells, and I headed for the track kitchen to find Charlie and make the final arrangements for shipping the three horses. This done, I went to the bar and found a smashed Mike Sullivan on the corner stool, propped against the cigarette machine.

I took out my wallet and gave him my card and two-hundred dollars.

"Mr. Santos said he'd pay you directly. I'm going to get a cab to the airport."

As I left the bar, the duck was sitting on a bench across the road, not fifty feet from Sullivan's old caddy. I nodded to her as Mike gave me my bag from his car. Knowing I'd have to go to the front gate and call a ride to the airport, I turned to her and said, "If you're going to the front gate, I'd love a ride."

"Sure."

As the golf cart weaved through the barn area, I asked her, "You always keep this close an eye on visitors on the backside?"

She appeared flustered and avoided my stare.

"Just making my rounds," she said as we reached the gate. She gunned the cart and headed for the security office without a further word.

When my taxi reached the airport, I was nearly an hour early for my flight. I took the time to hit the bar for a scotch and water and then call Santos on his cell phone.

"Everything okay?" he asked.

"I bought you three horses for a hundred and twenty-five grand. I'll bet you already know about the two I got from Gomez for eighty-five thousand. Matt Lewis had a chestnut colt named Cherokee Moon. I paid forty thousand."

"I thought you were going to call me first… you know, before the deal closed."

"Milos, this thing went so smoothly there was nothing to discuss. We couldn't have spent the money any better. You did a great job picking them out," I said to appease him. "I'll call you after I stop in Aiken tonight. The horses ship day after tomorrow. The vet was clean and I have pictures and scope results."

"You already had them vetted?"

"Of course. I'd never buy a horse until my vet had given me the okay."

"I have my own vet down there, Colin."

"I can't train off your vet, Milos. Remember, it's my way or the highway when it comes to the training decisions."

"Sometimes people who take the highway get run over, Colin."

"I'll look both ways before crossing, Milos."

He hung up without a word and I sat at the bar, staring at my cell phone. I felt a cold shudder run down my back as I ordered another scotch and thought about something I had intentionally not told Santos.

About the duck!

CHAPTER ELEVEN

The drive from Atlanta to Aiken takes about three hours. I passed the Augusta National Golf Club where the Master's golf tournament is played and crossed the Savannah River before entering historic downtown Aiken.

Aiken is unlike any town I've ever lived. Maybe it's because the lingering past hangs like the moss from the trees that surround the Aiken Training Center. The red clay roads around the training track and deep sandy trails through the fourteen hundred acres of Hitchcock Woods are filled with horses in the early mornings. Young horses jogging on hard clay to the track on a misty morning are the sounds echoing the best of my past.

It's a past ringing with the memories of the Bostwicks, Hitchcocks, Mellons, Iselins, Woodwards and Pulitzers, entertaining the likes of John Barrymore, Stewart and Joseph Alsop, John Jacob Astor and even Winston Churchill.

They dined at the old Willcox Inn, which opened in 1928, and spent their leisure hours at the Green Boundary Club, The Court Tennis Club and on the links at The Palmetto Golf Club, one of the south's oldest and most exclusive courses, even today.

Trainers such as Jim Maloney, Mike Freeman, Mack Miller, John Gaver, Buddy Raines, Woody Stephens and Scotty Schulhoffer honed the nation's brightest turf stars and most eagerly awaited two-year-olds, prior to the opening of Belmont Park.

During Aiken's heyday, racing fans throughout the world knew of champions Assagai, Hawaii, Shuvee, Lamb Chop, Kelso, Tom Fool, Stage Door Johnny, Summer Squall, Sea Hero and Pleasant Colony. These runners, and a long list of other legendary stars, were all Aiken graduates. One of the all-time great broodmare sires in American history, Blue Peter, was buried under a lonesome oak in the training track infield.

There also came from Aiken's shed rows a flood of training talent. Assistant trainers like Billy Badgett, Neil Howard, Steve Penrod, Paul McGee and dozens more lived in training barns, garage apartments and small cottages behind the huge winter homes of some of America's most influential families. Today they're household names in the Grade I racing world.

Talented and hardworking exercise riders and grooms came to Aiken to earn their first dollars. Many came straight out of college to toil under the tutelage of America's best trainers in the shed row barns belonging to Greentree Stable, Rokeby Farm, Phipps Stable, Buckland Farm and Kentucky outfits like Claiborne, King Ranch and Bwamazon Farm.

It was nothing to find Harvard, Yale, Sweet Briar and Hollins graduates working side by side with uneducated blacks and Mexicans under the same shed row beginning at 5:30 every morning. I was one of those college graduates who drank, worked, partied and learned in a setting not available to the younger generation in the horse business today. I learned that a real gentleman can fit in with the grooms as well as the elite.

As I walked through The Alley past the upscale restaurant The Bowery, and through the door of my favorite watering hole, Up Your Alley, I was praying I would get to see some of my old friends. Instead, the room was packed with engineers from the Savannah River Nuclear Plant, lawyers, realtors and new winter residents who, from their looks, were members of the horse show set. They were as far from what I remembered and loved about Aiken as could be.

"Hey, Colin, what the hell are you doing back here? It's been a long time," I heard from the bar.

Jamie and his two partners had converted the old building

in The Alley to a watering hole where socialites danced on the bar with exercise riders and blacksmiths a dozen years ago. He greeted me with a warm hug.

My pal, short of stature, sported a voguish goatee and, as usual, wore his barkeeper's apron. He had the great barkeeper's ability to recognize someone after a long absence and make you feel you got drunk and closed down the joint just the night before.

"Things have changed, right, Jamie?"

"Everything changes, Colin. I'm even making real money these days. But, yeah, it's not the same."

Over beers, we talked about old times, old friends and how jealous he was that I could see his coveted Celtics and Red Sox, since Suffolk Downs is just a short train ride from Fleet Center and Fenway Park. We both lamented the death of the old Boston Garden and talked of Cousey, Sharman, Russell and Bird. We were thankful there was still Fenway Park, even if Yawkey Way looked like a swap meet and street festival. Mostly, we were thrilled that the Red Sox had won the pennant after eighty-six years.

"They're all gone, the old-timers, aren't they, Jamie?"

"Just about, Colin. Pockets still runs the sandwich wagon and caters a few barbecues. What's left, those who got real jobs and stayed here full time, still go to the Variety for their weekly infusion of grease," he laughed, referring to the twenty-four-ounce T-bones and liver and onions at a run-down road house where race-trackers have eaten forever.

Bosses apparently still mix it up with help at the Variety. They love to argue horses, politics, breeding on neutral grounds. I rose to leave Jamie's, telling him I was going to try the Variety for old time's sake.

"Annie will be there, Colin. She's never had anyone serious after you two split up. All that time you lived together, I figured you'd be married by now. She's had some problems, Colin."

"What kind of problems?"

Jamie hemmed and hawed and finally said, "She'll have to tell you, but it hasn't been easy for her. She's developed a nice business. It's called the Saddle Doctor. The track gave her one of the small cottages that Mr. Maloney used for an office or something. Looks right on the turn coming home. She's always sitting on the porch, repairing tack and watching the horses train."

As I drove toward the Variety, I sipped on a take-out cup of scotch Jamie had slipped me. I pulled into the Variety parking lot and tried to cool out like a nervous colt after a race. The cup was empty before I knew it. I stared at the empty trying to think of a reason not to go into the restaurant and face Annie.

I sat staring into my empty cup behind the wheel of my car looking as the last of the diners walked to their parked cars. I felt frozen to my seat. Several times I tried to get out, but couldn't. Finally, when my watch glowed almost ten, I made my way through the near-empty parking lot to the Variety's front door.

Three tables were still occupied and a few old drinkers were at the bar. The Latin-Indian owners didn't recognize me as I walked into the dull light. In a small side room, three people drank coffee, chatted and ignored empty dessert plates. Lucy and Forest Williams were Annie's best friends. Forest looked at me as I stood by the door. Annie was laughing at a joke. It wasn't her old Julia Roberts laugh, but it grabbed me.

She looked up, saw me, and continued talking as if I wasn't there. I stood a moment and turned to go.

"Don't turn your back on me, Colin O'Hearn. You're not

going to walk in here and get off that easy," she called out, as if there was no one else in the room.

Forest rose and came over to me. "My God, what a sight for sore eyes!" he said, as he pumped my hand. I said something I'll never remember because I couldn't take my eyes off Annie.

With my arm around Forest's stooped shoulders, I walked to their table. Lucy warmly greeted me and offered her cheek half-heartedly.

"Wonderful to see you, Colin, after all these years."

"Thanks, Lucy. You and Forest haven't changed a bit."

Lucy looked at the tablecloth with a slight smile on her face. "Why do people always say things like that when they've got eyes and can see differently?"

"Because Colin is a gentleman, Lucy. Virginia born and bred, right, Colin?"

"Sometimes, Annie, even I can forget to be a gentleman," I replied.

"Only when it really counts, Colin," she snapped, her eyes blazing.

She'd changed over the years. She lacked the sharp aura and hardened physical look I remembered, although she sat erect in her chair. Working with leather had given her calloused and scarred hands. The lines in her face showed the rugged strength of a hundred good stories. Her scarred hands were folded in front of her.

"We'd better be going, Annie," the Williams said, almost in unison.

"I can get Colin to take me home, Lucy. You all run along."

"You sure, honey?"

" Honest. It won't be the first time the old stud has hauled me around," she smiled sarcastically.

It seemed like forever, but they said good-by and left.

I stood frozen until Annie said, "Take a load off your feet, Colin. You look like you've had a hard day. Matter of fact, you look like you've had several hard years," she said without smiling.

Somehow I knew that when I sat down, the ice was broken. Sitting directly across from her, I got the feeling that the aggressive, angry Annie was gone. Without my asking, she filled me in on her leather shop. She said she hadn't worked with horses for over a year.

My eyes were fixed on her face. I'd forgotten how different it was emitting confidence and character. Her fading freckles mixed with sunspots reflected a lifetime spent outdoors.

Her light complexion and reddish blonde hair made her a prime target for skin cancer. Her father, a general practitioner from Birmingham, had warned her about her fair complexion since childhood days. Nevertheless, Annie spent hours in the sun, dozing and reading. One of the perks of being an exercise rider was a day that ended at 11:00 AM when the last horse was cooled out and the tack was cleaned.

She wore her usual turtleneck with a crew-necked sweater. I guessed she was in Levi's with dirty loafers or topsiders, but I couldn't take my eyes off her wonderful warm face long enough to notice.

The years had been kind to Annie, but she still had that fierce look in her Irish eyes. There was a hard-earned softness to her mouth, and the slight smile it produced was encouraging.

We talked for almost an hour. I told her much more than she revealed to me about the time we had been apart. I told her life had been hard for me and took responsibility for my failures.

Lost clients, too much drinking, and more than anything,

gross mismanagement of what money I made or my father had left, really haunted me. I told her I hadn't set foot on the Virginia home place for years, but I couldn't bear to sell it. Gradually, I had added to the mortgage just to survive at the racetrack.

"Try never to sell it, Colin. You know what it meant to your father. It's your anchor. It probably keeps you from being a total failure and alcoholic," she pleaded.

I looked her straight in the eye and said something I never thought I'd get the chance to say.

"I'll never forgive myself for treating you as I did, Annie. It cost me every ounce of drive I had when I lost you."

There was a long pause and, as if on signal, we both took a long pull on our drinks.

"I won't fight with you, Colin. I've got other things I need to fight these days. Some were my fault, some not. You're not the only one with a cross to bear, mister. No one makes you feel sorry for yourself. You're a big guy, Colin. You are a smart and talented horseman, maybe the best I've ever been with. But only you can get your ass in gear and back on track. I could try and give you support, but it's your call, getting right with yourself."

I was going to ask her if she wanted to restart our lives together, but I didn't get the chance. I reached for the check and knocked it off the table. As I leaned over to get it, I glanced under the tablecloth.

The stab that went through my heart released a feeling I couldn't describe. They shone like the bright lights you see when hit square in the nose, and hurt just as much. Braces on both shoes. The bars through her heels, the old polio kind with metal braces to her knees.

My eyes went to hers as I lifted my head. She was tearful and then I realized my eyes were tearful as well. I tried not to, but it was no use.

"No! Not here, Colin. Take me home. I'll tell you about it when we get to my house."

She pointed to the corner, where two metal crutches leaned against the wall. I paid the bill on the way out.

Making her own way out the door, with one leg bearing most of the weight and the other swinging, she shunned my help. As we pulled into her driveway at a small cottage just off South Boundary, I realized for the first time in a long time that I felt sorry for someone other than myself.

CHAPTER TWELVE

By the time I walked through the front door of Annie's tiny cottage, I had somewhat regained my composure. She was sitting on a stool at the breakfast counter in front of a window that separated the living room from the kitchen. She already had a beer in her hand and was patting her black lab, Lee Roy.

In the old days when we both worked at Greentree Stable, the oldest groom in the barn was named Leroy. He was just a shade darker than the lab and was the dog's best friend, other than Annie. Not to confuse things, the groom decided he deserved first billing and instructed Annie that her dog was to be called Lee Roy with the emphasis on the Lee. He kept the standard pronunciation for himself.

Lee Roy was one of those wonderful labs with a huge broad head, a sign of his brainpower. His attitude was exceeded only by his dedication to Annie and a sex drive that kept him gone for days at a time. Annie constantly said that Lee Roy and I were a lot alike.

"Colin, I never want to discuss what happened between us at Saratoga, if we ever try to start over."

There was a deafening silence as she continued. "Isn't that why you came back to see me? Do you need me as much as I need you?"

I walked to her and put my arms around her and looked into her eyes. I could feel Lee Roy's tail slapping my leg, as if to say, "Go pal, you go."

I kissed her very softly; afraid to hurt her if I squeezed too tightly. We brushed the wetness from each other's cheeks. In the past, the moisture would have been from passion. Tonight, it was from our tears; tears of mending, need and understanding.

We smiled warmly at each other, as she whispered, "Forgive

me for needing your help. I'm not going to be very graceful, if you want me as much as I want you."

"I feel so stupid," I warned her.

"You're the last person I made love with, Colin. At first, it was because I was hurt mentally. Now, even if I wanted to have another, I'd never trust someone else to help me and get me through something I've wanted but never thought I'd try."

She buried her face in my shoulder and trembled. "Oh my God, Colin, I'm afraid I won't feel anything and make a mess out of everything."

I gathered her in my arms and carried her into a bedroom she'd converted from a glassed porch to keep from having to fight the stairs. "Not here, Colin. I've always kept our big bedroom upstairs, in hopes you'd come back someday."

She hugged me tightly as I carried her up the stairs. The upper half of her body was still sinewy with cords of muscle. I was oblivious to her legs hung which loosely across my arm. She passionately pulled at my hair and kissed every inch of my face and neck.

I placed her on the queen-sized bed and she began undressing me while I pulled her sweater and turtleneck over her head. As usual, she wore no bra. Her small firm breasts were hard with erect nipples. Her shoulders and arms were like a gymnast's, a reminder of the torture she must endure dragging her crushed legs.

"Colin, help me. Don't just spread my legs and use me. Let me be part of it, darling. Sit on the edge of the bed and put me over your lap and help me move with you. I want to know we're making love, watching when you come.

"From the looks of Mr. Happy," she giggled, "you're going to be able to come. I don't know about me though."

She moaned as I moved her up and down, back and forth, her head buried in my shoulder, as she sat astride my lap.

"You'll come, baby," I encouraged her.

"I never could feel much when I touched myself after the accident, Colin. But with you now, I really feel it. I think my dreams of being able to make love and come are real. Thank you," she gasped.

I felt her body shudder, just as it always had when we made love in the past. I told her my orgasm was the best ever. She rolled off me, laughing. "I'll bet you tell that to all the girls." It was probably laughter she held back for years. We began to stroke our damp and alive bodies. She wanted more. I meekly placed my head between her legs which I controlled and moved.

She begged me to make her come with my tongue. She cried out she was afraid she'd feel nothing and be dead to my touch. At first, her hips didn't move. Then, as if on signal, she quivered slightly. She cried out in passion and relief. She was still a whole woman, even if her legs had deserted her.

"I'm crushed, but not crippled. You've brought me back from the dark," she said. It was a happy moment for us both.

We must have slept for an hour in each other's arms before Lee Roy beat his tail against the foot of her grandmother's antique bed. Annie stirred next to me and gave me a shot in the ribs with her sharp elbow. I was instantly alert and had to resist jabbing her back.

"I'd be a proper hostess and let the bastard out, but there's no sense in us both going downstairs, and I don't want to slide down backwards on my boney ass if I don't have to," she said with a smile.

As Lee Roy and I stumbled down the steep and narrow

stairs toward the front door, I felt really good. It was like a huge block of granite had been lifted from my shoulders. I knew Annie's load was much the same as mine, maybe even heavier. She'd answered questions about her life and I was so glad to be part of it all.

I fixed two Diet Cokes, grabbed something from my bag and returned to the bedroom. She was propped up naked in the bed, with a big smile from ear to ear.

"You sly devil. You remembered I love a cold Coke and cheese crackers after a good roll in the hay."

I slid under the covers and pulled her close, looking into her eyes. "Tell me how it happened, Annie? I'd like to hear it from you, not some secondhand account."

"I was on a scatterbrained two-year-old filly by Halo, and you know how goofy they are. She'd had her first breeze a few days before and was ready to jump out of her skin.

"As I walked her from under the shed row, she was fine. When our set reached the chute and started to jog off, we were second of six.

"Holly turned her filly and started to jog, but Lonely Aunt, that's her name, started backing up. She hit the filly behind and went down on her haunches, almost sitting. When I got her feet back under her, she lunged forward. I went to her ears and she hit me in the face with her head.

"Colin, you know those damned chestnuts with white eyes you hate? Well, this bitch had more chrome on her than a '66 pimp Caddy. You'd have hated her. Maybe that's why I liked her so much. She was a real challenge for me."

"Don't blame me. I told you time and again, dark bays with no marks are money in the bank."

We both smiled and she went on. "I hardly remember

anything after that, but the boss, who was on the pony, told me later that I didn't let go of the reins, and she flipped all the way over on top of me. I was off to the side because I had the reins, and she pinned me right below the hips. Straight back, and she'd have killed me."

She didn't cry, but hung her head. "I'm sorry, Colin. I feel so bad."

"About your legs and all the hell you've been through?"

"Yeah. I wanted to be whole, if you ever came back. But for the filly, too. She's still around, but she's an outlaw. They drug her to train her and she's crazier than ever."

"She ever run?"

"She bolted to the outside rail and they pulled her up at Saratoga. Then they ran her at Keeneland in the fall and she won by a mile in 1:09 and change. In the winner's circle, she flipped and almost killed everyone. They sent her home and turned her out. She's back in training now, but she still needs medication to get her to the track. I heard they can't get anyone to ride her."

Annie sighed, "It's terrible. Baby, I feel so sorry for her. She's over in Greentree's barn. They just keep her around. Last I heard, the boss told the farm manager in Kentucky to breed her and forget about any three-year old campaign. I'm afraid to go look at her. I haven't been back to Greentree since the accident." She hesitated, "Oh, Colin. I'd love to go see her. Maybe it would get my head straight."

"You liked that filly, didn't you?"

"She's the fastest filly I've ever been on. I feel like I'm the one that messed her up for good."

"Maybe not," I said.

She reached over and turned off the bedside light.

After playfully kissing me hard on the lips, she said, "Don't forget Lee Roy. Let him in so we can get some sleep, just like old times."

CHAPTER THIRTEEN

When Martin Watson dragged his two hundred and sixty-five pound frame through the front door of Boston's FBI office the next morning, there was an e-mail waiting. Fred Hardy wanted him to call right away. He wheezed his way to his desk chair and made short work of spilling his coffee. Mary Ann was on the intercom, "Mr. Hardy's on the line for you."

It took a minute for Watson to get his coffee, doughnut and cigarette arranged in front of him. Finally, he picked up the phone. "What's on your mind, Fred?"

"I think I got a few blanks filled in after that trainer O'Hearn left here yesterday. My source at the track says he paid about a hundred and fifty grand cash for three horses."

"What's so wrong, him buying a few horses with cash?"

"It's not that he bought the horses, it's about one of the guys he bought two of them from. The circle is getting tighter, Martin."

After a short pause with no comment from Martin, Hardy went on. "The first horse he bought was on the up and up. The trainer is said to be a friend of O'Hearn's and he's clean as glass. Been around thirty or forty years and not a blemish on his record. It's the deal with a trainer named Paco Gomez that fits the money cycle."

"If you got something on Gomez, I'd like a copy."

"This isn't the first time Gomez has dealt with Santos. The records of sales and purchases, recorded with the Stewards and Racing Commission, show Santos bought several very expensive horses from Gomez a few years ago."

Watson took a long drag on his cigarette, coughed and said, "So what's the matter with a guy buying a few horses from Gomez?"

"On the surface, nothing. But, there's something strange that took place after the previous sales."

"Come on, Hardy, get on with it."

"The horses sold for a lot more than their racing value and then disappeared. None of them ever raced again."

"They disappeared... how, why?"

"Our people who know something about horses tell us that if they were to run after the purchase, they'd have to run where they could be valued. So, if it were a sham deal to wash drug money, we'd know. After a while, when they didn't run again, we started an inquiry. When we pulled Gomez in, he came up with a bunch of excuses. One or two died, one was sold for a jumper and a few as pleasure horses. They washed over a half million dollars and got off clean."

"Gomez has a long history around Miami, hanging out with known drug people. We have film of him with guys we'd love to collar. He's on tape a few times with Santos. We think they were talking about washing and delivering money. Maybe with horses again. We have a guy inside with Gomez."

"What about the drug arrests?"

"Gomez always ended up with an expensive shady lawyer and walked. Nothing sticks on him. He's covered with Teflon."

"Once I was sure we got lucky. There's a guy around the track we've been watching, Mike Sullivan. He's got one prior for taking an underage kid across state lines about ten years ago. He got drunk and took a sixteen year old girl to the Gulf Coast to gamble."

"He did six months and five years probation. He managed to keep clean until not long ago. He was among a bunch of guys we caught using the Internet to steal credit card information. He's on a leash until we see if we can use him to get Gomez." Hardy said.

"How's he figure in here?"

"He picked up O'Hearn at the airport and drove him to Calder. Sullivan heard from some of Gomez's grooms about the cash for the horses. We pulled Sullivan in late last night and he's terrified. He knows a lot about Gomez. Before we use him in the phone and Internet scheme, we're exploring his contact with Santos and O'Hearn. He swears O'Hearn is straight, just training horses for Santos. He can't prove it, but he thinks the horses really belong to our man, Vito Corsetti. That changes everything, if it's true," said Hardy.

"You think O'Hearn's clean?"

"Who gives a shit? He lies down in the mud with a guy like Santos, we can get him dirty. We'll go through his life like grease through a goose. If he's got nothing in the past we can use against him, we'll just give him a little bait and nudge him across the line.

"I hear he's a drinker and, until Santos came around, he was down and out. You get everything you can out of Sullivan. Take all the time you need with Gomez. Don't scare him off. I'm like you, the hell with O'Hearn. When we're through with him, Mr. O'Hearn's life will end up in the sewer. He'll do as we say… or else! " Watson said with a huge smirk on his face.

He got Mary Ann to run a complete history on Colin O'Hearn, warning her not to mention this to her husband, since he hung out at Suffolk Downs almost every race day.

CHAPTER FOURTEEN

I awakened early to the rhythmic "thump-thump" of Annie's bottom bouncing down the stairs. I lay still in the bed until she hit the floor. I listened to the handrail creek, and then heard the thump of her wooden crutches she used around the house. Remembering her pleading to be treated normally, I decided to let her start her morning business without my intrusion. After she'd cleared out of the bathroom and began moving around the tiny kitchen, I went downstairs.

Her damp hair and bright smile were eye candy. She'd lost the tired and pale look from the night before. We hugged and hung out for a little, enjoying being together, then began dressing for our trip to the track. The first light of dawn was breaking above the rustling, swaying pines as we pulled into the parking lot of Greentree Stables.

The first set of older horses was crossing the hard clay road between the barns and paddocks. I recognized Harry Walker, our old trainer, on his ancient lead pony in front of the horses making their way onto the track.

Harry pulled up his pony and stared at us before he realized that Annie had finally showed up at the stable. He had to have been surprised and pleased to see her. In the mist, he had no idea who I was. Rather than staying by the rail to watch the older set train he turned his pony around and jogged back to where we were standing. His eyes were glued to Annie. After he'd tossed the pony's reins to the ground, he dismounted and gave her a warm hug, saying, "Lord, darlin', am I glad to see you. God, we've all missed you around this barn. I see you sitting on the porch fixing tack, but never seem to get by since I'm always in such a rush."

His eyes looked toward the ground, trying to hide his lame excuse for not making the effort to see Annie after her fall. He looked up, glanced my way and did a double take. "Colin… is that really you?"

"It's what's left of me, old man."

"Well, we've missed your sorry ass around here too. This is a real surprise… you two here… together. What brings… ?"

"It's Lonely Aunt. Harry, is she still here? I heard maybe you were going to give up on her and send her to the breeding shed," Annie said, almost breathlessly.

"Right on both counts. She's here, but… I've given up on her as a racing prospect. The boss wants to breed her, if I can't sell her first. If she wasn't bad enough before the accident; she's even worse now. We'd really like to get her off the books and not have any of her crazy-ass blood running through any of our babies."

We made small talk as we walked to a three-stall barn at the back of the property usually used for quarantining ship-ins. Lonely Aunt glanced up from her hay pile. She dropped her head to continue eating, then stopped and turned her head back to the three of us standing outside the screen.

Harry and I stepped back, leaving Annie standing in the doorway. The filly, ears pricked, nose twitching as if searching for a familiar touch, cautiously took two strides toward Annie.

Annie teared up as she whispered, "It's okay Auntie, it's just me, Ole' Annie. Remember, you were sitting on me the last time we were together… "

I couldn't look at Harry, fearful that we'd both tear up.

The filly reached Annie's outstretched fingers and touched them with her upper lip. A second or two later, she moved in for a full pat. Annie leaned her crutches against the stall and grasped the screen with one hand, rubbing the filly's ears and neck with the other. We both instinctively knew we'd seen enough, so Harry and I walked out of the small barn, both looking silently at the ground.

Once outside I said, "Harry, you mentioned selling the filly. Is she sound enough to run again?"

"Colin, she's sound as a bell of brass, everywhere except between the ears. She's just plain dangerous, a total fruitcake. Just look at Annie in there. She'll flip on anyone who takes a hold or hits her in the mouth. Everyone on the track is scared to death to get on her in the morning.

"Annie says she's got real speed, Harry."

"It's a shame no one can rate her, Colin. She'll throw down eleven's one after another. When she ran 1:09 at Keeneland, she was seven wide the whole way, on the lead. She was all over the track. I closed my eyes until she got back to be unsaddled and get her picture taken. She flipped over in the winner's circle and chased everyone but the groom out of there. I brought her home and she's flipped twice, even with tranquilizer in the morning."

"What do you want for her, Harry?"

"The old man told me to do what I thought best. He just wants her gone. Would it be for you or a customer?"

"For Annie."

"To train or breed?"

"Probably both, Harry. It's about hope and looking ahead for her."

"For a customer, twenty-five thousand. For you, ten thousand and for Annie, a dollar and considerations."

"What considerations?"

"That no matter how good Annie gets, she'll never get on this mare. I'm serious, Colin. Give me your word that she'll never throw a leg over that filly, even if she gets one hundred percent well," Harry said with a worried and concerned look directed to me.

"You've got my word, Harry. There's one thing you have to do for me."

"What's that, Colin?"

"You can't tell Annie I have her. Just tell her some guy from Canada bought her."

"Okay, Colin. When do you want her shipped?"

"Charlie Pierce, a van agent from Calder, will arrange to pick her up in a day or two. I'll get him to call you tonight."

"That's fine. You looking for anything else?"

"I'm looking for an older grass horse. Sprinter or miler. Can't be too big. Suffolk's grass course is full of sharp turns and has a dip in the backside drainage area. Big horses lose it back there."

Harry had trained his share of years at Suffolk Downs, and laughed. "You don't have to tell me about that turf course!"

He thought a second and came back. "Colin, I've got a Manila gelding named Top Shot. He's won three or four allowance races and placed in the United Nations at four. He's six now and has won about three hundred thousand. I've been running him in New York for a fifty grand tag.

"The old man is terrified one of those milkshakers or blood dopers is going to claim him, cripple him and have to put him down. He's a nifty little horse, but with some suspensory problems recently. You'll have to go easy on him and not run him too often. He'll never quit; he's hickory, Colin. Knowing how you can hold a bad ankle with Jock's help... well, I think you'd be the perfect trainer for him."

We walked into the training barn and Harry had Top Shot pulled out. Barely fifteen hands, he was almost perfect.

I ran my hands all over him and checked out the suspensory ligaments.

"How much, Harry?"

"How about twenty thousand?"

I pulled out my wallet and handed him four cashier's checks, each for five thousand dollars. He looked at them and smiled. "That was easy. Fancy you with this kind of money. We heard you were on hard times, Colin."

I handed him another five thousand. "This is for you. Harry. Say it's for anything you want. It's from me to you for being so kind to Annie with the insurance and all. For old times."

A big smile came over his face as Annie approached. "Thanks, Harry for letting me see her before you sold her. Any idea when and where she's going?"

Harry paused and looked at the ground, "I think I've got her sold up Canada-way. Man's going to call me tonight and probably arrange a van for tomorrow."

"I hope she gets a good home, Harry. She's such a sweetie."

"After what she did to you?"

With a flashy smile Annie said, "Especially after what she did to me."

She gave the old trainer a kiss on the cheek, and I gave him a firm handshake as we said goodbye.

We drove to the track kitchen, arriving well before the break. We had a great time laughing with Pockets, a former groom who owns the kitchen and caters the best barbecue in South Carolina. His wife served us breakfast in the deserted cinderblock building down the street from the training track.

We drove to Annie's house in silence. As we got out of the car she said, "You're going to have to drive full out to get to

Atlanta for a noon plane."

When we entered the cottage, she smiled and said, "Hold me, Colin. Just for a few minutes."

We sat entwined, lightly kissing for a few minutes. She then followed me out to the rental car. I looked her in the eye, "What would you say, Annie, if I asked you to marry me?"

"You'd better think long and hard about that one, Colin. You'd have to drag me everywhere."

I laughed. "Oh, hell, who's going to drag you around? I thought I'd run around the country training horses in the spring and summer. Then I'd come back to you and spend the winter here in Aiken. I could break yearlings and you can keep sewing those busted saddles in that shop of yours."

"Colin O'Hearn, even a slick horse trader like you can't get that one past me. If I were dumb enough to marry you, I'd never let you out of my sight. Ever."

"Well, think about it, Babe. I've never been more serious in my life."

"Neither have I, you slick bastard. I just can't picture you being the marrying type… whatever that is."

She was still waving, leaning on one crutch with the other on the ground, as I pulled out. I felt lost and confused driving to Atlanta and all during the plane ride to Boston. When I got back to the cottage my message light was blinking, showing two messages. The first was from Charlie Pierce telling me the horses would arrive about noon in two days.

The second was from Annie.

"I'm alive, Colin. I mean really alive. God, I love you. Call me tomorrow. Thanks for coming back and giving us another chance."

As I got into bed, I thought my life was in line and that I

was straight with the world.

I couldn't have been more wrong.

CHAPTER FIFTEEN

When Milos Santos walked into Little Venice he was stopped by Johnny Carlino, the front bartender.

"Boss wants to see you right away."

Santos had been serving Vito Corsetti like a lap dog for six years, earning big money and prestige in the eyes of his peers as the accountant for North Boston's most feared mobster. When Corsetti said "jump," Santos answered, "How high and how far?"

A year earlier, Corsetti had set his heart on having a racing stable and asked Santos to find a trainer he could trust, one who could win races at Suffolk Downs while keeping his mouth shut. Santos had shared the boss's request with Jimmy Slacks, Corsetti's right hand man and chief enforcer.

Colin O'Hearn's name had come up at the bar in Little Venice and Jimmy had passed on what he'd heard to Santos, who he knew was looking out for a trainer. Both Carlino and Slacks loved to bet the horses at Suffolk and followed them closely.

Santos made inquiries and gathered information. The trainer was a loner, originally from Virginia. He had only a few horses. When Santos questioned his dwindling stable, he was told clients didn't like the fact that they couldn't tell O'Hearn what to do. The man was set in his old-fashioned ways. Nonetheless, he had an excellent reputation as a horseman. When Santos confirmed the trainer was broke and needed horses, he knew he'd found Corsetti's trainer.

Half a morning spent with Colin had confirmed Santo's opinion that he was a perfect fit for Corsetti. O'Hearn seemed easily managed with money. When Milos set him up to wash the quarter million, O'Hearn snapped up the bait without asking too many questions.

Now, however, it appeared O'Hearn could be a problem.

The man had gone off on his own and done what he wanted with Vito's money without checking with him. He hadn't expected Colin to be as smart and demanding in his choice of horses. Santos felt he was losing control. Still, he decided he'd short the boss on the cash part of the horse purchases and slip a few grand in his pocket. He'd never shorted Corsetti before, but he felt positive he could blame O'Hearn if any questions were asked.

Milos straightened his shoulders. Corsetti would want to hear about O'Hearn's trip to Miami. A shudder passed over Santos. The thought of getting caught lying to and stealing from Corsetti was terrifying. Jimmy Slacks would probably put a hole in his head and drop him in the Mystic River. He couldn't help it. He was a crook and that was all there was. He just couldn't shake the urge to skim from Corsetti. He'd be so easy.

Nerves and fear accompanied him into Corsetti's back office. Sweat trickled down his spine. There were white sweat rings under his armpits and the back of his collar was damp.

Vito Corsetti didn't look up from his meal as Milos entered the room. The old man was almost seventy and showed no signs of slowing down. He loved his hard-won status as the North End's most feared mob boss and protected his territory with every drop of his energy. He'd fought his way up the ladder and had no intention of losing any of his territory.

He tackled his pasta like it was his last, pushing it around a huge platter with fresh bread as if it might try to get away. His love of food was evident. At five-foot-ten, he weighed two hundred and sixty pounds. His huge arms were covered with thick, dark hair and his hands looked like sledgehammers. His long, black hair was greased up and combed straight back 40's style. He smeared his mouth with the wine-specked linen napkin tucked under his chin and looked up at Santos.

"What's your trainer up to? Do we own some horses yet?"

"He's bought three for almost two-hundred grand, Boss and they are really nice. He's gone from Miami and is in some place in South Carolina looking for a fourth one. Looks like he'll spend most of the money and we'll start with four good horses. We're right on schedule. I put some money in the account and gave him some for expenses.

"He's a strange one, Boss. You know those horse trainers. They always want a little extra for getting the job done. Not O'Hearn. He's straight as a string. But, Gomez and the guys selling got some commissions," said Santos, looking for a way to spread the money around.

"That trainer at Calder who trains for some of our associates cleaning up the cash, is he going to be a problem?"

"Paco Gomez has been around a long time, Boss. He called and said that O'Hearn was asking a lot of questions about the horses and he didn't like dealing with him. Too uppity, he claimed. He got a little on the side. O'Hearn's been around and knows how to keep everyone happy."

"What do you think too uppity means?"

"You wanted a trainer that was honest and smart. Well, smart guys ask questions. He had to know before he left that we were dealing below the radar with cashier's checks and cash, so he's no fool. I think the questions were all about the horses we bought from Gomez. He told me he wanted good horses for the money we are paying, so I knew he'd be asking questions."

Santos kept talking, "This guy is going to give us our money's worth, Boss. He's not only going to wash our money, he might make some real dough doing it."

"That sounds different. Making money while we're washing

money. It's been a long time since I won some races. This guy O'Hearn, what's he like?"

"He's a big guy maybe six-two and over 220 pounds. They say he's a mean one, but has a soft side. He's friends with a couple of queer trainers. You know, kinda protects them from the rough guys. He has a one-legged black guy who's been with him forever. Hell, he's bigger than O'Hearn, maybe six-eight and over 300 pounds. They're an odd couple and nobody messes with them.

"You know, Mr. Corsetti, he's smart. College, some law school and then he went into the Army. Jumped out of planes and all that shit. Like I said, a real tough guy."

"Protects queers? What the hell you got here, Milos? Is he one too?"

"Not that I can tell, Boss. I'd be afraid to call him one. In a way, he's an ugly guy. You know, he's got scars on his face. He looks kind of like a boxer with one big ear and a nose that looks like he's broken it a bunch. His hair's too long, kind of blonde and maybe some gray.

"Not a softy this guy, Boss. He's got that look. You know, like he ought to be one of us. Maybe like Jimmy. The other night he mopped up the parking lot with another trainer who gave him some mouth. The guy he left head first in the dumpster trains for your pal, Connie Tass.

"People stay the hell away from O'Hearn. They all say he's a horseman. He likes his horses and they like him. They run for him. He's a worker, but he's a heavy drinker, Boss."

Corsetti had become intrigued with his new trainer from what Santos was telling him.

"What kind of guy jumps out of airplanes and hangs out with queers? I want to meet him when he gets back to town."

More sweat appeared on Santos's forehead. A drop hit his eyelid, so he wiped it with his sleeve and said, "But Boss, you said you wanted me to handle this guy. You didn't want him hanging around the bar and getting on the Feds' film, you know, attracting attention."

"This is a restaurant, Milos. Open to the public. Be sharp. Have him come alone. Don't you or Jimmy bring him. When he gets here I want to eat with him back here. I want to know this guy better. I like some things that you tell me and some things I don't," Vito said while pushing away his dishes and standing to wash up.

Midway he stopped and half turned to Santos saying, "Milos, you might be catching something. It's cold and you're sweating like a pig. Cover up when you go out and send in Jimmy."

After Corsetti returned from the bathroom, Slacks was standing in front of his desk. The slim man in the perfectly pressed pants and cowboy boots. His greased hair was combed straight back and his tiny mustache and goatee were perfectly trimmed. He wore gangster gold, and too much of it.

"You want me, Boss?"

"Watch Milos, Jimmy. I've given him some room to hang himself, handling loose cash with no records. See how he acts, you know, spending or dressing different. I don't like all that sweating shit. He's usually not antsy. If he fucks me, I'm gonna cut his balls off."

When Slacks returned to his coffee at the bar in the card room, he had a smile on his face. Taking care of Santos would be an easy job. He'd never liked the smart-ass bean counter.

CHAPTER SIXTEEN

It was just after 4:30 when I danced over the black ice that surrounded Barn 15 the next morning.

"You lost, Boss?" Jock grinned at me. "Been a long time since you showed up before the horses cleaned up breakfast. You must have had a good trip. Did ya' find anything?"

"Things went great, Jock. I bought three nice horses in Florida and one in Aiken. I also picked up a project from Harry Walker," I said.

"Tell me… tell me what you got."

"I bought a young colt named Cherokee Moon from our old friend, Matt Lewis. He's a maiden special winner in his first start by seven lengths. He's a nasty chestnut with too much chrome and a white eye. He's got a little filling behind. Not the stifle, maybe a thoroughpin. You'll know what to do.

"I also picked up a solid old mare that needs a lot of care and oats. She's won seven and been stakes placed. She'll be an allowance filly, and might make a broodmare."

"I can't see that greaser from North Boston wantin' no broodmare," Jock quipped.

"Anyway, her name is Crystal Run. I bought her from a guy named Paco Gomez. He has a big claiming barn at Calder. Kind of a local big shot with fifty horses. There's something shifty between Santos and the guy.

" He also sold me a colt named Deeper River. He's an older dude who's has won about three hundred grand. He's got a set bow, but it's getting active again. I know you can hold him."

"I've seen that colt run on TV. He's been making the lead and dying the last few times I've seen him, Colin. Running wide, if I remember right. He might just be on his last leg," the old groom said.

"I figure I probably paid too much. Gave Gomez eighty-five

thousand for the pair and gave Matt Lewis forty thousand for
his colt. I think I can get him through his conditions with no
problem. Matt really needed the money, or I don't think he'd
have sold him to me."

I put my arm around Jock and walked him toward the tack
room. "Come on inside, old man. I've got a story about Aiken
to tell you."

Jock sat on the big tack trunk while I told him everything
about Annie, Lonely Aunt and the gelding Top Shot. He
shook his head sadly when I told him the details about
Annie's accident and recovery. He brightened up when I told
him we'd made up, leaving out all the sex stuff. He'd have
taken a whip to my head if I'd told him anything so personal,
especially about Annie, whom he adored.

When I got to the part about Lonely Aunt, he got up, walked
to the door and flung his coffee out into the aisle in disgust.
"You know better than to bring a crazy bitch into my barn.
Gonna' get me killed. Horse like that's a damn black cat, Colin ."

A frown creased his face. "When's that crazy bitch getting
here? I want to be gone and let you take care of her for a few
days ".

"The horses will be here Monday at noon, all except the
nutty filly. She's going to make a stop for a little refresher
course with a friend of yours.

"What are you talking about, Colin?"

"You remember John Willie, that shyster at the trotting
track in Aiken?"

"How can I forget that crook? Slickest poker player I ever
knew."

"Well, before I left Aiken, I called and told him all about
the filly. He said using one of those breaking carts, and then a

sulky, he'd be able to straighten her out. He said he'd expect to have her broken of her bad habits in about three weeks.

"When I talked to Charlie Pierce about picking up Top Shot in Aiken, I asked him to go by the trotting track and leave the filly off with John Willie. I'll go down and take a look at her when she's ready. I'll need to go see Annie about that time."

"Colin, you serious about you and Annie getting back together?"

"Jock, I've been drinking myself to death, pushing the envelope as far as I can, trying to make myself fail. I can't stand what I did to her."

"You can't make her live the racetrack life, Colin. Not in her condition."

"Maybe we can make it work, Jock. Sooner or later, we should go back to Aiken. We can buy yearlings and prep them for the two-year-old sales. Then, with what we have left in the spring, we can go to Monmouth for the summer. Annie can get a cottage near the beach. Maybe we can make some real money pinhooking and still get a little taste of the track in the summer."

"You mean I'm finally going to get that little house by the trotting track and keep all my stuff in one place? Get furniture, and the like?" Jock couldn't believe it.

"Yeah, old buddy. You can sit at your own fireplace and play poker with John Willie again." I laughed as I went out the tack room door and headed for the track kitchen to check in with Arch Hale and Steve Casey. It was Saturday, and I wanted to see what Arch thought about Lost Promise in the third today.

I also wanted to give both the short version of what I'd bought. I knew whatever I told them would be all over the backside after Steve got to the jock's room. But what the hell;

it should be better than answering a bunch of questions.

Arch had told Jock he felt there was a good chance with Lost Promise, but that I'd lose him through the claim box. That wouldn't be all bad. I could use the seventy-five hundred. After we chatted, I went back to the barn and called Annie.

She was down because I was gone. She'd called Harry and learned that Lonely Aunt had been sold as a broodmare. Harry's reference to "up Canada-way" was his crafty way of not lying, since Suffolk Downs is on the way to Canada.

I told her about Lost Promise running today and that I hoped she'd go down to the bar and watch the race with Jamie. She said she would and rang off, wishing me good luck and telling me how excited she was to have an interest in live racing again.

"It's like the sun's shining in my life again, Colin. I'm so happy!"

"Me too, honey. Maybe that old skate of mine will win today. If so, I'll send you half the pot for a savings account," I said.

It came from nowhere, but it was a perfect idea. I could almost see her beaming when she hung up.

Lost Promise's pre-race routine was the same I've used for years; bute four hours out and Wind-Aid one hour out. Before heading over to the paddock, I reached into my ditty bag and pulled out one of those round cartons of butter. Jock held the old boy while I coated the inside of each hoof with the butter. While other horses were "caking up" from frozen ice packing their feet, Lost Promise would be ice free when they turned for home. I took the tongue-tie and channel to put on in the paddock, but put the blinkers on before the long walk over.

As I was saddling Lost Promise, the snow started falling. Steve, who'd won the first race of the day, walked across the paddock in my colors of maroon and gold blocks with maroon sleeves. The colors had been in my family since Ireland, and I'd won over three hundred races in them.

"Fuck, it's freezing out here, Colin. Let's get on with this shit," Steve complained as I threw him up. It was Lost Promise's seventy-first start and he could care less about what was going on around him or how cold it was around the track. The bute took care of most of his aches and pains and he liked an off track.

"Just take your time and stay in the five or six lane where it's firm 'til the top of the stretch, Steve. Then set him down and mostly hand ride him home. You know you can't beat up on the old boy. He'll chuck it if you do."

I was just talking to hear myself talk. Steve knew exactly how to ride Lost Promise. He'd already won twice on him.

After the break, Steve took him to the far outside up the backside and was fifth through the turn. When they set down for the stretch drive, he went to scrubbing Lost Promise with the reins, hand riding. The old boy responded. He passed tiring horses struggling on ice-packed hooves and opened up three coasting home a winner.

As we took the photo in the winner's circle, a pall was thrown over the happy occasion. The clerk of scales clipped a tag on his bridle, indicating he'd been claimed. I felt a sad tug in my stomach as the new owner's groom took over and walked him toward the spit box for testing.

The seventy-five hundred from the claim and the forty-eight hundred purse, less Steve's ten percent, would give me close to twenty thousand in my horseman's account. The money made me feel a little better until I saw Milos Santos leaning against the clubhouse gate.

"Nice job, Colin. I bet your horse. Had the exacta and the

trifecta. Maybe I can buy you dinner tonight at Little Venice. There's someone I want you to meet," Santos said as he huddled in his huge overcoat.

"I'm really exhausted from my trip, Milos. Can I have a rain check for later in the week?"

"It's sort of a command performance. The old man really wants to talk to you about our new horses and a few other things," he answered curtly.

"I know about Little Venice. North End, in the old town."

"Yeah. Now go cash those winning tickets of yours; that's what I'm going to do. See you about eight."

As he turned to leave, I said, "Milos, by the way, here's the money left over from my trip," I said, handing him the battered yellow envelope.

After he turned away, I went to my favorite bar, deep in the clubhouse corner. As usual on a dreary, snowy winter day, it was deserted. The bartender, an old friend and supporter, was beaming.

"I had fifty on you, Colin. My old lady's going to be smiling. Your drinks are on me."

He put a double Dewar's on the bar. As I tried Annie's cell phone, I thought that Double Dewar's would be a great name for a racehorse.

Annie answered with a whoop. "I saw it, Colin. He won like a good horse should. I'm at Jamie's and everyone in the bar was cheering for you."

"Thanks honey but he's another man's horse now. He was claimed," I said, with sadness in my voice.

"I'm sorry, baby, but that's the claiming game. Here today, gone tomorrow." She wasn't trying to be flippant, just trying to make me feel better.

"I'm going to send you half the win and half the claim. Use what you need and open a savings account with the rest. You never know when we might need it.'

She thanked me, and we discussed Steve's ride and how good it was to be a winner again, especially together. Then we rang off.

As I walked through the blinding snow, I passed the spit box and could see Lost Promise cooling out. Thinking about Santos gave me a bad feeling. Command performance, my ass! I wondered how much of the cash from the trip would get back to his boss.

Jock was already cleaning out Lost Promise's stall by the time I got back to the barn. I gave him five, hundred-dollar-bills for the second time in a week.

"We can clean that stall tomorrow, old man. I brought your stake from the win."

"I wish you'd brought my horse back, Colin. I loved that old sucker," he said as he kept cleaning the stall after pushing the money into his pocket without looking.

"So did I," I said with a case of trainer's remorse.

CHAPTER SEVENTEEN

I'd been to Little Venice a few times with some horsemen, who, like me, held its macaroni and gravy in high esteem. I always felt like a tourist among the locals who packed the place. Tonight as I came through the front door, shaking the snow off my ski jacket, I was treated like anything but a tourist.

A tall, trim, muscular man in his forties who looked like a bodyguard straight out of a Robert Parker novel shook my hand. "Good evening, Mr. Hearn. I'm Jimmy Slacks. Mr. Corsetti asked me to show you to his office."

My eyes went right to his shiny slacks, which were pressed like a board, almost hiding a pair of brightly shined cowboy boots. The guy was either gay or he was searching me in an inoffensive but professional manner. We left the main dining room and walked through a pool and card room, then passed through a metal door heavier than the ramp on my old trailer.

A huge man sat at a table in the far left corner of the room. Obviously we were in an office, with a massive, cluttered desk in the center. The big man, dressed in an open neck, short-sleeved white shirt wearing glasses, smiled broadly as my escort said, "This here is Mr. Hearn."

I wasn't about to correct the dropping of the "O" in my name. I was too focused on the fellow who was obviously the famous Vito Corsetti. If Jimmy Slacks was Robert Parker's, Mr. Corsetti was straight out of the pen of Mario Puzo. The fact that his name was Vito sent chills down my spine.

"Good to meet you… may I call you Colin?" he said as I shook his fat, stubby, hand that felt like a catcher's mitt. I noticed a cheap Timex watch with a leather band, its buckle facing outward and face turned inward. His fat wrist almost enveloped the band, making it look ingrown. His waist gave his belt the same look.

"Colin will be fine, sir, and there's an "O", O'Hearn."

The old man took another slug of the red wine spilling more on his shirt that already looked like a road map.

"Mr. Santos tells me you won a race today. I hope 'ya can do the same for us... very soon."

Just then I noticed Milos Santos standing off to the left, ill at ease and erect like a cheap floor lamp.

"Glad to see you could make it, Colin," Milos said.

"Wouldn't have missed it for the world, Milos. I've eaten here before with friends. We all agree the macaroni and gravy is the best in town."

"Get the waiter in here, Jimmy. Some more wine, glasses, and something to chew on."

"Right away, Mr. Corsetti."

"Milos tells me you had a very successful trip on our behalf, Colin. Why don't you tell me about our new horses?"

Taking a seat directly across from Corsetti so I could look him straight in the eye, I began with Cherokee Moon and covered each horse, strong points and shortcomings. I talked about how I planned to run them, and since I hadn't seen them under tack, only estimated a timetable.

When buying and selling horses using an agent, it's better to be evasive about prices unless pushed when talking to the buyer or seller. Middlemen are known to add a few dollars to the purchase price under the table. I had no idea if Milos was dumb enough to try to put something over on this man, but he was the type.

My heart dropped when Vito said, "Milos tells me you had to spend most of the money I sent on purchase prices and expenses."

It was a question meant to trap me.

"There are always expenses. Trainers get a little extra and then there's an agent. In this case I dealt with two old friends. One's having a very bad run of luck. He's at the stage where I wanted to help him, so I didn't haggle on the price. Giving him a little extra now will pay off later. It always does, when you help good men in bad times," I said.

"Whatever arrangement Milos had with that Gomez character was obviously made before my arrival. I wouldn't trust that pile of shit any further than I could throw his fat, greasy ass."

There was a dead moment, as both men seemed surprised I'd talk about their friend in such blunt terms. It caused them to look at each other with doubt in their eyes as if thinking, "What have we gotten into here?"

Fortunately, the line of conversation was interrupted when a waiter carried a huge tray into the room, containing what looked like a sample of everything on the menu.

"Help yourself, Colin. Enjoy. That will be all, Johnny," Vito said. He ignored Santos, who was sweating profusely, small beads forming on his forehead.

Vito kept talking, while moving from entrée to entrée. "I was looking forward to meeting you and hearing about the horses from you personally, Colin. There's another item I want to talk to you about.

"I found another horse I want to buy. I know you want to look over any horse you're going to train, so I want you to go back down to Aqueduct tomorrow. I gotta tell you, I've already agreed to buy this one. If he pans out, he'll be the best horse in our barn, maybe at the track."

"Mr. Corsetti, there are many good trainers in New York. If you are gonna spend a lotta money, I'd like to find you a good one on my own. That is, if I don't like this horse," I said.

His face seemed to fall a little bit. "You don't seem to get my drift, here. I've settled on this horse and you go down and close the deal for me... that is if you want to train any of my fuckin' horses. You want to train my horses, Colin?"

"Yes, sir, but there's a problem with a really good horse at a track like Suffolk. You can win a race or two and then they write you out of the book and you can't find a spot to run him."

Corsetti ignored my warning. "His name is Sliding Scale. He's a stake horse... placed in a few stakes there this winter and won one at the Meadowlands. But, he bleeds like hell. He bled so badly in his last race he got put on some kinda vet list.

"The word is that you're the best in New England with bleeders. I'm going to gamble a lot of money that you can stop the bleeding and get him off the list here in Boston. Then when he's ready, after we try him a race or two, maybe we can win the Mass Cap. There's a lot of good shit you can use on race day at Suffolk."

I was surprised he knew anything at all about bleeders, let alone how to treat one.

He went on. "Milos will meet you where and when you want tomorrow. You all arrange that before you leave. He'll bring you the money to pay for the horse."

The old man then asked me about my family and a few other personal things. We ate dessert and drank the strongest coffee I've ever tasted, and, having spent so much time in New Orleans running horses at the Fair Grounds, I've tried some real strong coffee.

I told Vito about my father the Judge, and, of course, about Jock. He was interested in how my father, a former Irish steeplechase jockey, became a judge in Virginia. The story pleased him since he, like my father, was an immigrant. He seemed to appreciate anyone who made it the hard way after coming to America.

When the waiter came to clear the table, the old man said, "Jimmy, put everything left over in a few boxes for Colin. And Milos, see Colin to his car and make all the arrangements about meeting tomorrow."

"I can't thank you enough, Mr. Corsetti, not only for the meal, but for the chance to train some very nice horses," I said, rising and putting on my jacket and cap.

"The pleasure is mine, son. Just one other point. My name and the details of our business must remain in this office. I'm a very private man and don't take kindly to being talked about or discussed. If I ever hear that you've talked about me or my business, the circumstances will be very uncomfortable for you."

"I have no problem with being close mouthed. I'm a very private man," I said, holding my ground.

He rose and went into what I assumed was his bathroom. Jimmy Slacks appeared from nowhere and led the way through the bar and dining room to the front door. We shook hands and Milos joined me in the parking lot.

"What time can you take the shuttle tomorrow?" he asked.

"Meet me at the stable gate at 8:15. That way I can make the racetrack by noon. And Milos, don't forget the checks for the horse."

"The money will be in a leather belt. It's cash. Just wrap it around your waist for safe keeping, under that ski jacket of yours. They x-ray briefcases. Carrying cash is legal, but with all the 9/11 security these days they'll pull you out and ask a lot of questions. Just wear it and you'll pass right through."

"How much cash, Milos?"

"I think two hundred and fifty thousand. There's a bill of

sale and some other instructions for you. Take it to Barn 51 and ask for Carlos Reyes. He's been our trainer in the past, and he has the horse. He'll wait for you in his barn office all afternoon. Give the money to no one else."

I'd heard about Reyes, but like the guy in Florida, I had never met him or had reason to do business with him.

"Let's get something straight, Milos. I don't like this shit about carrying money in a belt; especially that much. Still, I told Mr. Corsetti I would and I will. I'm telling you, this will be the last time with cash."

He looked at me through the falling snow with a strange stare.

"Like the boss said back there, don't talk about our business to anyone. It would be dangerous. And Colin, with Mr. Corsetti, if you're in for a dime, you're in for a dollar." he warned.

I got into my truck, started the engine and the heater kicked on. The snow was piled high on the windshield and I knew no one could see into the truck until I started the wipers and the defroster warmed up.

As I pulled out into the snowy, deserted street from the Little Venice parking lot, a dark SUV pulled out to my right. It followed me out of the North End and across the bridge, then through Winthrop, turning off about three blocks from my cottage.

The dogs went crazy when I let them out, running and playing in the late-night snow that was now about a foot deep and still falling. Nadine stayed close to the edges, where she wouldn't be swallowed up by the drifts, but Killer looked like a deer as he bounded in high arching leaps.

While they played, I noticed that the light on the answering machine was blinking. There were three calls from Annie. I called her right back and told her of the dinner at Little Venice and meeting Vito Corsetti. I also told her about the trip to Aqueduct to look at Sliding Scale, and she was thrilled.

I left out the part about the cash. She's no dummy and it would worry her, as it should me. After we said goodbye, I let the dogs into the kitchen and fixed three fingers of Dewar's. I went online to punch up Sliding Scale's past performances and pedigree. Last year he'd won a sprint at the Meadowlands in 1:09 and change with a 108 Beyer rating. It had been a long time since I'd trained a horse with such blazing speed. I came down from my cloud when I saw that he'd pulled up and bled in his last two starts.

Getting this horse sound enough to start anytime soon was going to be a serious problem. Going through the security gate at Logan Airport with a quarter million dollars in cash in a money belt was going to be an even bigger problem.

I lay in bed most of the night wondering how I managed to get myself in such a position. It really didn't matter if I liked the horse. My inspection was window dressing. I was being used as a cash mule for the most powerful mobster in New England. Like me, Milos Santos, my owner on paper, was just another Vito Corsetti tool. The urge to escape my debts and lousy horses had led me to once again do something wrong and precarious. There was no doubt in my mind my training operation was being used by Vito Corsetti to wash dirty mob money. I could plead ignorance all I wanted, but I knew the truth. I've done some stupid things on my own, but this time I was on the wrong side of the law all by myself.

I vowed this would be the last time I'd be Vito's mule. Backing out would be slapping him in the face. If I went to the FBI with my story, I was positive I'd be floating facedown in the cold waters of the Boston Harbor. I'd been told as much, first by Milos and then Vito.

I drove to the barn at the crack of dawn, telling myself over and over that this would be the only time, just this once. I was in another world during training hours and Jock sensed my tension. We spent the majority of the early morning cleaning stalls and doing "make work" to pass the time.

"You don't want to go to New York today, do you, boss?"

"Naw, Jock, I've traveled enough. But Milos wants me to look at that horse and I have to. I'll be back late, so you take care of the stables, okay?"

After coffee with Arch, I drove home to give the dogs a run and change clothes, picking out my baggiest coat for my "walk" though security. I kept on my old khakis and boots from the barn and drove to the security gate at the track.

Milos was waiting with the money-belt under his coat as he leaned on his car outside the stable gate. I had a strange feeling as we talked briefly that we were now on different sides. He didn't trust me anymore, and I sure as hell didn't trust him.

Sitting in my truck at the airport parking lot, I took off my heavy ski jacket. I'd replaced my usual crewneck sweater with a baggy gray sweatshirt with "Virginia Football" across the front. I pulled down the sweatshirt over the money belt as I got out of the car and carried my ski jacket over my arm, slinging my green battered canvas Orvis briefcase by its strap across my shoulder.

I purchased my ticket and had almost no wait at the security gate. Throwing the briefcase and coat on the conveyer belt, I put my change and truck keys in the blue bowl and moved through the x-ray body scanner.

"Step aside, please," ordered the portly female guard, as she picked up her hand held scanner.

Almost in a state of collapse, I heard her say, "Use that chair and take off your shoes, please."

I thought I'd never get off my barn brogans. I fumbled and tried my best not to allow my sweatshirt to ride up in the back, revealing the money belt.

She ran the wand over my boots, which she left on the floor rather than dirty her hands. She allowed me time to put my boots back on before body scanning me.

"What's that?" she barked.

"What's what?" I asked, as I was sure I was about to shit my pants.

"That horrible smell, what's that?"

"That wonderful smell is a product of my livelihood," I laughed. "I'm a trainer at Suffolk Downs. I left work too late to change before the noon shuttle, which I may well miss if I don't hurry."

"Well, go on. The sooner you get that smell out of here, the happier I'll be."

I started for the gate, as a huge black guard called after me, "Hey, mister. Wait."

I froze, knowing I'd been caught.

He approached me carrying my coat and briefcase. "You might need these."

I thanked him and moved quickly, almost running toward the shuttle gate. The last thing I needed to do was look like I was fleeing from security to avoid capture.

From the time we took off until we landed at JFK Airport, my stomach was churning and my heart was in my mouth. I had a hair-raising ride along the Nassau Expressway and on to the Southern Parkway behind an Indian taxi driver, complete with turban, chatting in a non-stop, whining voice. The only words I understood were the ones concerning the fare, which I paid gratefully. Showing my Suffolk Downs identification and training license, I passed through the security gate at Aqueduct and headed for Barn 51.

Carlos Reyes's shed row was an uptown version of Paco Gomez's barn at Calder. Things were much neater and the barn was arranged in proper order. There were ten stalls with matching traps, and three grooms to look after things. Still, with the Latin music blaring and ragged equipment every-where, it wasn't my kind of operation. I thought of the old timers who once must have housed their outfits in this barn and now hated that those days were over.

As I walked down the shed row toward the office, a tiny man I assumed to be the foreman approached me. "Hola! Colin, my old drinking buddy. When Carlos told me you were coming, I couldn't wait to see you. It's been almost ten years since we worked together in Aiken.

"Tino Torres, my main man!" I exclaimed.

We hugged and patted each other on the back, then took a long hold to look each other over.

Tino had been a cut below the caliber rider who could make a living in the afternoon on New York's racetracks. In the morning, he was a wizard. Good trainers trusted Tino with the best stakes horses on the grounds. The little Jamaican had a perfect clock in his head and great hands.

Tino had a way of schmoozing the best from a tough, classy horse. A decade ago, he was a second string New York rider with a canny ability to win with the long shots top jockeys didn't want to ride. He was a favorite with the long-shot players and fellow barn employees alike for his paydays. When the big trainers came to Aiken each winter, Tino flourished as the track's best hand with yearlings and with the big, tough veteran runners with real class.

The appearance in the tack room door of a huge Latino man in sweats with Rastafarian locks cut short our laughter. "I see you know my man Torres. Now I think it is my turn to get to know you, O'Hearn." He motioned me into the tack room, closing the door before Tino could make a move to follow.

"Milos said you'd be here before three, and you're right on time. You have some papers for me to sign and a package for me?"

"I have both, but I'd like to look at Sliding Scale first."

"But the deal is done. Nothing you say will change things. He's done up now and I don't want the boys to take the bandages off and have to put them back on again," he snarled.

"Señor Reyes," I snapped, with the emphasis on the Señor, "I came here to examine your horse prior to purchase and that I will do, even if I have to take off the bandages myself."

I turned and walked out of the tack room, leaving the big trainer staring daggers.

"Tino, I have to look at the horse's legs."

"I took him down already, amigo. I know you well enough to know you ain't taking no half-assed look at a horse."

Tino held the big gray horse as I stepped into the stall. He reminded me a lot of Icecapade. He wasn't a huge horse, but broad as a Mack truck.

"This son of a bitch can run, Colin. But, God, he bleeds. If you take him and get Jock to do your bleeder thing with him, I'm going to the window." He laughed, but he was dead serious.

I was on my knees feeling the horse's ankles, which weren't too bad. They showed wear and tear, but they were cool.

"How many times you been into that right ankle, Tino?"

"Still got the eye, no, Colin? Maybe three times this season, before every start. I don't like that much tapping, but this man I work for treats every horse like he's a plastic bottle. He drains them and throws them away."

I stood and Tino put his hand on my arm.

"I need to talk to you, Colin. Why you doing business with this trainer? You know the best in the world. This man is very bad. I hate being here, but I owe him money and I'm afraid to try to leave him. He's told me he would really hurt me if I try to leave him."

There was genuine fear in the little man's eyes, almost desperation. "Maybe you can help me?"

"For the time being I'm stuck in Suffolk. I do need a groom now that I have five new horses. High-class horses. This horse may not be my best, Tino."

"Why are you staying in Boston, with those kinds of horses?"

"I have to for now. I may go back to Aiken over the winter."

"Help me, Colin. You must know somebody who's got something on this drug-dealing shit-heel. I'd love to be with you and Jock. Imagine, just the three of us with a small stable. What a dream!"

"You might be on to something, Tino, but be quiet and careful. I'll get back to you in a week. Hang in there."

"God love you, Colin, my friend."

I went back to the tack room to find Reyes at his desk, his feet on the only other chair in the room.

"What took you so long? I could have looked at five horses in that time."

"Maybe, but I doubt we'd be looking at the same things," I said sarcastically.

"Where's the money?" he snapped.

"These papers, the bill of sale and the receipt for the money must be signed first," I snapped back.

He signed both papers without reading them. For all I know, maybe he couldn't read. His child-like signature, made with almost stick figures, added to my doubts that he was literate. I took off the money belt and dumped the contents into a large paper bag he held. I made sure not to get my fingerprints on any of the bills.

"Don't you want to count it, Reyes?"

"Let me tell you something, Hearn."

"That's O'Hearn, buster," I said with venom.

"Oh, that's right; I heard you were a gentleman. O'Hearn, Mr. Gentleman Asshole. You get this straight: I don't have to worry about any of this money missing. One dollar short and you'd be a sorry man when Mr. Milos finish with you. If he don't get the job done on you, I do the job myself," he threatened.

I picked up the bill of sale and receipt, folded the money belt and put them into the briefcase.

Before I walked out into the shed row, I said, "Reyes, you ever lay a finger on Tino, and I will see that Milos and his friends make you disappear. No matter what he does or what your excuse, you'll never walk again if anyone lays a hand on my pal. That's not a threat; it's a promise."

I turned and walked out of the tack room. I paused long enough to shake Tino's hand and see Reyes staring furiously out the window. I'd had enough of Reyes and New York. My new horses would be arriving the next day and I wanted to be there with Jock. The finest competition and money in the country is in New York and California, but my best friends in racing, those who care the most about their downtrodden neighbors, are on the backside in Boston.

I couldn't wait to be back with them, even knowing trouble awaited me.

CHAPTER EIGHTEEN

On the trip back to Boston, I decided to take the bill of sale and receipt right to Little Venice in hopes that I could avoid Santos and talk to Vito directly.

Walking through the front door of the restaurant, the first person I saw was Jimmy Slacks. He lost no time moving from his bar seat to engage me.

"Colin, good evening. What can I help you with?"

"I have some paperwork for Mr. Corsetti and, if possible, I'd like to have a few minutes with him about a personal matter."

He returned to the bar, reaching behind the counter for a phone. "Mr. Vito says to come right back. He's looking forward to seeing you. You know the way?"

I passed through the main dining room and the bar full of drinkers, pool shooters, TV watchers and card players. I noticed the TVG channel with live racing was on several sets and my reflex was to stop and watch.

After knocking on the metal door, I heard footsteps, then Milos Santos appeared in the doorway.

"I thought you weren't going to show up here without me unless the man called you, Colin. We have rules and I expect you to follow them."

I stopped a foot from his face and moved closer.

"You know, Milos, I'm tired of you treating me like some little foot soldier of yours. I don't work for you. According to Vito, you're a bean counter," I whispered, stepping past him as I moved toward Vito's desk. He was talking into the phone with his back turned. He'd not heard me talk to Milos.

"Ah… Colin. What an unexpected surprise. You have some paper work for me?"

I had purposely not removed the gloves I'd put on before entering the restaurant. I had them on when I handled the paper in New York and had no intention of leaving a finger-print on any document relating to the money.

I looked the old man in the eye. "Mr. Corsetti, I took the job Milos offered me to train some horses. Those horses are far better than any I've had to train for some years and I'm thankful to you for giving me the chance to put together a first class stable." I paused and gathered my thoughts to make sure what I said was not misunderstood.

"I don't mind working around the bookkeeper to keep your ownership hidden, but I never dreamed I'd have to carry a quarter million dollars through airport security and deliver it to scum like Reyes. All of a sudden, I'm feeling dirty all over, dealing with the likes of Gomez and Reyes on a cash basis.

"I looked at the horse you sent me to inspect. He's a good solid racehorse at a hundred thousand. Your reason for paying almost three times too much for the horse is your own. My involvement in the purchase, apparently, was to carry your money through the airport and deliver it to that cheap Latino hood disguising himself as a trainer in New York."

I didn't slow down to give Milos a chance to interrupt. I noticed that Jimmy Slacks had silently appeared beside Milos. Vito had obviously summoned him.

"From this point on, Mr. Corsetti, I want you and your folks to understand that I am, if you want, your trainer. That's all. I haven't run a horse on your behalf, and will not do so until we have this agreement. I came to you in person and speaking frankly, I'm not afraid of anyone in this room. I do want your business and, above, all your friendship.

"I'm the most loyal friend in the world to those I respect, and I greatly respect you, Mr. Corsetti, but I will not be legally abused."

I stepped back a slight bit, to get Slacks in my line of

vision. I didn't give a damn about Santos, but Slacks was a very dangerous man.

"Jimmy, take Milos and wait outside. I'm fine."

As he turned to go, Slacks said to me, "I'll be just outside the door, my friend."

When the door closed and we were alone, Vito took a long drink of red wine and used a napkin to wipe his mouth. "So, Irish, you think you can walk into my office and lay down rules to me about how we are to do business? No man has done so for as long as I can remember. If you had not said that you respect me, you wouldn't walk out of here."

He paused and stared at me. His eyes, bleary with moisture and riveted on me, were meant to break me down.

"You think you're a tough son-of-a-bitch, don't you, Irishman?"

" Mr. Corsetti, I've killed some very bad men for the army. I've been trained to do things that would make even you blush. When it became senseless, I told them it was over."

As I kept talking, he never changed his deadly stare.

"I want to be your horse trainer and answer only to you. If you never want to see me again and I have to go through Milos about horse matters, so be it. However, I'd miss you. We're both strong characters. Let's have fun together, if you choose. You have my loyalty now and we can respect each other as friends. I've already done enough dirty work for you to land my ass in jail, but no more. There it is, take it or leave it."

"That's quite a revealing speech, Colin. You do have brass balls. Few in Boston would live after talking to me in such a way. I respect your courage. I want to be your friend and I still want you to be my trainer. My office is always open to you, but call first.

"There's one thing you must promise me. You must never tell anyone what was said here tonight. I will tell my men to give you a wide berth."

He stood for the first time in my presence. He extended his hand and grasped mine firmly.

"Stay my friend, Irishman. Never sell me out, or what has been said here will be forgotten."

He filled his own glass and a clean one for me. "To friendship and respect and most of all, loyalty between us, my friend."

"Always," I said as we touched glasses and drank to each other.

"There is one matter I need to discuss, Mr. Corsetti."

"It is?"

I told him about Tino Torres and his situation with Carlos Reyes.

"It would help us for you to secure the services of this man. For what it costs to get him, he'll make us a thousand times over in the conditioning and improvement of our horses. I've six horses to worry about, five of which are yours. Tino not only knows everything there is to know about Sliding Scale, he can improve any horse he trains with me."

"You have only the one-legged black man?"

"He's the best groom and ground man I've ever known."

"Ground man? What does a ground man do?"

"He's a leg man. He bandages and cares for the horses' legs and general health."

"And this ground man, does he feed and care for our horses?"

"If I'm out of town, he feeds them, but he follows my instructions. The horses are my life, and I take good care of them."

"Guard my horses as if they are yours, Colin. I have many enemies. Don't let anyone near my horses."

"My barn's not a fortress, but Jock and Tino will live in the barn and one will always be with the horses. When we have big races, I'll sleep with them."

"That makes me feel better. Do as the young folks say and kick some butt," he smiled.

Milos and Jimmy Slacks were at the bar with their eyes glued on the office door when I came out. They rose as one and took a different route than mine toward the office to avoid confrontation. Neither smiled.

I slept better that night after calling Annie and telling her about Sliding Scale. I didn't mention the cash or my talk with Vito Corsetti. She was really excited about my seeing Tino.

"I feel left out with Jock and now Tino sharing all this with you. Maybe I should move up there and be with you, when you think the time is right."

I was relieved she'd not pushed me about coming to Boston. She could tell by my tone I wasn't ready for her. I didn't want her involved in what I still feared was a volatile situation.

Vito Corsetti was a wise and cunning man. His soft and fuzzy response to my speech could have been real. If I was a betting man, I'd put the odds of his being serious at one in twenty. In horseracing, that's called a long shot!

CHAPTER NINETEEN

Neither the gunmetal gray skies nor the spitting snow, which seemed to be never-ending could dampen the pure joy and excitement of new, high quality racehorses in a backside barn.

Cherokee Moon, Crystal Run, Deeper River and Top Shot arrived on the van just after training hours the next morning. No sooner were they bedded down than another van arrived from Aqueduct with Sliding Scale and a passenger, Tino Torres. He was hanging out the open van door smiling ear to ear. The backstretch was buzzing as Tino helped me lead the sliding scale from the loading ramp to barn 15.

Steve Casey stood on the kitchen steps with a worried look on his face when he saw Tino. Steve was getting busier in the afternoons; he'd had a recent winning streak, and my new, better horses would surely boost his average and earnings. He sulked, but Arch Hale assured him he'd be making more money than ever and not have to suffer through so many long, freezing mornings for ten dollars a ride.

After the hugs and backslapping, Tino and Jock went with me to the tack room to talk. The little man and Jock walked down the shed row talking about our new horses. They'd been best pals in Aiken. The three of us together would make a formidable team and run a crackerjack shed row.

After we'd talked about old times for a few minutes, I got them to stop laughing and finger pointing long enough to go over the schedule.

Tino was new to my ways as a trainer, so some rules and duties needed to be set in stone. Most were no different from Greentree's in the old days. However, we weren't going to be having lazy days, like in Aiken. We were on the hot spot at the racetrack. Tight security and scheduling were important.

There are no forty-hour weeks under my shed row. Racing is not a job; it's a way of life.

I asked the boys to walk the horses after they settled down and had their traveling bandages taken off. They were then to be hand washed in the vacant wash stall, on mats, to get off the traveling grime. When dry, they'd be fitted with heavy winter blankets to keep them warm on the frigid New England nights.

Jock knew the routine, but I had to go over it with Tino. All new purchases or claimed horses go through a makeover in my barn. After they settle in for a day, we start by pulling all their shoes and trimming and treating their feet.

Most blacksmiths at the racetrack let the horses' toes grow too long, which pushes the shoes too far forward and can cause heel bruises. When they are ready for new shoes, the toes are cut back so that more heel will be protected, giving more support to the tendons and ankles. This often caused soreness in their feet for a few days. I have a special mixture of Bowie mud with DMSO, cider vinegar and bran to pack in the feet and draw out the soreness while conditioning the soles of their feet.

The Judge always said, "No foot, no horse." As a youngster, I watched him come behind a blacksmith and drag a nylon stocking over the foot and hoof to assure the surface was smooth and the nails were properly set and clinched. If the stocking snagged, he made adjustments. Today, any guild blacksmith would walk out of my barn and never come back rather than face such scrutiny.

My new horses are all given a five-day worming. The dentist comes and "floats" the teeth, to make sure they're not sharp and interfering with the bit. This also helps the horse to chew better and get more nutrients from the food.

If they show no signs of shipping fever, they're vaccinated with a five-way shot that covers east-west-tetanus and flu/rhino, as well as rabies and west Nile virus shots. These may knock them out for several days, but they stay healthier and train better in the long run. The five new horses had been x-rayed and scoped to make sure they were sound in those departments. I knew up front most of the problems I'd face. I usually need six weeks to turn a horse around with our program. It happens gradually and the horses keep training and racing, if possible, during the process.

The only new arrival ready to run right away will be Cherokee Moon. Matt Lewis and I do many things alike and his colt showed it. He'd be the first starter for di Vinci Stable.

Each horse was given a new halter with a nameplate. Their buckets were coded with their names so they use only their own buckets, limiting the winter colds and coughs that can spread like wildfire. A large training board hangs by my office and small blackboards by each stall with medicines to be given, feed instructions, and training plans for each day.

Each stall has a folding saddle rack and bridle holder, as well as a bandage box for every three stalls. Each horse has its own bridle, so adjustments aren't needed every day. Riders never saddle the horses in my barn. They're usually in a hurry and prone to costly mistakes. I like the horse to be saddled by his groom and standing tied to the wall ready to go, avoiding confusion and waiting. All wall chains have about six inches of baling twine at the end, in case a horse panics when tied. The twine can break if a horse pulls hard enough against it, avoiding a costly accident or injury. Avoiding injury by using common sense has saved the careers of many good racehorses.

With only five horses, there would be plenty of time for

Jock and Tino to get things done. In the old days, with two dozen horses and enough help, we got all of them out between 6:30 and 9:30 am with time off for the thirty-minute break while the track is harrowed. Six horses will be a piece of cake.

We always play classical piano or old jazz music at a reasonable level. Even if I wanted to stop the practice, the vets, other grooms and riders would raise all kinds of hell. For some reason, just about everyone, except the occasional Latino, loves my soothing barn music as a change of pace.

As I visited with Tino over coffee in the track kitchen, he asked, "How did you get me away from Reyes so soon? This morning he came up to me at feeding time and said, 'That gray horse is shipping out at nine. Get him ready and get your shit ready too. I don't know what that bastard friend of yours has going for him, but I got a call last night and you are to go with the horse and stay in Boston."

Tino grinned, "It was really great, Colin. The guy was so pissed, I thought he was going to have a heart attack. He cussed you up one side and down the other. Said he'd get even."

"What about all the money you owed him? What was that for?"

Avoiding the question, Tino said, "He said it was paid. The Boston guy scared the hell out of him, Colin. He said he couldn't get you and me now, but one day when we weren't looking, he'd do us both in. Let's stay out of that crazy bastard's way."

I left Tino, who recognized several friends from the past and began chatting them up at ninety miles an hour. I headed for an old barn at the rear of the stable area that was almost falling down. It was so far from the main track that trainers had to walk their horses to meet the freelance riders.

Charlie Clark and Grady O'Brien had four stalls in this barn. They survive on their pensions; Charlie's from the Army, and Grady's from some construction firm. They had few friends on the backside.

Because they live together as a couple in this macho community they may be verbally abused, but never in my presence. Several times I've come to their aid. Both are highly intelligent men dedicated to each other. They harm no one and I enjoy their company. Being gossips, they keep their ears to the ground and often tell me about good claims or others who want to claim horses from me. This gives me time to scratch my horse if I want.

"Speaking of the devil, look what the cat dragged in, Charlie," said Grady, who stood at least six-five and weighed almost 300 pounds. He was physically as soft as butter and just the opposite of Charlie who was a foot shorter and half Grady's weight.

"We've just been talking about you, Colin. Hell, the whole backstretch is talking about you," said Grady.

"I guess you heard I have a few new horses?"

Grady said, "Colin, you don't have just a few horses, if what I've heard is right. You checked in some of the best horses seen around here in a while. Some of the big guys used to having their way around here are mad as hell. They think they own the money and condition races and don't want anyone else playing in their sand box."

"Fuck 'em, Grady."

"He better not," snapped Clark.

Charlie walked toward me with a beer in his hand. "Here's your Sam Adams, Colin."

"You bet your ass, Charlie," I chuckled.

"I love it when you talk dirty, big man," he snipped.

Grady joined us. He pointed to me with his own beer and said, "It's not just the new horses, Colin. People have been talking a lot about your new owner. They say he's connected. That's not like you, baby."

Charlie chimed in. "Colin, something else is going on here, too. People have been asking questions about you. There was a man I didn't know in the bookkeeper's office asking questions about you. I can assure you he got nothing from Alice.

"Cozy Man Costas was talking bad about you to the guy in the grandstand during yesterday's races. I was having a drink, to try to wipe out the way our horse ran in the fifth, when I heard your name come up at the other end of the bar. It was the same guy I saw coming out of Alice's office when I was getting a check cashed. People kinda avoid us. They didn't notice me," he added.

"A man like that in a suit, asking about a guy like you is going to stand out like a sore thumb around here. You been paying your taxes? He looked sort of IRS, if you know what I mean," Grady said.

I changed the conversation. "I see you guys have been having bad luck lately. You had that horse break down last week and your old mare seems to be on her last legs."

"You come in here to gloat at us, Colin?" Clark said.

"Never, pal. You know better than that. You guys are two of the few friends I have when it comes to trainers."

"Well, I'll tell you one thing, Cozy Man Costas is no friend of yours. He's no friend of ours either," said Charlie.

Clark brought out a new round of beers and asked, "What brings you around, Colin?"

I gathered my thoughts and said, "I don't want more than six horses, or I'll have to start hiring new help that I can't trust. I have two horses of my own I need to sell."

Grady jumped. "Don't try to sell them around here, Colin.

We're flat broke and getting broker."

"Let me have my say, boys. I have Broken Heart, my five year old mare. She was second for sixty-five hundred last week. I also have a two-year-old that had one no-good start, but has some run. I raised him and like him. You guys need some fresh faces around here, so I thought you'd like them."

"Really, Colin, we have no money," Charlie said.

"I tell you what I'll do. Give me three thousand from your first win or claim and they're both yours. If they don't win, you don't owe me anything. If I hear you're playing with me and they keep running second, I'll kick that fat ass of yours, Grady."

"Oh, Colin, like I said, I love it when you talk dirty," he joked.

"Jock knows you might be coming to get them."

Charlie asked, "I see you have a cute new man. You wouldn't want to throw him in with the deal, would you?"

"Charlie, that's Tino Torres from New York. He's an old friend and a hell of a morning rider. He's also straight as a string. If you get in a serious jam, let me know and I'll send him over. He's not going to freelance though."

"That's not the kid used to ride in New York? Had all those long shot winners?" Grady asked.

"That's him. He's broken up and can't ride afternoons anymore."

"God, you are getting serious over there," Clark said.

"Serious as a heart attack, guys. Keep your ear to the ground, and good luck with the horses."

"God bless you, Colin," Grady said as I left the barn.

I was glad to have moved the two horses, but concerned to hear that strangers were asking about me. I'd have to have a little talk with Costas. Maybe I'll see him at The Shamrock again.

CHAPTER TWENTY

Fred Hardy, a smallish, rail-thin man in his late thirties, was born in Bangor, graduated from a middle-of-the-road prep school and then Rutgers. Making a case against Vito Corsetti could kick-start his federal career. Hardy was a bulldog of an assistant federal prosecutor. Breaking up a large scale money laundering ring and the indictment of Corsetti would put his career on the fast track to his own federal district.

Arriving at Boston's Logan Airport, he wore an expensive sheepskin coat, a plaid Bean shirt and black knit tie that went well with his tan corduroys and desert boots, giving him the college professor look. His neatly trimmed mustache, long, straight John Denver hair over his big ears and John Lennon glasses all looked staged. As usual, he wore a large rubber band on his wrist, popping it and rolling it around his index finger when he was in danger of losing his temper.

Though mild-looking, Hardy always seemed mad at the world. He'd never married and seldom dated. He made women feel uneasy and they almost never accepted a second date. His work and his struggle for advancement in the federal rat race consumed his life. He relished this return, even for a short time to his native New England. His parents had died in a house fire ten years before and he had only a few distant relatives scattered throughout the northeast.

He'd badgered his superiors to convince Martin Watson he could be of more help on the Corsetti investigation if he worked for a short time out of the Boston FBI office. He rented a dark, fed-looking Ford sedan and drove to a bland motel in nearby Saugus where one of the endless Indian Patel families rented rooms by the week. If the room was clean and had cable TV, Hardy, an avid sports fan, would be reasonably satisfied.

He drove to the train the following morning and caught the

green line to downtown Boston, then made his way to Martin
Watson's office on foot, walking with a strange gait that started
at his toes and rolled backward.

"I see you made it all right, Fred," Watson looked up from
the sports pages of the *Boston Herald*. Hardy, who kept up with
most things in the Boston area by reading its newspapers every
day on the Internet, preferred the broadsheet *Globe*.

"I guess you can keep up with the criminal element around
here better with that scandal sheet, Martin," Hardy snipped,
referring to the *Herald*.

Martin said, "I see you still got that chip on your shoulder,
Fred. I hope it doesn't hinder our investigation."

Ignoring Martin's remark, Hardy asked, "What's the latest
on Santos and our boy O'Hearn?"

"My sources at the track tell me O'Hearn made a trip this
week to New York and bought some fancy horse. All five of the
horses he's purchased have arrived at Suffolk Downs. I don't
know how he paid for the horse at Aqueduct, but according to
the scuttlebutt, it probably cost about three hundred thousand.
That means that he has moved a half million for our man,
Santos."

"That's a lot of money to be moving around without a paper
trail. If the cash isn't reported to the IRS, we could have a case
against O'Hearn," said Hardy.

"We may have a break on that front. All the paperwork is
in Milos Santos' name, but he's not about to make that kind of
money counting beans," Watson said.

"Yeah, Fred, but I'll bet those are Vito Corsetti's beans. No
telling where they came from."

"You know I'd love to get my hands on Corsetti. He's never
even been before a judge. He'd be a real feather in my ... our

caps," Hardy exclaimed.

"It gets better. My source tells me O'Hearn's been to Little Venice twice this week. According to my man, our horse trainer was seen being escorted directly to the fortress in the back that's Corsetti's office. Santos was there both times," added Watson.

In his organized manner, Hardy approached a clean drawing board on the wall and began writing names and drawing lines. They traced O'Hearn and Santos from the Barn 15 tack room, where they first met at Suffolk Downs, to Miami, back to Boston and then to Little Venice, on to Aqueduct and back to Boston and Little Venice. Three names, including Vito Corsetti's, were written on the lines as they traveled around the board.

"This is a start," Hardy said. "There are a lot of minor players who'll fill themselves in, but these three are the most important."

"Add a fourth name, Jimmy Slacks. He's Corsetti's body-guard who just happens to be shadowing O'Hearn recently. He hasn't been on him all the time, but he's been seen following O'Hearn from Little Venice to his house in Winthrop. They must want to know if he's meeting with anyone after he leaves Corsetti. Make a note that if you turn O'Hearn, you'll have to dodge Slacks," Watson warned.

They'd failed to include Colin's side trip to Aiken on the board. If either man knew about Annie Collins, they weren't telling.

Hardy took the break in the conversation after adding Jimmy Slack's name to the board to drop the ticking bomb he had discovered during his deep background search of O'Hearn.

"Mr. Colin O'Hearn is a strange man."

Hardy talked about Colin's academic and professional backgrounds, all of which Watson knew.

"I was going over his service record. He'd been in Desert Storm and then was assigned to the Special Forces detailed to the Pentagon. Everything was going good to that point, until a red flag went up."

"What kind of red flag?" asked Watson.

"The kind that says you and I don't have clearance to see his file. I went to my bosses and they were shut out as well. It took the Deputy Director of the Justice Department talking to the Assistant Secretary of the Army off the record for us to get anywhere."

"Where did things go from there?"

"Our man went to the office of the Army big wig who had O'Hearn's file. We weren't allowed to copy the file, but he did get a look at it and was able to take some notes. That was it. He was told that if anyone asked, the Army would deny that anyone at Justice had access to O'Hearn's file," said Hardy.

"I was called directly to the Justice guy's office. I couldn't take notes, just got an oral report and a strict warning. I can lose my job if it ever gets out that we have information from the sealed file. I don't know how Justice got the file open, even for a peep, and I don't want to know. Hell, I wish I didn't know what I learned."

"Tell me what you know, Fred. It will go no further than the two of us."

"Well, I didn't get any names, dates or even many places. O'Hearn spent some very hard time in Iraq as a sniper."

"Our man's a killer?" asked Watson.

"It just so happens that Colin O'Hearn is what the Justice Department referred to as a "killing machine." It seems he had some dirty duty which will never be revealed. After a few years, his assignments left him mentally unstable, or so they said. They watch him like a hawk ever since he mustered out," Hardy related.

"He has freelance killer credentials and more. This man was an honor scholar and a hell of an athlete at the University of Virginia. He was a champion wrestler in prep school and switched to the boxing ring in college. He was a Golden Gloves champion in the ring and went undefeated in the Army... never lost a fight. That's in his regular file. What he did after that, God only knows."

"How does this play with our investigation?" Watson asked.

"It's my feeling there were two reasons for the Army to tell us what they did. The first is to let us know what kind of man we're dealing with and trying to turn. The other is for us to be aware that his background is very sensitive. It seems they'll stop at nothing to keep O'Hearn's past activities buried."

"We'll never get this guy turned, Fred. We sure as hell aren't going to scare him."

"There's always a way, Martin. Maybe there's someone he is close to, maybe the black man or a girlfriend. He's never been married; maybe he's gay?"

"I know you're a hard nose, Fred, but maybe we should back off O'Hearn. This guy might be too dangerous to trap in a corner."

Hardy thought for a minute and said, "You know, Martin, we should watch him some more. Let's get the goods on him first and then decide how to push him. We might be able to recruit him. Hell, just think what it might mean for us to get Corsetti. We would surely get the credit, since it's our operation."

Watson thought for a moment before answering, "Fred, I think you're crazy as shit. The guy has never shown that he's more than what he is, a down-on-his-luck horse trainer with a drinking problem who's in over his head with some mobsters.

"Furthermore, I really don't think, knowing what I know now, that he's into anything really crooked. I'll tell you one thing Fred, you better leave sleeping snakes like this guy alone. You punch that nest with a stick, and you do it on your own."

"You giving up on the case?" Hardy snapped. "Just because one of the guys was a badass twenty years ago?"

"I don't give up on criminal investigations and you know it. I'm just saying we have to be careful, since we know that the Army has been keeping this guy covered up for all these years. I agree there's been some movement of cash, probably dirty money. We keep the principal players in this money laundering scheme in our sights."

Hardy thought for a second and then said, "Yeah, but who would get the credit?"

Watson shook his head, "Fred, you haven't learned anything from what we've been talking about here."

"I've learned one thing, Martin, I'm going to be making most of the decisions in this case, because you don't have the guts to play hardball with the mob guys involved."

CHAPTER TWENTY- ONE

I entered the bar at The Shamrock the evening after I bedding down my new horses for the first time. I noticed a loud buzz in the front bar. As Steve and Arch approached me, the tone of the room settled down noticeably. It put me on edge.

"What about the new guy you brought from New York?" Steve demanded.

"Is he riding in the afternoon?" asked Arch.

I took Arch by the arm and led him to my favorite table. Steve followed silently.

"Look, you two, calm down. Let's get a few things straight right off.

I went on quickly, to avoid more questions. "You both know I have some very nice, new horses. You do the job, Steve, and you'll get first crack in the afternoon until I tell you differently. The morning is another matter.

"Tino Torres and I have been friends since our days together in Aiken. He won't ride at all in the afternoons. He's banged up and retired. He will ride for me in the mornings, and no one else. He's on the payroll, part exercise rider and part groom.

"Steve, you have enough to do in the morning without a regular gig with me every day. This way, you can jump around more and give other trainers more attention in the mornings, getting better rides in the afternoon."

I waited for their reaction. "You still want him to breeze the one's he's going to ride in the afternoons, Colin?" Arch asked.

Being a very smart agent, Arch wanted Steve to set down his mounts before he rode them on race day.

"We'll have to work that out. I value your opinion very much. Yours as well, Steve."

Arch nodded, "What's your schedule?"

"Yeah, Colin, what have you got? Tell us about them. This

place and the backside have been wild with rumors," Steve said.

I turned to ask for a drink, and I saw Evan Kennedy walking our way with my regular scotch and water.

"Is this a private conversation?" he asked, as he put down my drink and pulled out a chair.

"It is if you're going to repeat any of it at the bar. I'm just getting ready to tell Steve and Arch about my new horses. I don't care if you know what I have and where I'm going, but the last thing I want is to tell every trainer on the backside my business."

I gave the boys a brief overview of the horses and when they might be ready to run. Steve didn't know whether to complain about losing the morning money or thank me for the new horses. He was a few drinks shy of showing his ass, so he stayed quiet and let Arch ask the questions. When I finished, they were off to cruise the bar looking for rides and free drinks.

"I have another horse staked out in the bushes, Evan. Might be the best of them all."

Evan had taken Jamie's place as my listening post, and he knew about my trials with and without Annie over the years. I told him about Lonely Aunt and how she'd messed up Annie. I explained we were back together and she might come up for the summer.

"Well, don't look behind you now, lover boy, but there's someone coming through the door who might like to hear about Annie, seeing as she'd gone and got herself all pumped up about you getting back from Aiken."

I knew he must be talking about Emmy. I'd been dumb to lead her on before I left. She pulled out a chair at the table, and Evan rose saying, "I've got to get back to the bar."

"How about a Sam Adams for me and another scotch for

Colin, Evan?" Emmy asked.

"How'd your trip turn out, Colin? I know about the horse part. I've been to the barn, met Tino, and he and Jock went over the horses with me. I think you hit the jackpot. I love the big, gray older horse."

"I guess I'd better start by saying my friend in Aiken and I are trying to fix things up."

Emmy looked into the beer Evan had just brought staring at the foam, taking a minute to say the right thing.

"When you didn't call when you got back and weren't at the barn when I came to look at the horses, I guessed as much. I'm sorry, Colin. I still think we can have some fun together. If you think I'm letting you off the hook that easy, you are crazy. You've got this big heart of mine racing like it hasn't for a long time. If I get the chance and you let your guard down, I might just put a lip lock on your Mr. Johnson."

She stood, her legs straddling her chair, and chugged her beer. "I'll be by the barn at the regular time in the morning, stud. Good luck." She turned and walked out the door.

I did the same, stopping by the bar to pay my tab. "One day you're bone dry and the next day you're drowning in women. That might be the best one you just blew off," Evan said.

"You may well be right, " I said as I left.

I was getting into my truck, when the door of another pickup opened next to me. A rugged looking man, as tall as me but thirty pounds heavier hit my door with his as he pushed me against my truck. I could see Cozy Man Costas get out of the driver's side and knew I was face to face with the Russian gangster Connie Tass.

"Get the fuck out of my way, buster," he snapped.

I pushed his door back against his leg and trapped him in

the doorway. He bellowed in pain, and pushed back. "You hit my car door," he yelled.

I heard Costas shout at me from the other side of the cab but was more worried about the big guy pushing against me. I grabbed the guy by the coat and slung him across the ice, where he went to his knees. "Get him, Costas," the man screamed.

"We've been there Cozy Man. Remember the dumpster?"

Cozy screamed at me as he tried to get the big Russian to his feet. Before they were both standing, I was in my truck and put it in low, spraying them with ice as I fish-tailed out of the lot.

It was too dark for me to see them as I pulled out into the traffic, but I could imagine the conversation behind me. I hadn't heard the last of this scrape with Tass. I wasn't worried about Costas, but knew I'd started something with the Russian.

CHAPTER TWENTY-TWO

The traffic was light as I drove past the Big Dig, took Somerset Street and parked in front of the brownstone where Ian Higgins had both his home and law office. The old attorney and racehorse fanatic was born in Ireland and went to law school with the Judge. He had been my "guardian" since my father's death, if I needed one. Right now, I needed the advice of a lawyer.

The Judge and Ian made a pact that the survivor would carry the other's ashes back to the little Irish town of Kells for burial. When he died, Ian made the trip to Kells alone, as I was in the Army. He's now in his late sixties and not in the best of health due to his ample allotment of Irish whiskey.

When the door swung wide and framed the small red-headed Irishman, his smile broadened as he welcomed me with open arms. His office has a library that gives his secretary space for a desk to work and to protect her boss. I followed Ian the length of the hall to a small elevator which provided access to the kitchen, living room and another study on the second floor. His living and guest quarters are on the third. Ian had installed the elevator five years ago when the three flights of narrow steps became too much for him.

When we got off on the second floor, Ian walked to the kitchen where he'd been eating the supper Ellen had left. Now fifty, she was a striking widow and is dedicated to the old man. It was a friendship that would never be consummated by marriage, as Ian is one of the last surviving, straight, rich, Boston bachelors. He enjoys women's company, but told me long ago he'd never marry.

"I assume you've interrupted my solitude at this hour to sell me a horse or something as foolish. You look far too healthy to be sick, and since you won a race and got the old gray horse claimed, you can't be broke. My grapevine says you may even be in the chips... so to speak."

He paused and I took over. "Can't I pay a friendly call when I'm not sick, broke or trying to sell you a horse?"

"Of course, my man, but it's been years since you've any other excuse to visit. Pour yourself a scotch and refresh my Bushmills, please. The Celtics are looking better and the Bruins are in first place. You must be after my box tickets which Ellen knows you can have any time I'm not using them."

We moved to the fire and big leather chairs in the living room. I'd cleaned up the dishes while pouring the drinks. He acted as if it was expected. I would have cleaned up after my father, and would do no less for the old man who now held that place in my life.

"Really, I love every minute you can spare me, Colin." He studied my face, "I have the feeling that this time you're troubled."

I told him everything that had happened in the last few weeks, except my lovemaking with Annie. I told him I suspected someone was following me. I also added I had just put Connie Tass on his ass.

"When you lie down with dogs, you attract fleas, Colin. I can only imagine the various groups who might be attracted to you, now that all of Boston knows you're training for Corsetti. You can start with the various law enforcement agencies and when you run out, you can look to Corsetti's enemies.

He then told me something that put me on my ass.

"I don't know if you know it or not, but I have been Vito Corsetti's personal attorney for 25 years. I don't go to court with him, but I advise him in other ways. It was me who told him about you when he started asking about getting back into racing. I told him to do it quietly, staying in the background.

"Corsetti's fellow Italian mobsters as far away as Providence see him as an aging mob boss with territory to be taken," Ian explained. "They watch him like a hawk. So do the Southie Irish crooks who're licking their chops. Then, add that Russian goon Tass."

"What's my legal exposure if the money I used to buy the horses was dirty, Ian?"

"At this point, if they're watching you, the FBI will try to entrap and use you against Corsetti. The white collar FBI boys are always looking for big cases for political and career reasons.

"Go on as if nothing had happened for now. Give me a week or so. I've got former students in law enforcement who owe me some favors. Let's start a plan right now. There are two important things you must do.

"First, don't carry another dollar or buy another horse for Vito Corsetti. Keep perfect, detailed records of your racing operation. Secondly, win some races and keep them happy. That way, they'll give you plenty of rope.

"Tass has hop-heads who will do anything for their next fix, or to make a name. Stay close to home. You're safe at the track. Anyone different will stand out to you there. If something doesn't look right, something's wrong. Look at the way a man dresses, even part of his attire. How he walks a horse, if he's pretending to be a groom or strange behavior by a friend or just someone with whom you do business. I feel sure the FBI will be keeping an eye on you. I have a very close friend in the Boston office. He'll give me heads up if someone from the outside is going to set his sights on you.

"Don't let your guard down for even a minute. What have you told Jock?"

"I've told him part of it. He's still mad at me because he told me not to get messed up with Santos in the first place."

"Tell him what he needs to know, what he needs to watch for. Don't tell the new fellow, Tino, much at all. I don't care how long you've known him. He was working for a connected man when you hired him. They may have something that friendship can't top on him. Watch him. Watch everyone now, Colin. Remember you're probably in trouble and you might be in danger."

He led me to the elevator.

Thinking for a moment, Ian said, "Colin, I already know your courage has no limits, and now Corsetti does as well. There is one thing you cannot do."

"What's that, Ian?"

"Never risk leading them to Annie. Try not to call her on a land-line. Buy a pre-paid cell phone. If they find out you love her and how vulnerable she is, anyone involved will try to use her. The feds especially will try to squeeze her up. The crooks will go so far as kidnapping her to get you to do what they want, to save their own asses.

"From now on, act as if your phones are bugged. Your house and tack room are probably going to be bugged, if they haven't been already."

Fear hit me between the eyes. I reached my truck and swore to myself that if anyone went near Annie on account of me, there would be a major bloodletting in Boston.

I pulled away from Ian's house and headed toward the bridge and Winthrop. A black SUV was on my tail. I raced through the next light and slammed on my brakes, pulling off to the right. The SUV passed me and slammed on its brakes. I sprinted to the driver's side door. It started to open and I jerked it open as hard as I could.

I was looking right into the barrel of a pistol held by Jimmy Slacks.

Cold, like ice, he said, "O'Hearn, we have to talk."

I got into the passenger side. The smoke and whiskey smell almost made me throw up. Jimmy's car was neat as a pin, but his ashtray was full and the car was fogged up. He took a long pull of whatever he was drinking.

"You and I need to talk away from the joint and all the nosey people connected with Vito, especially Santos."

He took another drink and continued. "There's gonna be trouble, man, and I'm afraid you're going to be in the middle of it. Vito don't know I'm here talking to you, but I'm gonna be talking mostly about others, not him. This is going to be kinda confusing, but you should know what you're into."

I was wishing I had a drink of my own when he reached into a small cooler on the back seat and handed me a Sam Adams.

"O'Hearn, you need to understand some shit and I need a friend, somebody I can talk to The bartender is my friend, but if push comes to shove, I don't know if I can trust him. For a while, Santos and I talked. But, he's the reason we're here like this. I don't know O'Hearn, I just think maybe you're a stand up guy and can handle yourself. If something breaks open, I'd rather have you at my back than any of the others. And you, Colin—you're gonna need a friend."

"Get on with it, Jimmy. What's on your mind ?"

"It's Santos. I know he's talking to somebody outside the organization. I just don't know whether it's the cops or the feds. Maybe it's worse… the enemy, so to speak."

He took another drink and went on, "You know that trainer you shoved around in the bar the other night? Well, he works for Tass, the Russian from the South End who's been messing with our business. When he got some racehorses and started dealing dope and making loans around the racetrack, we decided that we needed to be closer to his action. So, Vito got Santos to get you and some horses.

"Before we even get started you go after Tass's trainer, and he's not going to take that sitting down. He'll come after you, Colin. I want you to be ready. He's got a few men you might look for. If he sends a great big lug named Joe Dobbs, kick his ass and send him on his way. If he sends a tough guy named Miki Zepoff, you don't want to try him alone. You'll have to kill him. He's stone cold bad. Call me and I'll take care of him. Me and him are gonna have to get it on some day, but the boss don't want to let things heat up so fast. We're just playing around the edges now.

I let him ramble.

"Dobbs, he's a Russian too. His real name's Dombroski. The Feds are all over him, and from what I hear they might already own him. I think Tass will send him against you and not give a shit what happens. Sooner or later, he'll get rid of him. We've got someone on the inside with Tass, and that's what he's telling us. This guy don't know for sure, but he thinks Santos has talked with Zepoff or Tass, maybe both. If we find out for sure, well, you know what's gotta come down."

"Jimmy, just to catch you up, Tass gave me some shit tonight in the parking lot of the Shamrock and I put him on his ass in front of his trainer. I guess that's all the more reason he'll send someone after me."

I took a long pull on my beer. "Why tell me this shit? I don't want to be involved in any of Vito's business, not for all the money in the world. Thanks for the heads up, but I've got problems of my own without getting in any deeper with Vito.

I like the old man and I want to train for him, but that's as far as it goes."

"Sometimes you can't draw lines that thin, O'Hearn. You're in. You walk into the back room like you're one of the family and that makes you special. I just wanted to give you a warning about Tass and his people."

"I really thank you, Jimmy. I won't say anything to anyone about us meeting. And if it means anything, I agree; you shouldn't trust Santos. It would scare me to death if I had 'private business' and he had my books."

"The boss knows that and we're taking precautions, so to speak. By da' way... okay to call you Colin? That O'Hearn thing gives me trouble."

"You bet, Jimmy. It's Colin and Jimmy."

He started his car and then put out his hand. I shook it firmly and said, "I don't know much about these things, just maybe what I've seen in the movies or in books. But I think I'm glad you didn't try to kiss my cheek."

He burst out laughing. "What a smartass we have for a horse trainer." Looking at the ceiling as if talking to a third person, he said, "What am I gonna do with this guy? I gotta love him."

I got out as he put the car in gear and waved goodbye. When I returned to my truck, I was sweating like a pig. I was in way over my head. I just wanted to get back into my recliner under my horse blanket and start over again. I hated it. All I could think about as I drove home was what to do next.

While Colin and Jimmy Slacks talked, on the other side of Boston another clandestine meeting was going on. Connie Tass's right-hand man, Miki Zepoff, and Santos were huddled in a booth in a small Southie bar.

"So far, everything you've told us about Corsetti has panned out, Milos. But there's gonna be a time when Mr. Tass is going to ask you to show your true colors. We're sending that big lug, Dobbs, after your trainer tomorrow. I hope Corsetti gets the message that his men can't beat up on Tass people. You told us this guy you picked for Corsetti is a drunk and a loser, so Dobbs should mess him up pretty bad.

"If Dobbs screws up this job, Mr. Tass may ask for your help. He don't completely trust you yet, but after you handle a big job for him, you'll be on easy street. You'll be getting paid by Corsetti and have a nice retainer from Mr. Tass. When we finally get Corsetti out of the way, we are going to need someone who knows all the inside ropes to run North Boston."

"Nobody knows the North End operation better than I do, Miki. Make sure Mr. Tass knows that, too. I can run the business in the North End with my eyes shut. I have copies of all the books and know every contact. Don't take O'Hearn too lightly. He's a tough son of a bitch."

"That's fine with me. I've been telling Mr. Tass to get rid of Dobbs for a long time now. I don't trust him. He's screwed up several things we've asked him to do lately, so he's more of a liability than an asset at this point. Maybe, if he gets in trouble for messing up O'Hearn in broad daylight on the racetrack, he'll try to give up something to the cops to stay out of jail. We'll know. This thing with O'Hearn is just something Mr. Tass wants to do—smoke out Dobbs more than anything, and send a good message to Vito Corsetti as well. The sooner we get it on with him, the better we'd like it," said Zepoff smugly.

Santos pulled his car away from the bar and headed for his North End home after his conversation with Zepoff. He felt the noose around his neck, but was too greedy to see that he was putting himself between a rock and a hard place.

CHAPTER TWENTY-THREE

The following morning, I tried to put my meeting with Jimmy Slacks out of my head. It was one of those bright winter days when the slosh on the roadside and mud around the barn were evidence of a warming spell. The horses were enthralled by the break in the weather, playing as if it were spring.

Jock had blistered both Sliding Scale and Crystal Run. They stood with their heads hanging over stall guards in their cradles, taking out their discomfort on their hay bags. I threw a handful of crimped oats on each bag, teasing them before their lunch. After about a week their ankles would look like hell, but nature's healing process would soon be at work. What had been loose and mushy would be tight as a two-year old, and swollen ankles would be drawn down snug and sound.

Admiring Jock's usual masterful job, I watched Tino get ready to take Cherokee Moon to the track As I threw him up, I said, "Don't let him go too fast, just smooch him down the lane. He's going to run Saturday and all I want to do is blow him out."

"They sealed the track last night and it's sloppy, but firm underneath. You want me to back him up and gallop him to the half-mile and let him do it on his own?"

"Just don't let him leave Saturday's race on the track this morning."

I leaned on the rail and watched the jumpy chestnut colt buck and play with his neck tucked, fighting Tino's firm hold as he passed me. I knew the little man was in for a fight until he set him down to breeze.

As he passed the wire the first time, I knew Tino was in trouble. He swung Cherokee Moon slightly from side to side to take up his hold. Through my binoculars, I could see his toes pointed to the ground as he started up the backside, standing straight as a string. When he hit the half-mile pole, Tino eased over and dropped the colt's neck. Cherokee Moon took off like a rocket, causing Tino to rise up a little and take a firmer hold as they passed me at the quarter pole.

By some mystery of horsemanship, Tino eased the colt into a slower stride and they zipped past the wire in a nice quick move. They galloped out to the half-mile pole before slowing to a jog at the three-eighths pole. He jogged past me and nodded, telling me all I needed to know.

Other railbirds and trainers stopped and asked how fast my horse worked and I just shrugged. "You know me, Charlie, I don't even own a watch."

After I turned the corner and ducked into my tack room, I pulled my phone out of my pocket and called the clocker.

"Hey, Pete, it's me, Colin."

"Nice move. Real easy, pal: 49.2. He go like you wanted?"

"You bet, Pete."

He hung up and I smiled. I'd dealt with Pete for many years. I've never asked him to change a work or not report one. We never talked about it, but sometimes he'd report a slower time to be published in the *Racing Form*.

Jock had given Cherokee Moon a few turns around the shed row and begun washing him off in the sunshine by the time I spoke with Pete. Tino was holding the colt that was playing as if he'd never been out of the barn.

"He could have gone in a big number, Colin," Tino said with a smile covering his face.

"Great job, Tino. He had plenty left and should be just right on Saturday. Let sleeping dogs lie and don't talk about him around the kitchen. You guys don't want to rock your odds on race day."

As I turned to go back in my office, a huge man in a black topcoat walked down the steps from the track kitchen. He appeared to be heading for my barn and I had a feeling he meant trouble,... trouble for me. I stepped into the vacant hay stall and took out my cell phone. I hit the number for the stable security gate that was logged into the phone.

"Louie, this is Colin at Barn 15. Tell Charlie Martin to drive up to my barn and sit in his car by the track kitchen. I think there's a guy headed my way who might be trouble. Tell him not to show his hand unless I need him."

Before the man could get through the mush and melting ice, I could see the track security head climbing into his vehicle down by the front gate.

Tino was cooling out Cherokee Moon at the other end of the barn, when the man approached me with a full head of steam.

"Step into that empty stall, Jock. Trouble's coming and I want you to watch, but not be seen. I may need a witness."

I don't know why my stomach was so tight, as the guy got a few strides from me, but maybe my talk with Jimmy Slacks had me on edge. It had been many years since I felt physically threatened, but I knew this guy was trouble looking for a place to happen. I was more than ready.

The man in the overcoat rushed up, stopping three feet in front of me. We were the only two people in the world at that minute. I felt isolated and good as I drilled my eyes into his. I heard nothing as a focused heat filled my face. I could have been back in a boxing ring.

He was six-five and must have weighed about two hundred and seventy-five pounds. I noticed his shoes were made for street wear and his suit had that off-the-rack look from Sears. This guy was a foot soldier. His tie was pulled down and he was sweating like pig. His hair wasn't a buzz cut, but close. His teeth were spread in front and his nose had caught some punches.

"You O'Hearn?" he snarled.

Before I could answer, he was under the shed row where I'd backed up to make some room for us.

I turned for the office door and said, "Let's get out of the public and into my office."

My back was almost fully turned when he sucker punched me behind my left ear. Lights sparkled and flickered. A lightning bolt went off in my head and I felt straw on the palms of my hands. I was fighting for consciousness when he kicked me in the ribs.

I grabbed for a water bucket and fell backwards, holding on to an empty feed tub that was on the other side of the twelve by twelve stall. I knew he was almost on me when I heard something like, "this ass whippin' is from Connie Tass."

He never finished. I curled my fingers inside his collar like a vice. I felt soft, flabby skin and his Adam's apple. With my free hand, I grabbed his ear as hard as I could and pulled downward with a snap.

The better part of his ear came off in my hand. I grabbed what hair I could and pressed his face against the rough oak wall, shoving him the length of the stall as if planing the splintered wall. I then reversed him and did the same back the other way. He dropped to the floor, sitting and moaning, holding his head. I saw the ear sitting on the straw and picked it up, stuffing it into my shirt pocket.

The whole thing took about a minute. I went into his coat pocket and pulled out a gun. I went to his ankle and took his hideout .22 and dumped them both over the wall about eight feet from the floor. There was a space between stalls and I heard the guns hit the walls as they clattered their way to the bottom.

I've known lazy vets to dump needles in holes or over the wall rather than carry them back to their trucks. Through the years, the walls must hold thousands of needles and waste from drunks and junkies who hid in the stalls at night.

The big guy was sitting on the stall floor staring at the wall and moaning in shock. He was holding his ear with a handkerchief. I pulled him to his wobbling feet and got right in his face.

"Listen, you stupid fuck. Don't ever think you can come into my barn and hit me with my back turned and not pay for it. You tell that stupid fuckin' Tass he better send the first string next time. If that means your Zepoff goon, so be it."

Charlie Martin was walking from his car to the barn in a big hurry as I pushed the man toward him. "I saw him hit you from behind, Colin. Why's he bleeding so much? You cut him? Shit, look at his face. He looks like a porcupine with all those splinters. Must be a hundred stuck in his face."

Charlie had the back door of the cruiser open and the man inside as I said, "He came looking for trouble, Charlie. I've never seen him before. Jock was there. He saw it all. His ear is gone, so you better get him to the hospital. Write up something and I'll sign it. You know where to find me."

I watched as Charlie's cruiser wove its way through a crowded lane toward the security gate. I heard his siren as he hit the street and headed to the hospital. On the steps of the track kitchen Cozy Costas and several of his pals were staring at me. I returned Costas' glare before going into the tack room for a shovel. After a few minutes, Jock and Tino joined me in the empty stall.

I had so much blood on my hands that I gave the shovel to

Tino and showed him where to dig. In no time, he had enough room to get his arm ready to reach under the wall.

"Put your gloves on, Tino, there's no telling what's under there. You might get stuck with an old needle."

"A gun... no, two guns."

He pulled them out one at a time and threw them on the straw. "Don't touch them without gloves, Jock... You guys probably ought to get together on what to tell security and maybe the stewards and the cops. I'll give the guns to Charlie when he gets back. He'll know what to do with them."

After the boys left, I went into the office and cleaned up in the sink before pulling a spare sweatshirt from a hook on the wall. As I walked to my truck, people ignored me and asked no questions. I have a reputation for my bad temper, so I guess that's why everyone was giving me a wide berth.

On the way out of the track, I stopped by the guard shack and told them to tell Charlie Martin I was going to report what happened to the steward's office. The stewards who rule racing at Suffolk Downs with an iron fist, listened without asking a question. I left out the part about the two guns. I said nothing about the Cozy Costas and Connie Tass at The Shamrock.

I had a perfect record with the stewards. They've called me in a few times over a late scratch or a horse bleeding, but I've never had a ruling. They said they would read Charlie's report and call me back to go over it with me before they decided if there would be a formal hearing.

I called Ian Higgins on my cell while walking away from the meeting with the stewards. Ellen answered and told me Ian was teaching a class, and that she'd have Ian return my call. With a class until six, it would be late before he'd be back to the office.

I felt behind my ear and winced when I touched my goose

egg. This goose was carrying at least twins. I called Jock and asked him to cover at afternoon stables. My head was throbbing like a jackhammer, and there was no telling how much damage the big bastard had done to my ribs. On the way home, I stopped and bought a prepaid cell phone with a pile of minutes. My visitor from Tass was a stark reminder of Ian's warning about protecting Annie.

When I got home, I let my crazy dogs out for their run in the backyard and poured myself three fingers of Dewars' over ice before making an ice compress for my pounding head. There were calls on my machine from Annie and Santos.

I returned his first. "Did you work Cherokee Moon this morning?"

"He worked well in hand, in about .49 and change, Milos. He'll be entered on Saturday in the "A other than" and should have no problem. I know all the other horses eligible for the race and he's easily the best."

He asked if there were anything else I had to tell him and I gave him a rundown of the other horses. When I finished he asked, "What else is going on in your world?"

"Nothing that has anything to do with our business, Milos. I live a very quiet and boring life, except for my horses."

"Vito wants to know if you want to eat at Little Venice after the race on Saturday."

"Tell him I'd love to."

I fixed another Dewar's, fed the dogs and briefly rehearsed what I'd tell Annie. She answered on the first ring and we talked for over an hour. She wanted all the daily details about the new horses and Cherokee Moon's morning run. When she ran out of questions, I crossed my fingers and began lying.

"Annie, I lost my cell phone and had to pick up another one

today. Write down the new number, okay? And... uh, always use that number, hon. I'm thinking about disconnecting the number here at the house. Hell, I'm never here and all anybody ever gets is the answering machine. Seems silly to pay for the extra line."

I waited, hoping she wouldn't raise the question of how I'd use the computer and fax machine, without a land line. When she didn't, I breathed a sign of relief. After hanging up, I put a frozen pizza in the oven, showered away the dirt and grime from the fight and ate, not tasting the food.

I collapsed into bed, trying to plan the next day and what to do about Connie Tass. The Russian was obviously a man who held a grudge. I considered talking to Jimmy Slacks, but decided he might go off half-cocked and shoot the bastard.

CHAPTER TWENTY-FOUR

Martin Watson looked across his desk and wondered if Fred Hardy was going to have a stroke. For over a week, Hardy had been unable to make any headway investigating Colin O'Hearn.

"I even went to that restaurant myself to get the lay of the land and see if I could place anyone. All I got was a great meal and half drunk, which isn't like me. Just like you said, the pasta and meatballs were the best I've ever had. Neither Santos nor O'Hearn was there. I did see what a waiter told me was a table full of horse trainers from Suffolk Downs. Guess who was with them?"

"Cozy Man Costas, if I'm not mistaken," answered Watson.

"How did you know?"

"I have someone keeping an eye on him."

"Watson, why didn't you tell me?"

"You've been running around like you don't need me, so I thought I'd let you get your feet wet," said Watson.

Hardy sulked, "I guess you're going to tell me you've turned up something on your end?"

"A few things that I was working on before you arrived have brought something to light."

Hardy snapped his rubber band a couple of times and ran his hand through his hair. "Like what?"

"Like yesterday, somebody tried to rough up O'Hearn at his barn. The guy was huge. His name is Dobbs and he works as an enforcer for Tass. His real name's Dombroski."

Hardy asked, "How badly did he hurt O'Hearn?"

"Tass's big guy ended up in the hospital. O'Hearn broke out several teeth and rubbed about fifty splinters in his jaw while remaking his face. For good measure, he pulled off the thug's right ear."

Hardy was stunned. It was like he was working in another city on a different case. "What about a police report? What do we know?"

"The chief of security told the state police officer stationed at the track that there would be no charges. Apparently the guy hit O'Hearn when he turned his back and knocked him down. There were several witnesses, including the officer who took the guy to the hospital. I guess we know what kind of man we are fooling with in O'Hearn. I'm not going to brace him. They said he was a killer and I'm sure he could have killed Dobbs bare-handed if he'd felt like it."

"How are we going turn him, Watson?"

"Are you daft, Fred? The guy's a ticking time bomb. I'm going to watch him like a hawk. He's a drunk and doing business with the most powerful criminal in New England. Be patient and it will pay off."

"I don't work that way, Watson. I don't like anyone telling me how to run my investigation. I'm going after the washed drug money, and nobody's going to get in my way. I'm going to use some Miami tactics to get us to the bottom of this mess. We can get tough, too. Maybe I'll lean on Corsetti."

"You're not from around here, Fred. Vito Corsetti already knows who you are and what you're doing in Boston," Watson said with a sly grin on his face.

"How does he know about me?"

Watson shrugged, "My man inside Corsetti's bunch told me. There's talk about fitting you with cement boots if you push too hard. Go ahead on your own, hotshot, but be very careful. You're used to pushing around Cuban cokeheads. Boston's different. They invented the 'organized crime' label in the North End. You can't cross the street without them knowing it."

Hardy stared at his hands, popping his rubber band to stem his anger. "What about you? They know about you?"

"They've known about me since I started working the Whitey Bulger case seven years ago. They know who I'm after, and it's never been Vito Corsetti. They leave me alone as long as I don't put heat on them. That's your job, Hardy. I'm going to back off that crazy son of a bitch O'Hearn. He's done nothing to me and I'm not going to tear up seven years of work so you can get some political leverage in Florida," said Watson with some disdain.

Hardy was on his feet.

Watson continued, "My informants have made sure that Corsetti knows I only want Whitey Bulger. I've made a lot of progress, and my bosses know it. If I get out in front of you harassing Vito, I'll lose years of networking. No, Hardy, I'll never let your wild goose chase ruin my case. Bulger has killed more than a dozen men and I can prove it, if I can ever find him. Corsetti could be a help in locating Bulger. If Corsetti gets in a pinch, he might help me. Bulger's Irish and Corsetti's Italian. No love lost there, "said Watson, finally running out of wind and reaching for another cigarette.

"You don't care if I go after Corsetti and O'Hearn on my own?"

"I hope you get them both, if they screw up. I'll give you all the support I can from afar, but I hope we understand each other."

"Perfectly," Hardy said as he opened the door to leave. "I just wonder whose side you're on, Martin."

"Don't go there, Hardy. I've been with the FBI for more than twenty years. I bleed red, white and blue. I know how to play the game from the inside out. That's something I don't think you understand."

The two men parted ways with the lines clearly drawn. They both made phone calls when the other was out of sight. Hardy called his superiors in Miami while Martin Watson used his personal cell phone to make a call to the North End.

Charlie Martin pulled up to Barn 15 to talk just as I finished feeding, and we went to my office. "The guy's not pressing charges. He won't talk to the cops and was so scared he just clammed up. Said it was a misunderstanding over some money you owed him. He said something about letting bygones be bygones. When he left the hospital this morning, he paid cash."

Charlie cleared his throat. "Oh, Colin, the stewards want me to have the assholes from the state police shake your barn down. That includes your truck and Jock's and Tino's rooms and belongings."

"When are they coming?"

"It's supposed to be a surprise. I can't tell you… but in about twenty minutes, I'd be ready."

I had absolutely nothing to hide. No needles or drugs in my tack room. Sometimes Jock kept some pot for his bad headaches, but said he was clean. Tino ran to his room and the bathroom carrying a paper bag. He went over his new car with a fine toothed comb and finished just as the troopers in their jackboots stormed the barn.

The track provides all the regular security at Suffolk Downs, but the state police run the racing. About a half dozen troopers and plain clothes officers have the political plum jobs watching the "spitbox", the claiming procedures, and looking for illegal gambling and drugs. They search barns and offices without warning and are hated by everyone on the backside, not as much for their almost unlimited authority as for the way they carry out searches.

I got a cup of coffee and sat on the kitchen steps, watching the troopers tear my office and tack room apart. They made Jock and Tino shift the bedding up around the edges of the stalls and moved the stacked hay out from the wall looking for illegal aliens. In nine out of ten barns they would have found some, but not in mine.

When they got tired of tearing up the barn to no avail, the captain motioned for me to come to my office. I took a long sip of my coffee and casually threw the cup in the dumpster before facing him.

"I would have loved to have found something here. They say you're a tough guy, O'Hearn. Somehow I don't think so. Drunks are never tough guys. They're usually all mouth. I'm a pretty tough guy myself. So are all my troopers. You get out of line and I can prove something, you're dead meat. "

"Careful, Captain Carter, I got no truck with you. Don't come down here and start pushing me around. I'm a peaceful guy and you know it. For some reason, people who don't usually give me the time of day have been taking to pushing me around lately. I wish they wouldn't. Yesterday was a bad scene. I didn't ask for the guy to hit me without warning. He paid for it. I used to fight for a living and was pretty good at it. Could be again, with a little practice."

I didn't wait for a reply, but walked past the small crowd that had gathered between my barn and the kitchen. Inside, I could feel the shakes coming on, so I headed for the bar in the back.

After ordering a Sam Adams, I went to the bathroom. I looked in the mirror and saw real anger. It was different from "pissed off" anger. It was the kind I used to get in the service when people got in my face or tried to push me around. I didn't like what I saw and splashed cold water on my face.

I returned to the bar, finished my beer in two gulps and ordered another.

Just then, my cell phone rang.

"Hey, Colin, my man. It's John Willie at the trotting track in Aiken. I got this mare's number and she's ready to come to you."

The old man told me how much trouble he'd had breaking Lonely Aunt to driving reins. He walked behind her at first and then used a small cart. For some reason she liked it, after she got used to it. Matter of fact, he told me, that after she got used to the idea no one was going to rough her up, she was a quick learner. He told me how I could continue to win her confidence and keep her quiet.

"She's ready for you and Jock now. She don't walk the stall anymore and she's not hiding in the corner. Don't bite either, long as she has her pal."

My heart sank. I knew what he was going to say and I knew I was going to have to break a lifelong barn rule.

"Tell me, John Willie, has her friend got four legs and horns?"

He laughed. "You owe me five hundred for breaking this crazy bitch, Colin."

"That's not much, John Willie. It should be more."

He let out a bigger laugh and said, "The five bills are for the job I did on your mare. You owe me another ten bills for the goat."

I cussed him, laughing under my breath. He said a van was coming my way in a few days and he could get her to Aqueduct. The local Boston van would bring her the rest of the way. She'd be in my barn Sunday afternoon.

During feeding time, I told Tino and Jock about the mare and John Willie's goat. They almost died laughing until I told them they could clean up after the damn goat.

"Your worst worry, Colin, is these Mexicans. If they see that fat South Carolina goat, it'll disappear in a week for a cookout. Then what do we do with the crazy mare?" Tino said.

Jock joked, "Get a dog to guard the goat."

After Tino headed for the bar in the track kitchen, Jock asked, " Do you think we can get security to allow us to have a dog on a long chain in the shed row at nights?"

"I doubt it, Jock. That's the old days. You never see dogs on the backside anymore. Are you getting antsy, old man?"

"I think these new horses and that Santos guy are bringing us problems. I don't like you fighting and being on edge all the time. When that happened in the past, you drank too much. We've been running smoothly around here ever since we came to Boston. Never had this much on the line, Boss."

"I know, Jock. I don't like it either. Too many outsiders are showing up. Too many people getting into our business. I'm changing things. We have to tighten things up around here. Keep our plans and business between just you and me. I'm not too sure about Tino. He's probably okay, but he was working for a bad guy at Aqueduct. Something tells me we should be careful about talking too much around him."

"It's not just you and me anymore, Boss. We got Annie to think about, too. If we get that crazy bitch to the track, are you going to run her in Annie's name? Might draw the attention of anyone gunnin' for you."

"We'll cross that bridge once we see if we can keep the mare together in her head. If we do, we might have one of the best fillies on the East Coast."

"There you go again, Colin… dreamin'. Just plain dreamin'… ".

CHAPTER TWENTY-FIVE

Heavy snow had fallen during the night, but Saturday morning brought a break in the weather. The huge front-end loaders had been out since daylight clearing the racing surface for the afternoon races. Cherokee Moon was in the fourth race, scheduled to go off at two o'clock.

The morning *Form* had him second favorite behind a Kentucky-bred colt that had broken his maiden in his first outing three weeks before. Suffolk Downs is a notoriously slow winter surface, heavy with moisture and chemicals to keep it from freezing. Winning times can be as much as two seconds slower than Philadelphia and New York for the same class horse. After a heavy rain, if the track was floated and sealed, it might be called poor in the newspaper, but a horse can go six furlongs in 1:11 flat because the base is so hard below the mushy top. The exact same horse on a sloppy track that is drying might go the same distance in 1:15. Visitors who ship in horses see the times and think they're in a soft spot, but will usually get their hat handed them.

The backside had a chance to see that Cherokee Moon likes the Suffolk surface, if they cared to take notice. The locals would go by the published figures and not be impressed with the 51:2 clocking that Pete reported following our work on Tuesday. The slower time by the clocker caught my eye and I was sure Pete planned to pay off his car note with a wager on Cherokee Moon.

We decided to go with blinkers cut back to "cheaters" on the inside and a half cup on the outside. The "cheaters" were only slightly less than an inch on the rail eye and would cover just enough to keep Cherokee Moon from looking back at the jockey. The half-cup on the outside would give him no idea what was coming until it was too late to slow down. Although my long-term plans for the colt were to eventually teach him to race off the pace and close through the stretch when competition got tougher, I decided to take it one step at a time.

I closed his mouth with a figure-eight noseband over a tongue tie. I had to decide if I wanted a shadow roll to keep him from jumping the shadows and puddles. I didn't want them both, although some trainers would. It had turned cloudy and misty by race time, so, without shadows, I'd go with the figure-eight.

Tino led Cherokee Moon to the paddock after the third race, and I followed slogging through the ankle deep mud. As always, Jock waited with his pals in the kitchen bar where he could bet at the window and admire his work.

Cherokee Moon was all over the track going to the paddock, so I hooked on a second shank and took the right side to keep him in a straight line. As we entered the paddock, several of my fellow trainers who would never be seen in public doing a groom's job gave me hell.

"I'll lend you twenty to get a groom to run that horse, Colin."

"Take two of you to handle that runt?"

I could care less what they said. The safety of my horse and groom came first. Costas had a horse in the race that had the ten post, but he was all speed and would tire at the half. He'd be tiring from the second position because I planned to be on the lead. Although I didn't want him speed crazy; I wanted Steve Casey to ease him to the front and take him back, but not give up the front end.

When Steve came out of the jock's room wearing the black and white block silks of di Vinci Stable, I was alive with anticipation.

Before throwing him up, I said, "Break on top and get the

rail, then take him back and wait for that late running son of a bitch. Don't beat him up. I'm trying to quiet him down."

"What if he's not on the front end?"

"He will be if you let him. Just don't let him roll too soon."

The horses left the paddock and I went to my favorite bar for a Sam Adams before the start. I gave my "get to the window" nod to the bartender as he put down the Sam Adams and found the post parade on TV. I looked up to pay and he was gone, leaving the man at the other end of the bar to serve everybody.

I downed the Sam Adams and went to the benches near the finish line, where several trainers had gathered. I found a bench with no traffic and climbed up to get a better view through my glasses.

They loaded the starting gate from both ends of the eleven horse field. The outside horses were in, but Cherokee Moon was holding things up. Two guys locked hands behind his rump and he slid into line.

The starter gave warning and hit the button. Costas's jumped first and held the lead for fifty yards. Then down on the inside, hugging the rail, my chestnut rocket took off. By the time they reached the first quarter, he had a three-length lead. As they reached the half-mile pole, he was in front by four and Steve was giving him a breather.

I could see the favorite coming on the outside as they approached the three-eighths pole. His rider went to the whip and the big bay colt responded and reached Cherokee Moon's hip.

Steve just let our horse out a notch and went to hand riding him. He slipped off by a length and, at the sixteenth pole, Steve waved the stick by his neck and ear so he could see it. He widened the margin to almost three lengths at the wire. As they say, he won like a good horse should.

I got down to the winner's circle to unsaddle and Milos Santos appeared out of nowhere with Jimmy Slacks and Johnny Carlino, the Little Venice bartender. They were grinning ear to ear and obviously wanted to be in the win picture.

Tino took the blinkers off Cherokee Moon and escorted the three men into the winner's circle. I stood by the horse's head and put Tino on my left, and the others fell into place.

Steve looked down before jumping off after the photo and said, "I don't know how good this little shit is, Boss. I never hit him and he had a tank full of gas at the end."

I told him I loved his ride and his patience more. Some jocks would have tried to push the horse home by a dozen, but Steve understands me and how I train. It's about winning, not the show.

"The Boss will be pleased," Santos said as we walked towards the grandstand bar. I let him buy a round for the four of us, and then graciously said I had to get back to the barn. They started off, but Jimmy Slacks came back and put his hand on my arm. "Colin, that was really fun. I won a bunch, too. See you tonight."

When I got back to the barn, I called Jamie's bar in Aiken, where the race had been on TVG. Jamie answered on the first ring. I could hear a loud crowd in the background as he said, "Don't you ever lose? That's two in a row!"

His voice faded and I heard Annie say, "Gimme that damn phone, Jamie." She was laughing.

"Oh baby, baby, baby. You have brought fun into my life. What a nice horse! A real cutie he is. And I think he can go a route of ground, Colin."

"Hey Annie, take it easy. It's just a horserace."

"It was more than just that, Colin. You are back and we

both know it, baby."

"I don't know how good he is, Annie. Steve didn't rough him up; he just galloped. He's not nearly the best of the bunch in our barn."

I went on, "Annie, happy birthday tomorrow."

"I knew you'd remember. You're so good about those things. What are you going to give me, an engagement ring?"

"Not so fast, honey. I have my plate full up here now."

"Do you know how long it has been since I've been happy and had something to look forward to? God, I love you, Colin. Now tell me what you're giving me for my birthday."

"Your birthday isn't until tomorrow. I have a favor to ask. I know it's Sunday, but I need you to be at your shop in the morning so I can call you at nine o'clock. Be there at nine and I'll tell you all about your birthday present. You are going to die!"

"Jesus, Colin, how am I going to sleep tonight? Secret calls and surprise birthday gifts. I'm getting spooked. Is it that Italian guy you're training for that you think might cause you problems?"

I assured her all was well and she had nothing to fear. She said she'd be at the shop at nine and we rang off. I finished afternoon stables and went home to clean up before going to Little Venice to dine with Vito Corsetti.

The snow had turned to mist and the parking lot at Little Venice was slush when I pulled in at eight o'clock. Being Saturday night the place was packed. Jimmy Slacks and Johnny Carlino were holding court in Jimmy's usual spot at the bar. He motioned for me to go to the back and followed along behind me. The card room bartender, who also served the office, waved. He'd been at the races and wanted to talk. I went over and he thanked me for winning the race and letting him cash a big bet.

"I was going to bet ten across the board and Slacks told me to bet two hundred on his nose. I won about twelve hundred dollars. I've never won that much on a horse. Thanks, Mr. O'Hearn. Thanks," he said.

I felt a tinge of satisfaction and pride as I fell in behind Slacks. The big man was behind the table in the corner with a bottle of red wine, a glass and a pile of papers.

"You're a man of your word, Colin. He won easy, didn't he?"

"He did that, Mr. Corsetti, but they won't all be that easy. It's tough when a new owner wins his first race; he might think they should be all winners."

"Colin, with all the jerk-offs I've had training for me over the last ten years, I haven't won a race in ten."

"We'll do better than that, sir," I promised.

Vito motioned to a chair and I sat down. We chatted briefly about the other horses as we ordered. I usually order the macaroni and gravy, but this time I asked if he served arancini.

With a big smile, Vito said, "My favorite since a child, Colin. It's not on the menu. Where'd you learn to eat such a dish?"

"I trained several years in New Orleans. It's the dish of the house at Delmonico's. They fry those risotto balls and let them sit. Then they add the sauce that's cooked with broken up meat balls and sausage. It's just about the best dish in town. Not the best Italian spot in town, but the arancini can't be beat," I replied.

"What do you consider the best Italian restaurant in New Orleans?"

Before I could answer, Vito scribbled something on a

napkin and turned it over. "That would be Mosca's."

With great pride, Corsetti turned the napkin and pointed to one word, "Mosca's". Slacks laughed and Santos grinned sheepishly.

We ate like there was no tomorrow. The bread was some of the best I'd ever eaten. Like Mosca's, it was served piping hot, a thin loaf wrapped in a white linen napkin with all the real butter a man could eat. Good bread served in this manner is as important as serving barbeque on white butcher paper.

As we finished, the plates were removed and Vito spoke. "Jimmy, why don't you and Milos look over things in the other room and give me and Colin a chance to talk a little bit."

The room went silent and I could see both men lose their smiles as they reluctantly got up to leave.

"I'll be right outside, Boss," Jimmy Slacks said.

"You and Milos can take the night off. I'll get Carlino to run me home after we're finished here."

I waited for him to pour us both a cup of coffee.

"You want to tell me what happened at the barn, Colin?"

"Mr. Corsetti, I wish I had some answers. Several guys at the track had been telling me this big thug was asking questions about me and my owner, who they think is Milos. I've never said a word about you and di Vinci Stable.

"This big guy came around looking for trouble. He hit me from behind and gave me some stars to look at. After he kicked me in the ribs, I'd had enough. He went over the line."

"They say you pulled his ear off. Nice Irish boy like you, Colin? Street fighting?" He laughed halfheartedly.

From my shirt pocket I took the ear and put it in front of me. "I've done worse, Mr. Corsetti. It was all I could think of at the time."

"Jesus, son, you've made your point. After such a good meal, I don't need that for desert."

I put the ear back into the rag I had it in when I arrived. It was the kind of thing that caught the attention of a man in Vito's business. He knew for sure that I was a man to be watched and, in their way, respected.

"He was sent by Tass," I said.

He smiled. "You're right. Especially after being put on his ass by you in the parking lot.

"You're aware I've had Jimmy following you at arm's length. The feds are keeping tabs on you too. Jimmy keeps tabs on you both. It's a stupid little game. I wish someone would step forward so we could check the score.

"Do you want me to keep Jimmy covering your back?"

"I feel at home with Jimmy, but I don't trust Santos at all. He's weak and plays his hand without enough care. One day, we may have to change our way of doing business if he gets into mine, sir."

"Milos is a bean counter. He moves money, Colin. At this time, I have no one to replace him if I dumped him. Keep your eye on him. You may see something that wouldn't relate to you, but in our business would mean everything."

He ended our conversation by standing and saying, "I wish I had more friends like you, Irishman."

"Maybe we'll have another winner to celebrate soon, Don Vito. We have a grass horse, Top Shot. He might like the soft going here. I was going to wait for the turf course to open, but he's telling me he wants to run now. He's kicking his stall down."

" I'm really enjoying these horses. And maybe we'll have another winner. Yes."

He pumped his fist in the air as I left, and I thought, he's the nicest, most ruthless and cunning mobster I have ever known.

CHAPTER TWENTY-SIX

Winning a race does wonders for all the horses' connections. Even a tough old man like Vito Corsetti is moved by being a winner. I didn't care about Milos Santos, but it was good to see Jimmy Slacks and Johnny Carlino so thrilled to have their picture taken and cashing a bet. When I got to the barn I gave the boys each a crisp new one-hundred-dollar bill, their "stake" for the win. Old John, the ageless hot walker, also came by the barn looking for his stake since he walked the winner. He lived in an ancient station wagon full of newspapers and coupons, parked in a lot about fifty yards from Barn 15 against the outside security fence. His ragged clothing and whiskey breath, coupled with a body I doubt was washed over the winter, make him the butt of a hundred jokes.

Old John is just another of the Lost Souls on the backside. Few know it, but he practiced law as a young attorney in Natick where his wife, also an attorney, served on the city council until her death about fifteen years ago, They had no children and John, whose last name's Harkins, lapsed into a life of booze-induced depression. He closed his practice and resigned from his part time job teaching night classes at Suffolk Law School. Finally, he ended up in a homeless shelter until Ian Higgins learned of his fate. Ian sold his deserted home in Natick for a nice price and put the money in trust for his old friend. He allotted John, who by this time had fallen into a complete state of disrepair from drinking and creeping dementia a small pension. He'd give away most of what he earned to fellow drinkers and I had to draw down funds from his ample account at the bookkeeper's office and make him take it.

"Here's your fifty for the win, Professor," I said, when he walked into the barn. John knew we never trained on Sunday, but the win assured him enough money to buy a few drinks and a hot meal or two.

"You always share when you got it, Colin. Thanks."

"Hey, John, I'll give you five hundred dollars for all those coupons and papers you got stored in that old car out back," I kidded.

"You know better than that. Those coupons are for my wife, when she comes back, and the papers are my insulation against the cold weather. Gotta keep me and my cat Hoover warm," he mumbled, as he shuffled off in the direction of the kitchen.

He'd put ten dollars in his pocket to share with the other lost souls at the bar. The other forty dollars was hidden between layers of his filthy clothing and guarded by the stench of his unwashed body. As John hit the kitchen steps, I thought about how safe that money was in his smelly underwear.

It was almost nine o'clock when I called Annie's cell phone. "Happy birthday, lover-girl," I laughed when she answered.

"Thanks, Colin, but this better be good to drag me out of bed on my birthday and get me to down this deserted training track on Sunday."

"No one's around?"

"Hell, honey, the barn help's fed and gone home and this place is deserted except a big van at the ramp behind my shop. It's loaded with Dogwood Stables' horses, headed for New York. I don't know what they're waiting for. They've been loaded almost twenty minutes," she said.

"Look, Annie, I have a message for Nick, the driver of that van. I know it's a pain for you, but can you take your cell phone over to him? It's really important."

I could hear her put the phone against her crutches as she made her way to the van. She said something to Nick and handed him the phone.

"Hey, Colin. About time you called."

"I can't thank you enough, Nick. Annie's going to flip out when she sees that mare. It's her birthday present. Your money will be at the stable gate tomorrow."

He thanked me and handed the phone to Annie.

"Listen, Annie, I know you don't feel like walking up that ramp, but in that van is your birthday present."

She made it to the inside of the van and hissed into the phone, "You asshole, you bought me a goat! No, wait, there's a horse in a box stall behind... Oh, shit, Colin, you didn't! It's her! She looks great. She's looking fit, Colin. She's supposed to be a broodmare in Canada. You mean she's going to be my broodmare? Colin, she's nuzzling me. She's so calm."

She was breathless when I interrupted the babbling. "Let Nick get on the road, honey. I'll explain everything when you get off the van."

I could hear Nick start up the big diesel engine of the eighteen-wheeler as Annie made it back to her shop.

"Oh, Colin, I love you so much! You saved her for me."

I got her calmed down and explained everything. She had to be one of the happiest people in the world at that moment. I told her about John Willie and the goat and that the mare was coming to me in Boston to train.

"It's like a dream, baby. I can run her and then we can breed her. There is a God. Thank you so much. I can't wait to see you and show you how much I love you. What a wonderful birthday."

We talked a little longer and I explained it would be a while until we got together. Though disappointed, she agreed, but said, "If you think that mare's running and I'm not flying to Boston for the day, you're nuts."

"That's a deal, Annie. Now, get a set of your own colors made. John Willie says it won't be too long before she can run." After I hung up, I really felt good giving her something to look forward to.

I saw Steve Casey and Arch Hale trudge up the stairs to the kitchen. I followed them up the icy stairs over the crunching salt. Cozy Costas and Connie Tass were huddled in the corner. I avoided them and joined Steve and Arch.

Costas called out to me, "That was a pretty nice colt you beat me with, O'Hearn. It looks like the beginning of better things for you and your boys from the North End." I ignored him.

Charlie Clark and Grady O'Brien joined us.

"Congratulations, Colin. It couldn't have happened to a better man," greeted Charlie.

"I agree," said Grady. "And to show you how much we agree, we'll let you buy us breakfast."

We all laughed and ordered a round of Sam Adams to go with our food. We ate and poured through the *Racing Form*, talking about the overnight entries for Wednesday.

"We have your old, big mare in for a dime," Grady said.

"She'll win at a flat mile," I added.

"Think anyone will take her for ten grand, Colin?"

Raising my voice so that Costas and Tass could hear, I said, "She's worth a solid fifteen. She was in heat when she was third for me last time. I'd never have sold her to you, but I really needed the space. I hope no one takes her from you guys," I said.

The pair got up and walked out of the kitchen, leaving our table the only one occupied.

"Thanks, Colin. You think Costas took the bait?"

"I think it went down hook, line and sinker. Costas would love to take a horse of mine and move it up. I'll bet you guys put this one over on him."

Steve and Arch thanked me for breakfast and the beers before leaving.

"Colin, how well do you know Tass,?" asked Charlie.

"I heard he's a bakery owner from Southie with some Russian connections."

"He's a lot more than that. Don't let that bakery shit fool you, he's real trouble. I hear he's trying to take over all the bread sold to delis and restaurants that don't bake their own. He started in South Boston and has spread into the North End. They say he won't stop until he strong-arms everyone in town."

Charlie added, "That's not all. He has a trash pick up business and rents those port-o-potties you see on every construction site. Soon he'll be hauling crap from every site in the city."

"You trying to tell me he's Russian Mafia?" I asked.

Grady said, "I don't know about the Mafia thing, but he's very organized."

"How'd you find out about this guy?"

"There are plenty of gay Russians who hang out at the clubs in Boston. We don't make the rough scene, but we met a guy at a party once who told us that Tass was hung up on horse racing and wanted to get some horses at Suffolk Downs. We thought he might be a new owner for us, until we checked around and found out about the strong-arm thing. Grady was in the office making an entry and gave the guy's name and phone number to Costas. I guess he took it from there."

We made light of the conversation and went our separate ways. Maybe they'd be better off if Costas didn't claim the mare for Tass. When a sore loser like Costas discovers the mare is cooked he and Tass would be very pissed. They'll never get a dime back after claiming the lame mare.

CHAPTER TWENTY-SEVEN

Deeper River, the big stake horse with the old bow and dull appearance, was blooming more every day. The bow was much tighter and smaller, and even the cold weather couldn't hide the change in his coat. He was clipped and kept under a very heavy sheepskin blanket, making him look every bit a stake horse with a grade II victory and more than $300,000 in earnings under his girth.

The trick was the way Jock kept him done up at night. My special leg paint was applied in a single slow, downward stroke, never scrubbed. This avoided a blister and would sweat profusely into the first of two "no-bow" bandages. One was placed directly over the other. They were both wrapped snugly, but not tightly, in Saran Wrap. A standard standing bandage, wrapped firmly but giving enough room for expansion then covered the tendon.

Enough room for expansion was the key. The sweat would soak right through the first "no-bow" and settle in the second. When taken down in the morning, the outside bandage was still soaking wet, while the bandage closest to the leg was bone dry.

Getting and keeping fluid out of a bowed tendon reduces the swelling and keeps the skin tighter and firmer, giving the leg much more support. It's a tedious ritual, but training and grooming racehorses is a tedious job. Time means nothing to a good groom bent on seeing a horse with a problem get to the winner's circle.

The tighter Jock got Deeper River, the better he trained. He and the old mare, Crystal Run, were almost ready for a start. The tiny grass horse, Top Shot, was training even better and needed any kind of race I could find to keep him from tearing down the walls of his stall. I'd taken off his blinkers and been giving him long, two-minute licks with a shadow roll to keep his head down. Tino had him working in his hip pocket as he whirled past me and finished a full mile's breeze.

By the time we were finished and headed back to the barn, we began passing the first gallopers of the day. We'd breezed without telling the clocker. He would give us the number I wanted in the *Form*, and Top Shot would be ready to enter for Friday. Winning the race was not part of my plan. I wasn't going to get him hurt in Suffolk's deep, sucking surface. I just wanted to get the grass horse out of the barn and into some competition. Turf racing was still a month away, and I wanted him ready.

As the darkness faded and the first signs of light revealed the robot-like figures of exercise riders trying to get smaller, hiding from the bitter cold. One after another had a sarcastic remark as they passed.

"Couldn't sleep, Colin?"

"What are you trying to hide, Colin?"

"Charge him overtime, Tino, for having to work at night."

We were both smiling when we reached the barn and handed the colt over to Jock. Silently, Old John appeared out of nowhere, throwing a sweat sheet over the panting colt before giving him just enough water to wash out his mouth plus three sips. As the pair disappeared around the corner, Jock had Crystal Run off the wall following Old John's lead, giving her a turn around the barn to stretch her legs before braving the early morning cold.

"Tino, give the old mare the same thing," I said.

"You crazy, Colin? Breezing these horses a full mile?"

"You ride 'em, little man, and I'll train 'em."

When we started back to the track with Crystal Run really on her toes, I said to Tino, "She's been two minute licking, just like Top Shot. She's better than he is right now. He's still testing that bow and not giving me his all. This mare's gained weight and shows it. I'm going to run them as an entry."

"I know where you're coming from, Colin, but I don't like it," said Tino.

"Is that because you don't like what I'm going to do, or that you think I should run them in different races so Steve can ride both?"

"I don't trust either of these horses the first time over this track. Steve suits this mare. If one of those local thieves up here tries to hold her and play games, we could lose all we've been working for and she might really get hurt. We need a fresh face, someone we can trust to just let her run." he said.

"You're right," I agreed. Just before I turned him loose to back up toward the half-mile pole and break off, I added, "Find me a rider I can trust, maybe a young rider from Aqueduct."

I couldn't hide the way Crystal Moon worked. She pulled Tino the first three-quarters and jerked her head from his grasp the final two furlongs. Her final quarter was faster than her first. As I started back down the chute, following the bucking and playing mare, my cell phone rang.

"I can take care of the colt, but how the hell am I going to disguise what that mare did this morning?" asked Pete.

"Show her last half mile as her work and forget she went a full mile. You won't be lying."

"How fast do you think she went the last half?" he asked.

"Without a clock, I'd say fifty and change."

"You and that 'no-clock shit', Colin. I know you've got one in your pocket." He hung up laughing.

If the mare had been in a race, she'd have gone the mile in 1:40. It wasn't fast enough to win the Cigar Mile at Aqueduct, but fast enough to win an allowance race at Calder by five lengths. Crystal Run was back to her old stake form.

Tino hit the nail on the head. I decided to enter them both in the same allowance race on Friday and let Crystal Run try the boys. She'd rip their hearts out for three quarters and either steal the race or set it up for my closer, Top Shot. The boys at Suffolk Downs were about to get their first real taste of the di Vinci diet.

Just after training hours the van from Aiken pulled in, and Jock and Tino unloaded Lonely Aunt and the biggest damn goat I'd ever seen.

Jock pulled rank. "Last in, first out. Take that damn goat, and I'll follow with the mare."

"Jock, what's it gonna look like me walking up that road past all those barns and the kitchen with this damn monster goat?"

"It's gonna look like a little shit jockey from Jamaica leading his lunch."

The goat's head was almost chest high on Tino. She pulled him from one side of the road to the other, trying to go in every barn she passed. The whole backside was laughing. By the time they got to Barn 15, there were at least thirty people cheering Tino on from the steps of the kitchen.

I was in tears from laughing. Tino, his baseball cap pulled down low to hide his face, fought back mortification tears. I began looking over the mare Jock was leading. She was calm, collected, and gave no hint she'd been an outlaw. Her eyes never left the goat, and she paid no attention to her new surroundings.

These two were not the only new additions to Barn 15. A crusty old lead pony occupied the last stall in my shed row. I'd bought the old gelding from Grady and Charlie as we left the track kitchen Sunday morning. They had bought him for a dollar and promised to save him from the killers about five years before. They had pampered and overfed the spoiled gelding named Hard Rock. He'd be the perfect track companion for Lonely Aunt, when she had to be away from the goat.

I had a carpenter cut a big hole between the stall of the nervous mare and goat and her babysitter. A stall screen allowed them to smooch, but no heavy petting would be allowed. It cost me a case of Sam Adams for the carpenters, but was well worth it. The mare could nuzzle her new boyfriend without getting into trouble.

Within an hour the three were a model family. Jock had placed alfalfa in three corners and hung two buckets of water. Lonely Aunt was so tired and content after the long trip from South Carolina that she lay down after thirty minutes. The goat stood munching alfalfa, looking over the sleeping mare. Hard Rock stood patiently by the screen, in love.

I called Annie and told her everything about their arrival and how they'd settled in. I also told her about Hard Rock. She laughed at first and then went silent.

"It's okay, baby," she finally said. "I'm sad because I'm so happy, and also because I want to be there with you."

"Things are getting touchy here. A lot of rumors are going around about my new boss from the North End and people who don't like him. I'm also nervous about some other things that might spill over on me here at the track. What that big guy was doing in my face last week is still a mystery, " I said, knowing deep down inside that I wanted Annie nowhere near Suffolk Downs anytime soon.

Across town, a black SUV was parked a few spaces down from a dark blue van with tinted windows. It was just after two o'clock and the lunch crowd had returned to their offices, leaving the fifth level of First Boston Bank's parking garage deserted.

Jimmy Slacks confirmed there were no latecomers around before walking toward the van. The door locks popped and he slid into the smoke-filled interior, handing two envelopes to the driver.

"How much did I win for my two hundred dollars?" Martin Watson asked.

"The horse paid almost a dime. There's a little over eleven hundred dollars in the top envelope. Your regular payment is in the other one."

CHAPTER TWENTY-EIGHT

Just after dawn the sounds of big machinery and diesel engines cut through the otherwise silent morning as two front end loaders stacked the previous night's snowfall. One of the drivers hesitated, his bucket in midair. He'd noticed a large, dark object in his bucket. Dumping the load, he got down from his cab to get a closer look. A nearby dump truck driver cut his engine and stalked over.

"What the hell's the matter, Chuck?"

"Something strange fell out of my bucket." The driver walked closer and stopped abruptly.

"Oh, shit!" He turned to the truck driver. "It's a body, Steve! A big ass body!"

The truck driver walked to the operator's side, almost tripping over a long handled shovel lying in the snow nearby. The handle was black with maroon and yellow stripes. He kicked the shovel aside and leaned over the icy, frozen body of Joe Dobbs.

"Call the cops, Chuck. This guy's dead. From the looks of his face and head, I'd say whoever killed him used that shovel."

Chuck looked slightly sick and definitely pale.

"Wait," Steve said, glancing at the security office a hundred yards away. "We probably ought to let security make the call as to who should handle this. Since we're on racetrack property, it may be a state police issue, rather than one for the local cops."

He looked at the bloody shovel and blood on the ice around the body. "Wait here," he instructed the dozer driver. "I'll walk over to the security gate and tell them what we've found."

It was shortly after six o'clock when track security chief Charlie Martin saw the dump truck driver walk through the stable gate. He knew right away something was wrong.

"What's up? Did that old truck break down again?"

"You are not going to believe this, Captain, but there's a dead guy right over there by my front end loader."

"It's probably a bum that froze to death in the weather last night. It was five below. Art, you watch the phone and I'll take him with me and take a look."

The two men got into Charlie Martin's cruiser and drove to where the loader and dump truck were parked.

"There's a lot of blood, Captain. Blood all over this guy."

"Look at the size of him!" shouted the dump truck's driver. "Don't step on that shovel, Charlie. Looks like that's what killed him. Look at the blood all over the shovel's blade."

"Oh my God! It can't be," Martin said as he bent low over the body to get a better look at the dead man. "It's the guy I took to the hospital."

"You mean the one Colin O'Hearn busted up?" asked the driver.

"That's him. His name is Joe Dobbs. "

The truck driver pointed to the bloody shovel next to the body and said, "Captain, you know who puts stripes on his equipment?"

"Yeah, I know. You can tell Colin O'Hearn's stable colors anywhere. Everything in his barn, the pitchforks, the rakes and this shovel have those stripes on the end. If Colin had not beat this guy half to death last week and put him in the hospital after he pulled off his ear, I'd say there was no way he could have done this. Shit, now I don't know."

The Captain called both the state police and local cops. He told the locals to send out the homicide unit. Two Boston police arrived first, and a few minutes later the city's crime scene investigation lab pulled in. They were followed by a number of area cops and two detectives from the homicide division. Charlie knew neither but tried his best to fill them in on what happened the week before between Colin O'Hearn and the dead man.

While this conversation was going on, a state police unit assigned to Suffolk Downs arrived and Captain Norris Carter began to quarrel with the Boston police about who had jurisdiction over the crime scene. The argument lasted only a few minutes and the Boston cops took control.

When Captain Carter saw the dead man, he froze. He was told about the murder weapon and that it probably belonged to O'Hearn.

"That big mouthed son of a bitch. He'll be at Barn 15 right now. I'll go up and hold him for you guys. I can't wait to slap a pair of cuffs on that fucking wise guy."

Norm Smith and David Ross, the two homicide officers, tried to calm Carter down. "One of us will have to go with you. You stay here at the scene, David and I'll go with this officer to get the suspect. I'll put him in my car and meet you at headquarters," said Smith.

I was saddling Cherokee Moon for his morning gallop when an exercise rider, a friend of Steve Casey's, came running down the shedrow.

"Colin, wait! You gotta hear this. I was just coming to work, through the stable gate, and the cops were talking about a guy murdered last night in the lot across the street. It was that guy you beat up last week. I heard Steve say he was killed with your shovel."

"He's dead? That big fucker with the ear?" I asked, talking more to myself than Jock, Tino or the rider.

"Captain Carter is coming after you any minute."

I looked up the shed row and saw several cops, a man in a heavy overcoat and Captain Carter coming toward me.

Carter drew his gun. The man in the overcoat said, "Put that damn thing down. I'll handle this."

He started to say something and stopped. As they approached, I said, "Just let me put this horse away and we can go down to my office. There'll be no trouble from me."

I handed the reins to Jock. "Go slow with him, Tino, and the rest as well. Jock, you call Ian Higgins and tell him I'll probably be at the police station. Ian's number's on the wall next to the phone."

I turned to the officers. "What's this all about, Captain? And I'm sorry, I didn't catch your name?" I said to the other policeman in front of him.

"I'm Detective Norm Smith and we're here to ask you a few questions regarding the dead body we found across the street."

"Dead body? What's that got to do with me?"

"We've identified him as Joe Dobbs. Apparently you had a problem with him last week."

"You know, O'Hearn, the guy whose ear you pulled off at your barn here," snapped Carter.

"Look, I'd never seen that thug before he came in here and started pushing me around. I asked him if we could talk and he hit me from behind, then he kicked me when I was down. Three or four guys saw it. Carter, we talked about it," I said.

"Did you have to tear his ear off? I never heard of anyone tearing a guy's ear off," Smith said.

"It seemed like a good idea at the time. He was going to beat the shit out of me and I wanted to put an end to it."

Carter interrupted. "You didn't go that fast last night. You beat him to death with a shovel."

"Shovel?" I said.

"A black shovel with gold and maroon rings around the top was found by the body. It's covered with blood. You got a shovel that's painted that way, O'Hearn?"

"All my barn equipment hangs right at the end of the shed row in plain sight. It's not locked up. We paint it in stable colors so nobody will steal it. Look out the door. My shovel will be right there on the wall, where it always hangs, right next to the shed row rake."

Carter opened the door to the shed row. I could see a crowd hanging all around my barn area. There was no shovel on the wall. There were five other pitchforks and rakes, but the shovel was gone.

"Oh, damn," I said.

Smith looked me in the eye and said, "That's the understatement of the morning."

"I'll just bet your prints are all over that shovel," Carter sneered.

"Of course they are. I do stalls and clear out the drains, just like Tino and Jock. You'll probably find Old John's prints on there too."

"Look, O'Hearn, things don't look too good for you. I'm going to meet my partner at headquarters to see what else they turned up at the crime scene. I'd like you to come downtown with me and we can talk some more where there's not so much interference." Smith looked straight at Carter.

I knew only too well that the deck was stacked against me. I'd obviously been set up. Whoever did it knew exactly what they were doing. The shovel with my stable colors was a nice touch. The last thing I needed was to give these guys a reason to think I wouldn't cooperate.

"Detective, I'll be more than happy to come downtown, with you or in my own truck. Any preference?"

"I think you better ride with me, O'Hearn. It might look better for us both. You make the arrangements here. This could take a while," Smith warned.

Captain Carter, knowing he was no longer part of the procedure, started out the door. "You better look out for him, Detective. Cover your ears."

I got into the policeman's car, sitting in the front. Just as I slid in, he said, "I've got to put the cuffs on. It's procedure, but I didn't want to do it in front of your men and the other track folks."

"Thanks. Shows you've got heart."

"Sometimes, when I feel okay about a guy."

We drove through the stable gate and headed to downtown Boston. I could only hope Jock could get in touch with Ian Higgins. It wasn't yet seven o'clock. With luck, he hadn't left for court or law school yet.

A short while after Colin and the cop left the track and headed downtown, Jock felt someone tug at his sleeve.

It was Old John, shaking from the cold.

"I saw who stole that shovel from Mr. O'Hearn. There were two of them. I was in my car asleep when Hoover woke me, raisin' hell. I looked out the window where I'd scraped off the ice and saw the two men walking out of your shed row, just after ten. The smaller of the two was carrying a shovel... Mr. O'Hearn's shovel."

"Did you know either one of them, Professor?" Jock asked.

"Well, maybe. I've seen one of them around here a few times. Don't know him, though."

"It could help Colin a lot if you could remember the smaller man. Maybe if you saw him again?"

"Yeah, maybe."

CHAPTER TWENTY-NINE

Inside police headquarters, I sat in a drab room with the usual furnishings, a gray metal table with three metal chairs. Add a light fixture with a white metal shade that swings and the standard two-way mirror, and you've an accurate picture of the surreal setting for my two-and-a-half hour grilling.

Norm Smith and a second detective, Dave Ross, were taking turns with me. Somewhere after the first hour, one of them must have realized it wasn't the first time I'd faced such treatment. My training in hostile interrogation had begun at Fort Benning, was increased at Fort Bragg and then had been a semi-annual renewal affair at CIA Headquarters and the Pentagon in my Special Forces days. I tried my best not to laugh at their "good cop, bad cop" routine and never varied my story.

The Judge always said, "The truth is the hardest thing to tell, but the easiest thing to remember." I was telling the truth. I'd only seen this Joe Dobbs character once, the five minutes it took to send him to the hospital.

I had no idea how my shovel got to the crime scene. I was at home in bed, with only Killer and Nadine to back up my alibi.

"You ever think about killing a man, O'Hearn?" asked Ross.

"Of course."

"Why?"

"To save my life when I was in the Army."

"You ever do that, Colin… kill a man?" asked Smith, the good cop.

"I can't answer that."

"Why not?" snapped Ross, the bad cop.

"Just about everything I did while in the service is classified. If you can't get it off my service record, then someone at the Pentagon will have to fill you in. I'm not comfortable talking about those days. They have nothing to do with anything we have on the table," I retorted.

"Why'd you leave the service?"

"Pull my record. If it's not there, it's classified."

"We tried and we can't get anything that might shed some light on what makes you tick. It's true about being classified. They act like you're some kind of secret."

After about three hours, a small, preppy looking guy came into the room. He didn't say a word; he just leaned against the far wall and snapped a rubber band against his wrist from time to time. After a few minutes he said, "What can you tell us about Vito Corsetti and his band of merry men?"

"I eat at Mr. Corsetti's place, Little Venice, with one of my clients, Milos Santos, who is the accountant for the restaurant. The macaroni and gravy is the best in town. Bread's great, too. They make their own garlic butter. Love it."

"What about Corsetti?"

"Nice guy. Met him on occasion. He loves the Red Sox almost as much as I do."

"He like horse racing, too?"

"Most of the people I know, present company probably excluded, like horse racing," I said, getting more irate by the minute.

"Look, mister, I know these guys, and I don't mind being straight with them. I've been in this fucking chair over three hours and I'm tired of playing games.

"I had a scrap with the guy and they took him to the hospital. I said two lines to him before he jumped me. I grunted a few times, when I was kicking his big butt, and that was it. I have never seen or talked to him since and sure as hell didn't kill him. You all are smart enough to know that I know how to kill from my army training. It's what I did in the Middle East during Desert Storm. I don't need a weapon and I'm not dumb enough to leave my own bloody shovel at a murder scene only three hundred yards from my barn. Someone's made it look like it was me, but it wasn't me."

After another half-hour of the same type questions, there was a knock at the door. Ian Higgins walked into the small room, and I let out a sigh of relief. He led Detective Smith to one corner and said quietly, "I have information and a witness which will give you second thoughts about charging Colin with any crime at this point," Ian said.

The tiny Irishman nodded toward the preppy guy and with a stern look said, "Colin, meet Fred Hardy of the Miami Federal Crime Task Force. Mr. Hardy and I have bumped heads before."

There were nods and more silence.

Ian went on. "Gentlemen, I have a sworn statement properly attested to by one John G. Harkins. I might add that I've known Mr. Harkins for over thirty years. We met when he was a practicing attorney and law professor at Suffolk Law School. He now works part-time as a hot walker for Mr. O'Hearn.

"It seems Mr. Harkins was sleeping in his abandoned Chevy station wagon near Mr. O'Hearn's barn last night. About ten o'clock, he awoke and saw two men walk from the back of Colin's barn. One was carrying a shovel. He doesn't know the name of the person carrying the shovel, but he's seen him before. I'll have Mr. Harkins in your office this afternoon, or you can talk to him at the barn area where he is probably going to be more cooperative. He's not the same man he once was, but he's very aware of what happens around Barn 15. He's Colin's informal night watchman," Ian said.

Without saying a word, Hardy slipped out the door.

"What the hell's he doing here?" said Ross.

Ian ignored the question, "Look, you guys. Colin roughed the guy up, but killing him because they fought is very unlikely. Colin's the kind of guy who would do some long-term damage for the guy to remember him by, but nothing he's ever done in all the years I've known him indicates he would kill a man, except in self-defense."

Ross smirked. "Something to remember him by, O'Hearn? Like handing him his ear?"

The two officers stepped into the hall.

Ian looked into my eyes, "You gonna be alright?"

"I can't figure... "

Ian raised his hand, cutting me off. "Later, not here. Not now."

Smith and Ross came back into the room.

"We're going to let Mr. O'Hearn go for now," Smith said. "Don't leave town, and if anything comes up call us right away. Whether you like it or not, I don't think this is over. There was a reason Dobbs was killed. As long as you're associated with Milos Santos and his friends, you'll be subject to close watching. That FBI guy, Hardy, has you in his sights. I tell you this, not to give away information, but to let you know we're aware and are following their interest in you as well."

"Thank you, gentlemen. I'll go with you and give you the information about the man seen with the shovel and where to find John Harkins. He's a harmless old man who has lost all sight of the world. He'll be alright and clean up well for court," Ian said.

Before we left, I had a request for the officers.

"I know you guys will try to be careful not to let anyone know Old John is an eye witness. If someone would kill Dobbs, they wouldn't think twice of killing Old John."

When we got out the front door of police headquarters, Ian said to me, "Let's get a drink now."

We walked two blocks to a small bar called Art's Place. Ian and his friends wouldn't be caught dead in the joint, but I felt right at home. There were six bar stools and four booths. Three men huddled over their drinks and beers at the far end of the bar and an old man and woman sat across from each other about six inches apart in the last booth. They looked destitute and on their last legs. They could have cared less about us, so when Ian used his handkerchief to dust off a seat I slid in quickly, praying for the unlikely miracle of fast service.

Ian said, "Three fingers of Bushmill's."

I jumped up and headed off the bartender while he was still close to the whiskey supply. I returned to Ian, who had his face in his hands, then looked up and grabbed his whiskey before it touched to tabletop, drinking it in one gulp. I repeated the mercy mission to the bar and he smiled, though faintly.

Buffeted by the Bushmill's, he scrunched his face and said, "So, swear to me on your life that you will never tell anyone what I'm about to tell you."

"Of course."

"This may sound strange, but the lineup is a little different than you think. I've spent many years… hell, most of my adult life working the court system representing criminals and those who enforce the law. In Boston, we do things … different. There are the friends I associate with that have unsavory pasts."

He paused and I anxiously prodded, "Get to it, Ian… please."

"Every Thursday, I have a poker game with the same five guys… been going on almost twenty years."

He paused, thinking about what to say next, but I was silent.

"The other guys I play with are a *Globe* reporter named Lou Capps, the FBI agent Martin Watson and your Detective Norm Smith. The fifth hand is none other than your pal and my client, Vito Corsetti.

"I thought I knew everything, but Smith knows some things he's not saying. Watson's holding back on us and so is Capps who you have not met. But, Vito, my client and confidant with the attorney-client privilege, has told me everything. All I can say is that you will be cleared of the Dobbs' murder. Vito had nothing to do with it and Smith knows that. Just train your horses and let everyone else do their jobs. You're not a detective, and don't start playing one!"

CHAPTER THIRTY

I felt the world spinning as I was trying to understand what Ian was telling me about his Thursday night poker partners. He added, "It's not what you think; we just put our business lives aside and have a simple poker night. Vito and Watson have known each other since they were teenagers. Smith is younger, about Capps's age. Capps is the crime beat writer for the *Globe* and works with Smith all the time. I'm the graybeard of the game, and I know 'em all from various times of my life. It all just kinda came together a long time ago.

"The only one who doesn't figure is Vito. Smith and Watson should be trying to put him in jail, and Capps should be writing about it. I've been Vito's informal lawyer for years. I never go to court for him, just work quietly trying to keep him out of jail. Colin, we all really like each other… at least one night a week. I know it sounds crazy, Watson and Smith playing cards with someone the public sees as a criminal. With Vito it's no drugs and no strong arming, except with his enemies."

"How have you all kept such an arrangement quiet… all these years?"

"We play at Vito's. He has a whole block of property surrounding Little Venice. Different doors in and out all around the block. Then too, he runs the best damn eatery in the North End. Capps and Smith eat out all the time since they both have worked for years at night. I'm a regular at Little Venice and Watson just sorta drifts in and out of the game on his own. He's a very sharp but laid-back guy. He always covers his ass. We meet about ten when Watson shows up. When he gets there, the game really gets rolling."

"Why are you telling me all this? You want me to start playing with you guys?"

"Hell no. If one gets out, the game folds. That's the rule. I hear about everything if they're involved in my business. You're my business. I know that Vito and you had nothing to do with Joe Dobbs's death. Watson and Smith know it as well because I said so. None of them has talked with Capps unless it is Smith, and he's never going to say anything that might land in the press and hurt one of the other guys.

"Are you the reason Vito got on to me as a trainer?"

"Sure… and I own half of the horses you're training, so you better produce. Just do your thing, Colin, and keep your nose clean. No more fights, and no more taunting Tass and that bum that trains for him. We're looking at Tass for Dobbs's death. He was probably trying to set you up while trimming dead wood off his payroll. I personally think Dobbs was an informant for the cops. It's not something I'd ask either Smith or Watson, but my guess is Watson. He's got the money in 'house' to pay Dobbs and a lot of what Tass does is Federal. Still, I'm just guessing."

After I left Ian Higgins, his final words echoed in my ears. "Look, Colin, Boston and the North End are a world in themselves. Rules change from section to section. Many times, the law is bent or just overlooked if the long-term effect is to keep things on an even keel. Sounds crazy, but that's they way it's been for as long as I've lived here. Boston is Boston, and New Orleans is New Orleans. There are just a few international cities in this country. They have mixed cultures and even mixed languages. Old World habits die hard in places like Boston, New York, San Francisco, Miami, New Orleans, Montreal and even San Antonio. Don't fight it; enjoy it. In Boston, we do. Lighten up about who is eating and who is playing together."

I left Ian and drove back to my cottage to my dogs that were okay using the "doggie" door, but have yet to learn to feed themselves. Killer, like most whippets, will get mad when ignored and will tear up anything he can get his teeth into. Tonight one of my Bean duck shoes took the brunt of his anger and was torn to shreds.

My chores completed, I fell into bed with a bottle of burgundy between my legs. The more I thought about things, the more I felt like I was in the cast of a Broadway comedy. Still, murder's not comical, so I took a long slug on the wine, snuggled up to the two dogs and didn't wake up until I heard Killer slip though the door and into the dark morning. I made it to the toilet with my head pounding from the burgundy. It was ten 'til five, so I dressed and headed for the barn thinking about the day's racing.

By the time I reached the barn, Top Shot and Crystal Run had walked the shed row and had their baths. Both, as far as I could see, were in top form. Jock had the pre-race chores in hand without my having to tell him anything. He arranged with Emmy for the needed medication and made sure the blacksmith came by to clinch their shoes. Tino would take the filly over for the race, but I needed to get Grady or Charlie to help me with the colt.

When I decided to run the horses as an entry, I made arrangements with the jock's room to have a second set of di Vinci Stable silks made. In all the rush and havoc of the last two days, Arch Hale had to make the entry. Tino found a friend of his from Aqueduct, Libby Hunter, a "bug" rider for the mare. Crystal Run needed the weight break against the colts. She's a push-button mare who would take care of herself and a young rider at the same time.

Steve Casey was set to ride Top Shot. He'd need a clever ride for a solid effort in the mud. Since the grass is Top Shot's bread and butter surface, I had no idea how he'd run in Suffolk's deep, muddy going. I wasn't expecting much, but deep down inside I knew he had class and was dying to run.

Steve and Arch came by at the break, around nine.

"Are you crazy, riding that Hunter kid from New York on that mare? She hasn't won a dozen races in her life. I don't care who she rides for in New York, Colin, you should have run that mare against the other fillies when I could have ridden her," Steve whined.

"You know, Steve, I'm getting tired of you thinking every horse in my barn is yours. I give you a lot of rides, but if you keep coming around here telling me how to train my horses and where to run them, I can get someone else."

"He didn't mean any offense, Colin. He lets his ass overrun his mouth sometimes. Steve, I agree with Colin. Just do the job he asks you to do, and you'll stay up on the best horses on the grounds. Keep running your mouth, and we'll be out of luck," Arch snapped.

He turned to me. "Tell me about the kid, Colin. I could have gotten Hector Cruz, that little Mexican bug rider."

"His local connection to the Latin clique is the very reason I don't want him, Arch. He can't ride a boxcar with both doors closed, and he only does what Perez and Gonzolvo tell him. They run that side of the Jock's room, and you and Steve know it.

"Libby Hunter has won eleven races on horses the big guys won't ride. Some of the better trainers use her to breeze the best horses they have in the morning, and she makes the most of every ride she gets. She cared enough to fly up here for one ride, and I'm sure she'll do just fine."

At 2:20 that afternoon, I glanced from the clock in the paddock to the tote board. Even with the long lay-off and the fact that Top Shot was off the grass, my entry was favored at two to one odds. A pudgy little female rider trailed Steve out of the jock's quarters and walked up to me. She stuck out her hand and said, "Hello, Mr. O'Hearn, I'm Libby Hunter."

She was a just a shade over a midget, with short stubby legs. I asked myself how she could stay on a horse with those short legs. She must have read my mind.

"Don't let my legs bother you, sir. Have you looked at the other half of your entry, Top Shot? He has shorter legs than I do, for a horse and, he can fly," she said with a low, warm laugh.

I was dumb struck. "Libby, do you think I'd second guess you, if I flew you all the way from New York?"

"Thanks, Mr. O'Hearn. Now tell me about this lady I'm riding against the boys today."

"I think Steve's colt will be slow to make a move, if he does make one. He's going for position out of the gate to see if Top Shot wants to run. He'll be coming in the stretch, if he's a factor. You ride Crystal Run like she's your own. Get the feel of things and after the first quarter, let her pick her own pace. Most of all, take care of her. She might be short."

"I doubt it, Mr. O'Hearn. I hear you never run a short horse."

I was taken off guard. It was a nice compliment.

I threw Steve up first. As he walked out of the paddock, I put Libby aboard. She was so light, I was terrified I'd throw her all the way over the saddle and onto the ground. As always, I said, "God bless. Have a safe trip."

So far, all of them have survived, so my prayer appears to work.

As I left the paddock and headed for my lucky bar and a

Sam Adams before the race, I saw Johnny Carlino and Jimmy Slacks on the apron of the grandstand. Milos wasn't around.

I walked over, and they asked if we were going to win.

"I think Crystal Run will be right there. If the little horse can handle the track, he'll be coming at the end."

"Should we bet?" asked Johnny.

"I don't bet. With these low odds on the entry, I'd buy a combination, boxing both our horses against the field. If you win, you'll win big if a long shot hits the board. If you lose, you won't lose too much."

I hurried towards the bar and they made their way quickly to the nearest betting window. I turned the corner at the bar and Lefty Hamm, the black cat agent, was staring me in the face.

"How're they gonna run, Colin?"

"Probably short, Lefty."

"Shit," he said and walked off with his head bowed.

I decided a lucky drink was a waste of money after seeing Lefty. I wondered what more bad luck could come my way, with Lefty's hoax probably on me now. I figured we'd lose the race, but prayed both jockeys and horses would return safely.

I was hanging over the fence near the start of the mile and seventy-yard race. The horses would break a short way up the track. As they passed me the first time, Libby was trapped on the fence by three horses and I had to look for Steve. He'd broken sharp, but the mud from the other horses hit Top Shot in the face and he dodged to the outside and almost pulled himself up. Ten lengths separated Top Shot and the next to last horse. The leader finished the first quarter in a very slow 25:3.

I could see Libby trying her best to get out of the box. Crystal Run was pulling with all her might and Libby was fifth at the half mile pole. Top Shot was still last, at least thirty lengths behind the leader.

My eyes went from Top Shot to Crystal Run and I saw Libby stand straight up in her irons. She dropped the mare's head and helped her jump over the heels of the horse in front of her, the one holding her in the box.

It was a tricky move, one that took some daring. Now she was loose, outside of the entire field swinging wide into the stretch. I took a quick glance back at Top Shot and saw he'd passed one horse and seemed to be getting his footing.

At the eighth pole, five horses were still ahead of Crystal Run. Libby was pushing hard, scrubbing, but not hitting her.

At the sixteenth pole she was third, less than a length behind the second horse and three behind the leader. My eyes were glued to her when a guy next to me said, "Look at that horse on the outside. He's flying."

It was instinct. I knew he was talking about Top Shot, but he had to be out of it. They were coming right at me, as I hung over the rail at the finish line. Libby was now going after Crystal Run, whipping from both sides and keeping her straight as a string through the stretch. She got to the second horse and had a few more yards to catch the leader, who was giving no ground.

It was then I saw something I had never seen a "bug-rider" do in the past. As a matter of fact, Angel Cordero was the only rider who could make the move look as easy as Libby did. She whipped left handed, then three or four jumps before the wire, she switched to the right. I could see her move clearly. She perfectly timed the finish line and instead of hitting the mare, she flipped her stick and tapped Crystal Run under the chin, barely making contact. It caused the mare to raise her head and I knew she'd win the photo finish.

Three strides past the wire, Top Shot flew by both leaders. He'd finished a half length behind the first two. As I made my way to the winner's circle, I was stunned by how fast he had closed.

Libby pulled up and walked Crystal Run into the enclosure. She knew the photo would prove us the winner and was thrilled.

I smiled. "Where'd you get that move, Libby?"

"Angel taught me that tap one morning when I first started. I can't believe you picked it up," she said, as she headed for the weigh-in scales.

"Great win, Libby. We have to talk after you clean up," I called as she skipped her way to the jock's room, after they announced the winner and the lights on the tote board stopped blinking.

She'd used a move that no jockey at Suffolk Downs could do if they wanted. Steve was beside me as we watched Top Shot head back to the barn.

"That little kid can ride, but I almost caught her. Out of the gate my horse didn't handle the track at all. He was slipping and sliding until he got to the outside and got his footing. Then I was on a Rolls Royce. That's the fastest I've ever closed on a horse. If it was another sixteenth, we'd have won by five," he said, as he headed off to the jock's room to get cleaned up for his next ride.

"I've got your old mare for the 'girls' in the next race," he shouted as he hit the jock's room door.

I was glad Charlie and Grady weren't around yet to saddle the mare in the next race. However, I did notice Cozy Costas and Connie Tass standing by the rail, waiting for the horses entered in the next race. I was afraid that after all that had happened, Tass would claim the sore, old mare. He'd be some hot after she cooled out.

Both of my horses were walking and awaiting their urine tests when I walked by the spit-box. Since I had time with nothing going on at Barn 15, I went to the rail to watch the old girl running in the next race. Shortly after the break, the mare was on top by three and stayed there until the half-mile mark. Then she stopped like she'd been shot. After a few bad strides, Steve pulled her up and jumped off.

As I resumed my walk to Barn 15, I saw the horse ambulance pass me on the way to pick up the old mare. Lefty, the black cat, had been at it again today. He must have bet heavily on the mare.

They announced the winning order and the claimed horses right after the race. The dreaded news came over the stable's loud speaker. Costas and Tass had claimed the mare for ten thousand dollars. I was not going to The Shamrock to celebrate my horse's good fortune this night. I was trying to avoid an argument, as Ian had asked.

CHAPTER THIRTY-ONE

Fred Hardy and Martin Watson were sharing a sub at a small shop near FBI headquarters. The two were casual, almost friendly, since the killing at Suffolk Downs had put Colin O'Hearn in the spotlight.

Hardy, neat and tidy about his appearance, would never have tackled the meatball sub that Watson was dripping down a napkin under his chin. He'd ordered a tuna on a wheat roll, the six-inch size, as opposed to Watson's twelve-inch sandwich, served on a hard, white Italian roll.

"What do we do next about O'Hearn? After listening to you all, I guess there's not much reason to think he killed Joe Dobbs. Without him, I don't know how to get close to Corsetti. What do you think, Watson?" Hardy asked.

"Fred, I'm going to tell you something you can't repeat. If I hear it from anyone, I'll know it came from you, because no one but me knows it. Joe Dobbs worked for me. He was my informant in a case I'm trying to build against Connie Tass. I placed him in that organization after we arrested him a while back on a burglary charge. Neither Colin O'Hearn nor Vito Corsetti had any reason to kill Dobbs. Connie Tass must have found out he was a rat. I think we will lay Dobbs's murder at Tass's feet before long."

"Why didn't you tell me before? What the hell's going on? "

Watson smiled and put a tan folder on the table, well away from his tomato sauce and sub, before answering the last question.

"His American name is Connie Tass. Our research has him as Conrad Tabazoff. He came from Russia about six years ago through Canada, as far as we can tell. He's one of the top members of the Russian Mafia in New England. One report has him fifth or sixth down the chain of about twenty-five hundred connected Russians and Eastern European gangsters in New England. They're the biggest threat to the old-line Italian mob families.

"Tass is into everything. He looks legit, but, our research disclosed that, in addition to extortion, he's into loan sharking, girls and drugs. Even his bakery is involved. He's been trying to strong-arm his way into every mom and pop market and restaurant in the city. He's just now trying to push his way into the North End, and you know what that means."

Hardy brightened. "Vito Corsetti."

"Exactly. I've been waiting for all hell to break loose between the two."

"Maybe Corsetti killed Dobbs to send a message to Tass?"

"It's not likely he'd set up his own trainer if, in fact, O'Hearn is really working for Corsetti, and Santos is just a front."

"Tass would never do a hit himself. He has Nikki Zepoff, another Russian around to do his dirty work."

"We have to see what happens with Tass and Corsetti. I think O'Hearn is a lot more involved with Corsetti than he let's on. I think he's washed a good deal of money and you should go for that. He's your best bet to get something on Corsetti," said Watson.

Hardy had started the day depressed about the way his Corsetti investigation was headed. He was in a much better mood after his lunch with Watson. Now he had a new direction with new names to send back to Miami in his next report. That's what the Federal Strike Force loved, more names and progress. He now had both.

As I entered Little Venice, one person after another commented on the race. Jimmy Slacks signaled me from the bar. Johnny

Carlino and Milos Santos were with him. Santos offered to buy me a drink.

"Dewar's, three fingers on ice."

"Great win today, Colin," Santos said, "Sorry I couldn't get there. The boss had me running all over town. By the way, he was hoping you'd come by tonight. He has several things besides the race that he wants to talk to you about. I'll take you back."

After chatting with the boys a few more minutes, Santos and I headed toward the office. Seconds later, we stood before Vito Corsetti's desk.

"You gonna win them all for us, Colin? That was great. I've never won two races so quick. That Top Shot might have been the best in the race, if he'd had a decent start!"

He was really excited and rambled on about the race. After settling down, he motioned for Santos to leave. When we were alone, he said, "I need to talk with you about things other than horses."

I sat down in the chair directly across from the old man. His face changed and I knew he was in a different mind-set, now that horse racing wasn't the subject.

"I know the cops are full of shit if they think you had anything to do with killing that guy you beat up."

He said it as a fact and I'd bet even money he knew something I didn't.

"It's about that scumbag, Tass. That Russian's a real thorn in my side, to say the least."

Without actually admitting to any illegal acts, Vito talked about his business in the North End. He said Tass was trying to cut into his territory in the old Italian section of Boston.

"My people and I have been in this area for generations and

have always been looked up to. They have problems, they need money or help with politicians or cops, they come to me. In return, I get my share of their business and all of their respect. Then this Russian comes here and in no time, moves into the South End with his people. I got asked by the Irish to help run him out. It was a bad decision on my part, taking a pass on the Russians back then. Now they're my problem. I think Tass set you up by killing one of his own. The big guy that tried to mess with you and got killed was expendable to a man like Tass, or maybe he was a rat. Thank goodness that old man saw someone with that shovel."

"I'm worried about that old man," I said, "If they can get their hands on him before he testifies he's never going to have a chance." I was looking for a place to stash Old John and, in a roundabout way, was asking Vito for his help.

"If you want me to, I'll have Jimmy Slacks come get him or you bring him to me. We have several apartments above the restaurant and around the block. We'll get him to work at your barn by six. He can stay here at night until this thing blows over."

"Thanks, Mr. Corsetti. He needs help. Getting him off the racetrack at night is going to be a chore. Maybe if I tell him he gets to stay close to a bar, he'll be okay," I laughed.

He changed the subject. "I have a source close up in the FBI. He tells me you had plenty of chances to talk about my involvement with the horses and how we paid for them. He tells me, without lying, you got around involving me. I'm grateful for that. I wish more of my people knew how to walk such a tight line with the Feds. You said I could trust you and I do. I'm indebted to you, Colin. You have a large favor due in my black book. When you need it, call on me. I hope we can continue to enjoy our relationship at the track, and our friendship," the old man said.

I stood, preparing to leave. I wished Vito had offered me dinner. But the thought of going home, putting my feet up sharing a pizza with Killer, Nadine and Billy Eckstein was inviting. I'd have time for several relaxing drinks and a long call to Annie. It was then I remembered I hadn't called her after the race.

The dogs went through their usual terrier attack when I put them out after getting home. As I made the first drink of the night, the phone rang. I knew it was Annie. I wish I'd gotten through to her first, on the prepaid cell.

"How'd they run, Colin? I thought you would have called me by now."

"The mare won by a nose, baby, and the little horse was a fast-closing third, a half length from taking it all. I've been involved in something here that has taken every spare minute over the last three days. Let me try to explain. To be safe, let me call you back on the cell phone." She hung up without a word and picked up the cell on the first ring.

"What the hell's going on, Colin? Things up there seem to be out of control."

It took me an hour to go from Dobbs's death to the trip to the police station. After a while, we got to the horses. It was where we both wanted to spend our phone time. She cracked up when I told her about riding Libby Hunter and the move she made at the end of the race.

"Colin, you're not going to believe this, but Libby spent the last two winters down here in Aiken. She worked for Dogwood and has brought in things for me to repair. She's a hell of a rider. I'll bet she'll die when you tell her about us. Those itty bitty legs are better than none... right?"

"Cut that crap out, Annie. Nobody, and I mean nobody, has anything on you. I never even think about your legs. Time will cure them and you'll be good as new. You're the most beautiful woman I've ever met, Annie."

"You know just what to say, big boy. I'd forgotten how sweet you are sometimes. However, these crutches are still with me and probably will be here forever."

"I don't care, Annie. When I see you in my mind, I think of my soul mate, not just a woman. I see us together, now and forever," I said.

"When are we going to be together, Colin? Time drags without you. My life drags without you."

"We can't yet, Annie. Not yet."

We then talked about her filly. "I may get Libby back up here to ride her in a few weeks. Your mare's not that far off. She keeps herself fit. I don't want to breeze her much, because it'll get her all riled up. We've been taking her the wrong way with the old pony, every morning. She's fine as long as he's with her. I think I'll get Tino to blow her out tomorrow."

"Libby would be great, Colin. The filly only likes women, I can tell. She hates men."

There was a pause before we rang off. I was sure she had something else to tell me.

"Colin, the FBI came to see me today."

It took the next ten minutes for me to calm her down. She'd been afraid to tell me. Everything I said about the murder overwhelmed her and she was afraid to tell me about the FBI. I'd left her exposed and I was sorry. The Feds must have run my phone records and seen how much time we spent talking.

After she calmed down, my phone in the kitchen rang. Annie held on while I answered.

"No! I'll be right there."

I slammed down the receiver and said, "That's the guard shack at the track. There's a fire at my barn!"

I drove as fast as I could on the ice-covered roads to the track. The closer I got, the brighter the sky appeared. It seemed there were no vehicles on the road, except the fire, police and rescue trucks racing towards Suffolk Downs.

I thought about Jock and the horses. Tino would be okay. It was just ten o'clock and he'd still be up, probably in the kitchen bar. Jock went to bed much earlier, but the sirens probably alerted him.

A fierce wind was blowing out toward the bay and away from the barns when I parked my truck and ran the last block because of the traffic. I ducked through the high board fence near Barn 15 and was horrified. The fire was coming from Old John's old station wagon. Every hose on the backside, including the fire trucks and pumpers, was pouring water onto the roofs and sides of the barns. Horses screamed in fright. It sounded like gunshots exploding, as horses kicked the sides of their stalls in fear.

I raced into Barn 15 and saw that there was smoke, but no flames. Jock and Tino, joined by several race trackers from the kitchen, were standing in front of the stalls in case the roof caught on fire. To remove the horses when the fire was only in the station wagon would have resulted in total panic and mayhem on the icy roads outside the barns.

Within fifteen minutes, the danger was over. Our shed row and most of the stalls were soaked and flooded, but the horses were safe. There would be a huge clean up task, but it was a great relief that we'd dodged the most dangerous thing that can happen on a race track.

Jock was standing at Lonely Aunt's head. "She's fine, boss. But I thought that damned goat was going crazy. She screamed like an old woman. The rest are okay. The old horse is really cool. He kept the mare quiet when the goat wouldn't stop screaming," the old groom said.

When I was sure we were safe, I went outside and looked at the simmering mass that had been Old John's car and newspaper storage bin. I prayed he was still at Grady and Charlie's. It seemed that every trainer I knew was in the area, checking on their own horses or those of friends. I looked for Cozy Man Costas, but he was nowhere to be seen.

I walked up to the fireman in charge and asked, "There wasn't anyone in the station wagon, was there? Was the man inside?"

He looked back at the smoldering car that by this time was reduced to a charred shell and said, "We found the remains of someone, but we can't identify them at this time. Someone said an old man lived in that car. My guess it was him."

I walked over to the bench outside my shed row and sat next to Jock, whose head was almost between his knees. Tears stained his soot-covered face. My shoulders rounded, and I was cursing between sobs as I slammed my fist against the railing of the bench. The old man I'd been close to all my life put his massive arm around my shoulders, but neither of us could speak.

CHAPTER THIRTY-TWO

It took over an hour for me to fill in all the gaps for Norm Smith and Dave Ross, who got to the barn moments after the firemen received the call. They felt the same way I did. Joe Dobbs's killer probably set fire to Old John's station wagon when he was asleep to eliminate the only witness to their crime. In the back of my mind, I knew someone at the track had to have told whoever started the fire where they could locate the old man and when. There was no doubt where I intended to look for the bastard.

Before leaving the track, I called Ian. He'd called me several times on my cell, but I was busy with the cops. I have never in my life heard a man known for having ice water in his veins be as emotional as Ian was when we finally got to talk.

"John never in his life hurt anyone. We've got to get whoever did this, and now! I think we both know where to look. I've talked with Vito, Capps and Watson, and they all think we should start with Connie Tass. He's probably lying low for the time being. We need to send him a message.

"Ellen can do all the funeral arrangements for John through my office. I have his will and, it will surprise a few folks, especially people around the backside."

I was too upset to talk any more, so I hung up and headed to The Shamrock for a few tall Dewar's and hopefully a run-in with Costas or, even better, with Tass and his bodyguard Nikki Zepoff.

The Shamrock parking lot was full at eleven. I felt sure most of the racing crowd had gathered to talk over the death of John Harkins, as well as the near miss from the fire which could have easily engulfed the entire backside. Once inside the bar, I saw about six trainers at a long table a few feet from the restrooms. Costas was seated with his back to me. Someone must have warned him, because he turned in my direction and began to rise to his feet.

As he swung around, I said, "Costas, you and I need to take a leak."

I grabbed his left arm, letting my grip slip to his wrist, twisting his fingers back, pushing him into the bathroom. After I rammed a tall trash can under the doorknob, I threw him into the corner by the sink. His head smacked against the metal hand dryer as he fell to the floor screaming and cursing. I knelt on his chest and grabbed him by the throat.

"Listen to me very carefully. I think Tass is responsible for Old John's death. You get a 'hall pass' on this one, because I don't think you're crazy enough to threaten your own horses as well as the whole backside by starting a fire. But I've got a message for your fuckin' Russian. If he had anything to do with Old John's death, I'm gonna kill him. He'll never see it coming. Tell him he's dog shit and I'm gonna scrape him off my shoes, once and for all. But, I'm not even his biggest problem. He's got so many people after him on both sides of the law, his days are numbered," I said, slamming his head against the tile floor as I got off his chest.

I got myself under control and walked out the door. As I passed the bar Evan Kennedy said, "Do I need to send a doctor back there?"

"Not this time, Evan. Just put him out with the rest of the trash tonight."

I returned to my cottage and proceeded to get dead drunk. I slouched in my old recliner, my glance going from the dancing fire to my favorite Gilbert Gaul painting of the forlorn soldier trying to return home from the Civil War. I added fat wood to the fire and the surge of sparks and crackling sending

Killer to his bed in the kitchen and Nadine into my lap. As I stroked the fear from her shivering body and took a long pull of Dewar's, I shivered from hatred and a desire for revenge.

Losing a friend for no good reason is outrageous, but the cold murder of a helpless man is unconscionable. Twice I fell asleep only to be awakened by the popping noise of the fire scaring Nadine and my spilling of the drink in my lap.

Less than an hour before I needed to be at the barn, I watched the last embers of the fire die and finally staggered into the bathroom and turned on a steaming shower. I lay down on my back in the shower and let the hard, pounding water wash away my hangover, relentlessly punishing me for my night of mourning and self-pity.

The backside was overcast in fog as figures moved silently through the near-dark new day that seemed to offer little promise. The usual banter in the dawn hours was missing. The smell of ash and death filled the air. When I sat at our regular kitchen table, Arch joined me, his eyes drooping and sad, reflecting the senseless loss in the race track family. Trainers and jockeys would show up for the funeral Tuesday, a dark day.

"The fuckin' cops are already here this morning. You got anything new to tell 'em?"

"Let 'em do their thing. They'd be better off talking to the mobsters from Southie than wasting their time around here."

"Steve told me this morning that Costas is thinkin' about shipping out to Penn National. What the hell did you say to him in the crapper last night at Evan's?"

"I guess you can say I threatened him a little, but mostly I told him to tell Tass I was comin' for him."

Arch wrapped his gherkin pickle-sized lips around his coffee mug, giving himself a second to think. " Colin, you might get to Tass if you could find him alone, but he'll never be without Nikki Zepoff now. There's no worse killer than that Russian."

"Maybe not, but I'd rather have Jimmy Slacks on my side than three Zepoffs. That is, if Vito will ever turn Slacks loose."

"Just be careful, Colin… please."

"Anyway, I'm about through talking to cops. I just want to get back to training my horses."

"We riding anything this week?"

"There's a race for Deeper River on Friday. He's not at top form yet, but it's a race he should have something to say about. I need to run Cherokee Moon back, probably on Saturday. The following week I'll see if that filly of Annie's is ready," I said.

"When are you working the filly?"

"I'm going to get into her this morning, in about twenty minutes."

I killed the last of my coffee, and left Arch and crossed the road to Barn 15. I climbed on the pony as Jock threw Tino up on Lonely Aunt, and walked her around the shed row to settle her down.

"Tino, I'll go with you until you're ready. Then you break her off at the half mile pole. Drop her head at the three-eighths and let her do it on her own. I left her in the German martingale to give you more control. For God sakes, son, just don't let her get away from you."

"What do I do if she takes off and I can't stop her?"

"Just stop pulling on her and I'll be at the five eighths pole ready to catch you. Whatever you do, don't hook up with anyone. Hold up there a minute and walk her in the stall with me. Jock stood outside the door. "Okay, Colin, all clear."

I took a small syringe from my ski jacket pocket and

quickly injected three-tenths of a cc of Acepromazine into her vein and dropped the syringe over the back wall into the gap.

The tranquilizer should be just enough to take off the edge. It's against the rules and a thirty day suspension to get caught with a needle. It worked like a charm, and so did the filly. She was a lady the whole way, working a handy :37.2, with her head down, and pulled up without blowing enough to put out a match.

I passed Arch Hale as we left the back chute and he said, "I thought you said she'd be tough."

"It's like they say in prison, Arch. Age is the best rehabilitation device."

The filly had a line down her back and seemed to get a lot out of the breeze. Most of all, she wasn't stressed and didn't bleed. I was hoping I could get another quiet work, going five eighths of a mile into her, before she raced. If I could, without her bleeding or entrapping, she'd be ready.

Deeper River was the next horse out and was full of himself in the bright sunshine. He worked five-eighths in a minute flat, the perfect breeze. The big horse had completed the turnaround and was approaching his old form.

When I brought Deeper River back from his work, the two Boston police detectives investigating both murders were waiting for me at the tack room.

Norm Smith, who seemed to outrank Dave Ross, spoke first. "Colin, got a minute?"

"Sure, come on inside the tack room. I've got a pot of coffee on."

Arch, like all good agents, always brought a dozen donuts for the stable crew when his rider won a race. In this case, Steve had been on the show horse, but Libby had slipped Arch the money for donuts before she left for Aqueduct. Such gestures are not wasted on an old trainer and his crew.

"Have a donut and tell me what's on your mind."

"O'Hearn, what can you tell us about the fire the other night?" Ross asked, "And while you're at it, what can you tell us about this fight between you and Costas?"

"I can't tell you much about the fire, except my guess is that someone didn't want Old John to be a witness. I just sent Tass a message. Hell, you guys, we were down this road the night of the damn fire."

"When we talked to Costas this morning, he said you told him you were going to kill Tass." Smith said.

"All I know is, Connie Tass has a reputation for pushing people around. People say Dobbs worked for him. I was just reaching out, maybe wildly, but I wanted Tass to know I'm after him if he had anything to do with John Harkin's murder."

"For what it's worth, Colin, I never believed you killed that Dobbs guy," Smith said.

"I guess you never heard of a guy named Nikki Zepoff?" asked Ross.

"Not much. You hear things. I hear he's Tass's shooter."

Ross came back. "Any thing new with Vito Corsetti?"

"Does Corsetti own the horses you train?" Smith asked.

Thinking of what Ian told me about the "Poker Game," I wondered if Smith was aware that I knew he already had the answer to his questions and was just asking them for Ross's benefit."

"Di Vinci Stable owns those horses and, from what the paperwork says, Milos Santos is the owner. I've never looked into it, past the paperwork in the office. His checks are good and he bought me some really nice horses."

"Well, if you hear of anything brewing between Tass and Corsetti, would you let us know?" Ross asked.

"I don't get past the horses with Mr. Santos, so I'm not likely to ever hear anything like that," I said.

CHAPTER THIRTY-THREE

Leave it to Ian Higgins to come up with the best idea for the memorial service and wake for John Harkins. We gathered on the Clubhouse apron, near the Suffolk Downs finish line. From the looks of it, everyone on the backside wore the best they owned and were joined by a large crowd of locals in dark suits and camel-hair polo coats.

I introduced Ian to those gathered. The bent Irishman then spoke a few carefully selected words. "Our friend John Harkins never hurt a soul in his life, save himself. He was a troubled man, losing touch with reality when he arrived on this backside, where he finally found peace and real friends."

He told a few stories about the days when he and Old John practiced and taught law together. Many in the gathering stood and stared in amazement, never having been exposed to Old John's life before he arrived on the backside. Others, those dressed as swells, knew little of the downfall of their former friend and neighbor and were more shocked to learn of his late in life manner of living. Ian finished personal remarks with a stunning announcement.

"To most of you on the backside, John Harkins' life before you came to know and care for him is a mystery. His wife, also an attorney, was a member of the Natick City Council before cancer took her life."

Many of the Natick swells nodded in agreement.

"Before she died, not only did John have a practice helping the poor who could not afford a high-priced lawyer, but he represented his clients with skills that could have made him one of Boston's top earning trial attorneys. When his wife died, so did John's productive legal life."

The horsemen, grooms and jockeys stood mesmerized.

"As John fell deeper into his haze and further away from

reality, I watched over him and guided him toward the race-track. Men like Arch Hale, Colin O'Hearn, Captain Charlie Martin, Grady O'Brien and Charley Clark never questioned John's desire to drop out, and were always protecting his gentle, lost soul. God help the person or persons who took John's life if any of these men or myself ever get our hands on the bastards."

Ian cleared his throat and continued. "Several years ago, when he still hung on to some sense of reality, John asked me to make his will, to form a trust, and to serve as its executor. Contrary to what everyone thought, John did not die a pauper. He left everything he owned in a trust to build and maintain a medical and dental clinic and a legal service office to serve his fellow and future backside workers.

"Don't shake your heads. John knew this day would come, and I am proud to tell you that, as of his death, the John Harkins Memorial Trust will be activated. The rules of the trust provide that there will never be any direct funds allocated or spent on loans or grants to individuals except through free services to horsemen and their families, be they jockeys, train-ers, hot walkers or grooms. Never again will these folks want for a physician, dentist or attorney. My office or my designee will execute this trust and guard against the possibility of per-sonal gain by any employee from John's dream. To receive help, a person needs only to be in good standing with the Racing Commission and have valid state racing license."

The gathering stood silently with heads nodding, indicating that Ian had lost his mind. How could this old man living out of an old station wagon have done such an honorable act for his fellow workers?

"There are three provisions in his will that I will now carry out. First, his ashes will be spread across the track's finish line. Second, after the harrow has covered John's remains, the bar of the Clubhouse will be open and there will be a buffet to "wake" John Harkins and his life. Finally, we will begin building the clinics on a large lot outside the back gate which was purchased by the trust almost a decade ago for this purpose, as soon as the probate court allows."

Raising his voice in closing, Ian said, " The trust has funds of slightly more than nine million dollars, all that our friend had left in the world. It assures that John Harkins will be lending a helping hand to his friends and others who make their living on the backside of this racetrack for a long time to come."

The stunned crowd shuffled and mumbled its way close to the track railing as Ian walked as erectly as he possibly could, his cane in one hand and an urn of ashes in the other, onto the track. He crossed the finish line, his mop-like red hair blowing almost on end. The faint, gray spray of ashes mingled with the cloudy overcast day, falling as John Harkins wished. There was hardly a dry eye among those who watched with reverence. My lips moved with a prayer as Jock, Emmy, Charlie, Grady, Arch, Captain Martin and I huddled together.

Our small group stayed intact as we raised a few glasses and each made a toast to Old John. After voices got louder with conversation and jokes, we left together, walking ankle deep in mud and slush toward the tack room at Barn 15, where we knew we could privately salute our old pal. After about an hour and many rounds of drinks in the crowded tack room, a knock sounded at the door.

Ian walked to the center of the room holding a glass of Irish whiskey filled to the top. He silently raised it overhead and we all drank as one. Ian, tears still in his eyes said, "Now let's get on with the job of catching the fuckers who did this. Where do we start?"

In a small bar in South Boston, Milos Santos and Miki Zepoff spoke as they sat hunched over their drinks. Santos was not a vodka man, but he knew the Russian was, so he followed suit.

"Tass is impressed with you. He's glad to know whose side you're really on."

"I got no future with Vito Corsetti," Santos said. "He used to believe in me. Trust me. Now, I'm out of the loop. I'm afraid it won't be too long before a loop drops over my head. I'm a top accountant, and I know Vito's action like the back of my hand. I can be of great help to Mr. Tass. When he cuts out Vito, I hope I'll have some control of the action in North Boston."

Miki Zepoff was very leery of Santos. After he milked the turncoat accountant of all the information Tass wanted, he would kill the man. He'd make it look like Vito did it, after catching Santos stealing. He and Tass had been over the plan in detail before they agreed to meet with Santos.

He said to Santos, "Here's the first installment. That's ten thousand dollars to get you started. That's for a list of the top fifty people who owe Corsetti money and the amounts. If we can take over these debts by lending them money to get out from under Corsetti through our finance company, South Boston Financial Planning Group, we own them. They pay off Vito and we use them as our first line to get things started. We'll then take over other friends of theirs who are Vito's customers. It's simple, like a little merger, with us eventually taking over the loan business right under Corsetti's nose.

"After that, we'll ask you for other business we can cut from Corsetti. We're very interested in the restaurants and bars. Do a good job for us this time, and the next fee will be double."

Zepoff slid the envelope to Santos. They shook hands and Santo hurried out to his car. He sat for a minute before starting the engine and thought about what he'd just done. There was no turning back now. He'd worried for weeks that O'Hearn might tell Vito he'd skimmed cash from the horse deal.

Santos started the Lincoln Town Car and pulled away from the bar parking lot. He was so involved in his plans for the future, he failed to see the black SUV following him his entire trip home to Revere Beach.

CHAPTER THIRTY-FOUR

As I watched Tino leave the barn and head for the paddock, I felt deep down inside that Deeper River was as close to perfect as I could get him for his debut in the di Vinci Stable colors. The big horse appeared on top of his game, if his final week of training meant anything. I thought only racing luck would keep him from the winner's circle. It felt good to be back in the game I loved as I walked behind my horse toward Suffolk's grandstand and the saddling enclosure.

I nervously looked around for signs any of the "black cats" I always tried so hard to avoid. As I left the grandstand and walked through the small tunnel to the paddock, I knew I was just about home free. Suddenly, Lefty Hamm walked out of a rest room trying to get his stubborn fly zipped. He looked up just in time to see me. "We got a chance with the Riverman horse today, Colin?"

My heart almost stopped. "I've never run him, Lefty. You're on your own," I said as I failed for the hundredth time to give the poor, hard-luck, jock's agent a tip. I knew the black deed was done and something bad was in store for my rider, my horse, me or someone I cared about today. The thought of scratching Deeper River rather than face Lefty's curse flashed across my mind, but I quickly dismissed it.

As I threw Steve aboard, I told him to be extra careful with the horse. "I just have a feeling. You know, trouble around the corner and all that."

"Did you just run into Lefty?"

"How'd you know?"

"You always say that when you talk to Lefty before a race. You've been doing it for the five years I've been riding for you. It's bullshit, Colin, but I'll be careful," he said, as they called, "Riders up."

The bright-eyed bay broke right on top and showed good early speed. It was an added money race for non-winners in six months, and he appeared right from the start to be the class of the small field of seven. As he sailed past the quarter and the half-mile poles, he was skipping along two lengths in front. Turning for home, he opened up three on the field.

At the sixteenth pole, I saw his head jerk up as he took a bad step. My heart sank as he slowed and was a badly beaten fourth as they crossed the finish line. Steve barely let him get past the line before he pulled him up, jumped off and headed back to the saddling enclosure.

"What happened?" I asked as the colt favored his left front leg.

"Something low," Steve answered.

While he went to weigh in, I took Tino and the horse to the edge of the paddock. I cleaned off the mud and blood to find that he'd jerked a piece of meat the size of a silver dollar. It was hanging off his heel. After all our patient rehab, he'd "pulled a quarter."

It must have happened while changing leads in the stretch. It was my fault for not watching closer when I breezed him. I should have told the blacksmith to cut his toes back. I cursed hard-headed blacksmiths, who want a longer toe on horses for better reach. Most of all, I cursed Lefty Hamm for his damned "black cat" rotten luck.

Only Milos Santos was waiting for me when I reached the grandstand bar. Johnny Carlino and Jimmy Slacks weren't around.

"What happened?" Milos asked.

I showed him the blood on my hands and pants and said, "He pulled a quarter. He'll need at least six weeks to get over it.

Just bad racing luck."

"A lot of your luck's been bad lately. The murder, the fire, and now this. Better get yourself some shamrocks, Irish," he said, as he walked away with a bounce in his step.

It was a strange reaction from a man who, six weeks before, treated me as his new best friend. Maybe my getting close to Vito offended him. Ever since I gave him a break by not telling Vito he skimmed off the horse purchases, he'd acted strangely.

I went to the steward's office and watched the rerun of the race on tape. Nothing had changed; it never does. I don't know why I ask for a double dose of torture by watching my bad luck twice, I thought while making my way to Barn 15. Emmy had treated Deeper River at the test barn where he drew the "beaten favorite" test, usually given to big favorites who finish up the track after an apparent easy win was in sight.

When he got back to the barn, he looked as disappointed as the crew. Deeper River knew he should have gotten his picture taken. Many classy, older horses know all about winning and the rewards. They know if they go to the winner's circle and not straight back to the barn, there's a lot of love and treats coming their way. Maybe we just think we see these things in the horses we train when they do well. It adds to the mystique of the job. A true horseman trains racehorses not for the money, but for the love of it.

I walked through the front door of the house and let the dogs out the back, then poured my first three-fingered drink of the night. Nothing was going to spoil my enjoyment of good scotch, not even Lefty Hamm.

I buy my poison by the case and never allow my primary fuel supply to run low. I was mellow during my long talk with Annie. She was sad about the injury to Deeper River. Annie can teach both Jock and me things about treating injuries and sore horses.

We laughed and talked about how wonderful it would be training together with the horses again. After I hung up and put a steak on the Jenn-Aire, I leafed through the mail and turned to the morning's *Boston Globe*. I was fine until I got to the third page and noticed a one-column headline. "Bread Trucks Vandalized."

It was a strange story about two trucks owned by South Boston Bakeries having been broken into, while the drivers were servicing stores in different sections of North Boston during the predawn hours of the previous morning.

Vandals had dumped raw garbage inside the trucks and spray-painted graffiti on the outside. No one was injured and no suspects were detained, according to the police. Bakery officials said the bread and other baked goods on the trucks were destroyed. A photo above the story showed a bread truck with the letters USSR spray painted along side.

As I flipped my steak, I muttered to the dogs, "It's started guys. I only hope they leave us out of it."

I thought about Vito's horses and made up my mind that I'd hire a night watchman first thing in the morning. I was sure Vito would gladly foot the bill. I was thinking a war between the Italians and Russians had begun in earnest. When the phone rang Ian said, "Have you read the *Globe* or *Herald* today, Colin, my boy?"

"Are you referring to the story and picture of the trashed bread truck?"

"I thought that was interesting, after you explained to me the strained relationship between your owner and Tass."

"All hell's going to break loose, Ian. This is just the foreplay.

If I know Vito Corsetti, he won't stop until he baits the Russian into something really stupid that the cops can use to put him away."

"Killing two men at Suffolk Downs seems rather stupid."

"Starting tomorrow, I'm going to put a security guard on my barn until this thing blows over."

"I was going to suggest something like that. By the way, Colin, what happened to our horse today? He seemed to have things his way until the stretch."

I explained about the injury and how long the big horse would take to recover.

"Give me a call the first of the week and we'll eat. Maybe the Little Venice."

It was almost ten o'clock when I hung up. I washed the dishes, made another drink and sat down to go over the overnight entries. My cell rang, and I knew it had to be Annie calling back.

"Colin, I've been trying to reach you, but your phone's been busy." She was crying and I was scared.

"I'm sorry. I've been talking to Ian. What's the matter, honey?"

"Colin, I've got to tell you something. I've really messed up."

"Annie, you couldn't mess up if you tried, unless you're ditching me."

"But, Colin... I'm afraid you're going to be angry."

"What is it, darling?"

" I went to the doctor today. I... we're going to have a baby."

CHAPTER THIRTY-FIVE

I'm a forty-one year-old lifetime bachelor who's never had a savings account. I drink too much, live alone with two crazy dogs, and have the job security of a immigrant crop picker. As a thoroughbred trainer, there's plenty of work, but I have to move to get and keep it. Walking the floor with a drink in my hand, I occasionally stopped to stare into the flickering fire. Periodically I walked around the thawing back yard. Sleep was impossible.

The only woman I have ever loved was carrying my child. The thought of being a father, let alone being tied down in a marriage, sent me into a tailspin. Not even my hitch in the Army made me feel as trapped as Annie's news.

I wanted to run and not stop. If only I'd never crawled out from under that blanket or just thrown Santos out of my tack room, I'd be better off. If I felt this way, how must Annie feel? She was alone in her cottage and almost immobile. I considered her fears and felt more like a cad. During our several calls throughout the night we kept telling each other how happy we were then, and after long pauses, admitting we were both scared to death.

Neither of us could bring ourselves to even hint about the "A" word. But it had to be on both our minds. If we were cold and calculating middle-aged adults, we would know that we should discuss our options openly, but instead we talked in circles, avoiding any mention of abortion.

As the night sky lightened and the clock edged toward five, I gathered myself and left for the track. We had decided to make firmer plans during the week. I had agreed to breeze Lonely Aunt again and call her when I entered. She'd planned on driving up, but now she hedged. I mentioned the threat of a possible snowstorm, and she jumped at the chance to change her plans. She'd watch it on television. We were both relieved to avoid a face-to-face meeting, knowing it would result in a decision.

Jock, as usual, was singing to the horses as he picked up the feed tubs and carried them outside to be washed. He'd fed at four o'clock, then made his morning coffee and put something in the microwave for breakfast. The early morning is Jock's time with no loud talk, only the ancient sounds of jazz coming from his CD player. He hums all the songs, and if no one is around he even sings along. When the usual crowd arrives, he clams up and withdraws into a world I've only imagined.

Jock knows me better than any man alive, probably better than I know myself. After an hour of my moping around the shed row, getting tack ready for the day and writing instructions on the board, he put his arm on my shoulder and said, "Are you and Annie having problems again?"

"I can't go into it now, pal."

"Let me tell you something, Colin. You tell her to get that skinny white butt of hers up here to help me with that uppity bitch of a mare she owns. Mare hates me; she hates all men. When Emmy came by to check Deeper River after his race, that mare just hung her head out and almost pulled the woman into her stall. She's a woman's filly, she is."

He carried a set of tack to Sliding Scale's stall and said over his shoulder, "She's Annie's filly, she is. That's a dead cert."

Jock's ramblings put a smile on my face and the thought of being a father was almost forgotten as I crossed the horse path and climbed the steps to the track kitchen. They never cared if I brought my own donuts from the Winthrop bakery. The kitchen donuts were in a different league from my big yellow-edged, triple-iced breakfast treasures. The track kitchen served

Dunkin' Donuts, which were only iced once on the top. They would never do for a seasoned donut expert.

I poured my coffee, black with one Sweet 'Low, and took a *Racing Form,* never the top one, looking for good luck. My attention was focused on the field for Cherokee Moon's race. It looked like he had three or four to beat in a field of twelve. The track would be drying out by the fifth race and he'd have a good chance to make the lead from the seven hole. Three and seven are my lucky numbers, so I was pleased with my chances if Steve could get his mind on business quickly. I was smiling at the prospect of another win for di Vinci Stable when Charlie and Grady walked up to the table.

"We were hoping you'd be here this early," Grady said.

"What's up, guys?" I asked.

"The police were around yesterday. It was the same two, Smith and Ross, the local guys. They just asked questions about Old John. There was nothing we could tell them. We don't care about the locals, Colin... but yesterday late a natty guy from the FBI came by. He was asking questions about where you got the money for your new horses and if you ever had dealings with the drug crowd. Maybe they thought it was a drug deal gone bad that caused the fire and Old John's death. Anyway, we didn't tell the FBI fellow shit."

Charlie stopped Grady saying, "You know, Colin, Cozy was pissed about the mare he claimed from us. He ended up giving her away to some little girl for a riding horse. Tass is boiling mad at Cozy for losing his ten grand. Of course, Grady and I think that Russian money spends just fine. Here's your three grand, Colin," he said, handing a roll of cash to me, which I quickly put into my pocket.

When I got back to the barn, I gave Jock half the money

and told him to give a few hundred to Steve and Tino. The money was what we call, "found stakes." The morning's training took my mind off Annie, and I was where I belonged. The feeling of suspense, thrill of the test and money drives most trainers. It was no longer about the money for me. I'd put my share of the three grand in my stash and forget it until an emergency came up.

A few months ago, I'd have been all over the track dodging past due bills. Today, I'm thankful to Vito for making me more than just solvent. I love the action, even the danger connected to di Vinci. It was a major part of my make-up, pushing the envelope. If I have a child and a dependent woman on my hands, my life will never be the same.

Later I watched Cherokee Moon tear up the paddock. I looked Steve in the eye saying, "Strap your seatbelt on tight, Steve. When that gate opens, this squirrelly little streak of shit will be gone at the bell. You send him and look for the pine. Then lay his nose on that wood and don't look back. Six furlongs will go quickly today if his breeze last week means anything."

The white-eyed chestnut, with the markings of a damned Hereford cow, was all over the saddling stall. We fought over the chamois, saddle towel, pad, saddle and channel. I finally put on the over-girth, blinkers and the tongue-tie. I had some Vicks smeared inside my pants leg and forced inside the colt's nose, all the way up. He shook his head and almost dragged Tino and me to the lead pony. Then he seemed to settle down. He was smacking old Hard Rock's neck with his head and trying to push him all over the track as they headed toward the gate.

I'd briefed Tom, the starter, and he was ready when the colt walked up to the back of stall seven. He had the six and eight in line and waiting as Cherokee Moon strangely just walked into the gate and stood like a gentleman. The colt was all bluff and not much heart. I was sure if another horse looked him in the eye, he'd wilt.

Wilting was not a problem for Cherokee Moon this day. He beat the bell like a quarter horse and was a length up on the field after four strides. At the quarter pole, which he reached in 22.2, he had three on the field. The 45.3 seconds it took him to reach the half-mile mark was good for a six-length lead as Steve was just holding him on the fence. Either there was a shadow at the sixteenth pole or he was just playing around, but for some reason, he became airborne while leading by almost ten. He was a dozen lengths the best at the finish line and did the six furlongs in 1:10.1, the fastest of the winter meet.

The smile on my face reached from ear to ear. The winter track was at least a second slow, due to the deep, chemically layered surface. I had a stakes quality sprinter on my hands and he was only three years old. What a feeling for any trainer!

When the colt came back to the winner's circle, he looked sound as a dollar. Strangely, there was no one from di Vinci Stable around to be in the photo. As usual after a win, Barn 15 was a fun place to be as we waited for Cherokee Moon to get back from the test barn. When he arrived, he didn't blow out a match and had a ridge down his back. He played on the end of the shank as Tino gave him a few turns around the shed row.

"You ain't got to the bottom of this sucker yet," Jock said with a straight face.

"You know, Jock, life's funny. Two months ago I was borrowing money from you to feed the horses. Today, I've got money in the box, money in the bank and even some at home inside my old Gucci's. With six damned good horses in the barn, what more can a man ask for?"

"I don't know, Bubba... ask Annie," he said with a sly smile.

CHAPTER THIRTY-SIX

Few, if any, trainers breeze on Sundays. With the track almost deserted, it was a perfect chance for me to work Annie's filly almost in private, seven furlongs.

I rode the pony and Jock led the goat as our motley crew made its way from Barn 15 to the deserted main track. We wanted the filly calm at all costs, no matter what the embarrassment. There were several snickers and catcalls as we passed the kitchen.

Since Lonely Aunt was amazingly quick, Tino had his hands more than full. As a matter of fact, he had almost no control as the chestnut filly skipped through a half in :49, three quarters in 1:14 and finished the seven furlongs in 1:28 and change. She did it all on her own and pulled up calmly, like a good racehorse should. She was now set up perfectly for the mile race on Thursday. I couldn't wait to call Annie with the good news.

Annie had seemed preoccupied the night before when I called about Cherokee Moon's easy win. I knew she had a lot on her mind, but when I tried to be serious, she had changed the subject with small talk about her filly.

When I called her after the breeze, she'd been equally evasive, approving of the work before changing the conversation to visiting her father, the doctor. Her mother had died of cancer about three years ago, bringing Annie closer to her father. I could imagine his opinion of me, having broken up with Annie at Saratoga over another woman and now showing up in Aiken for one day and leaving her carrying my child.

"I haven't seen Dad in months. He really wants me to come. I told him the last time he called that I was seeing you again and that I was thinking about coming to Boston for the spring and summer. I promised I'd come and talk over some things with him before I came up. It's the least I can do," she said.

"Annie, don't you think we should make plans before you go talk to your Dad? I know you'll tell him about the baby, but we haven't gone over all the options. I'll fly down tomorrow and meet you in Alabama. We can talk things over and then go see him together."

"I don't want to do it that way. This is between my father and me," she said sharply.

In a shaky voice she said, "I have to run now, Colin. I have to close the shop and make arrangements for everything here. I'll take the dog with me."

"There's nothing I can do?"

"No, just hang in there and take care of my filly on Thursday. I'll miss you and call you on your cell to check in. Bye, baby," she whispered, and then hung up before I could say anything more.

It wasn't really a brush-off, but it was the closest thing to it.

Jock was doing afternoon stables, so I faced an afternoon alone except for Nadine and Killer. I tried a hamburger with Cape Cod chips, Sam Adams and the sounds of Ella Fitzgerald for lunch, but the hurt didn't let anything go down very easily. Nothing on television made sense and I didn't feel like a movie.

When I had called and talked to Vito Corsetti yesterday about the winning his race, he was guarded. There must have been something on his mind, and that worried me.

I'd just given most of my lunch to the dogs when the phone rang. It was Vito.

"There was an FBI guy named Hardy by here today. He wanted to talk about you and where the money came from to pay for the horses. Thank God Santos wasn't here. I just told him I didn't know or give a shit where you all got your money. I got a source inside the FBI who tells me he's trying to get you on a money laundering rap, hoping you'll roll on me. He's got nothin' cause I ain't done nothin' with you," he lied for the record.

Before I hung up, Vito asked if I could meet with Jimmy Slacks at a small bar in Saugus in an hour. He said it was a place where he doubted anyone knew me.

"There hasn't been this much action around here in a long time, Colin. There are big eyes watching my place day and night. The locals and the Feds are both poking their noses around here."

He seemed relieved to change the subject.

"I like the way our horses are running. I saw the late night re-run of that little horse's race if you could call that a race. He won by a mile. What was the purse?"

"About fifteen thousand. Your share will more than pay the tab for the month. That's three wins and a third. We've made about thirty grand in two months," I proudly pointed out.

"Just talk with Jimmy and keep your head down, son. Shit's starting to fly around here between that fucking Russian and me. I don't want you and the horses involved. Be really cool, Colin. You've got nothing to do with any of my business, hear?"

"Fine, Vito. Take care of yourself."

The Home Plate Bar in Saugas had Red Sox photos, bats with grime hiding the yellow tint of the wood and gloves like I used in grade school hung on the wall. The light was too dim to get a good look at anyone, so I stood by the cigarette machine for a minute or so to let my eyes adjust.

Through the filthy, heavy air I could see half a dozen old-timers at the bar, an old couple arguing at one of the tables, and Jimmy Slacks nursing a beer at the back booth. I made my way over to Jimmy after a nod in his direction and a stop at the bar for a Sam Adams.

"Glad you could make it," he said as we shook hands.

"Missed you at the races the last few times. Your pal Milos was there when the big horse got hurt, but no one showed up to get their picture taken on Thursday."

"Man, Colin. That little red horse is my favorite. I watched the rerun with Vito last night and I thought the old man was going to have a heart attack, he was so happy. That horse just flew. No one was ever going to catch him. And let me tell you, the way things are going right now, Vito needs a little good news," Jimmy said as he took a long pull on his beer.

"He told me it was shaky around your place with the Feds looking down your throat."

"That's why he wanted me to meet you away from the office. Some things are going down pretty soon you got nothing to do with. He don't want you to call or come near the bar until everything cools off. He don't want to be connected with the horses. That could be a headache in itself. You done lied to the locals and the Feds about Vito and the horses. Then that FBI guy Hardy tells him they got you on the money laundering. Vito said for you to just clam up about Santos and the money you got for the horses. You don't know nothin' from nothin'. Bad memory... huh?

"He wants me to talk with you about Santos. He don't trust him anymore. There's stuff happening that only Milos would know about. I shouldn't tell you, but people are coming in to pay off their loans early."

"That must be good," I said.

"Nah. We make our money off the vig. Sometimes they pay as much as two hundred percent. Money in the bank don't make shit. They ain't coming back like they should. The street says some of our accounts are doing business with Connie Tass. People who've been with us for years, even generations, are staying away from our bars. They don't want to answer questions or take out no more new loans. The bread business is one thing, but street money is another. What Tass is doin' to our loan business is a real problem."

He pulled at the beer, emptying the bottle, so I got two more. Jimmy continued, "Vito don't exactly know I'm telling you about the money thing, so don't say anything when you talk to him. Colin, I respect you. I mean, we're like friends. I know you're smart as hell and been around. Sometimes I need to talk to somebody. Except for Vito, I don't trust anybody now."

"Look, Jimmy, I have problems of my own and respect you as a friend. You never have to worry about me repeating what we say to anyone, even the boss. What you say stays with me," I promised.

"Well, the boss don't want you telling Milos nothing. Don't let him know we might be on to him if he's messing us over. Some of our ledger stuff is reaching the Russian. We can tell. The other night I followed Milos to a bar in South Boston. I know he met with Nikki Zepoff, the 'hitter' from Southie. I shouldn't even tell you, but the boss is worried Milos might talk about our horse business. He's worried about the cash for the horses. We think Milos is talking to the Feds to save his ass, and that means your ass. Vito's already told all this to Ian and some of the other right people. We got help on our side, but if somethin' bad gets in the papers, we got trouble. Vito… he's got a newspaper pal. That'll help.

"Vito's afraid someone might reach out to you. He wants you to be ready. He said for you to talk about this shit wid' that little Irish lawyer of yours."

I took a long sip of my Sam Adams and asked, "What could I need my lawyer for, Jimmy?"

"Vito said to tell you... the Feds... they subpoenaed all of Milos' records on di Vinci Stable this morning. Milos is down there talking with them as we speak. That fuckin' bean counter is dangerous to you and to us!

"Whatever you do, tell them nothing but the truth and as little of that as you can. Those are Vito's words. He trusts you. You've never done nothin' but good for us. Milos don't know we know the Feds have his stuff and he's meeting with them. Our guy on the inside says for you to be ready. Don't talk to the Feds without Mr. Ian, no matter what that little shit from Miami tells you." Jimmy finished his beer and stood up.

"I got to go. You be careful, Colin."

I was so confused and alarmed, I drank another Sam Adams, then another... and another. It was almost ten o'clock when I got home. The message light was going wild. I was hoping it was Annie. It wasn't.

"Colin, my boy, this is Ian. I'm gone for the evening. Call me at my office in the morning. Talk to no one, until we talk first."

CHAPTER THIRTY-SEVEN

When I called Ian after training hours, he asked me to come to his office that afternoon.

"What's your schedule?" I asked.

"My last class is over at noon. I have no court this afternoon and I've cleared my calendar after 2:30."

"Do you want me before three o'clock?"

"You bet. The Feds are going to be here at four."

"What Feds? What the hell do they want? I can understand the locals, if it has anything to do with Old John and the mess at the barn, but why the Feds?"

"I'll fill you in when you get here. Bring any paperwork about the horses and di Vinci Stable. Bring any checks, like bill payments and statements from the track, regarding earnings and disbursements. Make sure Vito Corsetti's name is on nothing you bring into my office. This is about you and your connection with the di Vinci Stable and Santos.

"This might be a fishing expedition, but it could be real trouble. Agent Hardy is very anxious to talk with you. They agreed to come here because I was going to stall them before bringing you to FBI headquarters. I wanted to get them on my turf and thought they'd fight coming here, but they agreed. They must have something they feel very confident about, son.

"Don't be late, and don't tell anyone we're meeting with the Feds. We have to be closed-mouthed from here on in. Make sure you don't talk with Santos or Vito. We can't be too careful."

When I hung up, I went to the track kitchen and sat at the bar. I ordered two hot dogs, chips and a Sam Adams. People stayed clear of me. I ate my lunch, and no one except the bartender said a word or came near me. I saw plenty of people I knew. I felt like I had some kind of disease.

Top Shot was jumping out of his skin, so I decided I'd look

for a race at a mile for older horses and hope the dry weather held up. Crystal Run was also nearing another start. I only needed two more breezes before running Sliding Scale. With two wins in three weeks, I decided to give Cherokee Moon three weeks off. Deeper River would be at least another month, according to Emmy, before his torn quarter healed.

Training and making plans for races made the hot dogs go down quickly. I was on my third Sam Adams when I looked at my watch and saw it was almost two o'clock. The afternoon traffic wasn't bad as I made my way past the Big Dig and arrived at Ian's office at 2:45. Ellen waved me towards Ian's office. "Colin, you win every race don't you?"

"I've been lucky lately."

As I passed her desk, she said, "I hope your luck will last today, honey."

I always wondered what the relationship between Ellen and Ian must be like. She'd been with him so long she's like an extension of the old man. I don't think anything happens in his life that she doesn't have input or an opinion.

Ian had his back turned to me, talking on the phone. He turned to face me as he hung up, "Colin, there's a lot of crap going on in your life, and none of it's good. This guy Hardy from Miami is a bulldog and he's set his sights on you. But I don't think he wants to convict you or take you to trial. He thinks you will help him with Vito before you'll go to jail. He's going make his plea pitch when he gets here.

"Hardy's bringing Watson from the local FBI office. He's got 20 years in at the bureau, and has no love for Hardy. I told you, from time to time he plays cards with me. They may both work for the FBI, but are nothing alike. Hardy will try to walk over anybody to get what he wants. With him, anything that will lead to an indictment is okay. I'm sure he thinks Vito does business with you under the table spending dirty money on the horses."

"Shit," I moaned.

" Colin, let's look at this from Hardy's point of view. If he can connect you to Corsetti's business, even legal, that's all he needs. You'll be their leverage. Guilty or not, they can charge you with a felony for lying to the FBI about buying horses for Vito. They think they can get you to testify against Vito in return for not going to jail."

"Felony?" I shouted. "I've never even committed a misdemeanor that I know about."

"Did Vito or his man give you cash to buy horses with?"

I thought for a second and decided not to get smart or play the devil's advocate. "Santos gave me cash to buy the horses and Vito is nowhere on the record as having anything to do with di Vinci Stable."

"Colin, when they come in here everything you say will either be taken down in notes or taped. If you tell the smallest lie, it's a felony and can get you four years for lying to a federal officer and four more for obstruction of justice. If you answer that you didn't know Vito had anything to do with the horses or that he never gave you money, then you will have committed a felony if they can get conflicting testimony from a witness or better yet, two. Personally, I think Santos is a rat and is giving you up as part of a deal. They wouldn't be closing in this fast if they didn't have a rat. If they do, you're dead. We have to satisfy them… or else! Did Vito ever give you cash or ever tell someone in your presence to take his cash and give it to you?"

" He told Santos to meet me before I left for New York to

buy Sliding Scale and give me the cash to buy him."

"How did you get the cash through the airport in Boston?"

"I wore it in a money belt. They didn't check."

"Why not just declare the money? How much cash did you have?"

"A little more than a quarter million. I didn't want to show it to them because they'd have asked questions. Carrying that much cash after the 9/11 security alerts, I'd have been on the grill all day. If I couldn't tell them exactly where it came from, I was dead and could have lost all the money."

Ian's voice was stern. "Colin, were you worried that the money on that day and the time you went to Miami was illegal, knowing what you do about Vito Corsetti and Milos Santos? The truth, Colin!"

"I was worried, to say the least."

"We may have to claim you were worried about the funds, but you didn't ask questions because you wanted to train the horses. It's called, 'Willful blindness or conscious avoidance'. It lays the groundwork for a good case showing a pattern of crime if they have witnesses or telephone tapes that show you knew the money was bad.

"Now, Colin, when they arrive, ask me before you say anything. Don't answer any question without at least looking into my eyes. I'll let you know if it's all right to answer. Son, don't tell them anything that's not absolutely necessary today. Don't volunteer anything and, for God's sake, don't get mouthy and start offering any explanations or information. Let 'em fish and we'll watch. If they ask you about Vito Corsetti, be evasive and say you met him at his restaurant with Milos. If you want to talk with me privately before answering, just tell me. We'll step into the bathroom behind us. Ask me a hundred times to step out if you need to. But, don't blurt out anything. You may think you're more clever or smarter than these guys, but you are not.

"They're professionals and have you in the dark. You don't have a chance of avoiding jail, in my opinion, based on what you've just told me. Let me help with the questions. Remember, you don't have to be guilty to be convicted of a felony. It happens every day. The Feds have no conscience when it comes to getting convictions," he said sternly.

"I've never been more concerned for you in my life. Get smart-assed with them, and you're dead. Make no mistake, these guys are here to hang your butt."

There was a knock and Ellen looked around the door. "They're here. Do you want coffee?"

"Send them in and no coffee," Ian said. "Make them ask for it. They're not getting anything free today."

I'd never seen Martin Watson before, but I recognized Hardy from the local police station. He looked like he came out of one of those machines in Arlington which crank out Young Republican Jaycees non-stop. We shook hands all around and Hardy said he was going to tape the conversation. Ian had told me it was a favorite trick for Feds to just take notes and avoid tapes, then lie about what was in their notes. He smiled at Hardy.

"That's fine. You won't mind my using a tape recorder as well so there'll be no confusion," Ian stated, as he pulled his recorder from his desk drawer and punched it on before Hardy could answer.

Home field advantage, I thought as we began.

Hardy looked me straight in the eye and snapped the first question. "Do you know a thoroughbred trainer in New York named Carlos Reyes? He's a witness for the government in an investigation that involves you, Mr. O'Hearn."

I looked at Ian. He left his seat and led me into the bathroom.

"I told you, no surprises! The first name out of his mouth is someone I've never heard about. He's identified him as a government witness against you. Shit!"

"He's the trainer in New York who sold me Sliding Scale. I paid him the quarter million. He's the one who took the cash and he's a real asshole."

Ian was seated on the toilet, staring at the floor. "Just stay with the game plan. Did you ever mention Corsetti's name to this guy, Reyes?"

"Never. I said some things about Milos Santos, but I never talked about Vito with anyone in the horse business."

My voice dropped down to a whisper. "I had some papers I brought with me. They're in a folder, at the table with the Feds. I left my pen in a special way so if it was moved, I can tell if someone has fingered my papers while we're in the bathroom.

"Ian, when I get back to the table, watch where my pen is. I left it half covered by my folder sticking out at an angle. If Hardy looked inside the folder we'll know that they've searched the folder behind our backs."

We returned to the table and my pen was six inches from the folder. I nodded to Ian. He smiled. It was good to know the good guys weren't so good.

I handed the papers to Ian and he read them again. He smiled again.

"Do you know this man, Reyes?" Hardy demanded.

"Of course. He's the trainer I purchased Sliding Scale from in New York on behalf of di Vinci Stable."

"How much was the purchase price?"

"Two hundred and fifty grand."

"By personal check or cashier's check?" Hardy asked.

"Neither. I paid for the horse with cash."

Hardy frowned, "We'll get back to how you came by the cash and took it to Aqueduct, but we have a problem. Reyes said the horse was purchased for two hundred thousand."

I looked at Ian and he raised an eyebrow before nodding.

"I paid the man two fifty. If he told you two hundred, then he lied to you and skimmed his client out of fifty thousand. Crooked, untrustworthy trainers pull that stunt all the time."

"Maybe it was you helped skim the man on your end of the fifty thousand?" Watson suggested.

"That didn't happen and I can prove it."

I looked at Ian, who had a pleased look in his eye as he passed the folder with my papers back to me.

"Here's the bill of sale, signed by both of us. You'll note the price was two hundred and fifty thousand dollars."

Hardy was irritated. "That's just a bill of sale. It means nothing."

I slid the receipt for the cash to Watson, who looked pleased. Hardy frowned when he saw the receipt for the cash, signed by both Reyes and myself.

"I'll need that back," Ian said.

It was time for Hardy to win one, so he pushed a paper of his own across the table towards Ian.

"This subpoena is self-explanatory. You have forty-eight hours to comply."

To calm my fears, Ian showed me the subpoena. I had to give just about every business paper, horse or otherwise, and my tax returns for the last five years to the Feds. This also included my phone and bank records, personal and business.

I felt invaded. It was the feeling you'd have if you came home and your house had been ripped off.

Hardy picked up where he left off. "How did you get the cash to Mr. Reyes at Aqueduct?"

"I carried it on the US Airways shuttle from Logan."

"Did the security officials ask you about that much cash?"

"No. They seemed to be more worried that my shoes had too much manure on them and that I smelled like horse shit."

Neither Ian nor the Feds thought my answer was funny.

"You can cut the humor, O'Hearn," Hardy said. "This is very serious business."

"I can assure you I'm as serious as a heart attack, sir. Both the female agent who made me take my barn shoes off and the man with the wand were very serious when they complained about my smell. The man's tag was Charles Williams and the woman's tag said Joan Riley. It may have been O'Reilly, but I'm pretty sure it said Riley. You can check with airport security. The date is on the bill of sale."

"How did you happen to remember the names of the agents?" Watson asked.

"There was a time in my life when I was trained never to miss a detail, especially being detained or questioned, sir. It's like the pen one of you moved to look through my folder when we were in the bathroom, out of your sight. Whoever moved it failed to place it back even close to the way I'd it arranged when I left."

Watson looked straight at Hardy. It was easy to see from the narrowing of Watson's eyes that Hardy had looked in the folder.

The home team had made a point. We may have had problems, but we were going to be a tough nut to crack. The Feds may be the big potatoes at the table, but the little potatoes are hardest to peel. I was in no mood to be peeled.

Hardy quickly tried to gain control of the questioning. "Do you know Vito Corsetti?"

"The owner of di Vinci Stable, Milos Santos, is the accountant for a restaurant called Little Venice. Corsetti owns it. I've been there three or four times and Milos has introduced me to Mr. Corsetti."

"What can you tell us about Corsetti?" Watson asked.

"Very little. He loves horse racing and the Red Sox. Since I do as well, that's what we mainly talked about. Oh… There is one thing about his business I do know.

Hardy looked hopeful, "And that is?"

"He has the best macaroni and gravy I've ever tasted. That is, with the exception of Mosca's in New Orleans. If I weren't afraid to wear out my welcome, I think I'd eat there every night."

"Does Corsetti have ownership interest in di Vinci Stable?" Hardy asked.

"The papers in the office, which I checked when I took the job, list Milos Santos as the sole owner. Mr. Corsetti loves to talk about the races, but he's never indicated he has an ownership in the stable… .Santos hired me."

Ian kicked my shin.

"Corsetti's not involved, not that I know of," I added.

"Why do you think you were hired by Milos Santos?" Watson asked.

"You'd have to ask Mr. Santos. Maybe because he liked the way I trained. Maybe he liked the fact that I had terrible horses and still won thirty percent of my races."

"What about the horses you purchased in Miami before the

Aqueduct deal?" Hardy continued.

"They've run well. They've won three races in five starts. Should have won four, but Deeper River grabbed a quarter and almost pulled his heel off."

Hardy was getting annoyed. "No, I don't give a damn how they've run. I want to know how you paid for them. Were they paid for in cash or maybe cashier's checks?"

I answered, after looking at Ian, "Some of both."

"What was the largest cashier's check?"

"Around ten thousand."

"Were any of the checks for $10,000 or more?"

"I don't think so."

"Didn't you find that strange?"

"Maybe strange, but not illegal, Mr. Hardy. I was broke, overdrawn in my checking account by more than a thousand dollars, and had to borrow money from my groom to feed my horses. No trainer in that condition would look a gift horse in the mouth. The man asked me to find five or six horses to train. If he wanted me to pay for them with pennies I'd have done so as long as it didn't break any laws."

Hardy leaned forward, "Mr. O'Hearn, since you think you know some law, did it ever occur to you that the cash you received and any cashier's checks under the legal reporting limit may have been obtained through illegal means and were being laundered?"

"Define laundering," I said, trying for time to answer what I knew was the most important question I'd been asked.

"I'm sure you know what I'm talking about."

Ian saw that I was stuck and chipped in. "We'll stipulate, for the record, that Colin has a general knowledge about laundering illegal money."

"You know, Mr. Hardy, it may have been in the back of my mind that it was strange Santos brought me money to buy horses in the manner he did. Santos is a CPA, and if he was doing something wrong, it would be his CPA ass in the sling. Me, I just wanted to buy and train his horses."

Watson broke in. "Just a few more questions for today, you guys. Mr. O'Hearn, did Mr. Corsetti ever tell you he had an interest in any of the horses you bought?"

Ian jumped in. "Asked and answered, Martin."

"No, Ian, we asked if Corsetti had an interest in the di Vinci Stable. This is different. I want to know if Mr. Corsetti gave Mr. O'Hearn money for the purchase of a horse. Or, in the presence of or to the knowledge of O'Hearn, did Mr. Corsetti instruct anyone else, namely Mr. Santos, to give him money for the purchase of a horse or horses?"

Well, there it was. If I said yes, I was tied to Vito in the horse business and I would be guilty in the eyes of the Feds for lying, obstructing justice and maybe even money laundering. If my answer is no, then I'm sure as hell guilty of lying and perjury.

Ian kicked my shin. "We want to think about that one before answering the question in the manner in which it was asked, Martin. You've thrown me one of those 'have you stopped beating your wife?' questions."

Hardy could barely contain himself as he packed up his notes and prepared to leave.

"Well, Mr. Higgins, you're going to have to answer that question and dozens tougher, before a grand jury or at trial."

"Maybe not, Mr. Hardy."

"We already know the answer, Ian," Martin Watson said to his old friend.

"How could you, Martin?"

Hardy turned on his way out the door. "Because we have a second witness, who has first-hand knowledge of Colin's relationship with Mr. Corsetti and his involvement with the horses you purchased. He's been granted immunity. These two witnesses will sink you, O'Hearn."

The door closed behind them and we sat stunned, not wanting to look at each other.

Finally Ian sighed, "I said no surprises, Colin. No fucking surprises!"

CHAPTER THIRTY-EIGHT

I stopped at the bookkeeper's office after leaving Ian's office, and after showing her the subpoena, asked Alice to copy all my records for the Feds. She frowned, and asked me how widespread I thought the investigation might be. I assured her it involved only di Vinci Stables, Milos Santos and myself.

"I told you those people were trouble, Colin, but you had to chase the easy money. I know you'd never do anything illegal and so do the stewards and the guys in the racing secretary's office."

"How the hell did they hear about it?"

"There was an investigator here earlier this afternoon. He got statements from the guys in the other offices, pulled the commission records and talked with the stewards. You know how it is around here, Colin. Everybody knows everybody else's damn business on the backside. You're going to be okay if what we gave them means anything.

"The only thing they made an issue of was whether anyone other than Santos had anything to do with di Vinci Stables. They took copies of the checks and all the other paperwork. Santos's name was the only one showing."

Evening stables went by in a blur and I decided I needed a break from everyone connected with horse racing and my troubles. I drove to toward the ocean and parked as close as I could to the waterfront. After leaving my truck, I walked aimlessly along the decaying Revere Beach boardwalk trying to organize my thoughts and quiet my fears. My life was going down the toilet.

I stopped at Kelly's Roast Beef to pick up something to eat. I had no appetite, but figured I needed to keep up my strength. Things were starting to look ugly.

Back at the cottage, the dogs begged with their eyes as I ate and listened to Sarah Vaughn and Jerry Vale. I could feel the scotches taking hold as my thoughts turned to Annie. I knew better than to call her at her father's. She'd get in touch if she wanted to talk to me. I called her cell phone and got the old message. I left a message that Lonely Aunt was in on Friday and Sliding Scale was in the fifty thousand dollar stakes race on Saturday. I was treating him with the "kitchen sink" as a bleeder. I said for her to pray I could hold him and get a clean test. With nothing left to say to the machine, I hung up. There was no way I was going to leave a message about the Feds.

Annie knew my bleeder jug by heart. It included Premrin, DMSO and extra lasix. What I was really counting on was my "China tea." The concoction was of Asian origin and had proven to be effective on known bleeders. I picked up the ingredients in Chinatown. Yunan-Pau came in a box containing eight small bottles. The dosage, which is completely legal and won't test, contains a brown powder with a tiny red pea which must be crushed, before warm water is added.

The powder first came to light after the Viet Nam War. The Viet Cong used it, stuffing it into gunshot wounds. The powder stopped the bleeding, or at least slowed it down. Our soldiers said the Cong could fight for hours before bleeding out or getting help.

Chinese stores sell it to women to help regulate their periods. After the legalization of lasix, Yunan-Pau dropped from sight. I finally found a chemist who explained the powder and the proper application. A lot of people have used the powder with no success. One needed to know both the dosage and the importance of timing the application. When Sliding Scale started down the backside of Suffolk on Saturday, I knew that, if it was possible to stop the bleeding problem, the

Yunan-Pau would get him home.

I turned my scotch-soaked brain to Milos Santos, who I felt sure was now a federal witness against me. I had to find a way to get Vito's horses away from Milos. If someone chopped down a tree and it fell on Milos Santos tomorrow, di Vinci Stable's hidden owner, Vito Corsetti, would be up the creek.

Ian and I had discussed the issue and decided a sale with new, clean cash was the best solution. If Milos was paid four hundred and fifty thousand dollars, a fair price for the horses, how would the cash get back to Vito? I warned Ian that Milos, feeling the pressure of being on the outside these days, might take the money and skip the country. Being robbed of that much money, Vito would 'sic' Jimmy Slacks on Santos. Now that Vito thinks Milos is selling him out to the Feds, he'll probably get Jimmy to take care of the bastard. That would create a worse problem. The horses would be put up for auction. Ian and Vito would have to find another surrogate to buy the animals a second time.

Somehow, we had to get Milos to sell the horses on paper with enough juice to pass muster with the stewards and the Feds, but without costing Vito almost a half million dollars to buy his own horses.

By the time I got to the track kitchen the next morning, I could see the stares and hear the whispering. I had squared things with Jock by giving him the short version of the Feds' involvement. I would never put him in a position of liability by telling him who owned di Vinci Stable. He knew nothing of Vito Corsetti and I planned to keep it that way. Anyway, Jock could put on the best "dumb darkie" show I've ever seen. The Feds would play hell trying to trip him up under oath.

Arch Hale was waiting for me in the track kitchen. "What

the hell's going on, Colin? Why are the Feds all over the track with subpoenas?"

"Arch, the less you know, the better off you'll be. I can tell you that most of this has to do with the murders still unsolved. Some of the locals, and even the Feds, are still looking at me since I had the beef with the guy who turned up dead in the snow pile. As to Old John's murder, you know as much as I do. They've subpoenaed all my personal and training records. They're just fishing." I shrugged and changed the subject.

"Anyway, I have horses to train. We have a good shot in the stake on Saturday. I'm sure you've seen Sliding Scale in the overnight."

Arch nodded. "I see you haven't named a rider on that filly you have for Annie Collins in the non-winners of two. Can we ride that filly?"

I shook my head. "No way. She's a crazy filly, Arch. She has this thing about women and I've decided to ride Libby Hunter," I explained.

"You know, Colin, Steve's going to be pissed. He has no mount in that race. He's done such a good job for you, he thinks you owe him the ride on all of your horses if he's open."

"I tell you what, Arch. You tell Steve if he's stupid enough to think he has 'first call' on my horses and insists on pushing me on my training decisions when I have got so much crap on my mind, he can take his tack down the road."

"Look, Colin, he had a chance to ride the two-to-one favorite in the fifty thousand, but I told him he should go with you. When we looked up that gray horse of yours and saw he got beat twenty lengths last time and bled, he went ballistic. I told him how good you were with the bleeders, but you know Steve. He's still hot under the collar about that little girl showing him up last time. He's pissed I passed on the favorite from New York and put him on your bleeder and doesn't want to ride him."

I glared at Arch. "You go tell your rider he can take the favorite in the stake and it won't bother me one little bit. Tell…"

"Hold on, Colin… here he comes. You can tell him yourself and I won't have to get yelled at."

Steve Casey took a seat. "Did Arch tell you I wanted to ride that filly in the third tomorrow?"

"He told me, but I have Libby Hunter on the filly. She needs a female touch."

"What the hell's the matter with my touch? This is the second time you've given away one of my rides to that kid. I see your horse is a bleeder and got beat twenty lengths the last time out in the big race. It's not fair. If I take the shit… I should get the good stuff too!"

"Look, Steve, I told you the last time you got in my face about my training choices that you could haul your tack. I see the guy with the favorite still hasn't named a rider. I'm sure you told him to keep the horse open until you talked to me. So, Steve, I'll name Libby on both horses and you ride the favorite. I'm taking you off my horses for a while. Don't come back under my shed row. Now, get the hell away from my table," I snapped.

Enraged, he shouted his response, "The way I hear it, Colin, you might not have a shed row around here for long. You can kiss my ass!" He walked away toward several of his fellow jockeys, who pointed at him laughing and giving him high-fives when he got to the table.

Arch Hale shook his head, "We have to put up with a lot of shit in this game, don't we pal?"

"Arch," I said, "that's one little shit you have to put up with, not me. You can take the riders at a second rate track like Suffolk Downs and throw them all into a feed sack and pull out any one. There's not much difference between them. They all think they're better than they really are."

"He'll be back, Colin."

"If I can get that little girl from New York to stay, will you take her book, Arch?"

He grinned. "That kid can ride circles around the jocks here. You get her to stay and I'll drop Steve and his big mouth in a heartbeat. You know how easy it will be to book an apprentice who can ride like she does? We'll make a killing."

When I got back to the barn, I called Libby Hunter at Aqueduct. She was really excited about the two rides. "I thought you'd never ask me to stay up there, Colin. I have a friend who gallops in the morning and ponies in the afternoon. She wants me to share her apartment in Needam. I told her I was hoping you'd ask."

I told Arch that Libby was coming when I went to the track kitchen during the break. He got up and walked to the jock's table, where Steve was holding court in his usual loud voice.

I saw Arch toss his condition book to Steve and say, "Fill it yourself, asshole. You're not smart enough to tell when you're well off with friends like Colin and me."

He walked out the kitchen door and down the steps without looking back. Steve ran after him, calling from the porch.

When I got home that night, my message light was blinking. I had one call and it was Annie. "Colin, I'm sorry I can't get you in person, but a message might keep us from saying things we can never take back. I have decided not to have the baby. It's too late for you to do anything about it. My father helped me take care of it here. It's over and I'm going to stay with Daddy. Good luck and leave a message about the filly on my machine."

CHAPTER THIRTY-NINE

I was in the tack room, getting ready to run Annie's mare on Friday with my stomach full of snakes. I was concentrating on the upcoming race, but kept thinking about Annie having an abortion without even talking to me. We've lost our only chance to enjoy a complete life together. There would be no way now that we could look each other in the eye without thinking about the reasons for terminating the pregnancy. My cell phone rang and I almost ignored it.

"It's me, Colin," said Annie.

I tried to say something, but was lost.

"It's over, Colin. I did it on my own because I knew you could talk me out of it and I was afraid... afraid of how I could handle life with you. There's so much going on with you now," she sobbed.

There was nothing more I could say that wouldn't hurt her at such a fragile moment. I vowed to myself I wouldn't answer in anger.

"Annie... are you okay?"

"I'm confused and uncomfortable, but it's over. I don't want to talk about it anymore. There's something I do have to talk to you about, though.

"The FBI found me at Dad's house yesterday. Some agent from Miami said terrible things about you. They suspect you of murder. They say you're tied up with the Mafia and have washed drug money. Daddy was with me while I talked to them. You can guess what he said. He blames you for so much of my pain."

I was silent on my end of the line.

"Colin, get over it. It's done. Daddy helped me with the doctor. Our life has to go on. Take care of your problems and yourself. I don't think it would have worked. I'm staying here with Daddy. He'll let me work in the clinic."

"Look, Annie," I said, "I'm so sorry I put you in such a position. I'm not going to beat you over the head for your choice. I would have loved to be the father of our child. It will always haunt me."

"I didn't tell the FBI anything, Colin. I just said we once were lovers, but now you're just training a horse for me. I said we were only together once in the last five years and I had no idea about who you were doing what with. They left here satisfied… I think."

"Your filly runs tomorrow, Annie. What do you want to do with her after that?"

"Just what we planned. Run her and see if she can stand up to racing mentally and physically. If she's shot like they say, make breeding plans for her. Maybe she'll earn enough to take care of my recent expenses."

"Send me your medical bills, Annie. You know I'll send you the money right away. Give me your father's address. I'll need to write you news about the filly… the kind you can't get on the Internet, that is if you still don't want to talk to me personally."

"Leave me a message about how she comes out of the race. I want this to be our last conversation. It's not that I hate you, Colin, it's just too hard. There will always be a part of me that loves you." She gave me her father's address and hung up. I sat in the tack room and stared at the wall for what seemed like hours.

The next day, an hour before Lonely Aunt's race, Jock stuck his head around the door. "It's race time, Colin. We have to tack up that filly. Tino is going to take our pony so she'll stay calm. I also got the paddock judge to let us bring the pony to her saddling stall."

"Thanks, Jock. Tom says we can keep out of traffic and take

her straight to the gate without warming up with the other horses. She's got the nine hole on the outside."

"You know what they say, Boss. Last in, first out."

I don't think I've ever wanted to win a race more than I wanted this one for Annie. She'd had so much fun designing her colors of cream and green. Three hoops around the green body and arms of dark cream. You could pick them out anywhere especially on the front end, where I prayed she would be.

I sat in my chair and looked at the needle in my hand. It had three-tenths of a cc of Acepromazine behind the plunger. I had never given a horse an illegal injection before a race in all my years of training. I knew Emmy had pushed the envelope for me many times. The lasix and bleeder jug would probably mask the ace, so there was little chance of getting a bad test.

The tiny bit of Ace had worked wonders taking the edge off the filly when I breezed her. She'd broken her maiden by twenty-two lengths at Keeneland in her first start. If I could keep her on the track, she'd blow away non-winners of two.

I went to the hay stall, emptied the syringe on the floor and threw it behind the wall. If I got a bad test with Annie's filly, it would have been cement proof she was right about me. Winning a race with this filly wasn't a good enough reason to cheat. I felt better, doing it the right way, but I was scared to death Lonely Aunt would flip over before the start. I thought of the danger to little Libby Hunter. I was sure I'd made the right decision this time.

I decided to use the figure-eight noseband, to keep the bit in place and make it harder for her to get her mouth open. I also decided to use the little ten inch French martingale, which was nothing but a strip of leather with rings on either end. It would help Libby keep her head positioned and give her better control. It was Jock who came up with the clincher.

We'd agreed to use the shadow roll along with the noseband. The sheepskin roll would keep her from jumping shadows and the harrow marks. When Jock started to put the shadow roll on, I almost had to bail out of the stall.

"What's that smell, Jock?" Tino screamed.

"What is that wet shit on the noseband?" I asked.

"The goat can't go with the pony, so I'm gonna fool her," Jock said, as he fitted the noseband. Lonely Aunt didn't move her head and seemed content.

Jock explained. "I've been letting the goat sleep on the shadow roll and I dipped it in goat piss before I tied it around the filly's neck last night for her to get used to the smell. It doesn't bother her and she thinks that old goat's right beside her. She can't see beside or behind her because of the blinkers," he laughed.

Jock knows his horses because he thinks like a horse. I couldn't wait to see Charlie, the paddock identifier, try to roll her lip with that stinking thing on her nose. It was certain to break the tension.

With Tino on the pony, I got Grady to help me lead the filly to the paddock. He took a shank on the right side, getting his huge body between Lonely Aunt and the stands. I took the shank on the left side and didn't use a lip chain to control her. I was afraid it would do more harm than good. The filly wasn't going to climb over Grady and I felt we could both keep her on the ground if she tried to flip. She couldn't be forced or manhandled.

As we walked, I tried not to draw in the foul air. When Grady first took the shank he stepped back, saying, "What the fuck is that rotten smell?"

I gave him some cotton and put some in my own nose.

"What a bunch of misfits we are," Grady said. "Here we go, a horse that smells like goat piss, a half-pint Jamaican on a half dead lead pony, a six-foot-seven queer and a man heading for prison all leading a crazy mare to the paddock."

"I love it. It's got game," I said.

The crowd was no larger than usual, but I couldn't help feeling they were crowding us. I felt like they were screaming at my filly, shaking their programs in her face, but of course they weren't.

Lonely Aunt walked like a perfect lady from the barn to the paddock. I'd waited until the last possible scratch warning for her arrival. I'd told the paddock judge I was going to be last, but to keep the stewards off his case, he had to make a show of scolding me.

I'd also told two of the stewards my plans and they said to forget the warnings, they were just making a show for the other trainers in the paddock. They were going to fine me fifty bucks for arriving late in the paddock, but it would be money well spent, allowing me to set my own pace.

"What the hell's the matter with this horse," the Paddock Judge snapped as he stepped back without rolling her lip to check her tattoo. "There's something dead in her mouth."

I held my breath and rolled the lip for him to see the tattoo. I'm sure he never got close enough to see the number. He was out of the paddock before we moved into the saddling area.

Libby and her valet were waiting for us.

"What's that smell, Colin? It smells like goat piss," said Libby, laughing.

Grady took the saddle from the gagging valet and passed it over to me without touching the filly's back until the last second. I was terrified the valet would slap the saddle on carelessly, as they tend to do. I eased it onto her back with only the slightest sign of a hump. As I tightened the over girth, Tino shoved the head of the lead pony into the stall to comfort and cramp the filly. We both leaned on her so she couldn't jump one way or another.

In no time she was tacked and I only had a brief moment to remind Libby of her instructions. She'd stopped by the barn before going to the jock's room, spending thirty minutes in the stall with the filly and the goat. I tossed her aboard and said, "God bless, Libby, and have a safe trip."

"I'll just smooch her, Boss. We have things figured out between us. She knows I'm not about to hurt her," she said.

I hurried out onto the apron to watch the race from the benches with my field glasses. I wanted to be close to the track if anything went wrong and I had to get to either Libby or Lonely Aunt.

A strange calm settled within me. I shut out the crowd. Grady knew better than to talk. Being a trainer himself, he'd been in my situation many times. I could hardly believe my eyes as Libby and Tino moved along the outside fence, far from the field. The filly acted as if she was out for a morning jog. Her head was a little high and she was shaking her nose, but I could see Libby through my glasses. She was talking to the filly, rubbing her neck as they jogged.

I was beside myself as they reached the starting gate. The other horses were almost loaded. Tom put his best two men on her head with instructions not to mess with her or touch her ears. Tino and the pony stayed with her until almost the last step. He handed her to the loader, then turned the pony and was rubbing butts with the filly. Lonely Aunt gave a half-hearted kick at the pony as he gave her a friendly but reassuring push from behind. I let out my breath as she stepped in and the gate was closed.

She dwelt! That's what the *Racing Form's* chart of the race said. What really happened was that she was backing up and reared at the bell, but Libby didn't send her or throw her off her feet.

The gate was opened and the field was gone. Lonely Aunt was left standing.

The nearest filly in the field was ten lengths ahead when our girl decided that she, too, might race today. I looked through my glasses and saw only Lonely Aunt and one other horse in my field of vision. I swept to the quarter pole and saw the rest of the field more than twenty-five lengths ahead. The thought dashed through my mind that they were setting a deadly pace, thinking they could steal the race and Lonely Aunt would never have time to catch them in the stretch.

Libby took her time, getting the filly on a straight course before she began to move. She was a length behind the field at the half mile pole and flying. Libby was quiet as a mouse on her, just leaning into the filly, making her confident. She was sending her with a true jockey's touch.

When they turned into the stretch, they'd only passed one horse. I moaned as she drifted to the far outside. As Lonely Aunt raced through the stretch she was barely a yard off the outside rail. She went past horses without a speck of dirt hitting her. Ears stuffed with cotton blocked out both the sounds from the stands and screaming from the other riders. She was past the leaders and across the wire before they realized she'd won the race. That was twice Libby had outfoxed the Suffolk riders.

As the others pulled up on the backside shaking their heads, Libby slowly eased her mount, letting the filly find her own way to stop. She was at the top of the stretch before turning around and starting back to the winner's circle. She was just making the first turn toward the paddock when the last rider had dismounted and weighed out. There were no other horses in the paddock area when she got back for the weigh-in and photo.

Grady, Tino and the winning pair joined me in a very proud moment. It was one of those wins that will always stand out among hundreds, yet would only be another lost chart in the *Form*. Trainers would read the chart and never notice that the time for the last quarter was faster than the first, a true racing rarity.

I wondered how many trainers would ask themselves and others, "Just how fast is this filly?" If they asked me, and a few did, all I could answer was, "Hell, I don't know, and I probably never will."

CHAPTER FORTY

The moment was too sterile for words.

Annie's cell phone rang three times before the message played. I tried to tell her about the race and about Lonely Aunt, but I couldn't get the words out. There wasn't a way to explain my feelings. The time for a message elapsed as tears came to my eyes and any possibility of sound clung in my throat. I clicked off and waited a few minutes to compose myself, leaning against the bar in the deserted track kitchen. The usually buzzing crowd had made their bets and now huddled around the TV screens, waiting for the eighth race. I took a large drink of scotch and tried to call again.

This time, I was ready for the mechanical voice. I described the race and how the filly was so well behaved. I ended by saying she would be getting a check for a little over eleven thousand dollars after the urine sample cleared and a second check for fourteen thousand from me for her other expenses.

That was it. Over. I knew she'd cry, because the filly that had almost killed her and left her chained to those metal crutches had come back to make amends. She'd play the video over and over again.

I finished off my drink and left the bar, walking down the steps in a daze and almost bumping into people crossing the road to my barn. Sitting on the bench outside my tack room was Lefty Hamm.

"What's up, Lefty?"

"They say you got all kinds of problems, Colin, but I think you gotta' know that I've seen this guy kinda following you. He was hangin' outside the paddock for both of your last two races and I seen him again when you wuz' getting' your picture took after that filly did 'em in yesterday.

"This dude's trouble. When I last seen him I was wid' this guy... I don't know him... he just hangs out at track. I asked if he knew this guy wid' the mullet haircut and he said he didn't want to... that he was some kinda gangster. This guy said his wife worked for some high up FBI guy and he'd heard about this Southie mug from her. Anyway, I jus' thought you would want to know I seen this guy stalkin' you."

"You say he was near the winner's circle when I was getting the win picture taken the last several times?"

"Yeah... jus' starin' at you... like in a trance"

"Wait here a second, Lefty."

I went into the tack room and found the unopened photo envelope that the track photographer sends with the post race winning pictures. I took the last two win pictures outside for Lefty to see.

"See anyone in these two pictures?"

"Look at that fucker wid' de mullett... jus' starin' at you, Colin... both pictures."

Lefty was right. In both photos, a large man dressed in a leather jacket with a blue "watch cap" was standing just outside the enclosure with his hands in his pockets. He had greasy black hair, short on top and long in the back, and one of the cruelest faces I'd ever seen. The nose was offset, probably from plenty of punches. He had only a thin line where his lips should have been and wore black glasses, the Buddy Holly type. This was one scary guy. I had seen him, but I couldn't place him.

I took a fifty-dollar bill from my pocket and gave it to Lefty.

"Thanks for looking after me, pal."

He took the money, shoved it into the pocket of his "P" Jacket and looked up at me, saying, " You know Colin... 'dis is 'de only money I made off you 'de whole meet. I hope it ain't 'de last."

He turned on his heel and walked toward the kitchen, surely to get drunk on my fifty. The thought of doing the same struck me for a moment... then passed. I went to my old tack trunk and took out the cheap, throwaway cell phone and prepaid calling card. I called Jimmy Slacks's number. He answered on the first ring.

"Talk"

"Jimmy, it's me."

"What are you calling on, man?"

"A cheap cell phone and a prepaid card. Untraceable. The throw away kind."

"Ain't no hair on you, Trainer."

Before he could answer, I continued, "Jimmy, I know it's against every good advice we've heard, but you and me and Vito have to talk. Everything we do from here on in depends on what we decide to do together."

"Let me talk to Vito. I'll call you right back. I got your number on the caller ID."

Like that, he was gone. They're like that... men who operate in secret. They laugh and have fun when nothing is on the line, but when the stakes are raised, they get very serious. No side talk. They talk like they're paying for conversation by the word. Maybe they are. In this case, maybe too many words would cost us our lives.

Five minutes later, the cell phone rang. I answered and the voice was not Slacks, but Vito's.

"Won another one, huh? Regular winner, every time."

He didn't wait for a response. "You know the sea wall, runs along the water in front of all those run-down stores at

Revere Beach?"

"Sure," I answered.

"Be there in thirty minutes," Vito said. "I'll be in Slacks'
SUV, the black one. Make sure nobody follows you from the
track. And, Colin, it better be good to get me outta my office!"

He was gone, just like Jimmy Slacks.

I took the photos and my small cooler that I filled with ice
and beer from my fridge. The drive to the sea wall in Revere
Beach took only eight or nine minutes. Not ten… I know
ten minutes and this was not ten. My heart was in my throat
because I knew the man in the photos. I'd seen him somewhere, but I just couldn't remember. I was sure he was bad…
really bad.

Truth be told, there was something about Vito's tone that
scared the hell out of me. I wasn't usually afraid of any man,
but this was different. Corsetti was dangerous. His word was a
weapon. He could kill you with his voice, his command.

I kept thinking I really wanted Vito as a friend. I liked him
as much as any man I'd been involved with in Boston, except
for Ian Higgins. There's a fading history hanging onto Vito
Corsetti. He's probably the last of his kind.

We'd made such a bond the night I'd confronted him face to
face after he'd used me to carry his money. He probably ruined
me with that errand, but I knew what I was doing. I can't
blame him for taking advantage of a fool.

I thought about these things as I wove my way through
Beachmont toward Ocean Avenue. The street signs passed
like galloping by poles on a racetrack. North Shore, Campbell,
Eliot, Shirley, Franklin. By the time I reached the sea wall and
saw Jimmy's car parked in front of the picnic area, I was
positive I hadn't been followed.

As I approached Slacks's car, with my keys in my hand, the rear door opened. The hunting knife in the sleeve of my ski jacket was my only defense if things got bad. In close quarters, my knife had always served me well.

I got in and had to stifle a laugh. Vito's huge frame was squeezed into the front seat. He was wearing a heavy overcoat with the collar turned up and a cap like my dad and most Irishmen wore. He was not very Italian looking, this mobster from the North End.

As I got into the car, Jimmy asked, "What's this thing you know that dragged the Boss and me out."

Vito spoke with an edge. " Talk, Colin."

"I think you already know, Vito."

"What do you think? Milos is a rat? I already know that."

"We can look at it three ways, Vito. First, you had him kill the fat guy to piss off Tass. Second, maybe Milos did it on his own to set me up. He thinks maybe I'm getting too close to you and that I know something that could make you very angry at him. I figure we both know he stole from you.

"Third, maybe he's thrown in with the Russians and was doing a job for them to prove his loyalty. He's already crossed you. He stiffed you on the horse deal for about eighty-five grand by overcharging you for the horses. Any way you take it, Vito, as long as I'm around, I'm a threat to him."

He thought for a moment before responding. "Maybe there's a fourth reason for this happening. Maybe I told Santos to burn you. Not telling me he was stealing was a mistake, even if you figured I already knew."

My knife was heavy in the sleeve of my jacket. I'd reached the point where I didn't give a fuck what these guys did. If they wanted to try me, they'd both be dead in a few seconds. I could cut both their throats before either could get a hand on a weapon.

Vito had turned in his seat, leaning against the door to study me. I very carefully looked him in the eye and said in my most icy voice, "You didn't set that fuck on me, Vito. If you had, you would never have taken me into your confidence. I'd like to think we're still friends and we all, except Santos, can walk away from this thing as friends.

"I don't really care why Santos killed Dobbs with my shovel and tried to set me up. I just have to make sure he doesn't send me to prison. You can take any course of action, just help me stay out of jail."

His voice hardened. "You have to give me your word that, no matter how hot it gets for you, our deal is still good. You can't bring me into it. We have to keep me above all the shit about the money. Be loyal, Colin, and I'll back your play. Oh, by the way, either Zepoff or Santos got to the fat man at your barn... Dobbs. But not us.

"And, Colin, figure out a way I can keep my horses. I don't want to get fucked out of half million dollars by Santos. I like having my horses. Figure it out... you and Ian."

Before getting out of the SUV I took out the pictures and handed a photo to each... different photos.

"Anything in the background strike you as strange?"

Slacks mumbled, "That fuckin' Zepoff!"

"I got him too. He's just starin' at you, Colin. Like he's markin' you."

Slacks almost spit out, "He's gonna kill you Colin...
that's what he does best. I'll get your back for a while, as long as it takes."

"How long's a while, and as long as what takes?"

Vito leaned closer to me as if he was afraid of being taped. "As long as it takes for my Jimmy-boy to take the cock-sucker for a swim… right Jimmy?"

As I took back the photos and opened the door to leave, Vito said, " Watch your back, Colin. Jus' know Jimmy'll be around. You probably won't see him, but he'll be around. Zepoff's good… almost the best. But my boy here's better."

He patted my arm and I shut the door. It was a game for these guys. My life and they play games. How did I end up with a hit man after me, and the law trying to put me in prison?

When I got back to my truck, I called Ian and told him what had happened. He said I needed to get to his house right away. Ellen was fixing dinner and could throw on a steak for me. As I drove to Ian's, I knew things were coming to a head. I wasn't going to get out of this mess unscathed. The most important thing was to avoid going to prison. Ian said they'd deal me out if I gave up Vito. But the hell with that, Vito would send me swimming if I ratted on him.

I knew I'd never give up Vito. Santos, maybe, but never Vito.

When I pulled up in front of Ian's townhouse, there was a dark Suburban parked out front with Feds written all over it. Two men sat in the front seat as if waiting for me. I left my truck and crossed the street, walking right past them. Neither one moved.

"Please let me get inside with Ian," I prayed out loud.

I climbed the steps as Ellen opened the door and ushered me inside.

CHAPTER FORTY-ONE

Ellen showed me through the outer office and into Ian's sanctuary. He was seated behind his huge, spotless mahogany desk. Ian was usually hidden behind stacks of files, tests and research papers from his law school classes, but not tonight.

"I've cleared the desk, so to speak, because I need to give you my full attention. Thank God we're on break at the law school and I'm without any pressing cases. Now, tell me exactly what happened when you met with our friends," Ian said with a hint of irritation.

I showed Ian the two win photos, both of which he'd already received and sent on to Ellen to have framed for his home and office.

"I have both of these; I don't need another set."

I took a pen from my pocket and circled the man watching me in both photos.

He studied them both and said, " It's the same fellow in both and he appears to be looking right at you… in both. Do you know him?"

"I've seen him someplace, but couldn't place him until Slacks and Vito… "

"I told you not to talk to Vito."

"We can deal with my breaking your rules later, Ian, but my life is at stake here. His name is Nikki Zepoff. He's a killer who works for Tass. Both Vito and Slacks agree he's looking at me like I'm supper. I think Tass feels I can trace Santos to him and hang the killings of Dobbs and Old John around his neck. Vito has asked Slacks to watch my back until he can come up with a long term solution for Zepoff."

"This is a fine crock of crap. As if I don't have enough problems to deal with! The Feds are waiting outside now to talk again, hoping to come to a conclusion in your case."

"Before they come in, there's something else we have to talk about. The other night we talked about the horses' owner-ship and the possibility of Santos taking the funds if they are sold. He can make a deal any time on them and run with Vito's money. What if Santos sold them to Tass and tried to run with the money? As soon as the papers were changed in the Stewards' Office with a bill of sale from Santos, Tass would be free to kill the bastard and take his money back. He could hold Santos in his office while his lawyer takes the bill of sale to the Stewards.

"If something happens to Santos before di Vinci Stable is taken out of his name and the horses' papers are transferred, Corsetti is going to lose a half million dollars and the horses."

"He knows that and is really upset. It's not just the money. He's really wrapped up in the horses."

"I think I may have an answer to that one. You are still his Authorized Agent on record... right? "

"Unless Santos has revoked it."

"That's why pencils have erasers and someone invented white out."

Ian hit a buzzer and Ellen came into the office.

"Ellen, I see on the front monitor the car with the Feds is still out front. Would you go out and ask Mr. Watson to join us, please?"

"How do you know Mr. Watson is in that car?" she asked.

"Because I asked him to be available. He's here as a favor to me and unless I miss my guess, a favor to Corsetti as well."

"Remember the card game... Colin? Things are not as black and white as they try to keep them these days. No one outside of North Boston, especially that wimp Hardy, knows that Vito and Martin are close. Friends scratch each others backs. I think you'll see Martin shit all over our Russian friend, Conrad Tass and soon."

I said, "I wish he shit all over Hardy's head."

"That, too, could be in the cards," he came back with a sly grin.

He stopped when the door opened and Martin Watson entered with cigar the size of a small rocket and a smile the size of Texas. "I'm freezing from waiting in that damned car. You better have some of that Irish whiskey."

I rose and shook his firm hand. The sparkle in his eye was evidence he was enjoying the moment.

"I assume you've briefed your client, Ian."

"I have."

"Well, then. Let's talk about a plea bargain and try to keep the lad out of jail," Watson said without a shred of humor.

For an hour, we drank and talked. Every once and a while they asked me a question or sent me out of the room like a disruptive child. Eventually, Ian convinced me I couldn't personally or financially afford to go to trial. I'd need a trial attorney with Federal experience. Ian, who didn't have the time for a long federal trial, said he could refer me to a very good past associate of his, but I should expect to be charged a hundred thousand dollars up front. A further deposit of fifty thousand would be needed for research, trial support and other paperwork. If I had to appeal, the whole thing could cost twice that much, and the end result would be being sentenced to four years in prison.

Secondly, Ian told me that in Federal court, unlike State Court, if I testified in my own defense and lost, up to four additional years could be added to my sentence for obstruction of justice. Although this isn't often done, it's a great tool the

Feds use to get a person not to testify in his own behalf and to encourage a plea bargain. I felt like I was involved in the gun-fight at the OK Corral with a water pistol.

In other words, with the evidence from tapes of my home phone conversations and testimony from Carlos Reyes and Milos Santos, I was a dead duck. They had me on both lying and obstructing an investigation. They were willing to gamble on a money laundering charge, which Fred Hardy wanted more than anything, just to get Vito into court.

They had two witnesses who would lie about anything asked. These witnesses would walk if they got Vito. It seemed that my walking away from this mess unscathed was impos-sible unless I pled and gave up Corsetti.

The two men called me back into the room and Watson opened the discussion. "Fred Hardy wants Vito Corsetti and a drug dealer in Miami, Paco Gomez, who is too afraid to testify against Corsetti. Hardy has his case resting on you. He's con-vinced you'll never give up being a racehorse trainer, go to jail and live the rest of your life a felon to protect Vito Corsetti."

Ian looked Watson in the eye, "What would you do in my place, Martin?" he asked. "I know it's a strange thing to ask, here in front of Colin and all, but you know Hardy and we both know everyone else involved. What would you do, my friend?"

Watson looked at me with a frown. "I'll deny I've ever been here."

Ian took a long drink of his scotch. "Right, Martin."

"I'll try to handle Hardy as best as I can. I'm trying to make sure he doesn't get his hands on Vito if you guys go to trial. Vito can never take the stand. You know why, Ian."

"Sure."

"Well, if I were you, Ian, I'd come up with some fancy plea

that would keep your man from testifying against Corsetti. The local Federal Prosecutor is one of your best friends and you've taught almost everyone on his staff. It will make the plea go down smoothly if you beg on your knees."

He continued, "I'll fight tooth and nail not to press for testimony from Colin, just take the guilty plea. I'll convince Hardy he can't nail Vito in Boston. I'll tell him that leaving Boston without a felony conviction will harm his career. He's gone too far out on the limb to come up empty and go back to Miami with his tail between his legs.

"I'll try to get Hardy to ask the judge for the minimum; maybe a ten-thousand-dollar fine and four to six months house arrest with a bracelet. The judge might want probation for a few years, and we won't fight it. Might work if you come up with the right plea." Watson wheezed as he stood.

We also rose from our chairs and Ian said, "We'll get back to you tomorrow. We have to move fast on this. Santos and the others involved are loose cannons."

"I agree," Watson said as he closed the office door behind him.

For several minutes we remained silent. Then Ian spoke. "You want the good news or the bad news?"

I poured a three-fingered scotch and put my face in my hands. "Bad news first. There can't be any good news."

"Things will go down just as Martin said. I can tell he's already talked with Hardy. He's told him what an uphill battle he's got with Vito in Boston. He'll deal.

"That means we avoid the legal cost, which you have no way to pay. That old farm you have in Virginia is all you've got. Anyway, you can't afford to go to trial and the Feds know it."

"You'll be confined at home with an ankle bracelet. I'll try for no more than a few months and see if I can get them to cut

the fine. You'll lose your voting and firearms rights. Most of
the states will never again give you a trainer's license as a convicted felon. There are a few that will make you wait a five-year
period after completing your sentence to reapply. I'll ask for no
probation, so you can try getting a trainer's license sooner."

Ian's voice warmed with sympathy. "You're facing a life-
altering experience. You'll become the butt of jokes and will
find out who your real friends are. You'll have no credit or
credibility and probably have a hard time finding any kind of
job, except as farm help or at a training center. You'll be banned
from all racetracks. Maybe you can get a farm trainer's job or
someday train steeplechasers from your farm, like the old days."

"Is that all?" I asked.

"No, there's Corsetti's problem with di Vinci Stable. We
can't do anything until that's settled and the horses have been
moved to another trainer," he said.

"Any ideas?"

"Yeah, but I have to talk with Vito first. You stay the hell
away from him, Colin."

"How are you going to handle it?"

"I'm going to try buying the horses from him for myself, at
least on paper. We both have old friends in the steward's office
and on the Racing Commission," he grinned.

"What about the good news, Ian?"

"Jock, Annie and I still love you."

"What am I going to tell Annie?"

Almost ashamed, he said, "Nothing. She called me the
other day and I filled her in on what you had facing you, Colin.
She had a right to know."

"Did you know she'd been pregnant?"

"She still was, when I talked to her."

CHAPTER FORTY-TWO

I left Ian's office after declining his dinner invitation. I sat in my truck for a few minutes staring into the night and noticed the black car was gone. The night was cold, the sky overcast, and there were no stars in sight. I'd never felt so alone in my life.

I straightened my shoulders and started the truck, refusing to continue feeling sorry for myself or to lapse back into the drunken depression that had laced my life for long periods in recent years. The next few weeks were going to be tough and there were a lot of unknowns. Ian, Jock, Arch and Evan … they'd stick with me. Maybe Vito. Annie was gone. Thank God she'd been saved the disgrace of having a husband who was about to be a felon and a child with a criminal for a father. What did Ian mean… she still was… ?

It was after ten when I pulled up in front of the little cottage in Winthrop. I saw it from a new perspective, realizing how much I'd come to love my home. I remembered Billy Eckstein's song about the soldier who came home from war to find his girlfriend gone and a sign on the door, "Cottage for Sale." It had sold over a million copies in 1946. Thousands of soldiers had gone through hell and come home empty-handed, with no cottage.

I let the dogs out, fixed a scotch and dug out Eckstein's album, "In the Still of the Night," selecting the second song and nodding along to the music, relaxing in my recliner and finishing my scotch.

My stomach rumbled, so I dug through the fridge finding left over veal and pasta from Little Venice. How I longed to drive over to the restaurant, but I couldn't go against Ian's advice again. I got away ignoring his advice once, but never twice.

I opened a good red wine to help the reheated meal and

dined to the accompaniment of Keith Jarrett's "Koln Concert" from 1975. Back in my recliner, I stretched out to the music, sitting in total darkness, Nadine and Killer at my feet. My mind drifted to Virginia, and I wondered what the old farm looked like. I hadn't been back in twenty years. I thought about the small Irish village of Kells where Ian and my father were born and raised. Maybe after everything was over, I'd move there.

Ian advised me to turn my racing license into the stewards voluntarily, heading off a ruling. If I ever applied for permission to train again, there would be no revocation. I'd arrange for the future of the horses in my care, hoping Ian could execute his plan for getting them out from under Santos and di Vinci Stable. My life on the backside was over.

The next morning, well before daylight, I headed to the barn at Suffolk Downs to talk to Jock. He was humming his way through morning chores. My heart sank as I looked down the shed row and saw six heads peering over their stall screens, eyes sparkling. I asked Jock to have coffee with me in the tack room. Knowing something was wrong, he quietly nodded and followed me.

"We got problems, don't we, son?"

"We sure do, Jock, and they're all of my own making."

I told him about my meeting with Ian and the Feds and what I expected to happen. I explained it would all happen quickly and we had to be ready to make the changes. We needed a new trainer for the horses. I'd have to leave the cottage. I figured I'd pack what I most wanted and needed and put the rest of the contents in storage.

"We've got a lot to accomplish, Jock."

He looked thoughtful. "I think you should ask Ian if Tino

can train these horses for him. He knows them all, and he's a pretty good hand, Colin."

I nodded. "You're right. I'd never considered Tino, but now you mention it, he'd be a good choice. It would be a hell of a start for him."

Jock sipped his coffee and studied me. "The gray horse is in the stake today. Is that going to be the end of it, Colin?"

"Looks like it. Ian wants me to plead right away if he can get me a good deal. He wants to move before the Miami Fed changes his mind. The local FBI guy is the only thing keeping me out of prison right now. The judge could sentence me to jail, regardless of the Feds' recommendations. If that happens… "

Jock stood up, as unwilling as I was to consider the possibility.

"Colin, get your ass out of that chair. We've got a stake horse to get ready."

I fell in beside him, going from horse to horse, feeling the front legs after removing the bandages. Jock took temperatures as we looked over each horse together.

Before leaving the tack room, I'd put on the three disc set of Harry Chapin and turned up the sound level. Harry made my heart race and cleared away some of the dread as I worked.

"Harry Chapin died far too soon," I said to Jock, as we refilled the hay nets. Libby and Tino had arrived and were tacking up the first set. I noticed they walked into the barn together and glanced at Jock.

"I think I know how you can rent that cottage and not worry about it, Colin," he said with a grin.

It was great having two morning riders, but I would have liked to drag out my last training day as long as possible. I was tying Cherokee Moon's tongue when I heard a friendly voice behind me.

"Can't you turn that damned old folk music down?"

"Good morning, Arch. Sorry I missed coffee this morning."

"Shit, Colin, I didn't miss you, but I sure missed those donuts.

"Steve's on the two-to-one favorite in our stake today. He couldn't wait to jerk my chain when he picked up the ship-in favorite from New York. There's two here from Aqueduct and one from Laurel. You already knew that, didn't you, Colin?"

"Yesterday."

"You think our little woman can handle the big gray son of a bitch today?" Arch asked.

"Arch, I'd rather have her on Sliding Scale any day. It's going to take a real rider to follow my orders and keep that bleeding son of a bitch going. If he thinks he's going to bleed, he'll stop before he does. I've used every trick in the book to get into his head. I've been using the bleeder jug when I breezed him, and put in illegal junk to make sure he didn't bleed. I can't use the stuff in the race, but I think he has his confidence back. I never let him breeze hard. That's why his times in the *Form* coming into this race have been slow.

"He'll be no better than eight to one, the way he bled before. I have a secret weapon my dad used thirty years ago that you just don't see around the track anymore."

"What now, Colin? What have you got up that Irish sleeve?"

"Libby," I called. "Come down to the tack room with Arch and me."

When we were all together around the coffee pot, I sorted through more than a hundred bits hanging from a chain on the wall. I selected a "Flying W" metal bit with a long leather strap attached to the ends.

"You ever use one of these, Arch? You use it with a regular 'D' bit and bridle on a horse that entraps or bleeds. You place this 'W' which looks like an angel food cake fork, into the mouth. The 'W' goes on before the bridle and holds down the tongue. The air, which is usually cut off, blasts into his throat, which is held wide open. He can't entrap, so he seldom bleeds."

"Why don't more people use this?" Libby asked.

"It's funny, Libby. It's like a special paint or a way of bandaging. Everyone can use the paint and bandages, but they won't listen to the guy who tells them it has to be applied a certain way to work. I'll bet a dozen trainers have borrowed my 'W'. They try it without success and they give it back after a race, never asking why their horse stopped or bled with it."

"This is where you come in, Libby. It's the ride and the trip that makes this thing work. You have to follow my instructions, or you'll have no chance," I warned. "There are only two ways this thing will work. One of these we can't try with Sliding Scale because he's a come-from-behind horse.

"The first way is to break on top and improve your position, as the Cajuns say. The second is for you to stay three or four lanes wide of the field. You can never let him get dirt in his face, wearing a 'W'. His throat will be wide open and he'll choke on the mud and dirt. The mud sticks in his throat, because he can't use his tongue which is pinned down so he can breathe."

"That's the craziest thing I've ever heard," Arch said.

"Trainers and riders are a hard-headed bunch," I explained. "They want an edge, but after they're given one they seldom follow instructions. They may just not want to send their horse on the front end or they think they look like fools, telling a rider to ride out past the middle of the track. So, they use the edge, but screw it up doing it their way.

"If Sliding Scale can handle this bit during the heat of a race, he'll gallop. I've had it on him breezing, but racing's different. Some horses panic in a race and this horse is one of them. The first taste of blood and he throws his head right up. I'll fix his taste buds, too, with some Vicks."

Libby smiled. "I've been around some of the best trainers in New York, Colin, and they never have to do the stuff you do."

"That's because they have better horses, Libby. I've never had a horse without problems, if he's a real racehorse. They all have holes in them by the time they reach Suffolk Downs. Trainers like me have to use imagination and old tricks to survive with a classy old horse like Sliding Scale.

"If you do what I ask today and ride this horse with confidence, you'll win your first stakes race. Remember, a classy old horse like this can tell if you're a confident rider. Shake him up, get stiff in the saddle or gator arm him and you're dead in the water."

Libby left smiling, full of herself and high on her ride.

"It's fun to play with old horses and young, willing riders. This might be the best horse I'll ever train," I said to Arch.

From his silence, I knew he wasn't going to ask questions, but rather let me tell him what I wanted to, in my own way. It was the best I could ask from a good friend, one of my few, if Ian was right.

As we started out into the shed row to watch the next set go, my cell phone rang.

It was Ian. "Meet me at the Steward's Office in fifteen minutes? I'm on my way. They're expecting us." He hung up without my answering. Command performance.

I walked behind Crystal Run and Top Shot as they plowed through the slop to the track to gallop. No breezing today.

I looked at the messy track, as I walked along side Libby on Crystal Run. "Look at the slop, honey. Don't let it fool you," I warned. "There'll be lots of shit flying today, but underneath it's as hard as Broadway. There'll be plenty of time and he'll be flying at the end. Just take aim after you're straight away and stay as far as you can to the outside."

"What are these jocks going to say, after the way I rode Lonely Aunt? We were brushing the hedge on the outside. We weren't even in the photo we were so far outside."

"If I told you it was worth three grand to ride along the outside, would you?"

"You bet, Boss. I've never had a three grand ride."

"Well, you will today. You go, girl," I called, as she jogged off.

I was standing outside the Steward's Office when Ian walked up.

"It's a done deal. I have the papers all ready. You, as the authorized agent need to sign in front of a notary. The other details have been worked out. di Vinci Stable will be mine. That's all you need to know. The stewards have no problem with it and neither does anyone else."

The whole transfer took less than ten minutes. Ian Higgins was the new owner of di Vinci Stable for the sum of fifty thousand dollars and other considerations.

"The man owed a fellow in Florida a lot of money for these horses and I paid them off directly," Ian told the steward who helped us. He was an old rider and would have done anything Ian asked. They'd known each other for over twenty years.

We walked from the Steward's Office to Ian's car. When we were alone, he said, "I talked with Watson and my friend in the

Federal prosecutor's office this morning. Hardy is in line and I have a plea that will get it done, if the judge accepts it."

"What's it going to be? Am I a liar, an obstructionist or a money washer?"

"None of the above," he said. "You'll plea to one count of misprision of a felony. It means you knew a felony was being committed and condoned it by not reporting it. It's not used much, but it's the best deal we can get and I'd rather you live with that than any of those other labels. It's seldom anyone gets jail-time on a misprision plea."

I was confused, but very grateful. "I guess I'm not a rat and will have the papers to prove it," I said, relieved.

"Don't get flip with me, Colin. This is the worst thing you'll probably ever face... I hope. Just be calm and grateful. More than anything else, you better show true remorse and get to work on a little speech for the judge at sentencing. He'll want to see you crawl and beg for mercy. Federal judges have big egos, especially this judge."

"You know him well?"

"He was in my class in law school and was a close friend of your dad's."

"When will all this happen?" I asked.

"Martin is bringing the plea bargain to my office Monday morning. We have a court date Monday afternoon at one o'clock. That fast enough?"

"What then, Ian?"

"I told Martin and a case agent from the US Probation Service that you wanted to go to your home in Virginia, where you are from and own property. After the sentencing, you'll meet with the agent who'll handle your case. He's already made a call to Virginia and your case will be transferred to the

Charlottesville office if the judge accepts the plea.

" Things will go fast, Colin. The good cases always do. You need to figure out what to do with your house. I can rent it for you if you don't have time. My guess is they'll give you ten days or so to be in the probation office in Charlottesville after your plea and the judge sentences you.

"The Virginia probation agent in charge of your case will attach your ankle bracelet and explain what you can and cannot do," he said, looking sadly into my eyes.

I nodded in understanding. "Ian, I've been thinking about the horses. I hope you'll consider leaving them with my assistant, Tino Torres. I've told you about him. He can get his license and he'd be a fine trainer. He knows the horses backwards and I'm just a phone call away. Jock's gonna stay on if you do. I'm going to trust him with Annie's filly. There's a stake coming up in a few weeks and she should at least hit the board, giving her the black-type she needs to be a much more valuable broodmare."

"I was hoping you'd want Tino to take over. So was Annie. She called and I told her about the plea. I didn't tell her your plans, but she asked. She knows Tino from Aiken and trusts him. They'll talk. It'll be okay, Colin, I promise," he said as he started his car.

"You ready to win the stake today?" I asked.

"I'll try to make it, but I have the plea meeting at the courthouse. You really think he's got a chance?"

"With some luck, a big shot at it all."

"That Italian partner of mine wants to keep the di Vinci Stable name and colors. The Irish in me wants to call it Kells Stable. As long as I still owe him for my half, he's got the leverage on me. Imagine me with an Italian partner."

As he started to drive off, I said, " I can't see Vito with an Irish partner."

CHAPTER FORTY-THREE

Depression hung in the air like a dark cloud as we prepared for my final race before the changing of the guard. When I told Tino of my pending fate and asked him if he'd be willing to take the reins of the stable from me, he fell silent. He tried to be reserved, considering my fate, but I could see that underneath he was pleased. I could tell as he worked, his attention was diverted from the race preparation to his future. I knew he hadn't the slightest idea how to handle the training concept, except the care of the horses. And that, he would find out, was the easy part. It's the human element of the game that is the ruination of most potential trainers.

I watched from the corner of my eye as he eased his way down the shed row, putting the cell phone to his ear. My guess was that he was calling Libby in the jock's room and telling her I was out as di Vinci's trainer and he was going to take over.

He'd looked genuinely hurt when I gave him the news and filled him in on the reasons behind the decisions that would forever affect our lives, his on the upside and mine on the downside. There would be plenty of time to fill him in on Ian Higgins and his future racing plans. Jock sat quietly as Tino asked about my schedule and how I wanted things done.

"I can't do this without Jock," Tino said. "These horses, this barn and the whole job; I can't replace you all."

I was seeking an answer when Jock spoke for me. "Tino, I remember when Colin went into the service, the year before the Judge died. His father called me to the big house and we sat in the kitchen. He told me he expected me to keep things going in the right direction so Colin would have the farm when he returned. It was the day he told me he was dying.

"I thought I could never make it alone," Jock said, sorrow in his eyes.

"That old man told me something I'll never forget. He told me everyone can be replaced. It's just like pulling your fist out of a bucket of water. It leaves waves and ripples, but never a hole. Things might be confusing around here for a little while, but there ain't gonna be no hole," Jock declared as he stood and left the room.

"Tino," I said, "I read people pretty well. This job's going to be a piece of cake for you if you remember all the things we've started with these horses and keep improving them. When you get new horses, talk to Jock and then do it your way. I've been watching you and Libby lately. You two look like a pair, a good team. Don't blow that. She's far too good for a man like you," I kidded.

"You don't miss much, Colin. We've been talking about moving in together. See what it's like, working and living together."

"I'll make it easy for you, son. When I go, I'll rent you all my cottage, cheap. I'll leave any furniture here I won't want in Virginia. I have a lot of my father's good stuff in storage that I can use. What's left in the cottage will be a starter present from me. I don't want any of it back, so throw it out or give it away as you see fit. I'll be gone sometime next week, after all the court shit."

Tino beamed. "Thanks for everything, Colin. I'll take care of your house and I'll talk with Annie about Lonely Aunt. Mr. Ian will be fun to work with and he can keep us up to date with you," he sighed.

We walked down the shed row to Sliding Scale's stall, where Jock was making his rub rag pop, and as usual, humming. "Like all the good ones, son, he knows he has a job to do today. Those old knobby ankles are as cold as ice and he feels great. He got the bleeder jug four hours out, with extra lasix," Jock reported.

In Boston, bute is legal on race day, allowing a horse to be without his usual aches and pains. Sliding Scale's major problem would be the bleeding and I'd taken every step I knew to get him over that threat. Just the same, being without creaky ankles or knees was a plus.

Coming up behind me quietly, Arch Hale said, "I think we've got ourselves a problem, Colin. I had lunch at The Shamrock. Evan told me he heard Steve Casey and a few other riders talking about messing up Libby. Seems they have one of the gate crew in their pocket. I figure he'll probably hold the bridle or get his head turned sideways at the break. If he's quick he can untie the tongue or have him backing up and rearing when the gate opens."

I frowned. "I'll talk to Tom and get him to watch as he loads them. You warn Libby and I'll check with her when she gets to the paddock. She's in the jock's room now and I can't go there," I added.

Arch left to see Libby between her rides. I could see Tino steaming. The thought of his new girlfriend getting hurt got under his skin.

"Look, Tino, if you're going to train horses, holding your temper and tongue are a must. We can get Libby ready for just about anything another jock can throw her way. I can't have you getting suspended for hitting anyone in the paddock. If you have that kind of problem, always take care of it outside the back gate. You know that. Anyway, if Libby's survived a hundred starts in New York, she can handle these pinheads up here."

He calmed down and continued putting the vet-wrap bandages over the special run-down pads I had fixed for Sliding Scale's long pasterns. I used emerald green bandages with dark green tape for luck.

As usual, my horse was last to arrive in the paddock. The valet was waiting with Libby's tack. We'd just finished with the over girth when my stubby little rider walked calmly past the male riders, who had a few choice things to say. As always, the paddock was crowded on stake day, but I had taken a few minutes to step into the grandstand for an errand.

I had on my corduroys, good luck tie and battered tweed jacket. Steve Casey was walking across the saddling area to the number five stall and had to walk right past me. I stepped into his way and said, "Steve, you hurt my horse or my jock and I'll retire you myself."

He said nothing, but pushed past me, knowing full well I was serious. I'd protected Steve dozens of times, breaking a few trainers' noses and blackening a few eyes when they gave orders to hurt him or my horses over the years. I figured he was getting the gate guy to do his dirty business because he was a coward and too long in the tooth to defend himself.

There was swelling under Libby's left eye as she turned for me to give her instructions. "Don't say anything, Boss. I'll take care of it after the race. Somebody's going to be dead meat after I get the job done with this horse."

We talked briefly. I told her what to expect in the gate and what I'd do if I were riding.

"I have my bag of tricks. No one is going to stiff my horse in the gate. New York was a lot tougher than this joint." She grinned with a showing bravado.

The trip to the gate was uneventful. I was glued to my glasses, standing atop the bench on the apron of the grandstand. Big fat Arch didn't dare balance himself on the bench and drifted toward the rail to watch the seven-furlong race that started deep in the chute.

After many years of watching races start, I was aware of every possible dirty move by a jockey, horse or attendant. When one of the gate crew approached Libby to steer her gray horse into the gate, she waved him off with her whip and called to Tom, who was leaning on the fence, watching the loading. He heard her and called for the attendant to back up.

Kept from getting his hands on Sliding Scale while loading, the attendant vaulted into the gate and grabbed for the gray horse's bridle with both hands. I could tell Libby was telling the attendant to take his hands off the bridle, but the guy paid no attention. In a lightning move, Libby flipped her stick, exposing the hard knob, and cracked the gate man a vicious blow across his forearm. The man jumped back onto his perch, yelling at Libby, but allowed Sliding Scale to stand quietly. Libby spun her whip to reverse it, and snuggled close to the big horse's neck.

Seconds later, the bell rang and the doors flew open. Libby took Sliding Scale back quickly and dropped to the outside of the field, in last place by five lengths. She gathered up her reins further and took a strong hold as the big gray began to run.

Steve Casey reluctantly hung back three or four lengths in front and to the far inside of Libby, who was almost standing in her irons. Casey's horse was a front runner. His trainer from New York must have thought he was getting jobbed. The charts showed he loved the front end, and the dark bay was pulling just as hard on Steve as our horse was on Libby. The difference was that Libby was letting her horse out a little and then reaching for him after a few strides, playing a game, while Steve fought his mount all the way.

I'd told Libby that if he was running well and far to the

outside of the field, Sliding Scale would have enough run to overtake the field unless he'd bleed. The big horse had his neck tucked and set. There was no sign that he was running stressed.

Nearing the half-mile pole, Steve took his mount sharply to the right and tried his best to get next to Libby. As he pulled alongside our horse, Libby went to the stick. In a flash, Sliding Scale sprinted ahead, but even further to the outside. The leaders went the half mile in :46 and change. Libby trailed on the outside, almost ten lengths from the leader.

Steve chased Sliding Scale even further to the outside on the turn with an all-out effort to catch Libby, who was moving smoothly and faster. Steve's horse began to labor after a taxing first half. He'd fought for his head the whole way, and was now done, appearing to have spit the bit.

The big gray and Libby hit another gear on the far outside at the eighth pole, where they collared the leaders. As she passed under the wire, still far on the outside in the twelve path, Sliding Scale was two and a half lengths to the good.

For the first time in five or six years, I looked at the odds board with keen interest before heading for the winner's circle for my last time. I checked the tote tickets in my pocket. I had bet $400 across the board on Sliding Scale and stood to make a pile, maybe enough to pay my fine.

When Libby returned, Steve had unsaddled and was the target of screaming from the New York trainer. When the man walked off in disgust, Steve stood staring at Libby from twenty feet away.

"You better not come in the room, bitch. I'm going to be waiting for you where he can't protect you," he threatened.

Our photo had been taken and Tino was headed for the spit box. I told Libby to be careful. She said Steve had hit her

across the face with his whip in the hall as she left the ladies
dressing room before the race. I knew she'd try to settle the
score, so I followed her to the Jock's Room. Before the door
closed, I noticed that instead of turning right into the ladies
dressing room, Libby charged through the door on the left,
into the men's room, where half the jockey colony would be in
the showers or in various states of undress.

Being an owner and trainer, I was barred from the Jock's
Room on race day. What I heard from inside sounded like
a Pier One brawl. Screams and cheers blared through the
half-opened, high window of the room. I was scared to death
for Libby, who would surely be suspended for her aggressive
actions against another jockey.

After a few minutes, the door to the Jock's Room flew open
and two valets and a security guard pulled Libby through
the door and into an area next to the paddock. They rushed
her through another door that led to the nurse's station and
various offices for racing commission officials.

According to Arch Hale, she was held inside until the next
race started and the crowd had left to watch. She was then
allowed to change before being escorted from the grandstand
and paddock area and told not to return without the Steward's
permission.

I checked the tote board and noticed that Sliding Scale,
thanks to my big bet, had slipped from twelve to one to seven
to one just before the race. He paid $16.20, $7.40 and $5.60.
The fifty-eight hundred dollars I won probably wouldn't pay
my fine, but it would go a long way toward it.

Before going to the barn, I went to bookkeeping and got an
account of my resources. Alice gave me the statement, which
I pocketed without looking. "Anything you want to tell me,

Colin?" she asked.

" I'll have the answers in a few days, Alice. Right now, I just know I'll probably be taking a break from training and turning my horses over to Tino Torres."

She looked as if she'd seen a ghost. "I'm so sorry, Colin. You know how much I love having you around. And Jock? What about him?"

"You'll be the first to hear the entire story," I said as I turned and left. Alice had saved my stable when I was dead broke. She'd allowed me to cash checks when I had no money to pay my help and bills. As den mother to many, she had the pulse on the entire backside. I knew she was fully aware of my situation, but, as Ian said, my true friends would never push me.

When I got back to the barn, Ian was there and already on his way to getting a load on. He'd watched the race on TV in the clubhouse and hurried to the barn after we'd won. He was talking to Libby, who had a mouse under one eye and a cut at the edge of the other. What other injuries she had incurred I could only guess.

"Well done, Colin, well done!"

He had an arm around Libby, consoling her. "I'll go to the Stewards with you and represent you for nothing. I'll bet you get a stern lecture and ten days off."

Just then Tino and Sliding Scale arrived from the spit barn. Libby ran to them and hugged the horse first. She then threw her arms around Tino and wept. They walked the horse around the shed row, wanting to be alone and cooling him out at the same time.

As they walked off, Tino said to me, "He never bled a drop, Boss. Best yet, did you check his time? A new stake record and a tick off the track record."

I heard him say to Libby, "If he'd gotten a decent ride closer to the rail, he'd have the track record now." They both laughed and hugged.

Arch arrived with champagne instead of the usual post race beer. He told me the whole story about the fight in the jock's room. Libby stormed into the room and caught everyone by surprise, many of them naked as jaybirds. She found Steve in the shower, buck naked. Fully dressed with her helmet on, she charged into the shower with her whip high and leaped on the naked Steve Casey, beating him all over with her stick.

"She had some well-placed strokes to his privates. Steve only hit her a few times with his fist. She held him under the water and almost drowned him before the other jockeys pulled her off. They said Steve packed his locker in disgrace. I asked around and they said he was heading to Penn National to ride. He'd never be able to face the other riders again after getting his ass whipped by a tiny woman. One guy told me Steve could hardly walk as he dragged his bag to his car. He said his face looked like an eggplant."

We couldn't say enough good things about Libby's great ride and Sliding Scale's valiant and game race. Jock stood and the others fell silent. Slowly, he looked around gathering. Ian, Tino, Libby, and Arch had been joined by Charlie and Grady. He raised his beer bottle and looked at me.

"To Colin O'Hearn, my son and the best damned trainer I've ever seen in my life!"

I stepped into the tack room in tears.

CHAPTER FORTY-FOUR

Monday morning, shortly after ten o'clock, I sat across from Ian in a small conference room in the Federal Courthouse staring at the legal papers.

"Do you want to read it over again before you sign?"

I shook my head. "There's no use. I don't agree with some of this, but it's the best we can do, I know. I don't have a lot of options. They have me by the short hairs. It's either this or jail or a hundred and fifty thousand dollar trial that you say that I'll lose. Yeah, I'll sign."

I took the pen from Ian and wrote my name beside his signature four different times. Next I filled out the pre-sentencing report, which contained every question Hardy and Watson could come up with. As soon as that was done, the paperwork was rushed to the judge.

By three that afternoon, I'd been through an intensive, interrogative grilling designed to confuse me and create contradictions in my answers. The Feds were far from happy with the results. At best, I figured they walked away with Milos Santos in their back pocket for a half dozen blue collar crimes and what little I'd been able to give them on the Dobbs murder investigation, which was still unsolved. The locals, Smith and Ross, were present, but they remained silent during the interrogation.

As the Feds left, a federal marshal escorted me to a set of offices in the basement of the court house. I held a number in front of my chest while being photographed from various angles. They took fingerprints and a DNA sample before returning me to the third floor where I sat and waited. A freestanding sign near the door announced that these were the chambers of Federal Judge Harold F. P. White III.

It was almost six o'clock when Ian came out. "He's ready for you now. They rushed the pre-sentencing report through in record time. I wanted this done today before word got out and someone had time to cause problems. It'll be all over tomorrow's papers."

"Papers?"

Ian nodded. "There are always reporters in the courtroom and little slips past them. Your case was added to the docket and I'd bet the court reporters alerted both the *Globe* and the *Herald*." He frowned. "Don't say a word to the press afterwards. I've filled in my friend Lou Capps on everything. If anyone approaches, refer them to me, even if you know them. Tell them you're gagged. We don't want to piss off the Feds. Even after your sentencing, they can make life hard."

"When will I be sentenced?"

"As soon as Judge White reads over the report and recommendations. Come on, we'll wait inside."

I followed Ian into the courtroom. A few reporters sat at the press table, but there was no audience. However, in the back row of the court room Jock sat with Evan Kennedy and Arch Hale. Tears came to my eyes. This was the worst, the most humiliating experience of my life. Thank God my best friends had come to lend their support.

The prosecution's table was heavily populated with everyone who'd been at the interrogation session and a few others I didn't know. The door to the judge's chamber opened, the bailiff announced his coming and everyone stood as a tiny, balding man in his seventies took his seat and adjusted his glasses. Slapping a file on the mahogany desktop, he looked directly at Ian.

"Mr. Higgins, you will bring your client forward."

I stood drenched in shame and unable to take my eyes

off the floor in front of me. I was terrified that the tears I was fighting would blur my vision and I'd trip and fall. I finally looked up when we arrived at the step six feet below the judge.

"Mr. O'Hearn, do you agree with everything contained in your plea?"

"Yes, Your Honor," I answered quietly. "I understand the plea and agree with the contents."

"There's more, is there not?" the judge demanded.

I stared at him, dumbstruck. I was dying to defend myself, but Ian had warned me that the only option I had was to express my guilt and remorse, or else... !

Ian spoke before I could respond. "The report speaks for itself, Your Honor."

Judge White frowned. "Counselor, if I want to hear from you, I'll ask. Your answer, Mr. O'Hearn?"

"Nothing is cut and dried, Your Honor. I'm here to plead and be punished for one of the most foolish things I've ever done in my life. I should have never condoned the felonious activity of my client and should have had the integrity to report him. I was wrong and I sincerely regret my actions. I'm ashamed and sorry for my crime and the terrible burden I've placed on everyone. I'll live out my life as a convicted felon and will do everything in my power never to exhibit any such behavior in the future. I beg you and the court for forgiveness and mercy."

"Nice speech, Mr. O'Hearn. You should have followed your father's example and gone into law. Now, Mr. O'Hearn, answer my question. Is everything you've done against the law included in this plea?"

I paused, sure that anything I said was going to be taken the wrong way. It was another of those, "have you stopped beating your wife" questions.

"Your Honor, no simple plea could include every moral, ethical and legal action in the life of a man like myself. I've killed men in combat. I've beaten men and taken advantage of others when I should not have. Your Honor, I have lived a flawed, but mostly honest life. I've tried to never lie, cheat or steal when it violated the law. With this in mind, I can honestly say I agree with this plea."

"Very well, I'll sign the motion and include in my court notes that I disagree with the plea and my reasons why. You have been charged and pled. I will uphold the plea and recommendations.

"In keeping with the plea request, I sentence you to four months home confinement with a tracking device and a fine of five thousand dollars. No probation will be required after the four months have been served."

He banged his gavel and said, "Mr. Higgins, I would like to talk with you and your client in chambers."

Judge White was taking off his robe by the time we closed the door behind us.

"Damn it, Ian, how did this happen? This man no more deserves to be here than the man in the moon. You should have come to me and I would have straightened out the Federal Prosecutor in a second. I feel like I've put a knife in the back of his father, one of my best friends. Sit down, Mr. O'Hearn. I want your attorney's accounting for this plea. At least, Ian, why didn't you go to court?"

"That would have put Colin's life in grave danger, Your Honor."

"Why do I feel Vito Corsetti's involved somehow here? Oh, hell, Ian, it's over now.

"Colin, your father was the most fair and honest man I've ever known. I'm crushed that we're here today. Please let me help in any way I can. Ian said you wanted to go to Ireland when your sentence has been served. That's why I didn't include probation, which is standard."

"Thank you, Your Honor, for everything you said about my father and for your help. I'll never let you down, I promise."

As he poured himself a drink from a brown decanter, he said, "One more thing, Colin. Did you really win a fifty thousand dollar purse on Saturday for this Irish jerk?"

"Judge, his horse sure did win the race on Saturday. He can afford to buy you a hell of a lot of pasta."

His Honor laughed, "At Little Venice?"

"No sir," I said. "I think he puts the feed bag on there for free."

Ian laughed, and as we were leaving, said, "That's what I thought."

The door closed and three reporters were waiting for us in the courtroom.

"No comment. No comment," Ian said again and again as we walked down the steps and left the Court House.

Jock was waiting to drive me to Suffolk Downs. When we opened the door of the tack room, Evan, Arch, Tino and Libby were crowded around a cooler of beer.

"We figured you'd check on the horses," Tino said. "We didn't want you to be alone."

I thanked them one at a time, and then I opened a beer and started my tour down the shed row. Jock was at my heels as usual. I walked to the end and started back to the tack room, one stall at a time.

I walked past Cherokee Moon, Top Shot and Deeper

River. Then, Sliding Scale and the lovely Crystal Run. At last, I slipped into Lonely Aunt's stall. I ran my hand under her blanket and she quivered, humping her back a little. She looked back and plastered her ears against her head. Boom. Boom. Like two gunshots, her back heels hit the plywood covering the back wall. She flashed her teeth as if to say, "No men in here. Get out."

"Just like her mother," I told Jock.

"Ian said she called. He told her about court and all."

"Should I call her, Jock?"

"Ian said no. Give her time, Colin. Maybe she'll feel better someday, but let her set her own pace."

"Too much water over the dam now," I said sadly.

CHAPTER FORTY-FIVE

I drove past the security gate, leaving Suffolk Downs feeling a little better about things. My horse had run well and won. My friends had been there to support me, both in the court room and at the shed row. The court appearance was behind me and the Feds were off my back, at least as far as I knew. No one in Boston gave a damn about me at this point, which was a distinct relief.

As I neared the cottage, I realized I was being followed. I stared at the rear view mirror, finally recognizing the van that pulled into the driveway behind me.

Emmy got out, a bottle of wine in each hand, and strode purposely to my truck.

"I waited until you got through with all that maudlin shit at the barn," she announced. "There's not a chance you're getting out of town without that date you promised."

She had been drinking and had lost all her inhibitions. I led her into the house, wending a path through the packing boxes that littered the entry and living room. Nadine and Killer barked sharply, upset at having been left outside all day.

"Why don't you let them in so we can get down to business?" Emmy suggested.

She opened a bottle of wine as I opened the back door. The dogs went into their usual assault mode, which Emmy totally ignored after giving each a quick pat on the head. Her interest was not with the canines.

She handed me a water glass half-filled with a fine beaujolais, then turned to fill one for herself. This was not the Emmy I was accustomed to seeing. She wore a black turtleneck with nothing underneath, her nipples straining to be noticed. Her blonde hair fell past her shoulders, soft and loose, begging a man to run his hands through it. A black skirt, cut high on the side to reveal her thighs, replaced her usual blue jeans, and black boots completed the sensual look.

A devilish smile lit her face as she enjoyed my lack of control over the situation. Holding her glass up to mine, we shared a silent toast. Never taking her eyes from my face, she took my glass, set both drinks on a nearby packing box and pulled me to her. The kiss started warmly, and then deepened with increasing passion.

I pulled back slightly, holding her lightly in my arms. "What brought this on?"

"You're leaving," she said simply. "If we don't share something for you to remember, I'll never see or hear from you again. I don't want that, Colin."

I studied her face. The small sink light was on in the kitchen, but the rest of the house was in shadows. Sliding my hands under her shirt, I massaged her firm, large breasts. She moaned with pleasure and pulled away enough to jerk the shirt over her head, then tugged my hand, pulling me off the box and leading me to the bedroom.

Emmy was running the show. She sat on the edge of the bed and began undressing me. I stopped her long enough to remove my barn shoes, and then she helped me with my pants. Without taking time to remove her skirt, she took me in her mouth. I couldn't remember such incredible pleasure. As I neared the edge, she stopped long enough to close the door, shutting out the dogs and the light from the kitchen, then slipped out of her skirt and lay face down across the bed, arching her body and asking me to get behind her.

She rubbed herself against me, igniting a fire. As she stroked me with one hand, she begged me to hold her breasts, encouraging me to squeeze them tightly. With her other hand, she rubbed herself. When we exploded together, I imagined flames shooting from the bed.

I rolled to my side, bringing her next to me, stroking her hair, her back, every part of her body I could get my hands on. As I began teasing her nipple with my teeth, my hand moved to her thighs, hidden beneath the quilt she'd hastily drawn up over her legs and belly. I pushed at the covering and her hand covered mine.

"Don't."

I rose on one elbow. "Don't? Emmy, I want to make love to you again. I want to see all of you, watch your eyes as we come together ... "

She hesitated. "Colin, remember when I told you about my husband? That he scarred me? Well, those scars are both emotional and physical. I'll hate myself for life because I let him to do it." There was a tremor in her voice. "If I move the quilt, you'll see something no one else has ever seen, something that may disgust you forever."

She held up her hand, as I began to protest. "I was young and stupid. We were stoned. He said if I did as he asked, I'd always be his and he'd always be mine. I believed him... We both got tattoos. Mine is much larger than his.

"He lied, of course. He left me and returned to Denmark. I divorced him never let him know that I was pregnant with Aimee. He doesn't know she exists." Emmy was sobbing, as she finished.

"Emmy, no matter what it is, it can't be that bad. Nothing about you could ever disgust me."

She hesitated and then turned on the small bedside table lamp. Taking a deep breath, she shoved the quilt to the foot of the bed.

I held my breath as I looked at her body. A dragon tattoo stretched from just above her knees to her navel. The huge head covered her belly and a long tail wrapped around her legs. Fire came from an open mouth that dominated the area between her legs. It was a hideous desecration of one of the most beautiful bodies I'd ever seen in my life.

"How could he… how could you let him?" I stammered as she attempted to cover herself.

"Don't you think I've asked myself that a thousand times? Where do you place the blame? Misguided love, the drugs, stupidity… take your pick. The bottom line is, I was mutilated and I live with it every day of my life. No court, no cops, no one can punish him for demanding complete control over my body. I took part in it, no matter how drunk or drugged I was, and I'll carry the responsibility and the results forever."

I sat up on the bed and once again removed the quilt. "Emmy, when I look at you, I don't see the tattoo. I see you and a beautiful body. Right now, I need you with me, in the shower."

I pulled her from the bed and toward the bathroom. "Never, never think twice about that damned thing when we're together. It means nothing to me, Emmy. It doesn't make your body or your passion any less beautiful."

I filled the claw-foot tub with hot water and eased her in with me. We sat for a long time, making small talk. I washed her and she washed me. We stood, pulled the curtain and showered, passion erupting once again, then dried off and returned to the bed, drinking more wine exchanging more kisses.

I poured several drops of wine on her stomach and watched it pool in her navel. Lowering my head, I began licking the liquid from her body over her protests.

"You don't want to do that, baby," she said.

I proved that I did, and followed the dragon's trail from top to bottom, bringing her to climax.

The next morning, as she dressed to leave, she looked from the dragon to me. "You know, I figured you might fight Cozy Costas for me, but I never dreamed you'd take on the dragon and win."

She laughed, and we shared a last embrace before she left for a long, long time.

CHAPTER FORTY-SIX

Milos Santos stared at the Tuesday morning papers in a state of shock, unable to believe Colin O'Hearn had pled guilty to a felony charge in Federal court the day before. Both the *Globe* and the *Herald* carried complete details of the plea.

The story appeared on the third page of the news section of the *Globe,* but covered the entire back sports page of the *Herald,* including a picture of Colin leading Sliding Scale into the winner's circle after Saturday's race. Both stories referenced O'Hearn's cooperation with federal authorities, implicating others in the laundering of alleged drug money from Miami, Boston and New York.

Setting aside the papers, Santos knew he had little time to remove himself from the immediate vicinity and inherent danger created by O'Hearn's information. He had to get out of Boston as fast as possible without leaving a trace. Until he was on the road he had to avoid an entire cast of threatening players: the FBI, local cops and, most importantly, Vito Corsetti, Jimmy Slacks and Connie Tass. If the law caught up with him, he wouldn't see the outside of a jail cell for years. If Vito or the Russian found him, he wouldn't live to worry about jail.

Santos packed his clothes and loaded the trunk of his car, then drove aimlessly back and forth between Boston and the New Hampshire line waiting for dark. The fifty-five thousand in his briefcase wouldn't last long. He needed more cash and he'd have to go to his Saugus bank to get it. Vito and Slacks both knew where he banked. His only chance to get to his money would be at the end of the banking day just after dark.

When he arrived at the bank, he parked in the back corner of the lot. He entered through the lobby's rear entrance and went directly to the bank manager to avoid any delay withdrawing his fifty thousand dollars. By the time he left, the bank was locked for the day and a teller had to let him out the front door.

Santos scurried around back and opened the trunk of his car. As he set the briefcase of cash inside, a plastic garbage bag was slipped over his head, blinding him. A second later, the bag was pulled tight with a vicious jerk. His arms were pinned leaving him helpless as he was pushed and shoved. His screams were muffled by the bag and his attacker ignored his efforts to escape. Santos knew from experience that he was a dead man. He stopped struggling as his last seconds seemed to drag by.

The assassin grunted and strained but said nothing. Milos Santos never heard the crack of his neck or the muted shot that put a bullet in the middle of his forehead. He was dead when the bullet entered his brain. The two men silently rolled Santos into the car trunk. They found his fifty grand from the bank and checked the briefcase. They took a box containing the rest of his money and various papers Santos felt important enough to bring with him on his ill-fated journey.

The two attackers walked through the bushes to their car in the nearby parking lot of a funeral home. They drove along Lincoln Avenue to Holyoke Street, then to Parkland Avenue, coming to a stop by Breed's Pond. The shooter threw the gun used to kill Santos into the pond, watching it hit with a splash and sink to the bottom. Returning to the car, he patted the briefcase of money sitting in the middle of the front seat and grinned at the driver. "How about a beer?"

The pair drove into the city, passed the Big Dig and pulled up in front of The Place, a popular South Boston bar. They were oblivious to the large black vehicle that had followed them from the bank killing ground and was now parked across the narrow street outside the bar. The driver turned off the car and removed the keys. "Better put the case in the trunk," he instructed the second man.

He opened the door, felt metal against his head and knew nothing more as his world exploded. The second man turned, startled by the muffled pistol shot. Before he could react, his forehead was shattered by a second bullet, bone and tissue sticking to the bloody car window.

Tucking his gun into his shoulder holster and retrieving the briefcase with the cash and important papers from the seat, Jimmy Slacks sauntered across the street to the black SUV. His boot heels dragged across the pavement, the only reminder of the violent night. As he pulled away from the curb, he punched a button on his cell phone, waited for a response and said, "Done," then snapped the lid of his cell phone shut.

The two dead bodies were discovered by a drunken patron leaving the bar shortly after the shooting. Detectives Ross and Smith arrived right behind the local cruiser. There were no witnesses and the victims were unidentified and unknown. The killing had all the earmarks of a mob execution cleanly done with no fingerprints or shell casings left behind.

The next afternoon Ross and Smith were called to the small bank in Saugus. The manager explained that a car had been parked in the back of his lot all night, so he'd called a towing company to remove it. The driver of the truck hesitated before towing the car and showed the manager traces of what appeared to be blood on the trunk lid.

Smith used a long screwdriver to open the trunk. Neither he nor Ross was surprised to find the body of a man, his head encased in a black, bloody garbage bag. When the crime scene investigator removed the garbage bag, they immediately recognized Milos Santos. He was shot between his eyes, with his face only partially remaining. His head rolled grotesquely from side to side.

After his night with Emmy, Colin O'Hearn went on a two-day drinking binge, something he hadn't done in years. Jock and Tino took turns watching over him as he silently drank himself through the bender, trying to escape the humiliation and disgrace of his court ordeal and very public conviction. Embarrassed and ashamed, he'd refused to hide at home. He rotated between his tack room, the Shamrock and the track kitchen bar. For the first time since he left the Army, drinking proved to be his salvation.

Martin Watson, Fred Hardy and the two homicide detectives listened as a hung-over O'Hearn accounted for his activities over the last two days. Many around the track had seen Colin at both bars and around Barn 15. His stubborn refusal to hide provided an airtight alibi for the killing of Milos Santos.

Even Hardy, who screamed and shouted at Colin during the questioning, admitted to Watson that the trainer couldn't have had any role in Santos' death. Had the mob accountant been killed before Colin's plea, the trainer wouldn't have pled and would have been the chief suspect in the murder. Colin had no reason to want him dead after the fact, much as Hardy wished otherwise.

The gangland murder of Santos meant that the Miami FBI agent had just lost his prime witness in Vito Corsetti's money laundering investigation. He was now destined to return to Miami with nothing to show for his efforts, other than Colin's misprision conviction, which wasn't particularly satisfying.

The gang killings pushed Colin's story off the pages of the

Boston newspapers and out of the minds of most readers. Only in racing circles did some recall that Colin had been the trainer for the di Vinci Stable, owned by the murdered mob accountant.

The murders and their aftermath jolted Colin sober. Jock and the crew were quick to forgive his binge. They realized how deeply the disgrace of the conviction and the stigma of being a criminal affected Colin, and how it would change his entire life. He'd failed his father and had ignored every honorable standard the Judge had tried to instill in him. Nothing he could do would cleanse his reputation or regain his honor. He was a fallen gentleman, a disgrace to the O'Hearn name.

Disheveled but now sober, I walked away from the questioning hoping I'd never see Hardy, Watson or the local detectives again. All I wanted to do was retreat to the farm in Virginia, put all of this behind me and decide what to do with the rest of my life.

I walked slowly to the Racing Commission's office under the grandstand. The meeting with the stewards went smoothly, and they seemed sincerely sorry to accept my license and my badges. From there I made the long walk to the bookkeeper's office on the backside.

Alice gave me my financial statement and closed out my account. It was difficult to maintain a businesslike attitude, given all she'd done for me over the years. I felt moisture on my cheeks as I walked away from my friend's office for the last time after a long hug.

I had Alice's track check for almost twelve thousand dollars in my pocket . Combined with the five thousand and change from my bet on Sliding Scale, it was a nice nest egg for

Virginia. I went home to do the last of the packing. A call from
Ellen that afternoon brought more good news on the financial
side. Ian had mailed me a check from di Vinci Stable for over
twelve thousand dollars: the ten percent purse money minus
my fine and court costs. The next morning, I made sure all my
bills on the backside were paid and then called Jock and Tino
into the tack room.

"I'm leaving," I said simply. "Jock, there's no need for you to
come with me. I can get along fine at home."

Jock smiled. "Boss, I was going to ask you if I could stay
for a while and hope it ain't gonna cause you a problem, being
alone down there."

"No, you guys just keep going. The movers will clear out
my cottage tomorrow and put most of my stuff in storage. I'll
get the things I need and head out when I get packed here. I'll
make arrangements for a place to stay when I get to Virginia.
Thank God I have the dogs for company."

"Tino, I've got a check for you from Ian. It's an advance to
buy tack, traps, screens and equipment for the barn. Anything
not covered by this five thousand dollars is to be charged. He'll
pay for it at the end of the month. I've rented a small trailer to
haul all my equipment to Virginia."

The following day I called the Boston probation officer, and
was filled in on what I was facing in Virginia. He gave me the
name and other information about my federal case officer in
the Charlottesville office. I had six more days to appear to be
processed and begin my sentence. It didn't give me much time
to make living arrangements.

Going by the Shamrock, the racing office and the track
kitchen to say goodbye to my friends was a gut-wrenching
experience. Arch Hale and Evan Kennedy fought back tears,

and we only allowed ourselves one final drink together to avoid another binge.

After I said goodbye and thanked Ian, I headed to Little Venice for one last lunch. I wasn't about to leave town without seeing my seedy friends. I'd called earlier and Vito told me to park around the back of the restaurant where I could pull into his garage and come into the office by the back door. Jimmy Slacks was also a convicted felon. It would be a probation violation for me to be in his company.

We both said to hell with the probation. Jimmy met me in the garage and we went into Vito's office through the storeroom. As usual, the Boss was at the big table in the corner, his glass of wine in one hand and a telephone to his ear. He motioned me to sit down and Jimmy asked what I'd like to drink.

"Sam Adams, Jimmy. I have to drive South tonight after I finish at the barn. I left my trailer there for the boys to pack. It's my last stop before I leave Boston."

Vito hung up the phone and extended his hand. "Thank you for your loyalty, Colin. I'll always be indebted to you. When I say I owe you I mean any favor is yours if it's within my power. But, you'd better hurry, 'cause I don't know how many months like this I can take."

Slacks brought the beers and we chatted for about thirty minutes like nothing had happened.

"I ordered you macaroni and gravy for lunch." Vito said.

We toasted and talked about the horses and how Tino was well suited for the trainer's job. I told him Jock was staying on to help Tino, and Vito was obviously pleased.

I finished my meal, savoring each bite knowing it would be hard to find anything as good in Virginia. As I laid my fork aside,

Vito picked up a yellow envelope from the corner of the table.

"The money Santos stole from me on the horse deal was returned just before he left my employ. It was more than I expected. The difference is yours, a bonus for work well done. I hope it helps making a fresh start easier." He pushed the envelope across the table.

I accepted the money reluctantly, knowing better than to say no to the powerful man's generosity. I doubted Santos had voluntarily given up the cash and I suspected the dead men at the bar in south Boston had been carrying it when they met their fate.

Vito looked at me, obviously wanting to say more, but waited for any questions I might have about the envelope or Santos's death.

My gaze went from Vito, then to Jimmy. I was terrified to broach the subject, but needed answers.

"I'd like to ask a question or two, but don't know how."

"Just spit it out. You're among friends," Vito said, as if he already knew what was bothering me.

"Will we ever know who really killed Old John Harkins and Dobbs, Vito?"

"I'm sure it was Santos. He was trying to kiss up to Tass, showing him he could be of use and that there was no limit to his bravado. That's what I found out indirectly through my associate in Providence, Carlo Parrino. Two friends of mine I regularly play cards with and who are involved with the investigation agree. They're both closing the case with that result, now that someone finished off Santos."

I pressed, "Do you think those two guys they found murdered in Southie... Tass's guys... I guess, killed Santos?"

"That'd be my guess. I don't think even Tass trusted that

worm," said Vito.

"You think the cops'll find out who killed Tass's men outside the bar in Southie?"

Vito hesitated, but Jimmy Slacks spoke up after looking at his boss first, " I hope not!"

I quickly changed the subject. "Do you think I have to keep worrying about that Nikki Zepoff guy that was in those win pictures?"

Vito answered, "That asshole's gotten the message, don't you think, Jimmy?"

"Definitely!"

I tucked the envelope in my jacket. Clearing my throat, I said, "About that favor… I need it now."

"That didn't take long. What can I do?"

"Well, Vito, I probably can't get Sam Adams in Virginia and I was hoping to get a case or two from you to wean me off."

The big man's laughter rang through the room. He sent Jimmy to the warehouse to put some beer in my truck before rising from his chair and giving me a huge hug. "Nice I should make such a good friend late in life, Colin, even if you are a fuckin' Irish. Don't be a stranger. Call me for anything else you need."

When I got to my truck, Jimmy had twenty cases of Sam Adams under a tarp. He gave me a paid receipt in case I was stopped and had to explain the amount of beer I was carrying. The last thing I needed was to have some small town cop arrest me for bootlegging.

"Thanks, Jimmy, but you're crazy to give me all that beer."

"Don't tell a man with a quick trigger he's crazy, Colin," he laughed as we hugged one last time.

As I drove to the track, I was glad I'd chanced lunch and a

final visit with Vito and Jimmy. Ian would have me strung up if he found out. Jimmy's criminal past could have cost me a four year prison stay for a probation violation.

I drove through the security gate to Barn 15, where I found Arch, Tino, Libby and Jock waiting. My trailer was packed and ready to hook up to the truck. I removed four cases of Sam Adams from the truck's bed and placed it by the barn door. Everyone laughed and we popped a round of beers.

Sam Adams in hand, I checked the horses for a final time with Jock by my side. I lingered at Sliding Scale's stall. "I've really grown to like this old guy," I told Jock. "Maybe they'll send him to the farm when he's done and we can breed a few mares."

When I got to Lonely Aunt, she didn't back up into the corner as usual. I rubbed her nose and she pushed my hand with her muzzle. I scratched her ears like Annie used to do, and she leaned into me.

I pulled out of Suffolk Downs for the last time and was well past Providence before the last tears dried on my cheeks.

CHAPTER FORTY-SEVEN

While driving through the night, my mind reached ahead to my Virginia hometown, wondering how much had changed in the last twenty years. I tried imagining myself on the peaceful farm outside of Staunton.

I'd checked the county's website. Based on what I'd seen there, about the only thing that hadn't changed was the population, which was still listed at twenty-five thousand. A brief tour of the site indicated small businesses were losing the battle to shopping centers and the big box stores like Wal-Mart and Target. The sleepy college town that once had three boarding prep schools now appeared to be an art-oriented cluster of revival projects.

I stopped for breakfast near Harrisburg, Pennsylvania. Four hours later I got off the interstate and drove through Staunton's hilly streets. Even my Internet research hadn't prepared me for what I found. There wasn't a store name I recognized. My heart ached for the town I remembered where the streets were safe and kids rode their bikes to the YMCA each day to play basketball or baseball, with their parents assured of their safety and welfare. The old "Y" was now converted into condos and that told the story of a new Staunton.

I made three passes around the center of town finally parking in front of Marino's, a small grocery store and sandwich shop which had escaped the restructuring of the business community. I didn't recognize a soul as I sat down at the counter and ordered a sandwich and a beer.

A few minutes later I was sitting on a stack of beer cases when a fellow drinker sat on the stack next to mine. Even twenty years away couldn't keep me from remembering Eugene Grimes whom I'd known since grade school. .

I smiled and said, "Hello, Gene. You haven't changed a bit."

He studied me a moment, obviously embarrassed. "I know your face, but darned if I can recall your name," he said apologetically.

"I've been gone a long time, Gene. Colin O'Hearn."

"My God, Colin, we were just talking about you at the country club the other day. I heard… " His words trailed off and he lowered his head to take a long drink of his beer.

"I hope you didn't hear anything too bad."

"You know, Colin, I don't think you'd know any of the guys at the club. Most moved here after the Judge died and you left for the Army. Somebody mentioned you being in the paper."

Again, he paused, and then released a sigh. "Hell, Colin, we've known each other most of our lives. No point in trying to hide things. I heard something about you going to jail."

"I'm not going to jail, Gene. I got crosswise with the Feds because I wouldn't give the bogus testimony they needed to entrap friends of mine in Boston. They don't give you many options when they want something. I pled out, got a fine and four months of home confinement with a tracking device. That's all. I've come back to take a look at the old home place. I'm hoping to fix it up and put a few broodmares out there."

Colin took another drink of his beer. "How long since you've been out there, Colin?"

"Twenty years. I don't know what to expect."

"You're not going to like it." He shook his head in disgust. "The farm is surrounded by low-class housing developments on all four sides. Must be three hundred apartments and town-houses, all with government-supported tenants. That whole area is really run down and the farm with it."

My disappointment must have been obvious because he held up a hand and continued, "That's the bad news. Here's the good news. There's not a realtor, developer or project builder who doesn't want that property and who wouldn't pay you an arm and a leg to have the land.

"That's how your name came up at the club. Somebody was asking how to get in touch with you. He wanted to make an offer on the land. The guy—don't know him, never met him—said he did an Internet search and you were in trouble."

The last thing I needed was the spread of bullshit information of that sort, even if I didn't plan on becoming a long-term resident of Staunton.

"Gene, you probably move in and out of every bar, restaurant and food store in town doing your business. Drop a few words for me. I'm home. I'm not a criminal, no more than a man caught pushing the envelope with the IRS, and I hope to see some of my old friends. If anyone feels I'm too low class to speak to me, that's fine. I'll take one old friend like you, Gene, over all the rest of the gossips. Especially since you own half the beer in this county."

He laughed. "If I remember right, Colin, you used to drink about half the beer in Staunton in the old days." He laughed and said he had the Miller Beer distributorship and would welcome my business.

I ordered two more beers and asked for help with my most pressing problem. "Gene, I need to rent a place to stay. I'd like a camp or small house in the country. Any ideas?"

He paused. "My brother Louis died last summer. He had a great camp on the Calf Pasture River in Marble Valley. You can't even see it from the road. It's three hundred acres and it's for sale. His wife would probably love to rent it while it's on the market. I'll call her tonight and get her to agree. It hasn't been used since Louis died. Matter of fact, they seldom used it when he was alive."

"That sounds perfect. I just want to be alone for the next four months while I play house for the Feds."

"How's that work, Colin?"

"I'm not sure. I have to be in Charlottesville on Monday, but let me give you my cell phone number and you can talk to your sister-in-law." I moved to my next priority.

"By the way, Gene, do you handle Sam Adams?"

"It's the best beer I carry, but I'll bet I don't sell a half dozen cases a month in the whole county."

"Hell, Gene, I drink that much a week," I laughed.

Half an hour later I headed north to the city limits, where the old farm was located. Gone was the small dirt road and a four-lane subdivision road had taken its' place. Houses were built within twenty feet of each other on both sides of the road. Small backyards had chain link fences to define the limits each resident could use for too many dogs, too many broken big wheels, swing sets and enough junker cars.

A mile further I came to the farm, or what was left of it. The weeds and grass were fence high and you couldn't see ten yards past the broken-down board fence, which had been left in perfect condition twenty years earlier. I drove into the clearing where the barn once stood. There was nothing left except a broken down crumbling chimney.

This had been the farm that had once housed the top thoroughbreds in the entire Shenandoah Valley, but you'd never know it. I opened my cooler and cracked a Sam Adams before walking over to the barn site, which was now a rise in the ground. A stately oak that had provided shade to the entire barn had been reduced to chips and bark.

I leaned against the fender of the truck, slowly absorbing

and accepting the fact that Jock and I wouldn't realize our dreams for the old farm. Twenty years of neglect had taken an irreversible toll on the property. Twenty years of "progress" had destroyed the peace and quiet of the countryside. This property is no longer home.

I finished my beer and then drove north of town to the Ingleside Golf Resort. The big hotel had burned to the ground right after I left town, and a new country club developed nearby. I took a room on the backside of the hotel overlooking the sprawling golf course where I'd caddied as a youngster. I'd walked up and down the mountainous course, looping one bag of clubs for a buck, or two for a buck-seventy-five, hoping for a quarter tip.

As I looked out over the course, which was now open to the public, my cell phone rang.

"Colin, I talked to my sister-in-law and she'd love to rent the camp. It'll be four hundred a month and that includes use of the three hundred acres. Plus, they'll take it off the market if you want to make an offer."

"Gene, I'm at the Ingleside Motel. Where can we meet so I can pay you and get the keys? I'd like to move out there tomorrow and get out of this town. I feel like a stranger."

"Meet me in the club bar in ten minutes. My warehouse is right up the road in Verona."

I walked to the 19th Hole and sat at a small table in the corner. Soon Gene arrived and came over. "I was going to put a case of Sam Adams in your truck, but you've already got more than I have in the warehouse," he grinned.

He put the keys on the table and saying he had to get home to dinner. I took a wad of money from my pocket. "Here's twenty-four hundred for six months, Gene. I do have one favor to ask. Will you try to think of that real estate friend of yours who may have a client interested in my property? I have no use for it now and could never move there with all those people around."

"Selling won't be hard. Someone's going to pay you a pile to develop that land. You'll make enough to buy the camp and a nice beach house in Nags Head."

We shook hands after he wrote down the name of his realtor friend. "Good luck in Charlottesville, Colin. Call me when you get back and I'll come out to Marble Valley for a few beers. There's still a few of the guys left who'd love to come out for a game of cards. You've still got friends here," he assured me, trying to make me feel better.

Nothing could make me feel better about the current situation.

CHAPTER FORTY-EIGHT

The converted farmhouse turned out to be just what the doctor ordered. As soon as I entered the big family room that dominated the first floor, I knew I'd be comfortable in the big, open space. At one end, a stone fireplace almost filled the wall, stretching up two stories. A big screen television and upright piano stood against another long wall, with half a dozen recliners for relaxing. Card tables were scattered around the room, inviting poker games. At the other end of the room was a breakfast bar and a heavy dining table that would seat a dozen people. Three ceiling fans gave the area an Old West barroom look.

The wall space was covered with a mixture of the usual fare of stuffed deer, bear and turkeys, interspersed with dozens of photos of guests who'd come for hunting parties or to snare the wily trout. I knew many of the people in the pictures from the time I had lived in Staunton.

I rolled out of bed at the crack of dawn on Monday and prepared for my trip across the mountain to the probation office. It took almost two hours to reach downtown Charlottesville and another half-hour to find a parking place in the Monday morning traffic. I made it to the Federal Building with only twenty minutes to spare. I passed through the metal detector and was frisked by a federal marshal who escorted me to the third floor, where I signed a register and waited for my case officer.

A small, hard-looking woman dressed in black jeans, running shoes and a golf shirt approached. She looked about thirty years old and I guessed her at five-foot-three and about a hundred and twenty pounds. There was a star on the pocket of her shirt and the inscription above it read, "Federal Probation." Her expression was angry.

" I assume you're Colin O'Hearn. I'm Carol Stearns, your probation agent."

"Yes, I'm Colin. Good morning."

She led me into her office, a standard, small, windowless area with a desk and a swivel chair, two straight-backed chairs and one bookcase. A young boy's photo sat on the desk with a few other trinkets. A diploma from James Madison University and a master's degree in criminal justice from the University of Richmond were on the wall for all to see.

There was no offer of coffee. "We both know why you're here, Mr. O'Hearn. It just amazes me that an educated man with your background managed to get himself into this situation. I can tell you this; do exactly what I say, follow the rules and be on time, every time. That means you must never be late for your monthly meeting. You must, without fail, file a detailed, timely report of your daily activities. That means sticking to a basic, set schedule. You must keep detailed records of every dime you spend or make. Is that clear? I'm going to have your ass in my back pocket if you ever screw up," she said with a cold edge in her voice.

She continued for another thirty minutes. "If you get in a fight, drive while drinking or get caught with a gun or other dangerous weapon, you'll spend the rest of your sentence in jail, plus a few extra years for breaking your sentencing guide-lines. If you commit a crime during this time, God only knows what Judge Harper will do with you.

"You're not Boston's problem anymore, Mr. O'Hearn. Your case has been transferred to my judge, and we both think you got off easy. Prove us wrong and be the angel I think you can. Walk away from any trouble. You're in my glass house now."

After I had filled out financial statements and had given

my life's history for what seemed like the tenth time since I'd entered the Federal system, Ms. Sterns asked, "How much cash do you have in your possession?'

I hesitated before answering, taking a leather bank deposit bag from my briefcase. "There is forty-four thousand, seven-fifty in this bag. I paid twenty-four hundred for rent last week."

She was stunned. "Where did this money come from?"

"I cashed out my racing and training accounts and collected client bills due me before I left Boston. I intend to put all but a small amount to live on in a Staunton bank today."

"Couldn't you find a cheaper place to rent than twelve hundred a month? I assume you put down first and last for a deposit."

"The twenty-four hundred pays me up for six months."

I went on to tell her about the camp in Deerfield's Marble Valley. I said that just keeping the place clean and mowed would be plenty of work for me.

"So you want me to list your job as farmer?"

"That's what I am. Animals are all I've worked with in my civilian life."

"I'm sure you'll be just fine in Deerfield."

She paused for a moment, as if she'd said something she'd like to retrieve.

"I'll be dropping in on you at home from time to time. I'll try to call ahead. It's way off my path to get to that side of my area. I usually go to Highland County once a month. Later this week, I'll come by your house and put the seal and computer on the phone. I'm warning you not to disconnect it, ever."

She put the black plastic bracelet, which looked and felt like a kid's cheap watch, on my right leg, fastened it with some special tool and smiled in satisfaction. She got up from the chair and walked to the door. It was the first time I'd noticed her great butt and fine figure. She caught me looking and said, "Keep your mind on business, Mr. O'Hearn. All you need to do for the next four months is stay out of trouble."

She smiled professionally and walked me to the front desk.

Ms. Stearns is one no-nonsense woman, I thought as I walked to my car. The black bracelet felt like a fifty-pound weight around my ankle. I carried the monitoring machine to hook up to my phone. When I stopped for a sandwich, I pulled my pants down as far on my waist as I could without flashing the public to hide the bracelet. I stopped and bought heavy, black, high-top socks and sweat pants, trying to cover my ankle.

That night, after staring at it in the shower, the damned plastic reminder of my criminal standing kept me awake. After the first few days, I realized the purpose of limiting my travel and keeping me within a hundred yards of the telephone was to drum into my head that I had lost my freedom, even if for a relatively short time.

I entered my time away from the house on my charts. I was allowed to leave home for business from seven in the morning until two in the afternoon, but seldom did. The rest of the time I had to be within a hundred yards of the monitor which Ms. Sterns had attached to the phone. Every week, I mailed a complete financial and personal report.

As time passed, hundreds of things happened that re-minded me I was confined, not by walls, but by guilt and the law. Never again could I feel I was normal. Leper might be too strong a designation, but socially, personally, and for business reasons, I felt soiled for life.

After the first month or six weeks, I stopped feeling sorry

for myself. I was well into my sentence and hadn't talked to anyone except Gene Grimes during the few times we had lunch and a few beers. I didn't count the clerks to whom I spoke to casually in stores and gas stations.

Gene called the first week in November and said a real estate agent had an offer on the farm. I made arrangements to meet him at the agent's office. The offer was better than I'd ever hoped, given the condition of the property. We ran through the settlement process in record time, paying off the small mortgage I had at the bank and signing the papers at a lawyer's office near the old courthouse.

I stopped by my father's old court room and sat in the back for a while, thinking about the old days, picturing the Judge on the bench, wondering how and why life had changed so drastically, and indulging in a fit of regrets. Finally I walked out the back door and down Lawyer's Row to the Planters Bank, where I asked to speak to the president.

I waited for almost a half-hour, watching the time closely, knowing I had to be home by two o'clock. Finally his secretary escorted me to his office. The man behind the disk greeted me stiffly, barely rising to shake hands.

"The name O'Hearn sounds vaguely familiar, but I've only been here a few years. I'm from our Richmond office," he explained.

"My father, Judge O'Hearn, served on the board of this bank before he took his seat on the bench. That's his photo on the wall outside this office and the Court House building across the street was his office for most of my young life."

"Oh, I'm sorry, I should have known that," he said, paying me more attention and putting aside the papers he'd been shuffling, addressing me directly for the first time.

"Look, Mr. Robertson, I have a small account here and want to add to it. Here's the number."

He punched my account number into his computer and sat straighter in his chair, as the current balance of almost forty-four thousand dollars showed on the screen.

"Yes, a nice account. How can I help you?"

I gave him my sale check from the property and watched his eyes widen in surprise when he looked at amount.

Before he could comment, I began issuing instructions. "I want a twelve-month CD for six hundred thousand dollars. I'd like a credit card with a fifty-thousand-dollar line secured by a ninety day CD. They are to be automatically renewed unless I personally contact you with other instructions. I'll be out of the country, but I will keep you posted as to where and how you can reach me. The balance of the funds are to go in my regular account."

Robertson was tapping computer keys as I spoke while the printer behind his desk spit out various forms. I reviewed the numbers, signed the CDs and then waited, while he got a deposit receipt for the checking account.

Our business concluded, I rose and looked down at him. "From now on, Mr. Robertson, I want to have my bank business only handled by you."

He nodded in agreement. As I turned towards the door, he cleared his throat and asked, hesitantly, "Mr. O'Hearn, why do you wear your watch on your ankle?"

"Just a habit, sir. An old, stupid habit." I grinned as I left his office.

For three months, three weeks and six days I never shaved and never stopped thinking about getting free of my bonds. The night before I was to make my final trip to Charlottesville,

I drank from the last case of my Sam Adams supply. That
morning as I sat across from Ms. Stearns, and the same
thought held my attention that dawned on me the first day we
met. She had a great butt and fine figure. This time, her smile
was rather sultry and not at all professional. I thought about
making a move for a split second, but reality set in and I was
tempted no further. I just wanted the hell out of that Federal
Courthouse.

.   The night before I'd packed my belongings and loaded
the truck. I left directly from the Courthouse, taking the
scenic route through the countryside, and picking up items
I thought I'd need in out-of-the-way places and paying cash.
After selling my truck, I made the final leg of my journey, the
Atlantic crossing, a passenger on a Greek freighter sailing out
of Norfolk.

CHAPTER FORTY-NINE

The freighter docked in Dublin just after dark on a cold wet night in December. I dashed off the ramp and through the rain. The process through customs lasted two minutes before I found a taxi to the train station. My final destination was the small village of Kells, but I longed to see the port city of Cork first. I would then drive the seaside route back to Kells, taking my time now that I was a free man in Ireland.

The train wound through the Irish midlands, finally arriving in Cork on the tip of the southeast coast of the Celtic Sea at midnight. It felt very strange being alone in a foreign country with no plans and not having a single friend or contact. I arrived, checked my guide book and tried not to sound like a tourist as I asked a cab driver to take me to the Jury Inn on Anderson's Quay. He studied me with a smile, then said, "My pleasure, Yank."

I wondered at the source of his amusement. I'd done some research on Ireland and the Kells area and thought I was outfitted properly. My rainproof duster, which reached my knees, was standard attire for an Irish winter, impervious to the rain and cold. My L. L. Bean hunting pants were rugged and practical, and my fleece-lined duck shoes kept my feet toasty. I'd dug out an old, felt, wide-brimmed steeplechase hat which sported several trainer pins, immediately identifying me as a horseman to any Irishman. While the hat was practical in the rain, I was hoping recognition as an American steeplechase trainer would open doors to Ireland's racing community. That was where my future lay.

The cabbie loaded my two rolling bags into his taxi, pulled away from the curb, crossed the street and stopped half a block down. The Jury Inn was on my right.

He unloaded the luggage and laughingly refused my

attempt to pay him. "This one's on the company, Yank. Welcome to Ireland."

I spent two days walking the streets of Cork, sitting along the banks of the Lee River and watching barges and tankers unload at the narrow docks. Finally, I picked up a long term rental car, checked out of the inn and headed towards Kells.

The drive along the beautiful sea coast was stunning despite the constant winter rain. I stopped to play tourist at Waterford, Wexford and Duiski before turning westward to Kilkenny.

There I settled into a small midtown inn around the corner from the fabled Kilkenny Castle and spent a week walking the streets of the town. After a couple false starts, I located a racing pub where I enjoyed drinking Guinness and watching the winter steeplechase racing on television. I was told that when the spring arrived, flat racing would return to the larger tracks at Curragh, Naas and Leopardstown, but for now steeplechasing was the only bill of fare. I filled my spare time reading books by John Connelly, Jenny Pittman and John Francome that I found at a tiny nearby bookstore. The local weekly paper carried a notice to let a cottage and five acres just outside Kells. I read the ad, jumped off my bar-stool, raced to the phone and rented the place sight unseen for five hundred Euros a month.

The tiny cottage was owned by a young family who lived across the road about a half mile east. It had been their grand-mother's home before she'd recently died. The cottage was freezing cold until I took the timer off the electric heater. My landlords, Irish born and bred, laughed at my lack of constitution. On the rare occasion of their visits, they shed as many clothes as possible, saying that my living room was a hothouse.

Well educated and friendly, they invited me to dinner and

my Wednesday evenings with them became an established part of my schedule. I dressed for the occasions in two sets of long johns since their cottage was colder than my barn in Suffolk Downs in January. The family sat around the dinner table casually puffing clouds of cold while eating. I chewed my food with chattering teeth.

After being in Kells for three months, I was well accepted as a daily patron at all three local pubs. One rainy afternoon, I was in a state well past sober when a very thin, bent, wheezing old man hung his cane on the bar and crawled on to the stool next to mine. I smiled and paid for the black ale the barkeep sat in front of him. He nodded before drinking, then said through lips covered in a yellow, almost caramel foam, "Hear you've got relatives in the Kells area," he said, without preamble.

"My father was Fergus O'Hearn," I said. "He was a steeple-chase rider who moved to the States in the forties."

The old man grinned at me and held out his hand. "Well, son, we're family. I'm Seamus O'Hearn, you're father's first cousin."

At his request, I called him Uncle Seamus, and we spent hours together at various pubs each afternoon talking about everything from family to horses. Many afternoons we'd go to the races at several of the small nearby local racecourses, mostly for point to points. It seemed Uncle Seamus knew every owner, trainer or old rider at whatever track we visited.

"What ever happened to that friend of Fergus's, a lad named Higgins. My mother was a Higgins and I remember her family was furious when the boy left County Meath, to join your father in some place in Virginia."

I told him Ian was now in Boston, a law professor at Boston College and a practicing attorney. I added that Ian owned a racing stable and I had trained him at Suffolk Downs.

"Well, if you ever talk to that rascal, tell him his Uncle Seamus could use a few Euros to keep him in Guinness for a month or two!"

One day Seamus asked me, "Colin, did you know that the greatest steeplechase horse ever to race was born and raised on the farm across the road from your cottage? He was born not 100 meters from your front door."

"What horse?" I inquired.

"Red Rum. I broke him."

And so it was, living in Kells, Ireland. Everyday more people heard that I was Fergus O'Hearn's boy. To them I was the famous American racing trainer, now retired, who wanted to begin training a few point-to-point horses next season.

At least three days a week I'd travel somewhere to a race meet. As spring arrived, so did better racing. I watched carefully and made notes, trying to learn the innovative conditioning methods of the Irish trainers. I also tried as hard as I could to appreciate the Irish style of race riding. I abhorred the flying elbows and the rider's inability to sit quietly during a race like their American counterparts. When I chided the Irish about their riding style, I never failed to point out that when they got to America, every rider from Ireland or England abandoned this native style. My firm thoughts and harsh disapproval of the Irish riding style were costing me some friends and even a few free beers, so I toned down my criticism. Soon I became used to the outlandish riding style, but never felt comfortable with it.

I joined the racing club and patron's bar at Gowran Park, where both steeplechasers and flat horses compete. I made a small circle of new racing and drinking friends. Several asked me to take out a permit to train their 'chasers. They were tired of having three or four horses in a yard of several hundred horses, as only a few trainers dominate Irish steeplechase racing. Not yet ready, I turned them down.

The racing club at Gowran Park had a golf course that spanned the infield and racing surface. Playing the course, your drive might go left and lodge in a hurdle. After being glued to Barn 15 at Suffolk for seven days a week, twenty hours a day, I was glad to spend some time relaxing, and my old passion for golf returned.

With the exception of the dull, tasteless cuisine, the ever-rising Euro and the loss of my beloved American television and the Red Sox, my love for Ireland knew no bounds. I was sure that nothing or no one could dislodge me from my peaceful new home.

One afternoon in April, my contentment was shattered. I received a large brown envelope from Ian.

Dear Colin,

By now you'll know we are distant kin. I hope that hasn't caused you to be run out of the village.

Our horses have flourished under Jock and Tino. Libby is the talk of New England, with her riding. Tino is currently third leading trainer at Suffolk Downs. Sliding Scale was second in the Mass Cap and both Crystal Run and Annie's filly have won local stakes. The goat, the old pony and Libby have all contributed greatly to Lonely Aunt's success.

Vito and Jimmy Slacks send their best. The Russian-Italian war has passed. Annie sent the enclosed to me. I took the liberty of obtaining a copy of the included document from the Birmingham Courthouse. I feel she wouldn't have sent it to me unless she wanted me to pass it on to you one day.

God bless and keep you, Colin. Come back to us soon. You are sadly missed.

Always,
Uncle Ian

Inside the envelope was a picture of Annie on crutches in the paddock at the Carolina Cup Steeplechase. A beautiful baby beamed from a harness around her chest.

Enclosed was a photocopy of a birth certificate. The child was born to Ann Collins of Birmingham in November. The child's father was identified as Colin Race O'Hearn of Kells, Ireland.

The child's name was Colin Race O'Hearn, Jr.

I took out my cell phone and began dialing the number Ian had scribbled on the back of the photo.

THE END